ALSO BY KAREN BROWN

The Longings of Wayward Girls

Pins and Needles

Little Sinners

THE
CLAIRVOYANTS

The
CLAIRVOYANTS

a novel

KAREN BROWN

Henry Holt and Company
New York

Henry Holt and Company
Publishers since 1866
175 Fifth Avenue
New York, New York 10010
www.henryholt.com

Henry Holt® and ⬡® are registered trademarks of
Macmillan Publishing Group, LLC.

Library of Congress Cataloging-in-Publication Data

Names: Brown, Karen, 1960– author.
Title: The clairvoyants: a novel / Karen Brown.
Description: New York: Henry Holt and Co., 2017.
Identifiers: LCCN 2016019129| ISBN 9781627797054 (hardback) | ISBN 9781627797061
   (electronic book)
Subjects: LCSH: Sisters—Fiction. | Ghost stories—Fiction. | Paranormal fiction. |
   BISAC: FICTION / Romance / Gothic. | FICTION / Psychological. | FICTION / Literary. |
   GSAFD: Suspense fiction. | Pyschological fiction. | Ghost stories.
Classification: LCC PS3602.R7213 C53 2017 | DDC 813/.6—dc23
LC record available at https://lccn.loc.gov/2016019129

Our books may be purchased in bulk for promotional, educational, or business use. Please contact your
local bookseller or the Macmillan Corporate and Premium Sales Department at (800) 221-7945, extension
5442, or by e-mail at MacmillanSpecialMarkets@macmillan.com.

First Edition 2017

Designed by Kelly S. Too

Printed in the United States of America

1 3 5 7 9 10 8 6 4 2

And he will find them divisible into two great classes—those whom we call the living, and those others, most of them infinitely more alive, whom we so foolishly misname the dead.

—C. W. Leadbeater, *Clairvoyance*, 1899

THE
CLAIRVOYANTS

She is young—dark hair, blue eyes, lashes long and dark, spangled with frost. Her skin the only brightness in the small, dim space. She lies on a narrow bed. Above it are shelves of aluminum pots and pans—their finish worn away from years of use. Dollar Store pots. The kind we played with in the sandbox at the awful nursery school when we were small. Some of them dented. Alongside those, a box of matches, and a lantern smelling of kerosene, a tin of deviled ham, a rusted can of green beans, a moth-eaten bag of clothespins. Amber-colored light seeps through a curtained window into a galley-like space—a small counter, a stove, a tiny booth like a restaurant, and a rod hung across one end that holds tattered clothing slipping from metal hangers. Beyond the curtains, a snow-covered vista, the sun very low behind shaggy pines. Ferns of ice etch the inside of the window. The girl must be very cold without any clothes. Her limbs lie fixed—one arm across her breasts, the other thrown out like an actress about to take a bow. Somewhere, girls her age awaken in giddy expectation of Valentine's Day roses and heart pendants and dinners out with their boyfriends at places with white tablecloths. She stares at a point beyond the ceiling. Come here, *she says.*

1

I was named after my great-aunt, a nun I first saw in my grandfather's barn on my seventh birthday. The barn was in Connecticut, where I'd grown up, and Auntie Sister sat in her black habit on a bale of hay in a shaft of sunlight. Pieces of her dark hair snuck out of her wimple. I knew her from the photograph my grandmother kept in her living room—Sister's pretty face framed by her coif, her head tilted to one side, her eyes laughing. My grandmother had two older sisters, Martha Mary, destined for the convent, and Rose, who would languish in the old Fairfield State Hospital in Newtown.

For my birthday, I'd spent the night with my grandparents, their house placed at the edge of my grandfather's thirty acres—land bordered by the Mile Creek Club golf course, Long Island Sound, and the woods where the Spiritualists by the Sea had their camp—a handful of seasonal cottages and a temple. That evening, as I sat with my grandparents on the back terrace, my grandfather had cocked his head at the drifting notes of their organ.

"That's the sound you hear on the astral plane," he'd said.

The smoke from my grandfather's cigarette rose over the privet hedges and swirled off toward the water. "I hear it," I'd said, though the sound had faded. My grandmother pushed back her chair, the metal feet scraping against the slate. She took me by the hand and told me it was time for bed.

My overnight visit was a rare treat away from my three sisters. I didn't know why I'd been singled out this way—none of my sisters ever were. Unaccustomed to the quiet—the absence of arguing, of Leanne's music, and of Sarah banging through drawers, slamming her closet doors, complaining about not having anything to wear—I'd spent a fitful night on the high guest bed, which had a horse-hair mattress, an acorn bedpost, a history of bodies stretched out in sleep, or sex, or death. And in the morning I awoke before my grandparents. The house was cold, and the light at the bedroom window was like rose-tinged water. I did what I often did at home when I awoke before anyone else—I crept into rooms in the house and rummaged through drawers and cabinets—and I discovered in the bottom drawer of my grand-mother's breakfront a child's white, leather-covered missal. It had gilt-edged pages, a silk ribbon bookmark, and colored illustrations—Jesus in all of them, a golden half-moon floating over his head. On the flyleaf Sister had penciled our name in cursive. I'd slipped the missal into my little overnight suitcase. I didn't think to ask my grandmother if I could have it. Once I'd asked for a ruby brooch I'd found in her jewelry box, and she'd told me no.

I'd never gone into the barn by myself before, but that morning my grandparents sent me off to play and, not used to playing alone, I had wandered along the pebbled drive, missing my little sister, Del. We were only a year apart and did everything together. Del was my mother's favorite—blond and pretty—and perceptive enough to try to include me when she saw she was getting more attention. If my mother noted how many flowers Del had picked, Del would pipe up: "But Martha chose the prettier ones!" Sometimes I was grateful for her allegiance; other times I resented it and found her disingenuous. Still, my mother thought Del was smarter, and it served me to let her think it.

That dull morning I walked the hedges' perimeter, hoping to hear the Spiritualists' organ so that I might report back to my grandfather. I'd gathered a handful of the white pebbles from the drive, and I was dropping them in the grass, leaving a trail Del would have pretended to follow, falling into the game. "Oh, look at this path of pebbles? Where will it lead?"

But Del was at home, coloring in our book, taking the pages I'd saved for myself. We lived at that time in a ranch house our father had bought for our mother, in a new suburb ten miles away, one we would vacate a year later when they divorced and our mother moved us into our grandparents' house for good. I reached the barn and passed through the wide, open doorway. The eaves ascended high above me, and barn swallows darted in and out of the shadow and sunlight, sounding their little *cheeps* and *churees* of alarm. Somewhere inside the vast barn were the animals my grandfather kept—sheep, goats, a cow, and a horse. I sensed their shuffling and smelled the feed and the dense, almost cloying scent of manure. I saw Sister, and I waited nearby for her to notice me. I thought she might be praying.

The interior of the barn was cool and peaceful, as I knew all churches to be. My mother took us regularly to Mass at the old Sacred Heart, where the pews smelled of polished pine, and the statuary of Joseph and Mary gazed smooth-faced and pitying. We dipped the tips of our fingers in holy water. The priest came swinging the censer. The little bells ushered in a deep, encompassing silence.

In the barn, I held my breath, waiting.

Sister's bale of hay topped a small stack near my grandfather's workbench, his mill, the coiled copper wire, and the copper lightning rods stacked in worn, oily boxes. The chill of the damp stone floor rose through the soles of my sneakers. At no time did Sister speak to me or offer any message about what was to come. I wish to this day that she had. She kept her head bowed, her eyes on her hands folded in her lap. Had she discovered my theft? Was she there to confront me and demand the missal back? Her veil fluttered, and she raised her head. Fearing her accusation, I fled outside, down the white pebbled drive to where my grandparents sat in woven wire patio chairs. Behind them the house's long porch trim was lacey cutouts, and to their left, beyond the privet hedge, the inground pool shimmered in the morning sunlight. I slid my hand into my grandmother's, and she held it in her lap's gabardine folds and patted it while they talked and had their coffee, the spiral of the steam shrouding their faces as they raised their cups.

Later, my family arrived—Leanne and Sarah, Del and my parents. Leanne and Sarah were jealous that I'd spent the night, and they refused to speak to me. Del put her hand in mine; she'd missed me, as I'd missed her. There was a cake and the seven candles I wished on and blew out. I waited in apprehension for Sister to emerge from the barn and join us, but she did not. I would eventually learn that in 1962, driving back to the convent upstate with three other sisters after a convention of the American Benedictine Academy, Sister had been in an accident. A blowing veil, perhaps, had obscured the driver's vision, and they'd all died on the New York State Thruway, many years before I saw her sitting in the sunlight in my grandfather's barn. This explained her smooth, youthful face when my grandmother's was creped and sagging, the outdated serge habit. It did not explain how I saw her, but I never questioned what most people might. A door had opened and I had left it open and maybe because of that, things happened the way they did. That was all I knew, and as a child all I cared to know.

2

On the day my mother deposited me in Ithaca, New York, to attend the university, I thought of Sister. I was leaving behind my home—leaving Del. In many ways I was happy to go. Why spend your life scrabbling at the sad bits of the past? There were things I would be glad to be free of, though I remained doubtful that freedom would ever really be mine. We drove, mostly in silence, past the lonely towns lining the Delaware River, the abandoned farmland along pot-holed Route 17. We drove through a gentle summer rain, and the grass seemed to glow with phosphorescence, like a radioactive charge, an anomaly of the sun dampening the gray sky with color.

"Look at the pretty hills," my mother said.

She had dressed that morning in a pressed, white, sleeveless blouse, her trademark Lilly Pulitzer skirt, a pink cotton sweater thrown over her shoulders. The Cadillac's air-conditioning kept the car's interior at seventy-two degrees, but every so often I would depress my window's button, claiming I needed to breathe, and the humid air would blow through the car, and my mother would raise a slender hand to her hair to hold it in place, and flatten her lips in irritation.

"Is this the highway where Auntie Sister died?" I said.

I had dreamed of the nuns driving in a sky-blue sedan with the windows down and the bright sun on the hood. The air on their faces was cool and smelled of cut grass. It caught in their wimples, invaded the seams, and soothed their scalps. Their habits flapped.

"I don't know," my mother said, her voice taking that curious tone I'd lately noticed when she spoke to me.

"Do you think they had the radio on?" I said. "Del always said they were listening to 'Kisses Sweeter Than Wine.'"

I hummed a few bars of the song. They were young women, wedded to God. Their mouths opened and drank in the sun and the wind. Under the black fabric their bodies surged in secret, betraying their vows. I used to pretend being pinioned in that faith, in the rules of their order. I'd feel my heart drawn out in wild longing with the words: devotion, ecstasy, rapture, and betrothal. Lately, I'd come to doubt I would ever find that sort of love.

I sang the chorus of the song out loud. My mother tightened her hands on the wheel. Then she reached out and turned on the radio so I might sing something else.

It was the end of August, only days before classes would begin. I'd spent the last two years commuting to classes part-time at Wesleyan, what must have seemed to my mother an aimless existence, the only one of her four daughters living at home. Leanne and Sarah had stumbled upon useful and regular lives. They had graduated from college, and Leanne was engaged and working at an advertising firm in New Haven, and Sarah had married and was already pregnant and had moved into a colonial house on a cul-de-sac in Stonington, and I pictured my older sisters' children, those destined to be born, growing up with toys we had when we were young—those Fisher-Price farms and airplanes and houses with miniature, limbless people and animals. They'd read their children the same books our mother had read to us—Sendak's *Nutshell Library*, and the Little Golden Books' *The Color Kittens*. They'd fulfill the promise of womanhood, slipping on their new responsibilities like pretty dresses—the traditions at the holidays, the joys of cooking and child rearing—and, unlike me, forget they were once unhappy teenagers.

My grandfather had died when I was eleven, and my grandmother had recently moved into Essex Meadows, a retirement community where she might be less alone, and free of her old house and its attendant memories. I supposed she'd wanted to force us all out by leaving, but my mother and I stayed—the two of us holdouts, believing that as long as we stayed, we were safe. But the old house, surrounded by its privet hedges and by Long Island Sound's wide, gray presence, provided only a semblance of privacy. Since Detective Thomson had paid us another visit, my mother had become even more distracted, distant, and I noted her relief when I agreed to move away to attend school.

Though it had been five years, the murder of David Pinney, a local teenager, remained unsolved, the case open, and every so often detectives visited, and we were questioned yet again, my mother's blanched face reflecting her irritation. I was summoned downstairs and asked to recall my memories of that summer—a time so far removed, and about which I'd talked so often, that my story seemed stolen from someone else's memory. Detective Thomson had graying hair and only half a pointer finger on one hand. Once I'd asked him if he'd had a bit of bad luck in shop class, and he'd smiled.

"Something like that," he'd said.

His missing digit intrigued me, and through the years we'd developed a loose sort of banter. "Did an evil witch demand it?" I'd asked, or "Were you held for ransom?" until my mother told me to stop.

This last time he came, I'd told him I felt like Cinderella, let out of the garret room to slide my foot into the proffered slipper.

"Does your mother keep you away from other people?" he'd asked me, leaning in, the buttons of his dress shirt straining.

My mother had been getting him a cup of coffee in the kitchen, and I'd almost considered playing along, whispering that I was a prisoner in my room just to see his expression, but then she came in with the cup on a saucer, and the look on her face—alarm, caution—prevented me from doing so.

Now my mother gripped the wheel of the car with white hands, and I sensed she wanted to get me to the school as quickly as possible before I changed my mind.

My great-grandfather had been an alumnus of the university where we were headed, a student of avian biology. Owing to his becoming someone famous in the field, and to the "enigmatic" quality of my photography portfolio, I'd been accepted as a transfer student. Years before, I had discovered my great-grandfather's notebooks in my grandparents' attic and had been intrigued—drawings on yellowed paper of various species of birds, with labeled coverts and scapulars and crowns. Among these drawings were others—landscapes that included figures standing at a remove, at the edge of a field, or a wood, their faces bearing the worrisome expression soon to become familiar to me—that of someone lost or forsaken. Along with the drawings were two slim, hardbound manuals—well-worn and filled with his penciled marginalia. They were published in 1907 by the Theosophical Society in Point Loma, California—*Psychometry, Clairvoyance, and Thought-Transference*, and *Psychism, Ghostology, and the Astral Plane*—both penned by "A Student."

It had been my great-grandfather who first leased the land to the Spiritualists by the Sea. In the late 1890s they'd arrived in wagons and pitched tents on the property. My grandfather had allowed them to expand, to build the temple and the cottages along the cart paths. What other relationship he'd had with the group remained obscure. We were cautioned as children to leave the Spiritualists alone, and I sensed that whatever they did in the camp was taboo. Every summer, we'd hear the organ's notes climb over the trees, signaling the start of their season, and we knew to stay away from that part of the woods.

By the time the dead began to appear to me again, at fifteen, I'd long been familiar with the manuals and the drawings. Cindy Berger, freckled, nervous, dead two years from leukemia, was the first. She appeared beside my grandparents' privet hedge, by the path to the pool. I saw Mrs. Harrington, my junior high school art teacher and a victim of spousal abuse, wearing her trademark silk scarf knotted around her neck, in the soup aisle at the Big Y supermarket. The old drunk, Waldo, found dead on the railroad tracks when I was twelve, appeared by the Mile Creek Beach Club gate on a summer afternoon. I didn't recognize some of the dead, but I soon learned not to startle at their arrival, to predict their appearance by the way the light seemed to waver and fold. I could distinguish them from the living by the way they stared at me, their expressions anxious and filled with longing, as if their appearances had been conjured by the despair of a lost love and the possibility of connection that only I might give. Their expressions compelled me to do this one thing for them, yet I refused. I continually let them down, believing they would catch on soon enough and leave me alone.

I was sure my great-grandfather had seen what I saw, and recorded his visitors alongside his sketches of the birds, their little clawed feet penciled in a violent grip, similar to the one my mother used on the wheel of the car. His manuals had become my own, their catechism one I memorized as a gullible child—*What is the ethereal double? Who travels on the astral plane? How does the clairvoyant receive messages from the dead?* Once all manner of dead began to appear to me I began to resent him for passing down his curse, and the manuals revealed themselves for what they were—the esoteric ramblings of a cult. It didn't matter that I had once believed in them. I felt foolish for doing so now. The Ithaca move came from my hope that the dead might not follow me out of the area, that perhaps they'd been summoned by the inept mediums affiliated with the Spiritualists by the Sea. According to "A Student," the people I saw were shells of themselves, trapped on the lower astral plane, manifesting in the places they once inhabited. I might be able to leave them behind.

My mother helped with my application, claiming she wished the best for me, but her eagerness also meant I'd played right into her hand. She wanted me gone, away from Del. Three years before, Del had suffered a psychotic break and had been admitted to a hospital for treatment. Though she'd recently settled into a kind of assisted-living arrangement called Ashley Manor, I hadn't seen her since our family's last attempt at therapy two years ago, and as the space between Del and me widened like an extending rubber band, my resentment toward my mother grew. I was being shuttled out of the way, while Del, still her favorite, was allowed to stay close.

"While you were in the kitchen, Detective Thomson asked me a lot of questions about Del," I said.

My mother pursed her lips but kept her eyes on the road, the river a dark, churning stripe beyond the guardrail and the dead summer grass. "He's a nuisance."

"He's been to talk to her at Ashley Manor," I said.

As I guessed she would, my mother glanced at me, concerned. "Your sister never mentioned that."

"She told me in one of her letters," I said.

My mother seemed to relax then. She sighed. "I don't think we can believe everything Del writes in her letters."

"Oh, I know what to believe," I said. "And what not to believe."

I saw the shape of her mouth like a rebuke. She suspected I did know, and held her own resentment against me for keeping things from her.

I was a prickly girl, difficult to love.

The summer I was fifteen, David Pinney died. After that, I saw the dead again for the first time since I'd seen Sister in the barn, and Del's behavior first bloomed out of control. She'd always been a little reckless—the result of imaginative plans and games that my mother couldn't help but marvel at. But her inventiveness took a self-destructive turn after that disastrous summer. Despite my admittedly distracted efforts to keep track of her, during the next year Del was caught with various boys—in cars, in a camper sitting in someone's side yard, in the Mile Creek Beach Club changing rooms. Her favorite place to take boys was a ravine off Mile Creek Road, the edge of someone's property where two cars had been abandoned—the springs and tufts of stuffing sprouting from the vinyl seats, moss and fern growing out of the rusted floorboards. There were drugs involved, too, and alcohol. I'd followed her and found our grandfather's old bottle of Glenfiddich wedged into a wheel well. When I'd confronted her she'd simply grinned, grabbed the bottle back from me, unscrewed the top, and taken a swig.

"You're such an innocent, Martha Mary."

The following year things worsened, and I'd wake at night to Del talking in her sleep. She always sat upright. Sometimes, she stood in the closet. I was half-asleep, and the talking rarely made any sense. I would awaken with only pieces of things—her tone, imploring or urgent, a word or two—*camellia* or *mirror*? *Broken branch*? I stopped trying to understand and I accepted the spiral of words that charted her forgetting everything—who she was, what she meant to me. It was a sad sort of relief to think that the only thing allowing me to slacken my watch over her was the understanding that she had moved into a place I could not follow.

Even my mother could no longer excuse Del's behavior as brilliance, and when I was a senior in high school and she was sixteen, she was sent away, to a place that had been founded in 1824 as the Connecticut Retreat for the Insane, then renamed the Hartford Retreat, and finally, more hopefully, the Institute of Living. Still the place couldn't shake the pall that came from the many lobotomies performed there from the 1940s to the 1960s. Gene Tierney, the actress who appeared in *Laura* and *Tobacco Road*, was admitted in the 1950s and suffered twenty-six shock treatments that robbed her of her memory. She tried to flee but was caught and returned. None of these things could convince my mother or my father that they had made a mistake sending Del there. They were resigned, convinced that this type of thing ran in the family—citing Great-aunt Rose, who had lived out her days in that Fairfield asylum in Newtown, long since closed down and abandoned to ruin.

Without Del, I worried I'd come home to an ambulance in my driveway, men from the hospital poised to chase me down and drag me in, too. Gone was the sister who posed beside me in photographs of our childhood, the two of us wearing Easter dresses or Christmas robes, identical except for color, Del with her blond hair and winning smile, me pouting and angry over some slight no one ever took the time to understand. I knew I was being selfish, that in some way Del had been taken in my place. If I had described my visions, I would have been the one drugged and shuffling through therapy groups and arts and crafts. But I wasn't brave enough to confess anything.

After almost six months of unsuccessful family therapy sessions, I drove alone to the Institute of Living to visit Del. I was preparing to graduate. It was clear that Del's participation in teenage milestones—the part-time job, the acquiring of a driver's license, the various mortifications of high school from her sophomore year onward—would be cut short. By then she'd been transferred to a residential house on the grounds. It was a spring day, the dogwood was blooming, and I waited in the lobby for over an hour, only to be told Del didn't want to see me. I was hurt, and furious.

I never tried to visit again. We wrote old-fashioned letters back and forth—a method of communication that let me couch my rancor in the false recounting of my life: details of shopping trips with our mother that I never took, a day with my father at museums in the city that never occurred, the date with a man I met at a play I never attended. I knew she'd see through my lies—lying was what we did best together, and so it was my best revenge to hide my life beneath a story of one. In truth, I rarely left the house. I'd gotten leery of the dead. They filled me with regret. And the living troubled me more. At least with the dead, there were no questions—just their longing, and my renouncing of it. I was an intermediary who refused to function in her role. Somewhere, grieving parents and siblings and lovers suffered, and I denied them any solace.

As I sat in the car, reassessing my earliest letters to Del at the Institute, my mother drove through Liberty, home of the old Grossinger's Resort, where, I imagined, throngs of astral inhabitants reclined on dilapidated loungers. As we passed through the seemingly empty stretches of Binghamton and Lisle into Ithaca, my mother hummed along with a song on the radio, and I sensed she had hopes that I would make a new start, and the pressure of her hopefulness was yet another burden. Perhaps she knew I was fleeing, had sensed, as I did, that the detective's questions seemed to have become more probing, more pointed, that his gaze had hardened, become almost wily, like a man who had a taste of something he liked.

He'd sat in a chair brought in from the dining room—he needed it for his back, he had said, and whenever he visited, my mother brought the chair into the living room, and he thanked her—"Ah, you remember"—as if her courtesy, too, were being cataloged in a file.

"I have a girl here, a Jane Roberts, who says you had a crush on David," he'd said.

I'd leaned forward and smiled. "My old friend Jane said that?"

Detective Thomson leaned forward as well. He cradled his coffee in his two hands, the missing part of his finger camouflaged by the others.

"Well, she doesn't want anyone to know," I said, keeping my voice low, eyeing my mother on the couch, her knees pressed together at the hem of her Lilly Pulitzer skirt. "About us."

"About who?" the detective said. "You and Jane?"

"Oh, good heavens," my mother said, slapping her lap, rising to her feet.

Detective Thomson leaned away, a flush rising from his collar. I waited a moment, watching my mother. "It's true," I said. "We had a little crush on each other, Jane and I. Maybe it was more than that. Do I have to tell you everything?"

My mother's jaw tightened and she sat back down, smoothing her skirt. "Is this what you wanted to know, Mr. Thomson? Is this what you've been digging around for? Some scandal? Some schoolgirl relationship between my daughter and her childhood friend?"

The detective had kept his eyes on me. Where once he might have smiled indulgently, this time he did not. "Are you saying you don't like boys," he asked.

"I'm saying if I had a crush on anyone, it was Jane. Not some boy I didn't even know."

"You're a clever young woman," he said.

It was July, and the drapes on the living-room windows blew in, carrying in the smell of salt, the tones of the Spiritualists' organ. Detective Thomson shifted in the chair, and the antique joints groaned. Outside, the Sound broke forcefully against the seawall. A strange little bird chirruped in the crab apple.

"No," I had said, cupping my upturned hands in my lap. "Del was the clever one."

Now, beyond my mother's profile at the wheel of the car, Route 79 wound alongside green swaths of hills still damp from the recent rain. This was an isolated valley with a poor yearly sunlight allotment and haphazard cell phone reception—another version of a sanatorium, a place my mother could tuck me away, the way you pressed a photograph into the back of a drawer—and be free of me. But I might be free of her, too, and I might find someone else to love me.

3

All the dorm rooms were filled by the time the university accepted me, so I'd rented an apartment in an old house, where a great elm cast a dark shadow over the porch. The house stood on a street of similarly grand old places, each shaded by a tree, their roots disrupting the cement sidewalks in front. Mine was a brick Italianate house with a wide cornice and elaborately carved brackets and window caps. The apartment was up a staircase that once might have been glamorous when the house was still a single-family residence. The place had been advertised as a "studio." I would be living in one room with a twelve-foot ceiling, a decorative fireplace, and an efficiency-sized stove, sink, and refrigerator—so small they seemed like playhouse furnishings. My mother, decorator extraordinaire, seemed not to have found any inspiration in the room, or else she didn't see the need to apply her skills to it. She scoped the space out, and then we left and found a used-furniture store nearby and purchased a couch that folded out into a bed.

"This will serve a dual purpose," she said. "You'll have room to move around once you fold it up."

She paid the man to deliver the couch bed, along with a table and chairs, which, when she tried to gain my opinion, I said were fine. In the short time since I'd arrived in town I'd changed my mind about being there, and I didn't care what we purchased. I went along, glumly, feeling myself resist confessing that we should forget the whole thing and head home. When Detective Thomson had stood, slowly, and, stepping toward my mother's front door, paused to look back at me, I'd felt that same small twinge of fear I'd felt five years before, the first time he'd come, and I knew returning home was no longer a choice.

On the sidewalk out in front of the used-furniture shop, a taped-up poster read HELP FIND MARY RAE SWINDAL and below that bold type was a photograph of a young woman wearing a formal dress, her dark hair styled into pinned-up curls that fell beyond her shoulders, like a prom queen or a princess. Her expression was droll, as if she knew the satin sheen of the dress, the bright smear of lipstick, provided only the impression of a beautiful woman. MISSING SINCE FEBRUARY 14, the poster announced. More of these posters, encased in plastic sleeves, flapped on telephone poles all along the street.

Driving in, we'd passed stretches of desolate space, open and wild-seeming, the trees dense on the removed hillsides, the occasional collapsed structures with weathered gray wood siding. I'd grown up surrounded by acres of professionally kept grounds, stone walls, and wild grapes. There'd been the rejuvenating smell of the sea. Here lay a landscape of despair. My mother sensed it, too. Her voice rose in pitch, into a false cheeriness that made her sound manic. My idea of a new start had quickly reverted to a keen sense of abandonment, similar to the feeling I'd had when I was first separated from Del. I'd had other friends, but none could take her place. We'd shared a bedroom our entire lives. She knew me better than anyone. And I'd found it difficult to sleep with her empty bed two feet away. Del's absence had been like a death. I'd been left behind, grieving and lost.

We stopped at Wegmans grocery store for staples, and the same plea to find Mary Rae Swindal was tacked to the bulletin board in the entryway. If my mother noticed the posters and their unnerving portent, she didn't mention it. The store was filled with students, young people who despite their familiar appearance—T-shirts, shorts, battered flip-flops—seemed entirely unlike me. In the car again, my mother commented on the number of young people we'd run into in the checkout line.

"Any one of them might be a new friend," she said, halfheartedly. While I had never been able to tell her why I felt so removed from the rest of the world, she understood that I did, that I was. Just as she'd named Del "exceptional," I was "introverted" or "reserved."

On the way out of Wegmans I'd paused at the flyer of Mary Rae Swindal tacked to the bulletin board, and as I reached up and touched the image, the bright glare of the grocery store, its heat, its smell of baking bread, gave way to the cold narrow room with the iced-over window, the nude girl on the bed. The cold struck me. My breath fanned out. My mother had already passed through the automatic doors, and I heard her calling—*Martha*, she called, as from a far-off place, and then she was beside me and had pulled my hand away.

"Martha," she said, sharply.

In my great-grandfather's manuals, there were passages about the psychometrist, how she perceives her images by touch, holding an item—a coin, a letter—in her hand, and how after a minute or two the external surroundings disappear and a series of pictures begin to appear. *Sounds, too, are heard. Perfumes smelled, and even the sense of heat and cold, dryness and moisture, are reproduced with surprising clearness.*

Back at my new apartment, the landlord, Geoff, came out of his place across the hall to meet us and introduce himself, almost bashfully, to my mother. They were nearly the same age. He had a British accent, unruly gray hair, and a dog named Suzie, a black-and-white setter that I shied from, and which, sensing my fear, Geoff kept on its leash. My mother, as if to prove to me that dogs were friendly, reached out to pat her, and the dog burrowed her head into my mother's crotch.

"I see you've purchased your bits and bobs," Geoff said.

He called my apartment a *bedsit*, and he charmed my mother with an easy, guileless smile and a pipe-smoking persona. After he'd gone she said he seemed just as friendly as he had on the phone.

"We know nothing about that man," I said. "Jack the Ripper had a British accent, too."

She opened the refrigerator and bent down to look into its depths. "You won't agree with me about anything, will you?"

"I'm here, aren't I?" I said.

She bustled up and down the staircase, hauling my boxes, revealing a sturdy stalwartness I'd never fully noticed before. We'd brought the basics—pieces of my grandmother's old Limoges china, some scarred copper-bottomed pots, and utensils.

"What more could you need?" my mother said, putting cups and saucers away in a cabinet above the sink.

We'd brought back a lamp and a small, ornate mirror that she hung beside the door.

"Now you can check what you look like before you go out," she said, like an indictment.

"I can ask it who is the fairest in the land," I said.

I wandered over toward the window and looked out at the tree-shaded street. I pressed my lips to the glass and closed my eyes.

My mother's plan had been to stay the night in a motel nearby, but she checked her watch and I knew she wanted nothing more than to leave me entirely and be on her way.

"This hasn't taken nearly as long as I thought," she said. She hefted her leather bag onto her shoulder and crossed her arms, resolute.

"What about our tour of the campus?" I said, hating myself for sounding so desperate.

She pursed her lips. "Do I need to do that with you?"

I followed her down the stairs to the porch, and then out to the street. A breeze picked up, moving the elm's heavy branches. A dog barked nearby, and I feared the scratch of its nails on the pavement, the jangle of its tags coming closer.

"Are you sure you should go?" I said. "It looks like it might storm."

And then in the flickering elm shade a woman appeared, as if produced from its shadows. She stood to the right of my mother's car in a coat far too heavy for the summer day—an eggplant-colored down coat, woolen gloves, a pretty cloche hat. Her dark hair held the semblance of the curls from her poster, but ice matted them together. Her fingernails were bitten to the quick, and she played with her necklace—an amethyst pendant, the kind of necklace I'd seen in my mother's Spiegel catalog as a child. The missing Mary Rae. I felt a jolt of excitement—I almost called out to my mother, who had already climbed into the car, "She's here! I've found her!"

But one look from the woman stopped me from saying anything. Any hopefulness I'd entertained about a new start dimmed. Her round eyes were blue, thickly lashed, and they stayed on me, beseeching.

"Now, Martha, I want you to be *happy*," my mother called out the car window. The Cadillac idled by the curb. She'd put on her large-framed sunglasses. Her lipstick was cracked, and her face lined under its makeup, and one day I would be older, as she was, and, like her, have no idea how vulnerable it made me seem. "I am! I *am* happy!" I said. The heat of the car's exhaust and of the sun on the hood were stultifying, and I leaned in and kissed her dry cheek, which smelled amazingly the same as when she would enter my room in the dark and bend down to kiss first me good night, and then Del, and say she was sorry for telling us she wished we'd never been born. We felt chastened when she did this—as if we'd forced her to make the declaration. And hadn't we, with our squabbles, our messes, the work that tending us required?

Under the covers I'd have on a floral, flannel nightgown with a lace ruffle on the bodice that scratched and sleeves that were too short. Del, in the twin bed beside mine, wore a matching nightgown. In winter, the heating registers clanked, snow piled up on the roof, and we were children.

"I think I can easily make it back by nightfall," my mother said, sounding like a character in a fairy tale. She rummaged in her purse and made a sound of surprise. "Oh," she said. "I almost forgot." She handed me what looked like a cosmetic case—tan leather with brass trim.

"It's a travel alarm clock," she said, brightly. "Your grandmother gave it to me years ago. I thought you could use it."

She gave me a smile, and her eyes brimmed with what Del and I always called *happy sad*. I didn't beg her to stay. I knew it was no use. Beyond the car, Mary Rae seemed rooted in the shade of the elm. My mother's car pulled away, and I felt entirely forsaken.

4

Up in my apartment, the porcelain taps to the bathroom sink and to the shower were cracked, and a small sign posted above the bathroom sink informed me, in what I assumed was Geoff's careful printing, that the pipes would make a loud noise when I turned on the shower, but that I should keep turning the taps and the noise would stop. At the spot where the water dripped from the faucet into the tub, there was a dark stain. Combined with the groaning pipes, the tub seemed the scene of a gruesome crime. I would get used to it soon enough, I supposed.

The couch bed and the table and chairs were delivered by two tired-looking men with packs of cigarettes sticking out of their shirt pockets. Despite my attempt to make friendly conversation, they said very little, as if they'd been warned by some superior not to talk to customers. Still, they left a lingering odor of sweat in my room. I unfolded the sheets and put them on the thin mattress. Out the window, the sight of Mary Rae in her heavy coat, the ice in her hair that refused to melt, surprised me. This was unusual—the dead never remained once I left their presence. A breeze slashed at the elm, thunder rumbled in the distance, and I smelled ozone. I went out with my camera and took Mary Rae's photograph.

I'd never told even Del what I saw. At one point, after I stopped believing the writings of "A Student," I stumbled onto *Occult Phenomena in the Light of Theology*, by Abbot Alois Weisinger—a theologian who claimed that in Paradise Adam and Eve possessed powers that were afterward lost to them, though some of these powers might have remained, weakened, latent in the gene pool, waiting to be revived. In the Spiritualists by the Sea camp, the mediums gave card readings, group readings in which attendees held hands and a medium summoned a personal spirit guide who might have a message for someone in the audience; I read about the Victorian spiritualist heyday that prompted the proliferation of these mediums. And I read about the popularity of spirit photographs in those days—*Mrs. French of Boston, with Spirit Son, 1868*, and *Moses A. Dow, Editor of Waverly Magazine, with the Spirit of Mabel Warren, 1871*—silly images taken by charlatans and tricksters—and this added to my unease about my own photography.

In my art class in high school, the year that Del went into the hospital, we'd been instructed to take the camera with us everywhere, and the first good image I captured was Mrs. Harrington at the Big Y. It was at night, and I'd gone there to buy spice drops—one of Del's old cravings. I used a 35 mm camera for class, and when I started down the soup aisle and saw Mrs. Harrington I'd hesitated, curious about what the image would reveal if I captured it on film, worried that even an attempt at photographing her would further prove my instability. But like my great-grandfather, who'd sketched what he'd seen, I felt the need to take that photograph, and the next day I developed the film in the lab at school. On the negative I could see the image, but I wasn't sure what would happen once I printed it.

Mr. Krauss, our teacher, squat and shaggy, leaned over my shoulder as I placed the paper in the bath. The image appeared, and he said it was excellent. He liked the surreal nature of it, the rows of soup cans, the strange saturated light that was arresting and eerie. He made no mention of Mrs. Harrington in her London Fog, her bruised neck, her bouffant hair flattened on one side. Just of the light, its quality. I'd felt a sharp disappointment.

"Unusual," he said, "this shimmer here," his pudgy index finger hovering over Mrs. Harrington's figure.

He liked the absence of people, he told me. I'd captured the loneliness of the place. But when I looked at the image, Mrs. Harrington was there, confused, as if she'd lost her cart in one of the aisles and as if the lost cart had been the only familiar thing in a strange land. Mrs. Harrington had had a daughter, a girl with long, thin appendages who sat in the junior high cafeteria alone during lunch, scribbling verse on lined paper, refusing invitations to join other tables. The printed image of Mrs. Harrington was the first I knew of what I had to do, like a calling. It didn't matter that I was capturing only absence—an empty supermarket aisle, a deserted, leaf-riddled road. I understood that lost love did that—uprooted you and left you abandoned.

While I'd been taking Mary Rae's photograph, Geoff came up the sidewalk with Suzie on her leash and smiled at me, hesitantly.

"Taking shots of the house?" he said.

"Yes," I said. "I hope you don't mind."

Geoff laughed. "I've got some stories about this place, if you're ever interested. It's got a history, you know."

"Ghosts?" I said, raising the camera to set Mary Rae in my sights.

Geoff put his hand on my shoulder, and I felt a flash of discomfort, then wondered if I was wrong to feel it. *Avuncular*, I told myself, an old high school vocabulary word I'd never thought I'd use.

"No, don't worry about that," he said. "I wouldn't have any renters if that were the case, eh?"

He went back inside, and I followed him, Suzie's nails clicking on the treads already marred by her ups and downs. We went our separate ways, into our apartments. It grew dark, and I knew I should think about eating something, but I wasn't hungry. The streetlights came on. Mary Rae tipped her head to meet my gaze, her pretty hair iced over. Though I wanted to ignore her, her continued presence was too baffling. I went quietly down the staircase, unused to living in such close proximity to strangers and leery of calling attention to myself. I stepped onto the porch, and then down to the sidewalk. Mary Rae began to move away from me, leading me along, stopping when I didn't keep up. I was afraid of getting lost. Though I had my phone, and it continued to pick up a signal, at that time I knew no one I could call, and this was before phones could direct you anywhere you wanted to go. Despite this I kept following her.

I pretended I was simply out for a walk on a late summer evening. I tried to focus on the trees arching over the sidewalk, the quaintness of the houses with their front porches, imagining how I would describe things to Del in a letter. The air felt cooler and the breeze, which had once seemed to promise a storm, kicked the leaves. We walked down one street, then another—Geneva, Cascadilla. Students had moved in, had hung their posters, had laid down their rugs, and were acclimating to the people around them. It didn't escape me that my fresh start so far involved none of those things; rather than making new friends, I was following a dead girl. I approached a party on a candlelit porch—laughter, banter, the group partially hidden by tall shrubbery. Mary Rae stopped walking and paused, lingering, as if she longed to join them; as if she sensed I, too, wished to go in.

I stepped back into the shadows of the shrubbery, as she did, listening. A woman laughed, softly.

"It's a beautiful night," she said. "God, I wish it would stay like this and never get cold."

Someone set a bottle of beer on a table. "You'd get sick of the sameness," a man said.

"I'm happy to be here with all of you. I'm just happy to be alive," the woman said.

There was a hush then, the laughter dying away. "Someone walked over my grave," the man said.

"Oh, stop," another woman said, her voice garrulous. "You're all so superstitious."

"I wish I would stop feeling guilty," the first woman said.

"For what?" the other woman said.

"Well, for Rae."

I felt a sudden apprehension. Mary Rae must have been the "Rae" the woman referred to, though her face showed no real emotion, just a placid, glazed-over expression, as if recollecting something from long ago.

"You doing okay there, William?" a man said. "You're pretty quiet."

"Yeah," William said. And then he stood and looked out of the screened enclosure. He looked past Mary Rae to me, standing there on the sidewalk. I'm not sure why I didn't flee. Did I think that I, too, couldn't be seen?

"Oh, hello," he said.

"Hi," I said. "Sorry, I was looking for my cat."

Del would have laughed at me. "That's all you could come up with?" she would have said.

Then the man, William, turned to the group, some of whom had risen from their seats on the dim porch to see who he was talking to.

"Anyone see a cat?" he said, his voice teasing. I suspected he didn't believe me. He looked back at me—for some reason I still hadn't moved.

"What does it look like?" he said. "What breed? Persian? Manx? Maine Coon? Abyssinian? Siamese?"

"Just a tabby." Could I have told him right then I'd been following his dead friend? What would that have accomplished? I looked toward Mary Rae, but she was gone. William raised his beer to me. "Want to join us?" he said.

Thunder sounded off in the distance, and then the porch door opened, and William stepped onto the sidewalk in front of me. Again, I smelled that pre-storm charge in the air. My grandfather would open the front door wide and stand before the screen, calling us all to him, and telling us to "Breathe. Breathe. Smell that?" Outside my grandparents' house, the horse chestnut leaves would be torn from the branches. The shrubs would buckle. The clouds would unfurl like great gray tongues. Our mother and grandmother would stand far behind us, safe in the hallway's shadows. "Get *away* from there," our mother would hiss, and we four girls would feel superior to the panic in her voice.

"You don't want to be struck by lightning," William said.

He was just being funny, but the mention of the lightning and the sudden disappearance of Mary Rae, the void she had left, made me uneasy.

"I'll be fine if I avoid trees, high houses, running water, and barns," I said.

"Or, you could come inside."

"According to Ben Franklin, to be safest indoors you're supposed to lie in a silken hammock in the middle of the house." I sounded odd, I knew that, but William laughed.

"We'll all have to face the risk then. No silken hammocks here."

The breeze buckled the porch screens. William's friends had grown quiet. "My grandfather sold lightning rods."

"You seem to have the pitch down," he said. "You've got me nervous."

I laughed, then. We looked at each other in the dark. I could see little of his face, his eyes.

"I'd better get going," I said. "But thanks."

I headed back the way I'd come, ignoring the voices that started up on the porch behind me. When I spun around once, playfully, William was still there, standing on the sidewalk, watching me go.

5

In Ithaca, I settled into a new routine—the walk to campus, the classes in historic houses named after university founders and benefactors, with open windows where gusts came through, occasionally dragging a leaf, flipping our notebook pages; the professors distant and oddly dressed, sporting clinking turquoise and silver bracelets, faded jeans, and the heavy shoes I understood would soon be needed to navigate the slush and snow. The area had been established in the late 1700s as the Military Tract, and its townships named by a clerk in the surveyor's office who may have read John Dryden's translation of Plutarch's *Lives of the Noble Grecians and Romans*. Homer, Hector, Ulysses. Even a village called Dryden, and another after his contemporary, Milton, which was where Mary Rae Swindal, the missing girl, had lived.

A report about her came on the television news one morning in the little diner where I often got my coffee on my way to school. I stood with a small group of students watching—the boys in their skinny jeans, skateboards under their arms, the girls with their phones out, calling friends. Later, I saw a copy of the *Ithaca Journal* with the headline about how the search for her continued. I bought it and brought it back to my bedsit. I read about the absence of new developments, and how yet another vigil was being held the next evening. There was the photo of Mary Rae, and quotes from her friends, and one from her mother, whom I imagined as a gaunt woman, her eyes red from crying.

"We miss our girl so much," the mother said. "We hope she will be home soon."

I felt a pang of sympathy for the mother, knowing Mary Rae would never be home. I'd tried, out of curiosity, to retrace my steps from the night she'd led me along, but without much luck. In the daytime, things looked off, and I had a crippling inability to get my bearings. I was often lost, and trying to squelch my panic. I must have seemed, to anyone who met me during those first weeks, strange and standoffish. Awkward. Other than Mary Rae, who made an almost daily appearance beneath the elm, I had no consistent visitors. And while I was conscious of having gotten what I wanted with this move away from home, I was apprehensive of my good luck. I found myself confusing new faces with those already familiar. I would smile and wave at someone, and, confronted with a stare or a hostile look, I'd realize my mistake. I'd get my bearings soon. And then I'd be able to be myself— whoever that new person was, waiting to emerge.

My photography workshop was the focus of my studies, even though I was enrolled in other courses—Romantic Poets, Women and Grief, a horrible statistics course that I might withdraw from. We were a small group, assorted and equally strange, if in different ways. When one of the girls, Sally Crowder, made the observation that we were weirdos, a few others laughed, softly, almost proud.

"Artists," Charles Wu said. He wore heavy-framed glasses and had dyed a white stripe in his hair, like a skunk. "We're artists."

I said little, preoccupied with my contact sheets. For me the work was less about art than about reassuring myself that what I saw existed in some form—just enough to assuage my fears about my sanity. Still, I was welcome in this group—we were all compelled to create images out of pieces of our own unique worlds. None of us saw things the same way as the other, and even if I wasn't sure I entirely belonged, I was grateful to be there.

I didn't bring any of my photography classmates home with me—even though Charles Wu kept inviting me places alone, then suggesting he walk me home afterward. I liked my privacy, and I often pictured living in the entire house alone, moving freely through all the rooms, enjoying a dining room and a kitchen at the back of the house, and this idea had taken hold so I'd almost forgotten that others living separate lives occupied these spaces—the elusive Professors Whitman and McCall downstairs, Geoff and Suzie upstairs in the room next to mine. Our lives did invade one another's in unwanted, unacknowledged ways. The floors creaked, and I listened to Geoff's slippered footfalls on nights I couldn't sleep—they shushed across the oak flooring, back and forth. Sometimes, at a deliberate, thoughtful pacing. At others, in a slow, anguished dragging. Once in a while I'd hear his dog Suzie's clacking nails trailing after. Each morning, though, Geoff emerged in the upstairs hall, boisterous and hearty.

"Come, Suze! Come on, girl," he'd say.

He was from London, and a craftsman. One day I chanced to open my door at the same time he did, and he stepped up to my doorway and peered behind me, asking if the place was working out. "Do you have any tea?" he said. "I'm out."

"I do," I said. "Would you like to borrow some?"

"Would you make it up?" he said. "Would you mind?"

He slipped around me and into the apartment, dragging Suzie by her leash. He sat at my little table and began to roll out a joint, the pot spilling to the floor by the chair legs. His hair was wild and gray around his ears. He wore a camel overcoat with soiled elbows that smelled of the cigarettes I'd seen him smoke furtively, like a teenager, at his cracked window.

"Maybe you shouldn't smoke that in here," I said.

"The tea?" he said. He reached over, cracked the window, and lit his joint anyway. His eyes were wide and dark, and I got the impression he was simply looking for someone to tend to him. In his youth he might have been the Heathcliff type—black eyes and hair, a rogue.

I put the water on the burner and stood over him in my coat.

"Sit down," he said, taking a long drag. "Tell me about yourself."

Suzie lay flat out with her noble head in her paws. I'd grown to accept that she would keep clear of me, and she no longer frightened me. Geoff held the joint toward me, sodden from his lips, and I hesitated, but only for a moment. I sat at the little table and he began rambling on, telling me about London and the chest of drawers he was making in his little shop on Ithaca Street, and how the woman who had ordered the chest was a ruthless bitch with a big house on the lake. Then he stopped and gave me a long look.

"Your hair is pretty in this light," he said.

I was flattered, even if he was nearly my father's age, and even if it felt slightly unsettling to be the object of his attention. I passed him the joint, the room sunny and filled with a languor that followed me to campus, late for class.

MY MOTHER SENT checks on a bimonthly basis and phoned regularly, ready with details of Leanne's and Sarah's perfect lives. Once in a while I'd get a call from one of them, and I'd hear the real story—arguments over a husband's inattentiveness, a car accident after too much wine at a luncheon. I continued to send letters to Del care of the Ashley Manor facility. I'd gotten used to this method of navigating the distance between us. Like the woman at the porch party, I felt guilty, and I had been prevented from living my life by my guilt, but the more I heard about Del's life away from me at the Manor, the less guilty I felt. Ashley Manor was a place from which she was free to come and go on a daily basis. It was also a structured environment that offered meals and medication supervision—a place she might graduate from once she felt more in control. She sounded happy in her letters and full of her usual plans to find an apartment on her own, to start classes at the University of Connecticut—all things she'd talked about before but that now seemed imminent.

I received a letter from her one day in September telling me about her new boyfriend, Rory. I was sometimes envious of her boyfriends—though she'd cycle through them so quickly, it was hard to keep track, and sometimes I wondered if, like me, she'd invented most of them. Rory, she claimed, was different. *I think he is going to pop the question,* she wrote. *Mother is all sorts of upset, and thinks I'm crazy for considering it. But who doesn't want a little house and a hubby and a garden full of vegetables and Peter Rabbit peering out of the shrubbery, and maybe a cat sleeping on a rug by the hearth.*

Unlike my mother, I didn't entertain the possibility of any of this. The Peter Rabbit reference meant she wasn't really considering it, and she found it all outlandish. Then I received another letter, two weeks later, in October. The leaves of the elm had brightened and had begun to litter the sidewalk and the porch. I'd find the leaves tracked into the vestibule, and sometimes Geoff would bring one, stuck to his shoe, all the way up the stairs. It had gotten cold; the grass, the windows, and the windshields of cars were sometimes stamped with frost. I was leery of winter, its portent like a trap about to snap shut around us. Del's letter arrived on a day the temperature dipped to thirty degrees. *Rory and I are running off together,* she wrote. *We're going to get married in Maine, where he has a cabin, and a friend who lives on a commune who is a religious figure in some church or other.* I thought apprehensively of the Theosophists who'd penned my great-grandfather's manuals. Del detailed the dress she was going to wear, *peasant style, with smocking and wide sleeves,* and the bouquet of mums she would carry—*a fall bride,* she said.

I pictured her marrying Rory, the two of them reciting lines of poetry in a ceremony attended by commune members. I doubted my mother, or Leanne or Sarah, or my father with his new wife, would consider attending, even if they'd been invited. Nowhere in her letter had Del extended an invitation to me. Had she gotten well enough to leave Ashley Manor for good—or had she been given some sort of overnight pass?

It surprised me then to return home from class that same afternoon and find Del sitting on my front porch. I recognized her old purple ski parka, which made me instantly leery. She wore a striped stocking cap, the kind that could hang down the wearer's back, or be wrapped like a scarf around the neck—a vintage piece she might have found at a Salvation Army store. Her hair had grown long, nearly waist-length, and she'd dyed it auburn, matching my own. Her face seemed bloated and her eyes too bright. I hadn't seen her in three years, and I felt a mix of emotions I couldn't have described. I swore I was happy to see her, but she looked at me askance.

"Liar," she said.

I felt instantly regretful, and she laughed. "I could tell you missed me from your last letter," she said.

I didn't know what I'd written to her—all of it was an invented mess.

"Where's your husband?" I said.

She laughed, again, flashing her bright teeth, her face altered in the time since I'd seen her. It had grown more mature, more filled with nuance I had trouble deciphering. Behind her expression lay the years of time we had spent apart. She was still the prettier sister. She said the Rory saga was a long one. She had left the manor of her own accord, taken the bus with money she'd saved.

"They just let you leave?" I said. "Or did you run away, like Gene Tierney?"

Del sang a little bit of the *Laura* movie theme, deepening her voice
to sound like Frank Sinatra. "Laura is the face in the misty light."
We'd spent long weekends as children watching old movies or singing the songs from our grandmother's Broadway musical albums—*My
Fair Lady, Funny Girl, Oklahoma!*

"I wasn't in shackles," Del said. "Sure I could leave!"

I found I was nervous, unused to Del's teasing outside of her
letters.

"I like your haunted house," she said. "I could have guessed this
is where you'd end up."

After our grandfather died, we had made a regular habit of sneaking into the Spiritualists by the Sea camp. A group called the Ladies'
Aid Society coordinated events and visiting mediums, and the
programs were held in the old wooden temple. The cottages, spruced
up each summer with paint and annuals, were, by the time we visited,
privately owned, or used as seasonal cottages. There were sessions
on "Meditation and Spirituality" or "Advanced Mediumship Techniques" or "Past Life Regressions," and a medium's cottage for
private readings. Del memorized all of the upbeat inspirational songs
played out on the temple piano, and when we mingled in the meditation garden, or in the gazebo placed on a spit of land near the
Sound, she would sing them, to the pleasure of camp visitors. With
her long, blond hair and her blue eyes, she could smile sweetly and
seem ethereal, while I sat beside her on the bench like her dark
opposite.

"Have you had any séances yet?" Del asked me. She dug a plastic
bag filled with spice drops out of her backpack. "Summoned any
spirits?" She held the bag out to me.

"Still eating this crap," I said. The scents of spices—clove, cinnamon, cardamom, anise, wintergreen—filled me with a strange longing for our old bedroom at our grandparents' house, for the way the
sun came in across the floor in the mornings, for the strange call of
the loon through our open windows.

Del chose an orange drop for me. "Clove," she said. "Your favorite."

Our eavesdropping at the camp had provided us with séance techniques, the language of mediums calling forth spirits from the ether, and Del had convinced me one summer to put these things to use in our grandparents' pool shed, corralling neighborhood children eager to hear from dead relatives, from recently deceased children's show hosts, from the local babysitter killed riding on the back of her boyfriend's motorcycle. Del always had a plan.

"What did we charge? A dollar?" Del dug around in the bag and pulled out a dark red drop for herself—cinnamon.

"We got up to two-fifty," I said. "I can't believe I let you talk me into that."

We'd been eleven and twelve—bored that summer. It was disarming to be the focus of Del's attention, her spotlight pointed on you, pressuring you to perform, to be who she wanted you to be. She was relentless about getting her way, annoying and a burden at times. But she also knew how to draw me in, to make something seem an adventure.

"Remember Mrs. Parmenter?" Del caught the red drop in her mouth, her eyes bright.

"She gave us ten dollars," I said.

Our grandmother's neighbor, Mrs. Parmenter, had shown up at the pool shed door. She wore a scarf over her head and dark sunglasses, and she wanted to contact her husband. We knew none of the details of his death at that time, only that he had passed away that winter, and though I did wonder why she would come to two children rather than visit the medium at the Spiritualists' camp, I brushed my concerns aside. She cut the line of children and stepped, a little unsteadily, through the wooden doorway smelling of gin and perfume, her lipstick dark and carelessly applied. The shed was tucked behind a privet hedge and faced a lane that led out to the main road. It housed the pool pump, life jackets and rings, cleaning supplies and tools. Towels smelling of chlorine hung on pegs, and folding lawn chairs, their slats bright green and white strips, were stacked against a back wall. The shed was naturally dark, with only one window we'd covered with a striped beach towel. Our candle was an old red glass citronella, stolen from a patio table. We were no-frills—no jewelry or fancy scarves. Mrs. Parmenter took in the croquet set, the galvanized metal tub we'd turned upside down to use as our table. We'd placed three low folding chairs around it.

"Here's five dollars for each of you," she'd said. "Let's get started."

I had given Del a cautionary look, but she'd taken the money from the woman's shaky hand and tucked it into her shorts pocket. It was dusk, and the sky beyond the curtained window was alive with last light, the darkness encroaching from the woods that backed the gravel lane. The shed flickered with shadow, with the eerie twilight. We lit our candle and Mrs. Parmenter sat down. She wore a narrow skirt and had to sit with her legs folded to the side. From her purse she removed a heavy, man's gold watch and tossed it down onto the galvanized tub.

"This was his," she said. "I thought you might, you know, need it."

"Perhaps," Del said.

She moved the watch out of the way, and we put our hands down flat on the galvanized surface, fingertips touching, and instructed her to do the same. Mrs. Parmenter's nails were long, the polish chipped. Del told her to close her eyes. She tilted her head at me—the oldest, and therefore considered the most responsible—her mouth a flat line.

"Why? So you can trick me?" she said. Then her expression changed and she complied, mumbling what sounded like an apology.

Her perfume was suffocating in the warm shed, an amorphous presence. Del summoned the spirits in her best medium's voice, a copy of Reverend Earline Morrissey's at the Spiritualists' camp. She said we wanted to hear from Mr. Parmenter, would he be willing to talk with us. And then Mrs. Parmenter interrupted Del, her eyes still squeezed shut.

"Oh no," she said, her voice harsh. "He doesn't get to talk. I want to give him a message. You let me know when he's here."

Del and I had exchanged a look. We'd never done this with an adult before, and the problems were immediately evident. Inventing anything seemed like lying, yet saying nothing would reveal us as shams. I pressed Del's finger with mine, giving her a warning to stay silent.

"I sense he is present," she said, ignoring me, proceeding with our usual script.

"I want a sign," Mrs. Parmenter said. And then outside a bird called, an evening songbird, and Mrs. Parmenter stiffened, hearing it. Tears formed in the corners of her eyes.

"He's here," she said, giddy and girlish. "He used to whistle like that. That tuneless sound. Yes, I know you're here, sweetheart."

Del's body trembled with nervous laughter, and I struggled to keep my own in check, my voice level.

"Yes," I said. "He is waiting for your message."

He wasn't there—none of the dead showed up at our séances. I played along with Del and felt guilty for our lies. Some of the children were suffering, confused and unappeased by the priests and ministers who insisted their loved ones had gone to heaven—a place I sometimes equated, wrongly, with the astral plane, and which they imagined as a cloud-filled oasis in the sky.

I expected Mrs. Parmenter would say how much she missed her husband, how much the children missed him. Already the oldest girl had come to us seeking him out. "Daddy," she'd said, "you promised you'd take me to the Civic Center for the Ice Capades. You *promised*."

Mrs. Parmenter seemed to gather all of her strength. "My darling," she said, her voice wavering and sweet. "Father March says that you're in hell, and I hope that's true. I wouldn't expect a priest to lie. I want you to stay there and know how much you've hurt—no—how much you've *destroyed* your lovely family. You stay there and think about that for eternity. You just settle in, the way you do, with your goddamn cigarette and your bourbon straight and your pressed boxer shorts and your 'just heading out to the office,' and that fucking plaid cap on your head, and you fucking rot there."

I pulled my hands away. Mrs. Parmenter took a deep breath, exhaled, and opened her eyes. In the candlelight she wiped her tears gingerly with her fingertips. Then she stood and smoothed down her skirt.

"Thank you, girls," she said. She stepped to the door and then paused. "How's your mother, by the way?"

Del drew her legs up and hugged them. The candle sputtered and made our shadows glimmer.

"She's fine," I said.

Mrs. Parmenter hardened her eyes. "So happy to hear that," she said, though I could see that she was not happy about anything.

She turned to step outside and had forgotten Mr. Parmenter's watch. I picked it up to hand to her, and she took it, grudgingly, and slipped it back into her purse. We'd watched as she'd disappeared through the gap in the hedges toward the lane.

GEOFF CAME OUT the front door and gave us a little wave. Del was checking out his boots as he passed by.

"Those are desert boots," she said.

"This is my sister, Del," I said.

Geoff paused on the sidewalk and shaded his eyes. "Lovely," he said, then he walked off.

"Cheerio," Del called out after him, imitating his accent.

She unwound the stocking cap from her neck and fiddled with the fringe of the pompom.

"Mr. Parmenter committed suicide," she said.

"At the Stardust Motel," I said.

"Supposedly, he was waiting for the woman he'd been seeing, and she never showed." Del stared at me.

"What?" I said.

"Never mind," she said.

I'd never told her about Mr. Parmenter's watch. This was years before the dead began to appear to me again, and at the time I believed I'd imagined it. When I'd touched the watch I'd seen a man stretched out on a bed, his hair dark and wet against his head, the pillow stained and his mouth open, as if in sleep, or in the process of a yawn or a scream. The motel room's paisley bedspread held its own dark stain, the man's feet shod in dress shoes and the thin dress socks the fathers all wore splayed at the bed's foot. And the terrible stillness, a slight wheezing sound that may have been last breaths, and then nothing, nothing but the cars passing on the turnpike, nothing but the dust and the spring day shifting through the blinds, and the long length of silence.

Del had goaded me on during the pool shed sessions—"Tell us what you see, Sister. What is he saying?" so I was forced to reply, to invent lies, and to keep the things I believed I was imagining to myself—vivid, disconcerting scenes, ones that would suddenly be presented to me while I sat in the quiet of the shed, smelling the citronella and the chlorine: an old man with a belt, beating a child on the back of his legs; a woman leaning over a toilet, spitting up chalky, white pills into the bowl; a dog locked in a toolshed, clawing at a door. The children returned with messages, with news of their accomplishments, with admissions, sometimes shyly expressed, so that I felt, at times, like the priest in the confessional. The Spiritualists by the Sea had taught me that there were places where others who purported to see what I saw gathered. I suspected that many if not most were liars and fakes, and was certain that to align myself with them would be a grave mistake.

"Think of the money we might have made if Mother hadn't caught on," Del said, in that wry, raspy voice I had missed more than I'd realized. I felt a twinge of sorrow, too, for all the time we'd spent away from each other, and for the way I'd let resentment color our childhood.

The wind swirled leaves around our ankles on the porch. I told Del to come inside, and she picked up her backpack and followed me. It seemed that she'd not come directly to Ithaca but had in fact taken a side trip to Maine with Rory. From her letters I'd gathered he was older, in his thirties, a gentle man who dyed her hair for her, and took her out places and always brought her back. I'd pictured his trembling hands in plastic gloves squeezing the bottle of dye onto the top of her head and tenderly distributing it through her roots.

"So what happened?" I asked her.

I'd showed her into my tiny bedsit. I'd told her she could put her backpack anywhere.

"What do you mean *happened*?" Del was sitting on my couch. "Where do you sleep?"

"What happened with Rory," I said. "Why did you call off the wedding?"

They'd had an argument and gone their separate ways, Del explained. "He was too controlling," she said. "Always wanting to have sex in the woods."

I leaned on the small counter, feeling the smallness of the room with the both of us there.

"Like some sort of pagan ritual?"

I told her the couch pulled out into a bed, and she removed the cushions right then, and marveled at the way the bed unfolded, as if it were something she'd never seen.

"He just likes to do it out in the open," Del said. "He's claustrophobic."

She sat on the mattress, trying it out. Then she spotted the travel alarm clock on the end table. "Oh look!" she cried. "Mother's little clock. She tried to give this to me in the hospital and I told her to take it back."

Del arranged the pillows and promptly fell asleep, which put an end to my questions. A feeling of both excitement and dread accompanied anything related to Del. She'd come to visit, which meant that

I was still someone important in her life, and that pleased me. But we hadn't spent time alone together in three years, and I wasn't sure I knew her anymore. It also occurred to me that Detective Thomson may have paid her a visit, that her flight to Maine with Rory had had another purpose.

Across our years of letters, I had never asked Del why she'd turned me away that day I'd tried to visit, and she had never asked me why I'd kept away since. It was as if we had silently acquiesced to a need to keep our distance from each other. That afternoon in Ithaca I watched her sleep, her hands pressed under her cheek like a child. The little travel clock on the end table wasn't really a gift intended for me, and I wished I had never accepted it. I felt a rush of animosity toward my mother, toward Del, but I tamped it down. As in childhood when she would propose an enticing plan, I was being lured back under Del's spell.

In the middle of the night I woke up and she was sitting on the edge of the bed in the dark having a conversation with herself.

"*You* told me that was what it was," she said, "and then *you* fell into the gap, and the bees interrupted, and the whole Sunday *I* couldn't find the place."

She cut the air with her hand emphatically, and when I spoke to her she didn't stop or seem to hear me. "Del," I said. "Oh, Del?" Clearly, she hadn't been managing her medication.

I should have expected this. In her letters she'd often talked about despising the medication and wanting to wean herself off of it. Yet it unnerved me. I dug the prescription bottles from her bag and read the instructions for dosage. I filled a glass of water at the sink and I handed the pills to her, one at a time, like a nurse at her bedside.

"You need to get those little plastic cups," she said, trying to provoke me.

"Your experiment failed," I said.

"This time," she said.

Eventually, as days passed, Del's drama seemed to level off. My mother called, and though it felt like childhood tattling, I told her Del was visiting. She pushed in a chair and crossed the kitchen floor and opened a cabinet. The old regulator schoolhouse clock chimed the hour.

"How is it going?" my mother said, falsely bright.

"We're having fun," I said. "I'm showing her the sights."

One Saturday, I'd taken Del on a tour of the campus. I'd gotten a map from the Campus Information booth, and Del had made fun of me for not knowing my way around. Another time, we'd hiked up wooded, spiraling trails in Buttermilk Falls Park. Yet another day, we'd crouched on flat rocks near falls that wet our faces. I'd even taken her across the suspension bridge over the gorge, clutching her hand, feeling myself drawn to the edge.

"That's nice," my mother said. "When is she coming home?"

Home meant Ashley Manor, I assumed, but still her question rankled.

"Soon," I said. I'd enjoyed having Del around again, and I even felt better with her near. I had willed the dead to keep their distance, and for a while even Mary Rae obliged.

6

I'd wanted to visit the Spiritualists by the Sea—it hadn't been Del's idea. I'd been reading my great-grandfather's manuals, and I wanted some proof of what was happening in the camp. While my grandfather was alive I didn't dare go against his wishes, but when he died I believed I would find him at the camp, and he would forgive me for defying him. That summer, I turned twelve. I was too old for Del's games of pretend, too young to care about the boys Leanne and Sarah entertained around the pool. My father had kept the ranch house in the suburbs and had moved in with his new wife by then. We saw him occasionally, staying in our old bedrooms during weekend visits. But the place had never felt like our house—not like my grandparents' had—and that summer my father and his wife had purchased a cottage on the Cape, and we were allotted a week with him there at the cottage, and then our visit with him was done.

My mother had continued her volunteer work at the church, and took shifts at the Prison Store, where they sold inmates' handcrafted tables and chairs, chess boards and jewelry boxes. Del and I always joked about messages in the merchandise—a hidden panel at the base of a wooden candlestick into which had been secreted a manifesto, admitting or denying the inmate craftsman's crime. The store was in a town plaza—between a bookstore and the one movie theater. Beyond this I wasn't sure how our mother kept herself busy.

My grandmother was occupied with her bridge club and her garden club. Often, neither of them was home and we were left unsupervised. We spent a lot of time in the house—reading our grandparents' old books, listening to French language tapes we found in the attic, and using the French around our mother to annoy her. The beach communities filled with summer people, and we spent our time on bikes, or walking the lanes to the beach club with our group of friends. Taking a detour into the woods wasn't much of a stretch, and Del and I stole down the gravel road through the woods one morning just as the Spiritualists' organ hit its first notes. We brought a backpack with sandwiches and pretended we were simply out for a hike. The woods were cool, just beginning to fill with bugs, and the sun blinked through the leaves as we walked. Neither of us spoke, solemn with the weight of our disobedience.

Occasionally, a car would come by, and we'd will ourselves invisible and step to the side, allowing it to pass—dusty Connecticut plates, some from New York or Massachusetts. The path through the woods inclined and we emerged at the top of a hill where the trees thinned to a meadow. Ahead the cottages began, brightly painted like gypsy wagons—peaked, wood-framed structures with gingerbread trim—miniature versions, I noted, of our grandparents' house, connected by narrow lanes. We saw towels and swimsuits on clotheslines, and floats and inner tubes stuffed under cottage porches. One of the lanes ended at a bulkhead, where a path led through rangy swamp rose bushes down to a rocky beach. Del and I paused at the head of the path, partly hidden behind the roses. The Spiritualists had dotted the sand with umbrellas, and children played in the Sound.

Someone opened a cooler and pulled the flip top of a can of soda or beer. Del and I surveyed the scene, surprised. This was like any of the other beach communities we'd been to.

The organ sound led us into a grove where the temple stood—a white clapboard building with tall windows and double wooden doors propped open to allow in the sea breeze. Inside, folding chairs made an expanding half-circle, and people had begun to file in and take their seats. That day, according to the placard at the front of the room, Reverend Earline Morrissey, a medium from New London, was scheduled to hold a spirit communication circle. We were told by a lanky man, who bent at the waist so we could smell the moth ball odor of his dress shirt, that children weren't allowed. Del, sensing my disappointment, waited until the doors had closed, then tugged me into the viburnum shrubs beneath the open windows where we could hear the event commence.

Reverend Earline said she was getting a message for someone named "Jean," and a woman, supposedly Jean herself, gasped, and Earline and Jean had a conversation—a back-and-forth about who the message was from (her grandmother's childhood friend) and what she wanted to say (she was the one who stole the silver sugar tongs). The hour went on in this way, with Earline calling out messages, and people claiming them—"Why, that's my uncle Gem" or "Oh! Mother! That's Susan Merriman, my mother." The messages were specific enough that they felt very real to me—the red bike with the basket, the boat named *Lucky Again*, a child's hatred of rhubarb, a man's quirky addiction to warm buttermilk. It didn't seem possible that Earline would make these things up. But there were also moments when she called out messages and no one claimed them, when she'd struggle with a message that the audience member couldn't understand.

"My mother never enjoyed going to the movies," a woman said, sourly. "She was agoraphobic. I think you have the wrong person."

In my great-grandfather's manuals, "A Student" had described how often messages were inaccurate, and how this made charging fees and offering yourself as a medium unethical. *To confuse the fitful and unstable sights and sounds of the lower astral plane, which seem so wonderful to the novice, with the steady, pure radiance of the Divine Spiritual Light is profanation!* The messages coming from the lower astral plane, "A Student" claimed, were always confused and misleading. I wanted to approach Reverend Earline with this bit of advice. I wasn't sure what reception I'd receive, but I was looking for acceptance at the time and was intent on corralling her.

As she finished up the circle, she called out one last message. "I have a message from an older gentleman. He is trying to speak to his daughter. Has anyone recently lost a father, or a father figure?"

Earline's voice, grating, high-pitched, rang out into the room. I heard a few mumbles, some shuffling feet. No one claimed the old gentleman, but I thought of my grandfather, and even though his message wasn't for me, I wanted to call out, to hear what his message might be. Del pinched my arm, cautioning me. I closed my eyes and smelled the fresh oil paint on the clapboards. "He is enamored of our organ, and once looked forward to hearing its notes in the evenings," Earline said.

The circle proceeded like an auction, the souls of the dead and their lost messages divvied up among this group of strangers. *How sad,* I thought. I waited for Earline to say more, but she did not. I planned to confront her once the circle was finished. Soon the folding chairs clattered along the wood floor. The attendees' voices swelled, and the doors fell open, and everyone came out. Clusters of people emerged, their feet moving past us. Del and I remained behind the viburnum, the large leaves keeping us hidden, until a pair of Bernardo sandals joined the group, and I peered out to note the woman's wicker purse—our mother's purse. She wore large sunglasses, the skirt and blouse she had on that morning when she left the house.

Del nudged me, having seen her, too. Our mother moved among the Spiritualists until we lost sight of her on the lane leading down between the cottages. We crept from our hiding place, but by the time we entered the temple, Reverend Earline had gone.

"She's disappeared into the ether," Del said, her eyes wide.

"Our mother, too," I said.

"Why didn't she answer when the old gentleman wanted to speak to her?" Del said.

We walked down to the little beach to sit in the sand and eat our sandwiches. I didn't want to believe then that it may not have been her "old gentleman."

"She must not want to hear his message," I said.

"Then why come?" Del said. She broke off bite-size pieces of her sandwich and put them in her mouth.

The Spiritualists' children were gone—all called in to lunch. I buried my feet in the warm sand. "There may be someone else she wants to hear from."

We couldn't conceive who our mother might wish to contact, who she'd known who had died. We knew very little about our mother's life. Sometimes, our grandmother would talk about old boyfriends our mother had spurned, boys who drove from college in their sports cars to the house.

"Drove five hours from Penn and she wouldn't even come downstairs to say hello," my grandmother had said.

"Maybe one of the old boyfriends," I said. This idea was tantalizing, and it overshadowed, somewhat, my regret at not hearing my grandfather's message.

We both knew that we couldn't let our mother know we were there, but it would be our mother, and the chance of eavesdropping on her, that brought us back down the wooded gravel road again and again that summer, hoping for a glimpse of her in the medium's cottage, eager to hear her claim a message in the spirit circle. If she ever returned, we never saw her, and once we were caught playing clairvoyants Del lost interest. Eventually, my attraction to the Spiritualists ended as well. I'd grow to dislike the way their mediums drew people in with false hope and provided paltry messages that might not have come from anyone they knew. Those of the lower astral plane were tricky, tiring, and deceitful. You could trust the messages just about as much as you trusted the things you saw in your sleep.

7

Del's visit extended to over two weeks. On the days I had classes I didn't know what she did or where she went, and when I asked she was always vague. "Here and there," she'd say. "Out and about." It was my responsibility to shop for food, to buy shampoo and soap. Del would add things to the list—razor blades, rat poison, clothesline rope.

"What *is* this?" I said, shaking the list at her.

Del stood at the mirror trying on winter hats from a pile she'd thrown on the bed. I had no idea where she'd gotten them. "I was kidding," she said. "You don't joke anymore. You've gotten old."

"I don't think this is funny," I said.

Del turned to me wearing a faux fur Russian hat. "Because you're worried I'm crazy." She pulled the hat's flaps over her ears.

"You look it wearing that," I said.

I crossed out her ridiculous additions to the list, folded it over, and tucked it into my purse.

I came home from Wegmans, lugging the bags up the stairs, and discovered her setting up an old television, fiddling with its connections.

"Does that even work?" I said. "Where did you get it?"

Del explained that she'd found it for free on the side of the road. "And it does work," she said. "The sign said it did."

Another day I came home to find her reading in an upholstered chair, its cushioned arms curving to end in the carved heads of ducks.

"How did you get this up here?" I asked.

"Good ol' Geoff," she said. "Don't you love it? It's a gift for you, from me."

I didn't say that it left less space in the apartment or that it seemed a little threadbare. I didn't ask where she got it—if it had been left out in the rain or was covered in animal hair.

"Don't worry," she said, returning to her book. "The stains aren't blood."

ONE AFTERNOON SOMEONE knocked on my apartment door. Both Del and I were home. It was Halloween, and Del had purchased a bag of candy corn, which we ate in handfuls. The television was on, and I was trying to read poems assigned for class—Wordsworth and Shelley, the print so small on the thin page of the anthology that I kept losing my way. At the sound of the knock we startled and eyed each other warily.

"Maybe it's Detective Thomson," Del whispered.

She'd confessed that he had visited her at the manor, "with his shiny shoes and his suit," she had said, scowling. "I'd almost forgotten all about him."

He'd asked her the usual questions, and she'd done her best at "dazed and forgetful."

"I kept asking him to repeat the question," she'd told me. "Then

I would spend at least three minutes thinking it over before I answered."

She'd stared through me, disconcertingly, imitating her interview behavior with the detective. "You're good at that," I'd said. "You didn't even blink."

We'd both laughed about Detective Thomson's growing bulk, his white legs that showed above his socks when his slacks rode up. Neither of us mentioned the sense that he'd sharpened his focus—mentioning Jane Roberts and some of the others we'd hung out with that summer. We didn't admit to feeling afraid, but there we were, startled by a knock on the apartment door.

Del answered the door with a lavish flourish, her hand filled with candy corn. "It's a visitor!" she cried. "We're not alone!"

Geoff stood in the doorway, surprised. He seemed a little cautious around Del. Since she'd been with me, his visits to my bedsit had stopped.

"I've been invited to an outdoor party," he said, clearing his throat. "I wondered if you two would like to join me."

Del put a piece of candy in her mouth. She held her hand out to Geoff, but he declined.

"What does that mean?" I asked Geoff, rising from the couch where I'd been reading.

"Outdoors? A party?" Del slapped my shoulder, as if I needed waking up.

It had grown quite warm the last day or two—a welcome Indian summer.

"A cookout?" I said. "Or something?"

"Yes, yes," he said. "You know, to celebrate All Hallows' Eve. Grilled meat and that sort of thing."

Del laughed at me. "Are you dense, Martha? Yes, we'll go with you!" she cried. She put the remaining candy corn in her mouth, wiped her hands on her jeans, and grabbed her backpack. "I look OK, right?" She smoothed down her T-shirt. There was a stain on the front, but she let down her long hair from its clasp, and it fell over her shoulders and covered the spot. "Oh, do we need costumes?" she asked, concerned.

Geoff began to speak, but Del cut him off.

"That might be fun," she said. "We'd have to stop to pick something up, though."

"You can just wear your Dr. Zhivago hat," I said.

Geoff stepped into the room, waving his hands. "Hold on, now. No one mentioned costumes were required."

Del went to the bureau and began opening drawers. "No costumes at a party on Halloween. That's a first."

I clutched my book to my chest. "Who's going to be there?" I pictured a group of older men and their wives, and Geoff showing up with Del and me, looking like his two lost daughters.

"It'll be a nice group," Geoff said. "Some artists, some students."

"I do have a paper to write," I said.

I didn't want to be around students with Del. She drew the wrong sort of attention. Charles Wu, with his wool blazer, his torn T-shirt, would ask to be introduced to her. But I also knew how bored she must be getting, while I was in classes or at the library, wandering around town, waiting for me in the little apartment; I had gathered that Ashley Manor sponsored a lot of activities for its residents. Del slammed the bureau drawer closed and tugged one of my wool sweaters over her head.

"You can go," I said.

"I can't without you," she said. "The day would be ruined."

"Yes, you'd be missed," Geoff said.

I understood that neither of them wanted to go alone with the other. I hadn't begun the paper—hadn't even planned to write it for another few days. It was a poor excuse. I set my book on the couch.

I changed into a pair of jeans and grabbed a sweatshirt. I took my bag with my camera. I met Geoff and Del downstairs, where Geoff's car, an old Volvo, sat sputtering by the curb. The car had once been white, but rust, and a general accumulation of road dust and dirt, had transformed the paint into something dull and gray. It was a windy day, and the elm sent its bright leaves down onto the hood. In the tree's shade Mary Rae stood, irresolute, twirling her necklace. I refused to look at her face, at that bald expression of longing, irritated that she would continue to appear to me, as if she might force my hand.

She wanted to be found. And I hated to envision the state she'd be in, what might have happened to her. I had no idea where she was, and the idea of coming forward with the details that I knew seemed ridiculous. In the days after David Pinney disappeared, we'd learned that no one had thought to look for him. His father, his only parent, hadn't reported him missing immediately. "He's had his share of trouble," his father was later quoted to have said. "I figured he'd run off with some friend or other."

I felt a chill in the air, and I knew the warmth of the last two days was gone and something else was blowing in. You could hear the Cornell chimes, ghostly and partly out of tune. Del was already in the front seat, so I climbed into the back, the door groaning on its hinges. The leather upholstery was cracked, and the floor mats were encrusted with dirt and dried leaves and sawdust that I assumed came from Geoff's work in the furniture shop. I knew I was sitting in dog hair but was grateful that Geoff hadn't brought Suzie along— possibly in deference to me. He lit a cigarette and headed out of town, down Route 13, so that it wasn't long before we left the houses and the university, and Ithaca itself, behind.

"This will be a taste of the countryside," Geoff called out. He had the windows down, and the air blew in and whipped my hair over my face, making it hard to see where we were headed. I breathed in the smell of the dried leaves and roadside grass. We drove for what seemed an endless time, the road swinging in long, lazy curves past an old drive-in, its white screen blocked by tall spruce; past Cinda's Bridal Shop, where the dresses were lit up in the two front windows—fuchsia

moiré and the white sheen of synthetic silk falling in cascades from
the waists of headless dressmakers' dummies. A growing sense of
anxiety pervaded the whole outing—we knew nothing about Geoff,
and he could have just lured us into his car, and was now transporting
us to some remote location to do whatever he wished with us. Del
and I would be two more missing persons on the news.

My chest grew tight, my face numb. The road went through harvested fields filled with stubble, crossed a bridge over a stream into a
small village. Main Street consisted of turn-of-the-century houses
decorated with mums and carved jack-o'-lanterns, a funeral home, the
post office, a stone library. We approached the one intersection, its
four corners occupied by a gas station, a diner, a church, and a grand
Victorian house behind an iron fence. Geoff slowed and stopped for
a red light, and we passed an old wooden three-story building with a
sign that identified it as the Milton Hotel.

"This is Milton?" I asked him.

Geoff's eyes, dark and alert, appeared in the rearview mirror.

"Yes," he said. "My friend lives here. She's a painter. She teaches
at the university. It's not far now."

"This is where that girl is from," Del said.

We hadn't discussed Mary Rae, but obviously Del had seen the
flyers, and possibly read the newspaper accounts. There'd been no new
discoveries, no new quotes from the girl's mother hoping for her safe
return.

"You know, maybe she met someone and took off," I said. "She
might be sitting in a motel in Florida with some boyfriend watching
the news reports."

Geoff eyed me again in the rearview mirror. "Not likely she'd
take off."

I sensed he wanted to say more but thought better of it.

"I heard she was murdered," Del said. *"Macabre."*

Her earring caught the late afternoon sun, and I reached out and
moved her hair away to expose it.

"You still *have* those?" I said.

Del shook her head and Jane Roberts's Tiffany earrings flashed—pearls and tourmaline. *"Mais oui,"* she said. "I always carry them in case I'm invited to a party."

The light changed and Geoff pulled away from the intersection, turning soon after down a gravel road that proved to be the driveway of a picturesque yellow farmhouse. Dried sheaves of corn leaned against a lamppost, buttressed by bales of hay and lit jack-o'-lanterns, their grins toothless, their brows arched in ironic expressions of fear.

"Welcome to Windy Hill Farm," Geoff said.

We pulled alongside a Camaro with a crystal rosary hanging from the rearview mirror, a GTO with a new paint job and racing stripes, all of the cars sporting various stages of rust.

"It's the night of the dead," Del said.

Geoff laughed and put the car in park. "The poor souls are freed from purgatory, allowed to return to their old homes." He shut off the car and the keys jangled as he stuffed them in his pocket. "My grandmother used to say that after supper they would spread a clean cloth on the table and set chairs up for their returning loved ones. They'd recite the *De Profundis* and go to bed and you'd hear one of the townsmen ringing the bell."

"What was the bell for?" Del asked.

"To warn everyone that it wasn't safe to roam the streets at the time of the returning souls."

I worried about Del reading too much into the All Hallows' Eve thing.

"It's just an outdoor party," I said, trying to make her laugh.

Geoff opened his door and slid out of the car. The driveway gravel crunched under his boots. "Whatever it is, we're here. Come on, I'll introduce you to Anne."

I had thought it was kind of Geoff to invite us to the party, but now that we were there I wondered why. Some people subscribed to the notion of "the more the merrier," and as Del and I climbed out of the car, I told myself that was the case with Geoff. But was it odd that he would single us out? He walked ahead of us, his gray hair blowing around his head.

"He must have noticed we hardly go out and he feels sorry for us," I said, my voice low.

"Maybe this is a coven," Del said.

"And we're virgin sacrifices," I said.

Del snorted. "Speak for yourself. I was scourged and led down into the vault a long time ago."

As children, Del and I had read how the corrupted vestal virgins were taken to a vault furnished with a couch, a lamp, and a table with a small amount of food. They were sealed in and left to die. We used to joke that we'd sneak in a book to read in our lamplight, and we'd discuss which one we'd take.

We followed Geoff across the lawn to a path that led around to the back of the house. There the brown grass was interrupted by scattered trees—ash and maple—nearly barren of leaves and roped with strung lights. In the center of the lawn, surrounded by folding chairs, was a bonfire, the smoke unfurling across the harvested cornfield like gray ribbon. Stone steps led to a terrace, where a linen tablecloth covered a card table for a makeshift bar. About thirty people stood clutching bottles of beer or wine goblets, most of them young, a few others mixed in who were clearly not—men with graying hair, like Geoff, sporting button-down oxfords and suede slip-ons, women in bulky cardigans, glasses dangling from their necks on beaded strings. Geoff was greeted heartily by everyone, and he gave a sheepish wave and led us up the stone steps to the back door.

"Is Anne inside?" he said to no one in particular, his hand on the sliding glass door.

"I'm right here," a voice answered, and an older woman stepped from a group of younger ones who all seemed preoccupied and sad. Anne tossed her arm around Geoff and kissed his cheek. "We're all trying not to be morose," she said, not to him, but to me and to Del.

She took both of our hands in her own, her hand so light it felt insub-
stantial. "Anne Whiteside," she said.

"It's nice to meet you," I said.

Anne wore a bright patterned headscarf. Beneath it I could see the
delicate bones of her skull. It was evident that she was ill. Anne looked
at me, her eyes clear and searching. Del was surveying the yard, taking in the groups of people, the illuminated lights between the trees,
garish and out of place, like carnival lights.

"I'm Martha," I said. "This is Del, my sister."

"You look like twins," Anne said. "Are you?"

Del roped arms with me and pressed her cheek against mine. "Yes,"
she said. "We are."

"That's interesting," Anne said. "I love twins. Maybe you'll let
me paint you."

"We're not," I said. "We're not twins."

Someone started some music—it sounded like an old recording
of a plaintive, classical cello piece—and it filled the backyard, the
swirls of blown leaves, the line of pine trees beyond the shorn fields,
with a sense of haunted sadness. Despite the few days of warmth it
was too cold, really, to be outside, but everyone had put on sweaters
and jackets, and were fortifying themselves with alcohol, moving their
chairs closer to the bonfire. Geoff had gotten a glass of bourbon and
ice. He looked at us. "I don't really see the resemblance."

Anne seemed affected by the music. Her eyes grew wet. "Well, I
see it," she said.

Del fluffed her dyed hair. "I'm not as curly."

"Well, you're curvy enough," Geoff said.

Del laughed out loud, one of her exuberant laughs that offset the
sad cello.

"She said 'curly,'" I said.

"Regardless," Anne said. "I would like to paint you."

I couldn't discern where the music was coming from—and then
I saw speakers in two of the lower-story windows. From this angle

you could see the house's blistered paint, its peeling wood siding, the way the house, like the landscape, seemed dead or dying. The wind picked up and jangled the glass bulbs of the strung lights together.

"Who's playing this awful stuff?" Geoff said.

"I like it," I said. I did like it. But Del gave me a strange smile, as if she thought I was making it up.

Geoff and Anne went down the terrace steps, and it was just Del and me. There had been years of birthday parties when it was just Del and me, separate from the others—in paneled basement rec rooms, a long table covered with a paper cloth holding soft drinks and bowls of chips, the paper streamers drooping from the ceiling. Maybe our clairvoyant game had left its mark on the neighborhood children, or word had spread about us in the hallways at school. Were we really able to see their dead? Or was it all an elaborate hoax? The other children didn't like either possibility. We were invited by their mothers out of a sense of decorum.

In our teenage years, Del was sneaking off to upstairs bedrooms at parties, slipping away with boys in cars, leaving me to find my way home alone. She was a wonderful mimic, and she could pattern her conversations with boys on those she overheard with other girls, with actors on television—none of it very original. She learned to flirt at an early age and it annoyed me only because it seemed so dishonest. Much like her role in our clairvoyant game—Del was a fabulous fake.

I stood by her on Anne's terrace. She had no qualms about abandoning me, but I wouldn't leave her side. No one approached us, and I wondered why we'd even come.

Del said she wanted a whiskey sour, the drink our parents had at the cocktail hour.

She stepped over to the bar. "I just love them."

I knew she was making fun of me for claiming I liked the music. I followed her to the bar and poured myself a glass of red wine, the glass monogrammed and too flimsy to be used outdoors. When I turned around, a man was so close that I nearly spilled wine on his wool sweater. Del was behind me at the bar, filling a glass with ice.

"Did you find your cat?" he said.

He had one of those smooth-cheeked faces that flush in cold weather. The kind that mislead you, instantly, into believing the person is younger than they really are, or that they retain a child-like innocence, and, so, are incapable of having any ulterior motives. His eyes were almost a gold color—a brown like ale. He was tall and broad-shouldered in his corduroy jacket, but the most unusual thing about him was his wide-brimmed beaver-skin hat. I wasn't sure how he recognized me—it had been dark the first time we'd encountered each other, and I wouldn't have known *him* without the lost cat reference. I considered pretending I wasn't who he thought I was, but he was watching me, almost waiting for the lie. I suspected he would have a quick comeback, had even planned it out before I replied.

"I didn't find her," I said.

"I'm sorry," he said. "Hopefully someone's given her a new home."

And then Del appeared, taking my glass of wine, jumping into the conversation. "Or she's been mauled by a loose dog, or struck by a passing car," she said. She looked up at the man over the rim of her glass. Before we'd even introduced ourselves, Del was there. "Remember that book about the four kittens we used to have when we were little?" she asked me. She reached out and grabbed my wrist. "The house cat, the ship's cat? The alley cat had to live through the traffic in the streets and the bad weather, and fight off the other bigger, angrier cats? I used to say that was me." I could feel Del's cold fingers.

"No, I don't." I pulled my arm away. "Where's your drink?"

"You were the housecat," Del said. "Muffy, or Miffy. Sipping milk from a china saucer." Del held her hand like a paw and stuck her tongue out in a dainty way to imitate the cat sipping.

"I'm William Bell, by the way," William Bell said. He held out his hand and I took it in mine, aware of the heat of him, the brightness of his eyes.

"Martha," I said.

"Or Muffy," he said.

Del held her hand out once he'd released mine. "I'm Delores, her sister."

William seemed hesitant to take her hand, suspicious of another lie.

"We came with Geoff," I said. "I rent an apartment in his house."

"Sure, Geoff," William said.

I wondered if Geoff had mentioned me to him. I wondered, then, what Geoff might have said.

"The girl was from here," Del said. "The missing one."

I could rarely predict what Del would say, or to whom. It was almost a comfort that this much of our relationship hadn't changed.

"She is," he said. He looked around him as if to assess the group of people. "Most of these people grew up here."

"Did you?" Del asked.

William slipped a hand into his jacket pocket. "I did," he said. "Born and reared."

"So all of you knew her? She was a friend?"

Del sipped my wine, and I wanted to reach out and dash it from her hand.

"Everyone knows everyone in a small town," he said.

I understood then the somber tone of the group, the absence of costumes—that this was a sort of vigil for Mary Rae.

"Oh, we know all about small towns," Del said.

I wasn't sure when I might join the conversation. Should I mention where we were from, or tell him I was a student? Should I ask him what he did for a living? But Del continued on.

"We can see if your friend has a message for anyone," she said. "My sister and I can contact her."

William had raised his beer to his mouth. I'd seen him glancing around for a way to excuse himself, but now he lowered the beer and angled his head at Del. "Pardon?" he said.

I should have stepped in and interrupted, but I found myself unable to summon the words to stop her. She went on to explain about the Spiritualists by the Sea, and how we received our training there as young girls. "I'm sure Martha wouldn't mind a session. If your friends are curious, that is. Some people gain solace from a medium."

I could feel my face redden. "No parlor tricks today, Del," I said.

Del looked almost flirtatious. "She's just being modest. We're really very good."

William clutched his beer with both hands. "The majority here don't talk about her in the past tense," he said. "I don't think anyone is seeking closure."

"I'm sorry," I said to him.

I watched him walk off across the lawn with a sense of a missed chance.

8

I did like boys. The story I told Detective Thomson had been just that—a story with a small bit of truth—one afternoon Jane and I had gotten high and kissed in her bedroom as practice for the boys we planned to take each other's place. I'd started it, and Jane had been embarrassed after—so much so that she'd begged me never to tell anyone, her eyes filled with anxious tears.

The sun lowered, and the sky darkened, and gray clouds slipped quickly across the horizon and out of view. Someone had added wood to the bonfire and tightened the ring of folding chairs around it. A grill on the terrace sent up smoke, the source of the grilled meat.

Del drank the wine back in one gulp.

"Another?" she said. She held the glass by its stem and twirled it. "This is fancy."

"I can't believe you said that," I told her.

"It's the night when lost souls return home," she said. "It would be a perfect time to do it."

"How do you know she's dead?" I said. "You can't talk like that here with her friends all around."

"Oh, I have it on good confidence that she's dead," she said. "And she may be stuck in between worlds, or have some last words. She may want to name her killer."

Mary Rae had stopped at the porch party that night, lingering, as if she wanted to join them. "Where did you hear this?" I asked Del.

"I have some friends who talked about it," she told me.

I went to the bar and poured myself a new glass of wine. Del reached for the bottle. "Stop it," I whispered. "Just stop it." I grabbed the bottle back from her. Her medication clearly prohibited the addition of alcohol. "What friends? Where did you meet them?"

Del sighed. "It's too hard to explain," she said. "They live in the encampment. And I know you're going to ask me 'what encampment,' but I'm not even going to try to describe it. I will take you there."

"What?"

"They want to meet you anyway."

"Who?" I said.

"Sybil Townsend," she said. "She reads cards."

"Not a very original name," I said, laughing. "She reads cards in the encampment?"

"Yes." Del spun her empty wineglass in her hands, and I took it from her and set it on the bar.

"You're going to break that," I said.

I worried that Del had lost the plot, as Geoff would say. I should have kept a more careful eye on her. The concerto spilled through the window speakers, and we could hear the low voices of the people around the bonfire.

"Sybil read my cards," Del said. "She said someone close to me is in touch with the dead girl."

"That's ridiculous," I said. "That's just not true."

Geoff was walking up the sloping lawn. "You two tending the bar?" he said. He uncorked the bottle of bourbon, and I could smell it, and smell the dead leaves, the drying hedges around the terrace, the bonfire smoke. "Come down to the fire. Get something to eat. It's warmer."

Del and I grabbed plates—vintage Spode china depicting an autumn scene—and stood in line for grilled chicken threaded on skewers with vegetables, warm bread. We followed Geoff back to the fire, and Del and I took open seats, separated from each other. Geoff introduced us to the people sitting nearby—a woman named Lucie, tiny, almost frail, wearing a man's coat that seemed to dwarf her; her boyfriend, Joseph, burly in a heavy plaid shirt. I recognized Lucie's voice as that of the woman at the porch party. A woman to my left introduced herself as Alice.

"This town is cursed," Alice said. A tremor moved through her, from cold or fear, I couldn't say. Her long, dark hair reminded me of Mary Rae's—she wore the same style of curls.

Joseph, as if to corroborate, told about people they knew, presumably from high school, a litany of tragic ends—Jerry Zelnick in his blue Pontiac on Trumansburg Road, Cary Belton in his Camaro in Ellis Hollow—boys who thought it impressed someone to drive without headlights on dark country roads. Alice mentioned a teacher shot by his daughter's boyfriend, the boyfriend's subsequent suicide over his own father's grave.

"Carl Sutton," Joseph said.

"And maybe Mary Rae," Alice said. She started to cry, softly.

A few seats down, Del wrapped her arms around herself as if she were cold, and a boy sitting next to her gallantly draped his coat over her shoulders. The girl named Lucie rose from her chair and knelt down beside Alice and hugged her.

"Mary Rae is her best friend," Joseph said to me across Lucie's empty seat.

"I was the last to see her," Alice said to me. "She spent the night at my grandmother's house. We got drunk on beer from the cellar refrigerator, and then we went out into the snow in the backyard with my old batons. Mary Rae threw hers up and dented the house's siding. God, we laughed so hard we wet our pants. We made snow angels."

Alice briefly covered her face with her hands, like a child playing peek-a-boo or counting for hide-and-seek.

"When we couldn't find her at first I just knew it was my neighbor who took her," she said. "Me and Mary Rae used to watch him go out all dressed up. He wore these flashy silk shirts and polyester pants and aviator glasses. We watched him through my bedroom window and made fun of him. 'There goes Lonesome Ricky,' Mary Rae used to say."

Alice's eyes filled with tears again.

"One time we snuck into the drive-in—Bobby Sorel had his father's car, some big sedan, and we both fit curled up in the trunk. When Mary Rae was missing I kept picturing her wrapped with duct tape in Lonesome Ricky's old rusty Grand Prix, listening to him singing disco music."

The wind rattled the branches overhead and sent sparks skittering out of the fire. I'd visualized nearly the same thing about Geoff— minus the duct tape—driving Del and me off in his car.

"I don't know what to picture anymore," Alice said. "It's all a big nothing."

Now might have been the time for me to mention the girl in the narrow room with the icy windows, but I doubted this information and its accompanying image would be welcomed.

"Did you tell the police about him?" I asked her. "Lonesome Ricky?"

"Yeah," she said. "That poor man worked for New York State Electric and Gas for thirty years. His only crime was being stuck in the seventies."

Geoff had left his seat and was up at the bar again. Del was talking to Anne, beside her, and I worried she would repeat her offer of our clairvoyant services. I caught William watching me, wearing the expression of someone trying to puzzle things out. Alice and Lucie kept me distracted with their reminiscences about their lost friend— how she'd gotten a job at the Viking Lanes bar, how she'd started classes at the community college, how on New Year's Eve they'd all gone out to the Hill Top Inn.

"She looked so beautiful," they said. In the photograph on the telephone pole, Mary Rae wore curls, a fancy dress.

They told me how they were all champion twirlers—competing all over the state in high school. "Mary Rae was so good," Alice said.

"The best of the three of us," Lucie said.

They described their costumes—the short skirts and sequins, the warmth of the gym during practice. I'd lost sight of Del—she and Anne had walked out of the bonfire's ring of light. When I looked behind me, cold air struck my face. The house's downstairs windows were lit up, and the sorrowful cello piece had come to its close.

Just then a man in a police uniform came around the side of the house. He approached the fire, his badge glinting, and I wondered if he was mistakenly in costume. Everyone quieted. Overhead, something dark took wing, and the man in uniform ducked, as if he, too, sensed it passing.

"Officer Paul," Joseph said, his voice terse but polite.

The officer came right up to the fire and held out his hands to warm them. He was tall, trim, his shirtfront tucked neatly into his belt. His ears stuck out below the band of his cap, large and vulnerable in the firelight.

"Good evening, folks," he said.

Around the fire, every face seemed marked with trepidation. William kept his face averted, as if investigating something of interest in the woods. This was probably the sole officer on the town force, the first responder to the accident scenes, the one who had come to the doors of houses to report the deaths they'd just cataloged. "No news," he said. "Just checking a report of a noise disturbance. Playing your music a little too loud?"

The concerto's close had ushered in an eerie silence, and we all just looked at one another.

"The professor around?" Officer Paul asked.

Someone suggested she had gone into the house, and he started up the lawn toward the terrace.

In his wake, someone cleared his throat, and someone else made a remark under his breath.

"He's such an asshole," Alice said. "As if any of us would ever do anything to Mary Rae."

I suppose I hadn't considered their involvement in her disappearance until Alice mentioned it, and then I felt—what? Sympathy? Understanding? The days after David Pinney was finally reported missing we waited for the discovery of his body. The uniformed police came around to houses in the neighborhood, asking questions, and we were called downstairs to sit in the living room when Detective Thomson made his first appearance, the chair brought in from the dining room, his trousers riding up to reveal his brown socks, his white legs.

"Who usually swims with you in your pool? Any neighborhood kids? What are their names?"

Answering, tearfully, my heart racing, Del clinging to my hand, to our mother's hand.

"My girls are distraught," our mother said. "Must you continue to question them about this? They've told you all they know."

The days had moved forward then, one into the other like a train chugging off from the station into the city, the world a blur going by. And then that train stopped, and I got off, and first Cindy Berger, and then the other dead—lovelorn, languishing—began to appear to me, and it was senior year, and Del was in the Institute. Detective Thomson continued his rounds of questioning.

Where were you on the afternoon of Friday, August eleventh?

At home.

At your grandparents' house?

That is home.

What were you doing?

Reading. Upstairs.

Anyone with you in your room?

No.

Anyone else at the house?

There were kids swimming outside, but a storm came in, and I think they all left.

Why weren't you swimming?

I didn't feel like it.

Did you have an argument?

No.

Well, did you talk to any of the kids?

Sure.

What did you say?

I don't remember exactly. We played croquet for a little while. Then it seemed like it was going to rain, so I went inside.

You didn't invite anyone in?

No.

Why not?

I'm not allowed to have friends in the house when no one is at home.

Whose rule was that?

My grandfather's.

And, I'm sorry, he passed away several years ago, is that correct?

Yes.

But the rule stands?

Yes.

What book were you reading?

The World as Will and Representation.

(silence)

Schopenhauer?

I understood Alice's anger.

"Screw Officer Paul," I said.

Alice squeezed my hand.

"Have you seen my sister?" I asked her.

The other girl, Lucie, touched my shoulder. "Don't worry," she said. "We're all friends here."

I understood that it wasn't just Mary Rae's disappearance, but the mystery of it, that had these girls frightened, clustered together around the fire. Beyond the firelight the ring of pine woods did feel ominous, a place where the dead might hang back from the brightness, hesitating to emerge. I scanned the woods, and I thought I could see figures, waiting patiently in the shadows. It filled me with a rare dread—I'd never been afraid of them before. I stood to look for Del or Geoff, and my head spun from the wine.

I moved out of the circle into the cold night air and began to walk across the lawn. Suddenly William emerged from the darkness behind me, reached out for my arm, and held it, loosely, near the elbow.

"Hang on," he said.

I startled, felt the heat of his hand through my sweatshirt. I faced his amber-colored eyes, his square chin. "What?"

Had Del done something or said something more? He let go of my arm. "It was nice of you to listen to the girls back there," he said.

"It's terrible," I said. "What's happened to your friend."

"At some point, though, you have to move on," he said. "They refuse to do it. It's frustrating to have to hear it over and over. The last night, the last phone call, the last birthday, Christmas, New Year's."

I could tell he was older than the girls, old enough to see them as immature. I didn't want him to know I was closer to their age than his, to view me the same way.

"You think I'm being harsh," he said. "I guess I am."

"I think you're honest," I said. "I can't fault you for that."

I stepped toward the terrace and warmth of the house's lights, intent on finding Del, but William grabbed my arm again, this time more forcefully, perhaps surprised that I was leaving him.

"Wait," he said. "Could we talk sometime?"

"About what?" I asked. The pressure of his hand on my arm lessened now that he had my attention. A gust of wind blew my hair over my face, sent a spray of embers up that forced a few people back from the fire.

"Anything at all," he said.

It was as if I had amazing things to share, and that out of innumerable nameless women he might encounter—passing by on the sidewalk, or in their cars—and even over Del, I was unique, and chosen. It was a powerful thing, this being chosen. Strong enough to urge me to assume I had the upper hand, that I could control what I'd give and take. I told him I had to find my sister, and he asked if he could call me. I knew nothing about him—who he was, what he did, why he was even there. Still, I wrote my phone number on an old miniature golf scorecard I found in my bag, and we separated at the terrace steps. I went up to the door and into the glare of the kitchen, where Anne sat with a cup of tea at the counter.

She raised her hand, weakly, in greeting. "I had a wonderful chat with Delores," she said.

I found Anne difficult to read—the thin line of her pressed lips, the trembling teacup in her hand.

"I hope she didn't bother you," I said.

"Not as much as that irritating police officer," she said.

The kitchen was as warm as its lights had promised from outside. Anne gestured to a bar stool beside her. "Sit," she said. "I found your sister very intriguing—given my circumstances."

I didn't want to sit with Anne. I felt certain I should find Del, and Geoff, and head home. I kept picturing the dead waiting in the fragrant pine shade—souls who knew Anne, family members, friends, Mary Rae herself with her dismal longing.

"I'm looking for Del," I said. "Do you know where she is?"

Anne took a sip of her tea. "I'm going to die soon," she said. She set the cup down on its china saucer and gave me a look that startled me at first—it was the look the dead gave me, full of worry, and need.

"I'm sorry," I said.

Anne laughed then and did her weak wave. "Oh, well, it's not your fault. I do wish I could work more—there's suddenly so much I'd like to finish. I'm sorry about that. And this whole horrid thing about Mary Rae—such a lovely girl." Anne's eyes seemed questioning. "I'd like to stick around long enough to find out who did this to her," she said. "I'm open to any little hints."

"Del is full of stories," I said. I measured the steps toward the glass doors to the patio and escape. "You can't really believe the things she says."

Anne continued to appraise me. "I do," she said over the rim of her shaking cup. "I believe her."

When you've spent a long time in hiding—quiet, resourceful, and almost always unsure, questioning yourself and your own sanity—and someone tries to coax you out, it's a rush of emotions impossible to take in at once. I felt gratitude, relief, an overpowering surge of release, and then cautiousness. Anne's voice turned soft, kindly.

"I believe you," she said.

The kitchen felt too warm, and my head spun. "I really would like to find Del," I said.

Anne set her teacup down in its saucer, where it settled with a brittle-sounding crash. "She met one of the local boys here in the kitchen," she said, curtly. "They may have gone out front."

I thanked her, and I felt a tinge of regret for not providing her with what she wanted. I didn't know who killed Mary Rae, and I didn't want to know those details. I couldn't have realized then that they would become very important to me later.

I went back out the doors to the terrace, down the steps to the yard, and around the side of the house. Geoff was there in the glare of someone's headlights.

"Oh, there you are," he said. His voice was slurred. He'd had too many bourbons. "Your sister is taking off."

Along the gravel drive the maple trees' leftover leaves were like torn golden paper in a car's headlights—a red Firebird, its dual exhaust fanning white smoke around our ankles. Del stood by Geoff, her face lit up. I suppose I knew what she would do before she did it, and still, there was nothing I could do to stop her. The driver reached over and opened the car's passenger door and Del slipped into the car. I smelled pine tree air freshener. And then she shut the door without a glance back, and the car took off, careening down the gravel drive like a getaway vehicle.

9

Geoff wasn't ready to leave the party, but he took pity on me and gave me the keys to his car to look for Del. I was panicked, and furious with her for taking off.

"I'll stay here with Annie," he said. "She can give me a ride home tomorrow."

I suspected it was the bourbon that made him so generous, but I would come to find out that he was often generous with his car. Before I drove off he leaned down to my window, provided simple directions—a few landmarks for finding my way home—and said, "Randy's a good sort," referring to the driver of the Firebird. "Don't get all up in arms."

I made it down the gravel drive to the main road, and then circled around town, past the diner, past a park with an old-fashioned bandstand, its intricate woodwork glowing white. The streets were dark but dotted with children walking in groups, their Halloween costumes disarming in my headlights—genies in chiffon and spangles, princesses in blue satin, the long dresses dragging around their shoes. As I drove past them some looked at me from behind their masks—creatures with fangs streaked with blood, monsters with distorted faces, even more friendly cartoonish characters—but their eyes darted, alive and frightening, behind the molded plastic, and I felt a sense of being lost in some strange, in-between world. I had the window rolled down, and I smelled wood smoke and burned pumpkin. My fury at Del compelled me to circle the grid of streets, and looking, in Geoff's Volvo wagon, like a crazed housewife—desperate and near tears.

Del didn't have a cell phone, and I didn't know the town well enough to find her, although I could guess where she'd gone with the driver of the Firebird—some unmarked road leading to a lakeside, or up a rutted, abandoned cart path to some dark field to have sex. I could only hope that Randy was, as Geoff suggested, "a good sort," and I gave up, finally, and found the main road out of the village, following Geoff's directions back through the empty stretch of open land, past the garden store with its sheds for sale, its lawn statuary, its jewel-colored globes shimmering. Del wasn't an innocent. She always went after what she wanted, while I waited behind, the cautious bystander, embarrassed by the virginity I kept a careful secret. "Sister," Del would call me, after our great-aunt, and it annoyed me just to think about her saying it.

At my apartment I parked in front of the house, half-expecting Mary Rae to be standing under the elm, but the street was quiet, save a few bands of older trick-or-treaters who probably were planning some mischief. I had hoped to find Del at home, and the porch light was on, but the house rose, hulking and unfathomable over me, its windows all dark. I climbed the staircase and put the car keys under Geoff's mat. Suzie, on the other side of Geoff's door, poked her nose at the bottom, sniffing me out. My sweatshirt hadn't been warm enough, and I was chilled. Inside my apartment I turned on the lamp, put on my warm coat, and lay down on the bed. We'd stopped folding it up every morning, and it had become a landing place for books and bags, a place where we lounged to read or talk. I must have fallen asleep, and I awoke when my cell rang. I answered expecting Del—a plea to come pick her up back at the party or at the local Viking Lanes. Instead, William's voice filled the apartment, clear and deep.

"Is that you, Martha?" he said.

I sat upright, nervously, his voice ringing out of the phone as if he were beside me. "It's you," I said.

He laughed. "Yes, William, from the party."

He said he was sorry for calling so late, and although I had no idea what time it was, I suspected it must have been past midnight. Del wasn't home yet, and I was relieved to have the place to myself to talk. William said he was a bit of an insomniac, and he was going to try to wait until morning to call, but there wasn't anything else of equal importance to do until then. He felt we were connected somehow—though he wasn't sure why he felt it. My head swam, the confession so intimate I didn't know what to say back. I couldn't let silence be my only reply.

"Maybe there is something unexplainable at work," I said, and instantly regretted it. "I'm just kidding," I said, which was just as bad.

"It's fine," he said. "I'm not suggesting anything *otherworldly*."

I leaned back onto the pillows on my bed. I didn't hear the footsteps on the stairs, but Del burst into the room.

"It's snowing!" she said.

Out the window, in the streetlight, snow was whitening the branches of the elm. I was so unnerved by William's call, I didn't care where Del had been, what she'd done. I kept seeing his eyes on me at the party, and the way his cheeks reddened from the cold.

"Who is 'D'?" he wanted to know. "And are you 'M'?"

He was reading off the scorecard, where my sisters and I put our initials. My older sisters and I were competitive miniature golfers and played with our father on a course near his ranch house every summer. I told him I was "M," the one with two holes-in-one. I didn't say that "D" was for "Daddy" and not "Del," who had always refused to play.

Del had turned on the TV and made hot chocolate spiked with Kahlúa. She sat a few feet away from me, shushing me every so often so she could hear, dropping handfuls of candy corn onto the bed for me. I told William I was an art major, and then I told him about my Women and Grief course.

"We listen to tapes of keening women from Ireland and Greece," I said. "I can barely stand it."

"I can understand why," he said.

I tried to explain how it was so awful I wanted to laugh, and how hard it was not to. At that point, Del gave me a look. "My sister says I'm crazy," I said.

"You're interesting," he said.

He said he, too, was an artist, and he taught at the university. A photographer. "Like you," he said. He'd heard of my work—abandoned places, landscapes—from another professor. I asked him who, surprised, and he brushed this off. "Just another professor in the department." I didn't want to seem as if I was encouraging him to gossip, so I let it go.

"I'm just an adjunct," he said. "I'm hoping to find something more permanent."

I asked him what his work was like, and he said he'd been inspired by Ted Spagna's sleep studies. "Something like that," he said.

All very vague, but at the time his hedging and easy side-stepping hadn't been obvious to me. I would push him away, ruin it, if I was too inquisitive, but it was difficult to negotiate closeness over the telephone. I was struck, then, that this was something out of the ordinary—a man calling me up in the middle of the night to talk.

"Why abandoned places?" he asked.

I could make out his breathing on the other end, waiting.

"You'll have to see for yourself," I said.

Below my window, beneath the elm, Mary Rae waited, though for what I hadn't yet decided. I wondered how well William had known her, and then decided it was wrong, at this point, to bring her up.

"The places must seem like the women on the tapes," he said.

"Yes, keening," I said. We were both quiet for a moment, deciding what to say next.

Del turned off the television and stood in the center of the room. She, too, had put on her coat, and I made a mental note to ask Geoff about the heat.

"Let's call it a night," she said.

"It is three a.m.," William said. He'd heard Del, and it rankled that somehow she had become part of our conversation. "I have class tomorrow. Do you?"

"No," I said, though I did. I wasn't ready to run into him in person on campus, to have him take my arm again and lead me into the Green Dragon for coffee. Talking to him had filled me with some sense of promise that I might become someone other than myself, and I wanted time to fashion this person. When I hung up the phone Del came out of the bathroom in a T-shirt, and slipped quickly under the sheets of the bed. We had a few blankets, including the afghan my grandmother had crocheted for me, and she pulled them all up. Beneath the covers I could feel her shivering. She smelled of cigarettes, and a cologne that must have been worn by the Firebird guy.

"That was him, wasn't it?" she said. "The weirdo from the party?"

"He's an artist," I said, sounding like Charles Wu. "Besides, a Fire-bird? Really?"

I could tell Del was falling asleep. "He had on a leather jacket," she said. "A 1950s hoodlum jacket."

"What was his name?" I said.

"Don't know," Del mumbled.

"Randy," I told her. "Geoff said his name was Randy."

"Are you sure he didn't say he *was* randy?" Del said.

"No, he said he was a good sort," I said.

"It's snowing," she said, and fell quickly asleep.

10

William called every day that week. We learned how to interpret each other's silences, which direction to take our resumed words—back to our childhoods, or simply to daily occurrences to fill the spaces in our conversations.

"I slipped off the steps of my porch today," I said. Then I worried he would think me ungraceful or foolish.

"She fell arse over tit!" Del cried out so William could hear. She was imitating Geoff, something she'd begun doing unconsciously, without any malice.

"Oh God, Martha. Are you all right?" William asked, and I was touched by the caring in his voice and by the sound of him speaking my name.

He invited me to one of his classes, but I had a class of my own at the same time, so I left mine a little early and stood outside his door. The inside of the classroom was dark—the lights were off, and he had a slide up on a screen, an Edward Weston nude. He was talking about the work, his voice different than the one I'd become accustomed to on the phone—not its sound, but its tone, more goading. The students' replies were soft and tentative, as if they were a little afraid of him. Did I know the man in the room at all? Before the class let out I left. I worried about his calling me that night. How would I react? But when he did call, he was the same as always, and I relaxed.

By then our talking had become spotted with whispered intimations—things taking on a double meaning, the equivalent of him pressing his thigh against mine under a dinner-party table.

"Anne is right," he said. "You'd be a perfect subject."

It had been a Wednesday evening, two weeks after we'd met.

"Do you even remember what I look like?" I stood in front of the mirror by the door and looked at myself talking on the phone as if I were someone I didn't know. Had he overheard Anne mention wanting to paint me? Or had he spoken to her about me?

"You had a few buttons undone on your blouse," he said.

"Could you see anything?"

"Do you want to know if I was looking?"

"Obviously you were looking." I was not at all bothered by his looking.

He told me after classes that day he'd gone out for a walk, and had crossed a brook, and had found that the stones at the bottom were the same color as my eyes.

"I could be wrong," he said. "It was such a brief meeting."

He said we should have the predicted coffee somewhere, or lunch, if I wanted. But I was imagining something else. The old rules didn't seem to apply to us—all that holding out interminably, waiting for something to be proven. I had no reason to dicker with my body. I'd done that enough with boys at home—pushing them away after a kiss good night, expecting more from them—a dinner date, an afternoon watching old movies, a gift or two—before I gave more. I wasn't sure why I'd behaved the way I had, why I'd refused them all. Even poor Charles Wu. I was determined to overcome my hesitation. William was, after all, a professor who found me *interesting*, and I had heard yearning in his voice. I invited him to come to my apartment. There was an awful halting silence, the kind that is so long you worry the other person has been disconnected. But then his voice sounded in agreement, and I forgot completely about what his indecision might have been.

During all of this Del had refused to return to the manor. Our mother called and lectured me about keeping Del in my apartment. She bought an airline ticket for Del to go back. "We worked hard to get her in that place. Your father pulled strings," she said. "She's going to lose her spot. And then where will she be? A homeless person."

Our mother, in that big empty house. I wondered if both Del and I were banned from returning home—if we could even view the old house as home anymore.

A week after the party at Anne's, I had talked to Del about going back. It was a Saturday, and we walked through the slush from my apartment to the bakery, and we went inside for éclairs and coffee.

"Don't you miss your boyfriend?" I asked her. We'd taken a round café table in the corner by the window, and Del flipped through the newspaper someone had left behind.

"No," she said. "He's not my boyfriend anymore."

I thought about the Firebird guy, Randy, but decided not to mention him. I didn't know if Del had continued to see him. Often when I left for class she'd be asleep, and when I returned the apartment was empty, and she'd be gone for hours. If I questioned her she only half-answered, and William would call, and I'd get distracted. I hoped she hadn't been visiting Sybil Townsend in the encampment. I'd made it clear that she shouldn't go back there, that it wasn't the best thing for her. Some days I'd get out of class and she'd be waiting for me on campus.

"Surprise!" she'd say. Her roots had begun to grow out—her true blond showing through, and she often looked out of place in her faded purple parka. Students passing her would eye her, though Del never seemed to notice or care.

"We need to get you a new coat," I said.

That day in the bakery she had on a dark green wool duffle coat she claimed one of her Milton friends had given her. "You remember Alice, right?"

She tore sugar packets and dumped the crystals into her coffee. The shop window steamed up behind her, the people beyond it on the sidewalk blurred shapes trundling past.

"How do you get to Milton?" I asked her.

"The bus?" she said. She raised the large mug up toward her face. "Or someone picks me up."

In my preoccupation with William I'd lost track of Del. I pushed her éclair on its china plate toward her.

"It's a nice coat," I said.

"It's Mary Rae's," Del said. "She left it at Alice's house."

She set her coffee down and picked up her éclair. At the table next to us a man blew his nose, and she set the éclair back on the plate without taking a bite. I'd never thought she'd wear a dead girl's coat, though there wasn't any proof yet that Mary Rae was dead.

"Well," I said. "It's warm and new-looking."

"There's nothing in the pockets. No clues. I checked."

I sorted through the sugar packets spread on the tabletop. "That's a relief."

"We want to find out what happened to her," Del said.

I lifted my cup to my mouth and the coffee was bitter and hot. Del had used all of the sugar.

"You know, all of us," she said. "The girls in Milton, and Anne."

The bell on the door rang as people came in—husbands and wives with small children for doughnuts, couples with their arms linked.

"What about your friends in Connecticut?" I said.

"I should just stay here. I can get a job," she said, her voice sounding almost plaintive. Del, as far as I knew, had never held a job before.

The cars sped past us in the new slush, their tires wet and churning. I wondered if life at the Manor was dispiriting and lonely. Once, I'd driven by the place—an old house with a porch and a newer addition with large plate-glass windows where everyone gathered for Ping-Pong. Del twirled her hair. She told me she could stay with Sybil in the encampment.

"I don't think that's an option," I said.

"Or with Alice. She lives with her grandmother, though. Her mother might move back from Florida and then I'd be in her room—sort of awkward."

Del told me the whole story about Alice and her mother, whose name was once Hester, and who'd changed it when she turned eighteen to Erika. Alice's mother had moved to Florida when Alice was little, and she arrived home every so often to "recharge." Erika had a tan, and long, dark hair, and wore beautiful clothes that made her seem like a bright bird against the backdrop of gloomy Milton. Summers, she set up lounge chairs in the backyard and she and Alice spent hours there sunbathing, planning when Alice would move to Florida with her, planning the name Alice would change hers to when she turned eighteen: *Vanessa, Brooke, Tiffany.*

"But Alice never changed her name?" I said.

"I guess not."

Then, with a mischievous look, Del confessed that Professor McCall, who lived downstairs next to Professor Whitman, had gone out of town on leave and was looking for someone to sublet her apartment. Geoff had told her this.

"But you'd have to talk Mother into it," she said.

My immediate reaction was irritation that Geoff hadn't consulted me first. But I knew he saw Del as an independent adult.

"When did Geoff tell you this?"

Del spun her coffee cup in circles on the tabletop. "He saw me yesterday and he told me about the professor. She'd left to take care of her sick mother in California."

I wasn't sure I wanted Del so close by, but I couldn't have her living in some encampment with a self-proclaimed medium named Sybil. She picked at the chocolate on her éclair and stared out the window.

"You'll have to talk Mother into it," I said.

Del wore her sly look.

"Well, she's a big pushover," she said. In our childhood years, our mother had relegated Del to my care. "Watch out for your sister," she would remind me. "Include your sister," she'd say when I had friends over swimming, or if I went bike riding into town. To my mother Del was always in need of watching, and part of my job had been to pretend that was true, to hide the fact that Del had been off on her own for years, doing whatever she wanted to do, and keeping much of it a secret.

The day Del was admitted to the Institute had been a dreary November one, wet and cold. I was a senior in high school. My friend Jane Roberts was driving me home from school, and we passed Del walking up the street in that same awful purple parka she'd shown up wearing in Ithaca, her hair and pants legs blowing back, the fallen leaves eddying around her feet. On her face was a look of purposeful concentration. Jane slowed, but I told her to keep going, and she drove up the hill to my house, and I got out. My mother was in the doorway wearing her cashmere car coat as if she were heading out to the store. My father's car was there as well, which was unusual. After their divorce we rarely saw our parents in close proximity to each other, and our father never came to the old house. But that day he was there in the driveway, sitting in his new BMW with the engine running.

I'd heard our mother talking to our grandmother, and talking on the phone, endless days of consulting friends and doctors—*a threat to herself or others*, she'd said. So far, she'd been told that walking around town and refusing to bathe didn't merit the kind of help Del needed. But I understood someone had "pulled strings," and I saw what Del was walking into that day, and I let her walk.

Inside the house, brushing past our mother's perfume, past her lip-sticked mouth, I went upstairs to my room to discover Del's clothes packed in a suitcase. Leanne and Sarah were away at school. They would find out later that Del was gone, and to them it wouldn't really matter. It would be a relief to know they wouldn't see her walking past the park where they hung out with their friends on their school breaks, wouldn't have to hear our mother try each evening to urge Del out of her dirty clothes, to wash her face and hands. They wouldn't wake in the night and find her sitting in their rooms, or wandering up and down the stairs. We had gotten used to these things, but it would be just as easy to become used to something else.

Our mother called me downstairs. I stood in the upstairs land-ing, and she begged me to come down. "You'll have to convince her to go to the hospital," she said.

I thought of her walking the neighborhood streets like one of the dead. I thought of David Pinney. I told Del I would ride with her to the Institute. That she wouldn't stay long, and that when she came home we'd go to the beach, and take the gold bedspread to lie on in the sand. We'd spread on Bain de Soleil, and our lives would continue on much as they'd always been. I couldn't know that too much time would pass for this to ever happen. I opened my father's car door and she got in. Only the neighbors watching through their bay windows with their evening cocktails would have seen this—a father and two daughters going out late one afternoon to the drugstore, or for ice cream. In the doorway to the house my mother had turned away.

When I got home that night my mother was in the living room in the dark, with my grandmother across from her on the brocade couch. The regulator clock's pendulum echoed. My mother still had on her lipstick, and her coat, tightly cinched. When I came in, she pushed herself from the chair and took off the coat. She went into the kitchen and emptied the dishwasher and put the dishes away. She climbed the back kitchen stairs, slowly, and shut the door of her bed-room. She'd remove her makeup with a special lotion and rub cream into her hands. She wouldn't cry until she crawled into the big bed and covered her head with the woolen blanket. I had hated my mother then for loving Del more and for expecting me to be the stronger one.

Now, I watched Del pick the chocolate off her éclair with her fingers and eat each small piece, and thought of my mother, who'd called yesterday and left a long message imploring me yet again to talk Del into returning to Ashley Manor. "Maybe she seems to be doing well," my mother said. "But just remember what used to go on. Do you want that responsibility?"

It wouldn't be too difficult to convince our parents that supporting Del here was a better alternative to the manor. Del's adventure the night of the party at Anne's gave me a small twinge of apprehension. But Del was taking me up on my promise that day in the car, and she knew I wouldn't refuse her.

"Maybe you can sign up for classes in January," I said.

Hopeful and happy, Del bit into her éclair and licked her fingers.

11

William Bell came to my apartment on a Friday night in mid-November. I watched for him from my window, through the branches of the elm. Del had moved into the professor's apartment, and the light from her window downstairs shone out onto the snow. Though I'd spoken to Geoff about the heat, the house remained cold. I had a fireplace in my apartment, and Del had one in hers, but Geoff had stated emphatically that we were not allowed to use them. I pictured hibernating bats with singed wings filling the winter sky above the house. We put large, lighted, pillard candles in the grates, and these gave, at least, an illusion of warmth.

The cold was bitter, different from New England's. Outside the city the wind spilled across the sweeping, open land dotted with abandoned farm machinery and old houses buckling in on themselves. You wouldn't think such houses were habitable, but once in a while there would be a tacked-up sheet in the doorway, or plastic nailed over the windows, and the trace of smoke from a chimney. William wasn't from anywhere else. He was born in Tompkins County, and except for the time he spent in Buffalo, acquiring his degree, he'd lived here all his life—most recently in the house on Cascadilla Street, where he'd rented an apartment and had held the gathering the night I met him. His father, who'd died two years before, had sold and repaired lawn mowers in a shop behind their rented house in Milton, and before that he was a famed attorney with a drinking problem. They had an enclosed front porch with an air hockey game, and gnome statuary on the front lawn that William, an only child, believed came alive at night. His mother had been gone since he was four years old, but before she died she grew apples and sold them from a small roadside stand, Macoun and Winesap and Cortland, and William had made change from a small metal tin. I supposed, from these aspects of his life told to me over the telephone at night, I knew everything about him. "*Mon pauvre orphelin*," I said to Del.

Del flopped down onto my couch, folded up for William's visit. "Poor orphan? And what are you? His new mother figure?"

"We're friends." I rummaged through my bureau drawers for an outfit, holding one sweater, then another up to myself in the mirror. "I like him."

"What do you like?" Del said.

I knew his interest in me was what made him special, and it embarrassed me to be so needy. I spread a red lamb's-wool sweater on the couch.

"It's not Christmas," Del said, and I balled the sweater and stuffed it back in the drawer.

"Don't be the one who loves more," she said, softly. "Remember Mr. Parmenter."

"I don't think that's a good comparison," I said.

Since Mary Rae, nothing out of the ordinary had appeared in gloomy Ithaca.

The town's dark pall, its strange, shifting cloud patterns, and the fluttery lake-effect snow that went on for days seemed to create a no-astral season. Nothing could materialize in such weather.

I told Del not to worry about me.

"Such an innocent, Martha Mary."

"Oh, shut up," I said.

So far, we hadn't discussed David Pinney, or that summer, and I wondered if, like Gene Tierney, she'd received too many shock treatments. Had that summer been entirely erased? Had her act for Detective Thomson not been an act at all? This would be the best scenario, and I decided not to press her for whatever slip of memory remained.

The night William came over, Mary Rae was absent from her spot beneath the elm, and I was grateful. He walked down the sidewalk and stepped onto the porch, and I found myself rushing down the stairwell to meet him at the door, tugging him by the arm in from the cold.

"Come here, you," I said.

His cheeks held the flush I'd noted at Anne's, and he wore the wide-brimmed beaver-skin hat. We stood on the old, worn Persian rug in what had once been the vestibule, the walls papered in brown, with tiny pink roses. The woodwork was brown, too, mahogany glowing in the weak yellow overhead light. There was a coatrack and an umbrella stand and a small, rickety antique table. The whole downstairs smelled of Del's incense, and I knew my urgency was prompted by a fear of her emerging from her apartment and saying something that would put a damper on all my plans.

William looked around, somewhat sheepishly, and removed his hat with one hand, grabbing it at the crown and revealing a mass of coppery curls. "Nice place," he said.

"Your hat is different." I should have said something else.

He looked at it in his hand. "Well," he said. "I guess it is different. It was my father's hat."

Del called him "Indiana Jones."

He hung his hat on the coatrack, and I worried that he knew Del had made fun of him. He was someone alone in the world, without family or ties. I didn't wait to kiss him. It felt natural to ease the sadness about his mouth with mine. His lips clung and trembled, kissing me back. His hands were cautious, suspended midair alongside my hips. I took his hand.

"Up here," I said. I pulled him up the stairs. His face was bright, his chest heaving under his coat.

Upstairs in my apartment, by the wavering fireplace candlelight, we kissed some more, and I undressed for him, a somewhat awkward striptease that I performed without any prompting. I'd assumed this was what he wanted from me—we'd talked around sex every night on the phone, and I'd decided to give up my hold on my virginity.

"You'll have to tell me how it is," Del had said before she left that afternoon. She'd smiled at me, though I sensed something hollow and distracted in her teasing.

I suppose my behavior was spurred in part by what I'd seen in movies, and what I'd imagined Del had done in the Firebird guy's car, or in the woods with Rory, her back against dead leaves and fern, or with the myriad other men she'd had sex with, mostly in cars, she'd said, which were preferable to the woods, though she loved the woods. I understood that the cars in the ravine had been the best of both things. I'd expected that the offering of my body, stripped of its clothes, would be enticement enough. Yet William stood by, his face marked with surprise. I took his hands and placed them on my waist. He slid his palms up and down my body and felt the raised bumps on my skin.

"I can't warm you up," he said.

So I pulled off the cushions and unfolded the bed, and we climbed in under the blanket and the crocheted afghan. William kept his clothing on until I asked him whether he was going to take things off, and he reluctantly, it seemed, removed his shirt and his pants and tossed them aside. His belt buckle clanked to the floor. He told me he'd brought me a poem, and he reached down to retrieve it from his pants pocket. He had copied it out from an old college anthology onto a sheet of paper, he said. The paper rustled, and my heart contracted from the sweetness of his motives. When he read his voice was the same soft hum I had grown used to over the phone. What I caught of the poem were a few images—a nest fallen into the mud, a rabbit's bones, an empty house—and I suspected he thought the poem would resonate with my artist's sensibilities, though I couldn't explain it was less the abandoned landscape than the presence of the dead that inspired me. After he finished, he carefully folded the paper. The words hovered, ghostly and solemn in the dim room. He asked me did I like it, and then why I thought it was good, and other things, until I found myself watching his mouth, craving it, even.

"Am I talking too much?" He shifted to his side and placed his head in his hand.

"Maybe," I said.

I had thought he wanted me. But when I touched him he took my hands away, like a correcting parent. I was resigned to kissing him, and even that he interrupted with a story about his motorcycle, a Triumph he was eager to ride again in the spring.

"This is different," he said.

I wasn't sure if he was making fun of me.

"Than what?" I felt awkward then for having taken off my clothes. He must have seen this on my face.

"Than I expected," he said. "Not that it isn't wonderful."

Under the blankets his hands moved, barely skimming the surface of me. He talked about the two spaniels his neighbor had at his house, and the way they came when you were sitting in a chair and settled their heads under your hands. His father had had a brown retriever that would lie in the dust of the garage floor while he worked on the mowers. Some people, William said, are happier working with their hands. Gradually, his eyes closed and he fell asleep, and I was left wondering about his discussion of dogs and their flanks.

My bed was lumpy with springs, and I had a certain angle in which I slept. But with William taking up the space, and my body burning from his fingertips, I could not sleep. Was this how Sister had sometimes felt? She'd entered the abbey at twenty-six, maybe worried she'd be an old maid—that she'd never find anyone but God to love her. I closed my eyes and tried to picture myself alone in a chaste bed, consumed with desire for something ineffable and bodiless, but lying beside William I knew you could not separate the two—body and desire. The elm cast shadows on my white plaster wall, and its branches, sheathed in ice, clicked together like bones. Beyond this sound was the silence of the snow. Was poor Mary Rae still waiting out there in the cold?

That first night with William, I envied Geoff. I tried to breathe in and out, regularly, to feign sleep. I considered slipping out of the apartment, down the stairs to Del's. But she would press me for details, and I didn't want to confess that nothing had happened. After a while, I slid from the bed and went across the room to peer out the window. Mary Rae's frozen hair framed her face, her eyes luminous. "What do you want from me?" I wanted to ask.

William and I were each similarly connected to our art, and though William was more taciturn about his work, I felt some tie to his approach that I couldn't explain. He'd said that, like me, he still shot film. He liked the way film captured light. He liked the old lenses. We'd talked for a long time on the phone about our cameras and our preferences. I enjoyed making prints—I didn't tell him why—and I thrilled to see the figure I'd photographed appear, though others saw only the light and some sort of golden glow that seemed to tremble in the location of my subject.

I sat by the window and pressed my face against the glass. After all of our talking on the phone, I didn't know this man in my bed at all. Perhaps he didn't want me pliable, eager to have him. Maybe he wanted me to play hard to get, to dole out pieces of myself—a mouth, a breast, a hip. Maybe he wanted me to object, to refuse him so he could force me. His sleeping, slack expression revealed nothing, and I felt a small, pitiable stone of fear. What was his interest in me? I wanted to wake him and demand an answer. But I carefully slipped back beneath the blankets. When I finally slept it was near morning, and I awoke to find him watching me in the gray light. We were like sentries who had traded places.

"Here we are," I said, a little too cheery.

His cheeks flushed. His breath came out in a white cloud. The candles in the fireplace had burned down to flat saucers of wax. He sat upright, his bare chest exposed, and my grandmother's crocheted afghan swaddling his waist, multicolored and gaudy.

"What time do you think it is?" he said.

"Do you need to leave?" I asked.

He ran his hands through his hair. "Do you think," he said, "I might be someone you could actually have feelings for?"

"Well." I sensed his staying or leaving was dependent on my answer, but I didn't know what to say. Del had cautioned me against revealing any true feelings, of having any feelings at all. I knew experience had taught her this—but I also knew Del didn't want a man's love and wouldn't have known how to return it if any had offered it. A boy had flowers delivered to our house once—a dozen roses. My heart had sunk when I answered the door, when Del pulled out the card with the boy's sloppy handwriting. Later, when I'd asked her what she did with them, she said she'd taken them to the cemetery and put them on David Pinney's grave. Back then, before the Institute, these were the kinds of things she said to me. "I like to get your goat, Martha," she'd said.

I had thought William and I wanted the same thing—that neither of us needed any real declarations of feelings, that what we felt could remain unspoken. I considered pulling him down under the blankets and warming him up, but even that seemed like coveting his body.

"You look cold."

His chest rose, pale against the afghan. "That's your answer?" he said. I felt like one of his students, bullied to provide a better response. But he didn't make a move to get up and leave. I felt sorry for him then. He was a nice man who thought we might have a normal relationship, and I'd tarnished it by not having the courage to voice my feelings. There was nothing I could do, honestly, that would change the situation. I didn't dare attempt to touch him, for fear he would recoil from me.

"You don't have to stay," I said. I rolled away from him, to the metal edge of the bed. Geoff would be waking with his Saturday morning routine—toast, black coffee in a china cup, listening through the wall with buttery crumbs on his fingers. I thought of Del, her ear pressed to the other side of my door. William heaved himself out of bed. He was tall, and his body unfolded, a sound of cracking joints and rustling sheets. He found his clothes, and the fabric slipped over his arms and legs. Finally, he put on his shoes, big boots that clomped on the wood floor. I rolled over and he was standing by the bed.

"Ask me not to go," he said.

"Tell me you want to stay," I told him.

"Tell me to kiss you," he said.

"Do you want to kiss me?" I was confused.

"I want to kiss you more than anyone I have ever met," he said, but he made no move toward the bed.

He went out the door and thumped down the stairs. I didn't get up and lock the door behind him. I lay there for a long time before sleep overtook me, wondering whether or not to believe him.

12

When I awoke it was early afternoon. Weak sunlight marked the end of the bed. And William was there, sitting in the duck-carved armchair. He was watching television without the sound, and the station wasn't tuned in well. He ate from a carton I recognized from the Korean place in Collegetown. Beside him on the floor was a camera—an old Leica, his favorite, I would learn. I was suddenly afraid of him, coming into my apartment without asking, and I feigned sleep, my heart thudding beneath the blankets. In my Romantic Poetry class we'd read Keats's "The Eve of St. Agnes," Madeline awakening in the poem to Porphyro's lute. Then I remembered William's work—the sleep studies—and I wondered, crazily, if he'd photographed me and captured my astral body rising up to mingle with those on the astral plane.

As if he could sense that I was awake, he smiled at me, wide and happy, and that quickly his presence seemed perfectly normal. I hadn't seen him smile like that before, and I thought we were embarking on this adventure in which each day would be marked by the new things we learned about each other.

"You're back," I said. It was as if he had chosen me again. My body was warm; my limbs slid across the soft sheets. Did he know of the tradition on the eve of St. Agnes? He said he did not.

"Virgins fast all day. They make sure that they kiss no one. At bedtime they remove their clothing and lie down on their backs with their hands beneath their pillow and say before sleeping: 'Now good St. Agnes, play thy part, / And send to me my own sweetheart, / And shew me such a happy bliss, / This night of him to have a kiss.'"

William put a chopstick full of noodles in his mouth. "And?"

"They see a vision of the man they're going to marry."

"And you're a virgin?" he said, looking skeptical.

My face must have gone blank. I hadn't wanted him to guess that.

"You're very beautiful when you're sleeping," he said.

"But I'm awake now. Does that mean you'll leave?"

He brought the food over to the bed and sat on the end.

"Are you hungry?" he asked.

"Not really." I wanted some kind of explanation for his presence, but he seemed perfectly at ease, as if it were a natural thing. He took a mouthful of food. I watched him chew, and he pointed to the television.

"Do you remember this show?"

I looked at the screen and couldn't make anything out. "No," I said, propping myself up to get a better view of the images beneath the static. My grandmother's afghan slipped down my body.

His face changed, quickly, like clouds moving over the sun and the shadows lengthening on a lawn. "You're still naked under there," he said.

He set the food down on the floor. He pulled me onto my knees and put my arms around his shoulders. I tasted the food's spices on his mouth. His breathing caught, his body's tension shifted like something coiled and tight, releasing. His hands were cold, but it felt wonderful, his hands and mouth moving, his groans. I didn't worry about what made him change his mind. I thought: *He came into my room while I slept.* He fell back into bed with me and fumbled with his belt, with the clasp to his pants. His entry was hurried, knifelike, and though I was prepared for it I may have cried out. He stopped suddenly, surprised. But then I pretended that nothing was different or wrong, even though at that moment I understood it to be. *My deflowering*, I thought, and then I knew I would never be able to tell Del a thing about the moment, that it was mine, not something I could share.

William and I stayed in bed all that day. Geoff came up the stairs and slipped his key into his lock. I wondered what Del was doing, but only briefly, and with no guilt for having forgotten her. Once or twice I may have heard her footsteps on the stairs, a gentle tapping sound. Maybe she really was listening at the door, but William held me in his hands. I felt my body transform, heighten and strain and sigh. The light moved, watery, across the foot of my bed, across the worn oak floor. It settled in the lap of the duck-carved chair. We let the room grow dim and darken and match the outside. When the streetlight came on, we watched the snow falling in it.

"Does it ever stop snowing here?" I asked. His hand was heavy, pressed to my bare stomach.

"It's winter," he said, as if this were an answer.

My stomach rumbled, and he said we needed to feed me, and so he pulled me up and my nakedness was light and airy in the dark. I stood on the foldout bed. He slid off the end and stood in front of me, and I was suddenly shy, unmoving under his gaze.

"Look at you," he said. "Galatea."

I was still, like marble.

William put his hands on my hips. This moment would stay with me for a long time after—the press of his thumbs, his cradling of me. He leaned in and kissed my hipbones, my thighs, and I gave in to him. I didn't need food. I wanted to be ravished. This was, for the most part, what became of us. My desire, and William satisfying it. I should have known better—desire brought suffering.

Maybe our movement in the room getting dressed, putting on our boots, alerted Del—she was at the door with her distinctive knock, a pattern we used when we played clairvoyants as children, rigging a lever to make a banging on the underside of the galvanized tub. Some patterns were warnings from the dead, and others, like this one, were more benevolent. "I miss you" or "I'm thinking of you." I looked at William. "It's Del," I whispered.

"I can hear you in there," Del said. "I was just heading out for a walk. Want to come?" I opened the door to Del on the landing in her new coat, its large hood pulled over her hat. "Finally," she said.

William shrugged on his corduroy jacket and took a long time with the buttons. He put his hands into his pockets, as if searching for a pair of gloves, but came up with nothing. Del and I waited in the doorway until he was ready. "Are you going to be cold?" I asked him.

He pulled me in close and wrapped his arms around me. "Not with you," he said.

I buried my face against his chest. He told Del he liked her coat, and she explained it was a dead girl's coat.

"She got it from the Salvation Army," I said.

We went downstairs and out into the snowy street. William wore his camera slung under his jacket. I'd left mine behind. The houses lined up in their rows, their roofs thick and white, the lampposts and power lines and tree limbs all leaden with snow. The snow falling was bewitching and oddly warm. William held my hand, and I let him, conscious of Del watching. Every so often he stopped and pulled me in to kiss. A passing car's headlights would light us up.

"This isn't the usual way things go with you," he said, quietly. "Is it?"

"This is out of the ordinary," I said.

I believed we were both feeling the same thing at the same

time—but I knew very little then. I was dangerously close to confusing the sex for love. Thankfully, I never admitted to it. Del had walked on ahead, and she looked back at us.

"Lovebirds? Really?" she said, in her caustic way.

William looked at me, his eyes soft and questioning. "You trust me, don't you?" he said, as if he needed reassurance. He let my hand drop. I had to retrieve his hand and tell him to stop it, and I knew then that I'd succumbed to something unnameable, marked by this reclamation, this rush to reassure.

We stood on the sidewalk, under someone's porch light. Inside the house we saw people watching television, just their feet in socks propped up on a coffee table. They'd never removed their jack-o'-lanterns from the porch. Nearly buried by snow, you could make out the carved grimaces. All around, things were caught unprepared by the snowfall—a rake propped on a fence, a child's bicycle tossed down on the grass. On the porch a pair of socks, pulled off and abandoned, frozen stiff in their contortions.

We kept walking, past Johnny's Big Red Grill, where a group of students spilled out, singing a pop song, and I had a sense of watching what should have been my life from a distance. We'd been walking behind Del, who steered us past the railroad tracks, into an end of town I had never been. She stopped at the head of a path, and we joined her. Below us a creek, not yet frozen, rushed in the dark. To the right were scattered twinkling lights, and a soft din of conversation. I sensed low-built dwellings coated with snow. There were several fires burning. The place smelled of wood smoke and the dank creek mud.

"Where are we?" I retreated a few steps, tugging on Del's arm.

"This is the encampment I told you about," she said. "I want you to meet Sybil Townsend."

William turned as if to head back toward town.

"These people know me." Del was slightly exasperated.

"My feet are getting cold," I said.

I didn't want to meet Sybil Townsend, especially just then. William stepped toward me and slid his two hands up under my coat, under my sweater and T-shirt. His hands on my skin, the press of his fingertips, were somehow consoling, familiar.

"Oh, let's just go with it," he said, quietly, into my hair. "She can tell us our fate."

Sybil Townsend and her abilities were all a game to him, as such things had been to Del and me as children. Del seemed to have forgotten we'd once played at this. William held my hand and we followed Del down the path worn muddy by others' footsteps. The enclave consisted mostly of tarps strung on two-by-fours. Sea breezes had aired out the tent encampment erected on the Spiritualists by the Sea site, and those balmy nights had filled with fireflies. Here people huddled in the harsh cold. Strung bulbs, or Christmas lights, powered by a small generator, lit some of the dwellings. Under the tarps, or around the fires, the people sat in aluminum chairs, the kind with plastic slats, on low-slung canvas chairs, camp chairs, the type you took to an outdoor concert or a kid's sports game or the beach. On end tables were small shaded lamps and tinny radios. I looked for tarot cards, for hands linked in communion. I listened for whispered messages from the dead.

The people eyed us warily from inside the tents. They were dressed in layers of clothes that made them look lumpy. We kept walking down the narrow paths, one leading to the next. The snow fell, landing in their fires and hissing. The mud sucked at my boots. From the tents came the smells of humans—stale breath, refuse, the odor of a dirty clothes hamper—all mixed with the wood smoke of the fires. I had a disorienting feeling of having stepped into a separate world with its own time and place—a ghost camp. We arrived at a site removed from the others, a larger community fire. Around it, the people laughed and passed a bottle. They smoked and their exhaling formed large clouds about their heads. When they saw Del, they greeted her, all at once.

"Well, if it isn't Delores," a man said.

Del went up to a figure whose boots smoked on the rim of the fire.

"Where've you been? Come back for another reading?" he said.

We stood beside the group, the warmth of the fire on our faces. Still, I couldn't shake the cold that seeped down the back of my neck.

"So, what do you have for us?" someone asked. Was this request for a gift a kind of password or mode of entry? I couldn't distinguish between the men and the women. Their voices were deep and gravelly. They wore knitted caps, some with pompoms, some striped and bright. They seemed like children sitting by the fire. I pictured Del here with these people, placid in their midst, her old boyfriend, Rory, adding a broken chair leg to the flames.

"I brought my sister," Del said, and as an afterthought, "and her friend."

"That's it?" someone said.

Del laughed. She pulled a bag of candy corn out of her coat pocket and dropped it in the man's lap. "Where's Sybil?"

Snow blew softly around us. The sky was a black and starless bowl rimmed with the lonely shapes of trees, their remaining withered leaves. Someone leaped up, startling me—a smallish man with a gleeful face. He disappeared into one of the nearby tents and emerged with Sybil Townsend, who made her way toward us cloaked in layers of what looked to be long skirts, a knitted poncho draped over it all. She was small, wizened, though with a youthful, quick way of moving. She wore a scarf wound around her dark hair.

She approached me with her bare hand held out, and I hesitated, not wanting to touch it. In the sudden quiet a throat cleared, raspy, horrible. Her eyes were flinty in the firelight. The smallish man hovered near Sybil's shoulder, his round face lit up.

"Take her hand," he said.

William hadn't said a word, and when I looked at him for some sign of encouragement he put out his own hand and shook Sybil's.

"Nice to meet you," he said. "I'm William."

Sybil seemed flustered. "Nice to meet you, too, Billy."

William took his hand away quickly. "William," he said.

"I know what it is." Sybil folded her hands together, clasped over her heart.

The first of Sybil's tricks was a more malevolent, gypsy-like version of Reverend Earline of the Spiritualists by the Sea, who'd worn Diane von Furstenberg sheaths, coiffed hair, and expensive costume jewelry. Someone had called William "Billy" before. I'd been indoctrinated in the methods of the Spiritualists by the Sea mediums—their calm, inquisitiveness, their ability to read body language, movement, the small adjustment of pupils to pain, sadness, joy. But so had Del, and she was watching me, waiting for something more, as if she had discovered my secret. Her gaze made me feel unhinged. I might have given in and told them all what I heard, what I saw. Was this what I was doing with William? Giving in to the feeling of bodily closeness because it kept me grounded?

The cold came in through my boots. I'd thought I could leave the dead behind, but they were here, summoned by Sybil Townsend's shoddy tricks. Behind me, in the tent from which Sybil had appeared, an open flap served as an entrance, and a woman sat within clothed inappropriately for the weather—in a sundress patterned with faded flowers. The snow seemed to land on her bare arms, and she appeared not to care. Her hair was cut short to her head, and she peered out with the look I'd come to associate with the dead. Others, woeful, seemed to keep a respectful distance. I could have summoned them closer and held my own spirit communication circle. And what if I had agreed to help them all? To connect them to their living in some grand spectacle? *A woman is looking for her daughter, given up for adoption in Seneca Falls in 1955. A man who died in a fire caused by a gas heater is seeking his father, Herbert.* William wouldn't have believed me. I might have consigned myself to this ragtag group and never have seen him again.

And then Mary Rae stepped toward us in her down coat. Her pretty curls lay on her shoulders, frosted with ice. I felt a surge of panic. But rather than continue toward me, she addressed William.

"Oh, Billy, don't," she said.

Sybil reached out to me again.

"Don't touch me," I said angrily, loud enough for everyone to notice. "I'd like to go. My feet are cold."

What did Sybil see when she looked at me? My aura, my etheric double, its bulging edges signaling neurosis? I'd slipped back into a reliance on the manuals, and I grew even angrier.

"Take her home," Sybil said to Del.

She shuffled away and someone gave her a seat at the fire. Del turned us back down the path and behind us we heard sad, cackling laughter. We made our way up the embankment, listening to the creek slough its banks. In a week or two, the temperature would dip and its surface would still and thicken. Underneath, the rainbow trout would sit, dumb and cowed, waiting for spring.

"I'm sorry if I was rude," I said, once we reached the road.

The streetlights overhead, the passing cars, distanced the encampment, as if it hadn't existed.

"She seemed mostly concerned," Del said.

"I thought she was going to read our palms," William said.

I slipped my hand into his. "Why don't those people go to shelters or get help?"

"They want to be there," Del said.

"I don't understand," I said. "Who are they?"

"They're people," Del said. She stopped in the street. She didn't say "like me," but I understood it anyway.

"I don't want you going there anymore," I said.

We walked the rest of the way home in silence. I held William's hand. Del went into the house in a huff and slammed her apartment door. Upstairs we met Geoff in his plaid robe and slippers. His ankles were bare and white. He seemed dazed, standing on the landing. The cold followed us in on our coats.

"Good morning," he mumbled, standing as if he'd been chased from his room by something to which he did not wish to return. I put my key in the lock and regretted seeing him like that.

Inside my apartment it was still cold, still gray, still dark.

William sat on the end of the bed. I sat down beside him. The evening felt strange now—almost unreal. He seemed to have distanced himself, and I didn't know how to reclaim him. I kept seeing Mary Rae's figure approaching him. "Oh, Billy, don't," she'd said, as if he were a bad child. All night the snow had been like powdered sugar falling through a sieve, like stage snow, pretty and harmless, but as we sat side by side at the end of my bed it turned to ice and slanted against the window.

"It seemed as if you saw something there," William said. "I can't explain it. Something happened."

I lay back on the bed. I was tired. My life before William seemed now like loneliness. Everything had changed. I might even confess the truth. William lay alongside me. His closeness, his curiosity, suffused me. But I confessed nothing.

"My sister makes odd friends," I said.

"I wanted to photograph those people, but I didn't want to ask," he said. "They might let you. You should think about it."

After a short time he rolled from the bed and stood and went to the door. He was leaving, and I was afraid I would never see him again. I felt tied to the slope of his broad shoulders, his soft hair curling over his collar, the fingers of his hand on the knob.

"Don't go," I said.

He faced me, and his expression was hard to describe—satisfied, almost canny, a look that I should have paid attention to.

I went to him and put my arms around him. I kissed his warm mouth. He sighed in relief. His hands fell back into place on my body.

Had he wanted to discover me, unknowing, in my bed? And had I wanted to be discovered, awoken and vulnerable, aroused from sleep? We held each other, believing we knew what the other thought. We could imagine anything about each other, even a past we might never confess. And maybe this was what love was—what I'd wanted all along.

13

The summer David Pinney died Del was fourteen and I was fifteen. His family owned a cottage in the Spiritualists by the Sea community, and he ended up that summer with a group of us who would meet to swim in the old house's pool—me and Del and Jane Roberts and a handful of others we'd known since we were small—local kids who would show up each summer. When we were younger they'd arrive at the privet hedge gate, and my grandmother would wave an arm to welcome them. Leanne and Sarah were part of the group then, and my mother, who would sit with my grandmother at the iron table in the shade, the two of them with iced coffees, their voices low, in earnest discussion of my father—my mother claiming she was at the end of her rope, my grandmother telling her to divorce him already. There'd be orange life preservers tossed in the grass, a blue plastic boat the little kids floated in, a set of croquet mallets in a stand, and towels, flapping on the backs of chairs, on the hammock.

If a boy did a back flip, my mother would inhale, sharply, and bolt upright in her chair, waving her hand.

"Oh, you there! Someone, one of you, tell him not to do that."

She'd have on her usual large-framed Giorgio Armani sunglasses. Her hair was dyed a reddish shade of auburn then, short and soft around her face.

My grandfather complained, saying we trampled his lawn, saying it wasn't a public pool, saying we had the Sound to swim in with our friends. But after he died, and we'd grown older, there was no one to monitor our comings and goings. Leanne and Sarah had stopped swimming, choosing to spend time with boys home on vacation from Loomis Chaffee or The Gunnery. My mother thought we were old enough to monitor ourselves. Younger children weren't allowed to freely roam, as we had been. The group of kids at the pool was always only our group.

The pool was one of the first installed in the area in the 1950s, oval-shaped, inground, placed at the base of the sloping backyard that joined the woods on one side and the tamed and rounded holes of the golf course on the other. From the pool a path of flat stones led through the privet hedge and up to the house, where large horse chestnuts and maples threw their shade, and my grandfather's delphiniums waved on tall stalks. He'd never been a real farmer. He was an entrepreneur who sold lightning rods, traversing the New England countryside in a shiny Cadillac, quoting installation prices for barns stacked with freshly mown hay, for clapboard houses with mourning doors. When my mother met my father he was my grandfather's employee—a young man who climbed the old slanted roofs, nailed the copper wiring and the bracketed rods to sides of silos, to widow's watches, his boot heels slipping on slate and loose asbestos shingles.

David Pinney was new to our group, someone to pay attention to that summer—his shock of blond hair, his lean, tan torso, his daring on the diving board. I'd seen him at the Spiritualists by the Sea camp a few times when I'd gone without Del. He'd be on the beach with his friends, and we'd watch each other. I'd become friendly with Reverend Earline, and we met to talk in the temple, and sometimes I'd see David Pinney walk past the open doors and peer inside. *Looking for me*, I'd thought. Not all of the cottage owners were Spiritualists, and David's family probably viewed the old camp as a novelty, the spirit circles and the organ music quirks of the community. What had once been cart paths were now narrow, tarred roads with rustic street signs on wooden posts: *Osprey Lane, Sea Breeze Way, Nehantic Path.*

It was hot the summer David died, and the sun had burned the grass. The heat of it along the pool's concrete rim scalded the backs of our legs. The meadows were filled with black-eyed Susans, and overhead the horse chestnuts and honey locusts swayed. There'd been the sound of the wind through the leaves, and the Spiritualists by the Sea's organ, its notes almost mournful. Reverend Earline and I had a falling-out—I'd accused her of being a fraud, and she'd been hurt and confused, and decided we should no longer meet. That had been weeks before, in June. The day I'd left, walking home tearful and angry through the woods, David trailed me. When I stopped to confront him he paused as well, lit a cigarette, and then walked back the way he'd come. He appeared at our pool the following afternoon, and no one questioned his arrival. A month later it was as if he'd always been part of our group.

The neighborhood boys in the water performed for us, the girls, rimming the pool in our bikinis. Dragonflies dipped near the blue, chlorinated water. One boy, Curtis, had the best pot. He kept it hidden in a plastic bag in his towel, and after he swam he'd pull it out and roll a joint. Not everyone smoked with him, but those of us who did became closer than the others—me and Del and Jane, a girl named Katy Pepperill, another boy, Paul Grant. David didn't smoke. He kept to the fringes, mostly kept to himself. People took other drugs they didn't share—Jane would show up, her eyes glassy from her mother's Valium. Paul would bring beer in a cooler, or a stolen bottle of Captain Morgan rum, and someone would ride a bike

to the beach clubhouse and get Cokes, and I'd slip into the old house
for glasses. We'd swim, and then sit on the patio with our drinks,
like imitations of our parents.

That summer became a foggy, blurred succession of days—all of
them blissful, filled with laughter, with our own clever mocking of
one another. It was July when girls began to disappear with various
boys—usually into the barn, or around to the back patio, where my
grandfather's flower beds had become overrun with weeds. You'd
notice someone was there a moment before, and then you simply
forgot about them. No one looked to see who was with whom—and
it was only if they were caught appearing together from around the
corner of the house, holding hands, or a boy's arm thrown over the
girl's shoulder, or a girl's bathing suit bottoms on inside-out, that
we'd know anything at all had happened.

I didn't like any of the boys that way—they were boys I'd grown
up with, friends. But I noticed David Pinney, simply for his sun-
bleached hair, his habit of hanging out beneath the diving board,
watching everyone in his quiet way.

"He's mysterious," I told Jane.

It was the first week of August, the heat unbearable, and we were
all in the water, Jane and I lounging on the steps. She'd stolen a bottle
of Krug champagne from her parents' anniversary party, and we'd
chilled it, secretly, in the freezer. Every so often I slipped inside and
refilled our glasses, and then the bottle was empty, and I brought it
out of the house and threw it into what we'd begun calling the "bottle
pit," a patch of woods behind the barn that bordered one side of the
golf course. It hit another bottle, the sound of shattered glass carrying, and Del came around the side of the barn and stood, staring at
me, her hands on her hips.

"Why didn't you share?" she said.

"It wasn't mine," I said. I came unsteadily up the hill to the edge
of the barn and joined her.

"You're drunk," she said.

She had on Leanne's pink bikini. She'd been sunbathing on the lawn and had the top undone, and she held the strings up on either side of her breasts. Her blond hair was long and loose down her back. The boys loved Del, but she didn't pay any attention to them yet. We joked that we were the vestal virgins; we needed to remain pure so as not to corrupt our clairvoyant powers.

"Mother is going to have a fit," she said.

Our mother had suspected we'd been drinking last week and had given us a warning.

We came around the barn and Jane was swimming her laps, and a few of the girls were on the hammock in the shade with Paul, and David Pinney was under the diving board, watching everyone. Del returned to her towel, and I slipped from the edge of the pool into the water at the deep end. It was so cool, I wanted to stay submerged. Jane's legs, white under the water, kicked up little waves. David Pinney's navy blue suit trunks and the lower part of his tan torso wavered in the deep end. And then he slid down into the water, and we were suddenly looking at each other, and I knew for sure he had picked up my interest in him, like an electromagnetic wave. We both surfaced at the same time, and I swam over to the board and looked at what he saw from that spot—the whole of the house against the sky, the points of the copper rods, the canopy of trees beyond, the lawn rolling out in all directions, the windows glinting with the sun like mirrors sending messages.

"This is a nice view," I said.

He laughed, and his voice was low and pleasant. In the confusion of other voices I hadn't had the chance to notice.

"So is this," he said.

I watched the way his eyes shifted to my breasts, and I felt the heat in my face. Del called me then, stood by the rim of the pool, her towel wrapped around her. The sun moved behind a cloud. She told me she was going to the beach, and was I coming with her, and I told her no. She stood, waiting, but I ignored her, and then she rejoined Katy and a few others, all of them crossing the lawn, moving toward the pebbled drive. Del looked back once, and I waved to her, and she must have believed David Pinney was harmless, a quiet boy who kept to himself. Maybe she thought we were talking about school in the fall, or our favorite movies, or books, or songs—the sorts of things you talked about with regular boys. David's face and mine were so close he might have kissed me there in the pool, but he didn't.

"Meet me in the barn," he said.

He pulled himself out onto the pool's rim, the water dripping from his suit. He dried himself with a towel in the grass and started up the lawn toward the hedge, his back speckled with water dripping from his hair, his arms swinging by his sides. He didn't once look back at me, as if he knew, from the moment he'd been next to me in the pool, that I was the kind of girl who'd be intrigued and, once hooked, would never refuse him.

14

⁘

William began spending every night in my apartment, and it seemed natural that he would simply move in—although when he did he brought very little with him, claiming his old place was furnished and that he didn't need many things. Owing to his orphan status, I didn't press him. It seemed incredibly bohemian to live the way he did—free of all the material encumbrances that defined my life growing up. My own clothing overwhelmed the bureau my mother had purchased for me. When I made tea William handled my grandmother's dainty Limoges with exaggerated tenderness. "I'm just a mug sort of person," he said. His choice of vessel would have been a large stoneware cup, medieval-looking and clumsily crafted—something my family might have used to hold screws on a shelf in the garage. Then I felt like my grandmother, passing judgment on my father for not being *our kind*.

At first, William and I stayed home alone evenings—watching my little television or reading. Once, we went walking together, as we did that first night, and the groups of students and their revelry seemed a species entirely different from my own. The sex was a given—the reason we never felt the need to leave the apartment. It was part of our day—like heating soup for lunch, or brushing our teeth at night. I loved the regularity, the way we'd created our own little world, a bubble broken only when one of us had to leave, or Del came to the door. More often than not I found a way to avoid her. I told her I had a sore throat or I was too tired to go out. She never argued. She'd taken my relationship with William in stride, though I suspected she wasn't entirely happy about it. When I felt twinges of guilt for avoiding her, I reminded myself it was her decision to move to town; I didn't have to entertain her.

William and I liked the shadowy elm, its familiar rattle of branches, and the way its shape, cast by the streetlight, moved against the plaster ceiling. Mary Rae was often out there, and I grew resentful, as if she were spying on us. It was clear from her appearance at the encampment, and her leading me to William at the party my first night in town, that they'd known each other, though I wouldn't have gone as far as to assume they'd had a relationship. When I tried to ask him about his past girlfriends, and mentioned Mary Rae, he seemed confused, almost angry.

"Why would you ask me that?" he said.

I couldn't say that I'd never heard anyone else call him "Billy."

Then, as if Mary Rae could read my irritation, she stopped appearing.

When William wasn't teaching, he was working in the lab on the photographs for his new series. He came in some nights after a long day and he flung himself onto the bed and began to talk, full of stories about our future together—how we'd one day buy a house in the country, like Anne's. How we'd set up our own studio, and have children and dogs and a swimming hole reached by a path across a field, then through the woods. I liked the sound of his voice and let him ramble on. Slowly, his dream of the future became my own.

I wondered if Geoff minded the sound of William talking, or if he sat by the wall and listened in his plaid robe, his eyelids heavy, soothed by the sound, as I was. Sometimes, as William talked, he touched me, his hand moving over my body like a blind man's over Braille. I bit my lip, willing his hand to move higher up my thigh, between my open legs, the waiting unbearable. He asked me to tell him not to stop. I did anything he asked. I never questioned the bruises I found on my inner thighs, my arms, the marks on my breasts. The more urgent the sex, the more desperate I believed his love for me. These things, hidden beneath the layers of clothing necessary to survive the winter, never seemed to matter. What kept me moored to him was the sound of his voice at night, his roaming hand. I believed I had gotten what I wanted—I was loved finally, unquestioningly. I became complacent.

When William and I finally socialized together it wasn't with his colleagues, as I would have thought, but with his old friends in Milton, the town where he'd grown up. At the center of this circle was Anne, his mentor, who had retired from teaching due to her illness and hosted regular gatherings at her farm, Windy Hill. The first invitation was for Thanksgiving. William came in from shoveling the walk with Geoff and announced that Anne was hosting dinner.

"Really?" I said. "Do we have to go?"

I'd thought we might have our own small feast at home. I'd even looked up recipes, thinking I might duplicate Thanksgivings from my childhood before my parents' divorce, when even the preparations were extravagant, and the little ranch house was filled with cooking smells, and my father would wrap his arm around my mother in a boozy sort of embrace.

William looked annoyed. "I don't want to go alone."

As with the All Hallows' Eve event that Geoff had taken us to at Anne's, I felt in some way manipulated to attend.

"Who will be there?" I asked William. "Can I invite Del?"

William said he had no idea who'd be there—that he hadn't asked. "She *is* your sister," he said. "I suppose it's all right."

That evening, I tried to find Del to tell her about the plans, but she wasn't home, and on Thanksgiving morning there was still no answer at her door. By afternoon it had grown so cold, everything frozen over. I was worried about Del, but William brushed over my fears.

"She's probably visiting Sybil Townsend, learning card tricks," he said.

"What if she's missing?" I said.

I wished I had gotten Del a phone, although I knew she wouldn't have kept it charged and wouldn't have carried it with her at all times. It began to grow dark. William asked me if I was ready.

"I have to take a shower." I stepped into the bathroom and turned the taps to the shower. The pipes groaned, and I left the water running to heat up.

William sat in the duck-carved chair. He often did, to read, and he was looking over student essays. "What have you been doing all day?" he said. He kept his eyes on the pages in his lap.

"I was in the lab." William was always curious about my work—always asking me if I would like him to take me to sites he'd found. I suspected his interest was more competitive than he would admit, and I mostly refused.

I stood in the light from the little bathroom. I'd taken off my clothes, and the water was running in the shower. He looked up at me, and his expression changed—his eyes softening.

"You want to kiss me," I said.

He shuffled the pages, slowly, his eyes still appraising. "That and more," he said. "We have to leave in fifteen minutes, though. We're riding with Geoff."

I went to him and moved the essays from his lap, slid my legs alongside him, and took his face in my hands. He groaned, a sound I loved to urge from him. Meanwhile the shower ran and the apartment steamed up—the cold windows by the chair, the chrome fixtures on the stove, the mirror hung beside the door. We'd often made love in the chair—William's head leaning against the upholstered chair back, and me moving over him, clutching the carved ducks' heads. I would close my eyes and then open them to find him watching me, intently, and sometimes I found it disconcerting that he would see me in the moments I was least in control. That night he kept his eyes open in the darkening room, the steam swirling around us, and I didn't protest or ask him not to look at me, as I often did. It was funny how you expected the moment of orgasm to be joyful, but really, his eyes revealed so much more—a strange mixture of joy and pain and sorrow. Once I mentioned putting the mirror behind the chair, so I could see what I looked like, what my own eyes revealed. William never moved the mirror, but I knew he didn't judge me for my request or think me strange; rather my desire to see my own expression was just another thing he found *interesting* about me.

That night I kissed him in the fog of steam, and he lifted me off of him, almost abruptly.

"I don't want to make Geoff wait," he said.

I felt out of sorts, reminded of the first night he refused me. "Come in the shower with me," I said, tugging on his arm, but he pulled away and gave me a look I suspected he gave his most ignorant students.

I took only a few minutes to shower, then I dressed, shivering with cold. Neither of us spoke. We went downstairs and I knocked on Del's apartment door, but there was no answer, no lights, and no smell of incense. Geoff was waiting for us in his car at the curb, exhaust spilling out and blackening the snow.

"You'll have to help me watch for black ice," he said as we climbed in.

I made a sound of concern, and he chuckled.

William pulled the passenger door closed. "Black ice is transparent," he said to me. "We'll know we've hit it if the car is spinning."

"Where's your sister?" Geoff asked.

"I don't really know," I said. "Maybe she's with Alice's family."

The thought of Del seated at a dining-room table covered in a lace cloth with Alice and her grandmother and Erika—tan and striking against the gray scene through the picture window—didn't make me feel any better. Next, Del would be planning her own trip to Florida, she and Alice with Erika in her convertible speeding along some palm-lined boulevard.

As we drove it grew dark, making the ride to Anne's feel longer than it had before. Although I'd driven the route myself, I wasn't ever sure where I was. I shouldn't have gone without Del. On Main Street I barely recognized the landmarks I'd driven past in my search for Del on All Hallows' Eve—the bandstand, the Agway, the funeral home, the diner—all of it transformed by the snow, by the deserted quality of the town's roads. Anne's house, too, seemed changed, the snow's sheen lit by the lamppost, the lights beaming yellow from the house windows. The same cars from last time were there—the Chevy Nova, the Camaro, Randy's Firebird, a pickup truck—now splattered with salt and sand thrown by snowplows. I had thought the Milton girls would be with their families—but it seemed that they were as displaced as Del and I, and Anne was their family. I had a vague hope that Del would be there, but then I wasn't sure how I felt about that. We walked up the ice-coated walkway to the front of the house. Geoff opened the storm door and we stepped inside.

After days in our cold apartment, the warmth of the place struck me immediately. We'd stepped into a room with low, beamed ceilings and white-painted walls. There were shelves of old books, a fire in the hearth, and two long green velvet couches in an *L*. On one wall were what I took to be Anne's work—portraits of nude women done in an impressionist style in oil. The colors were subdued, the texture of the paint heavy. Along the main wall, high above the door frame, mounted heads of stag and elk peered down at us from the shadows.

"Her trophies." William laughed.

Down a narrow hallway was the kitchen—I could hear everyone talking all at once, not garrulous or cheery, but subdued—still tinged with the tragedy of Mary Rae.

I slipped off my coat, and William took it. Geoff went down the hall calling, "Hello!" and then, "Well, surprise, surprise."

Del slipped past him and appeared in the doorway wearing an apron with I PUT THE FUN IN DYSFUNCTIONAL printed on the front. I felt angry, almost left out.

"What are you doing here?"

"Cooking dinner," she said. Her hair was twisted up on the top of her head. A few stray pieces had fallen loose.

"Since when do you know how to cook?" I said.

"I needed something to do with my time," Del said. She tugged on the apron. "Isn't this funny? We should get one for Mother."

"When would she wear it?" I said, and Del laughed, though it was hesitant. She didn't know our mother had nearly quit cooking altogether.

What was Del's life like at the manor—had she had a job there? If she knew little about my mother's and my life, I knew just as little about the last three years of hers. I'd allowed her to become part of mine again, and then I'd met William and practically abandoned her. William moved behind me in the hallway and grabbed my shoulders.

"God, it smells fantastic!" he said.

He'd never seemed to care about food, and I felt like a bad housewife in a sitcom, the one who'd burned every dish. I began to protest, to ask him why he never wanted me to cook, but he maneuvered me out of the way and stepped around me. Del and I were left to file behind him, down the narrow hallway into the kitchen.

15

School had let out a few days before Thanksgiving, and students had flocked to the public transit system for home. Our mother had said she was going to Leanne's for the traditional feast. She'd called yesterday, and there'd been a moment on the phone when I thought she might insist Del and I join her, but she did not. Instead, I heard her open a kitchen cabinet, listened to her sort through the glass casserole dishes on the shelf.

"Leanne didn't invite us," I said.

In the old house's kitchen, my mother ran the electric can opener. She would be assembling her traditional canned green beans *almondine*.

"You said you weren't coming last time we talked," she said.

I stood in front of the window and fogged the glass with my breath. Below me, Mary Rae tipped her face to meet my gaze.

"You told me you weren't having Thanksgiving," I said.

My mother clanked the side of the can of green beans against the glass dish. "I said I wasn't hosting."

Del hadn't attended family gatherings for three years. The first year she'd been in the Institute, and the doctors had recommended she skip the holidays at my mother's. The following Thanksgiving, all of us girls went to our father's house. He claimed he'd invited Del, but when I arrived—to find Leanne with her new husband, Sarah with her fiancé, and my father and his wife, all of them at the bar in the family room, mixing gimlets—my father told me Del had other plans.

"With whom?" I said. I stood in the foyer in my coat and considered heading home. My mother would spend that holiday with my grandmother, and at least we would be three women alone.

My father came around the bar with a frosty glass and handed it to me.

"Oh, let her take off her coat first," his wife said. Her name was Jill, a name for a character in a children's beginner reader, Del would have said.

That year, Jill tried too hard and served what to Leanne and Sarah and me seemed exotic dishes: individual acorn squash halves stuffed with mushrooms and rice, bleu cheese mashed potatoes.

"I miss plain corn," Sarah said. The three of us had offered to wash the dishes, and we were alone in the kitchen.

Leanne finished a glass of wine and re-poured. "Wasn't maize a Pilgrim staple?"

For once, we had been united, though it was in our dislike of the food and at Jill's expense. If not for Del's absence, one I felt obligated to fill with her scornful comments, we might have continued to get along.

I ran a dish towel over the china plate Sarah had set in the drainer. "I'm pretty sure Squanto wouldn't have enjoyed green beans *almondine*," I said.

Sarah washed another plate and handed it to me, her pink nails shiny with suds. "Why don't you let Leanne dry now?" she said.

Last Thanksgiving, we'd all gathered at the old house. Leanne and her husband had picked up my grandmother at Essex Meadows on the way over, and my mother had gone to the manor to get Del. Sitting in a rocker on the cold front porch, I waited for them to return. My mother and I had potted mums the month before, and their colors were bright against the painted gray boards and against the dried grass of the lawn. Inside the house, my grandmother oversaw preparations, and Leanne and Sarah's husbands watched football in the den. When the Cadillac turned down the pebbled drive, I stood and went to the car. Del hadn't come.

"She wouldn't get in the car," my mother said. "She wanted to know where you were."

My hands and face were numb from standing outside. "You told me it was better if you went alone."

"How could I know?" she said. Her eyes were angry and sad at once. I followed her onto the porch and she tore off her gloves. "It's probably for the best."

Inside the kitchen my grandmother sat at the scarred farm table, her arms covered in flour. Leanne crimped the pastry crust. "A chore for a three-year-old," Del might have said. I knew that as long as I was separated from Del, I would channel her dry observations.

Yesterday, on the phone, as my mother put together her green bean dish, I'd paced my small apartment. Del hadn't mentioned going home for Thanksgiving—she hadn't acknowledged the holiday at all. Perhaps she knew her absence had become part of our family's holiday ritual, and Leanne, this year's Thanksgiving hostess, wouldn't have wanted to change that. Del often knew more than I gave her credit for.

"Don't worry about us," I'd said. "And don't worry about Christmas, either. We're fine here. We have a lot of friends to make plans with."

Appropriating Del's new life seemed perfectly acceptable. I'd had no plans to mention William to my mother, who had attempted a protest before I'd hung up the phone. Still, I'd worried. Should I have convinced Del to go home? Even if we would have arrived at the big, empty house, and headed upstairs to our old bedroom as if we were visitors to some roped-off scene from our childhood—we belonged there more than at Anne's. I felt in some ways like a fugitive.

16

⌒

After the meal, Anne sat in the living room on her green velvet couch with a glass of sherry. She wore a red head scarf, a white sweater, and white wool pants, and she looked beautiful, if drained. Alice was there, along with Lucie, and Kitty, another girl, whose parents owned a farm in Cortland. Kitty's mother sold Mary Kay cosmetics, and Kitty wore lipstick I was certain came from her mother's product samples—*tuscan rose* or *sienne brulee*. I greeted them all in a friendly way, but they were cool toward me. They'd been so open the night I met them. I could only surmise that it had something to do with Del.

Anne patted the couch next to her, and I sat down, and all of the girls but Alice got up and disappeared down the hallway to the kitchen. Anne took a sip of her drink and set it down on the coffee table next to a small wooden box painted to look like a miniature bookcase. I asked Anne what it was, and she told me to push the button on the front. When I did, a mechanism lifted a panel at the top, and a black dog holding a cigarette in his paws emerged to the tinny sound of "Smoke Gets in My Eyes."

"It was my mother's," she told me. "Isn't it funny?"

I told her I liked it, and she grew serious.

"It's yours then," she said. "When I die."

Although I tried to object, she pushed the button again, and the melody played and the dog's head appeared. Anne took the cigarette and handed it to me. I couldn't say I didn't smoke.

"It was going to be Mary Rae's, but now it will be yours."

I accepted the light she gave me, and then I held the cigarette between my two fingers like an actress playing a part. Alice sat on a pillow in the corner of the room, braiding the pillow's fringe. I knew she had to have been listening.

"Maybe one of the others might like it," I said.

The girl stood, unfolding like an agile bird, and left the room to report to everyone in the other kitchen, I assumed.

"They have their little tchotchkes picked out." Anne set her cigarette in an ashtray, a black ceramic cat's head, its mouth yawning open, its painted eyes bright and shrewd. Smoke spiraled out of two holes in the ashtray cat's nose, and I wondered who had claimed this memento.

All the girls wore their dark hair long, and it was often difficult to distinguish among them, especially after a few glasses of wine. Alice's hair was heavier, a reddish mane that she often played with—her fingers lithe and slender and always moving. She had a sprinkling of freckles, and that afternoon wore a plaid wool skirt and tights, like a school uniform. Lucie was so tiny she seemed like a child, and whenever Joseph came into the room she rushed up and grabbed him and pulled him down with her onto the couch. Kitty was the rudest to me. She was tall and dark-eyed, her lipstick bright, and when I would catch her watching me she'd continue to stare for a beat before she looked away. There was another girl, Jeanette, who came in late, letting in the smell of snow. She caught sight of me and quickly pretended I was invisible.

The music on the stereo was Aaron Copland's *Appalachian Spring*. Geoff played host, making rounds with the wine bottle, refilling glasses, so I didn't know how many I'd had to drink. The more I drank, the less I monitored Del, who shouldn't have been drinking at all. She was often nestled on the couch between two of the girls, or with Randy, who was surprisingly handsome, fair, and chiseled, and who wore a pair of cowboy boots he must have owned since high school—the toes misshapen, the heels worn down. Joseph wore, like William, a stretched-out sweater and corduroys with a hole in the knee. His hair was longish and stringy, and he became boisterous when he drank too much. The empties littered the floor around the chair where he sat, sometimes with Lucie on his lap. It was clear to me that William was older than everyone there, save Anne and Geoff, and I wondered about his connection to all of them.

"What are we doing here?" I wanted to say to Del, but she never caught my eye. She had found acceptance with the Milton girls—replacements for the sisters who'd snubbed the two of us all of our lives. Maybe we had both found a way to be happy. That the Milton girls ignored me didn't hurt my feelings. I had William.

The focus of the evening, I gathered, was to give thanks to Mary Rae's memory. The girls told more stories about her—these less complimentary than the ones I heard on All Hallows' Eve—how she slashed an ex-boyfriend's tires in high school, how after an abortion she decided never to have children and would only care for the children of others as her penance. She had been attending Tompkins Cortland Community College and wanted to one day run a child care center. It seemed unfair that Mary Rae, the object of so many stories, was unable to correct anyone or set the record straight.

I wanted to know who had gotten her pregnant, but Mary Rae, listening in from the ether, knew their talk had turned to gossip, and if I indulged them they'd find other cruel things to say about her. The whole discussion felt wrong.

"She misses us," Kitty said. "Yesterday I found a rose petal in the snow in front of my house."

"Where could that have come from?" Lucie said. She seemed the most practical—looking for reasonable explanations.

"A florist delivering roses to your neighbor for her first anniversary was careless," I said.

"The spirit has spoken," Del said in her medium's voice.

Del had obviously been talking about the Spiritualists by the Sea and our childhood séances.

After the meal, the girls all stayed together in the living room smoking clove cigarettes, the smell competing with the roasted meat, the wood smoke. No one seemed queasy about smoking indoors. William spent time in the kitchen with the men. When I managed to slip away from the living room, I found them all leaning against the kitchen counter with cigars and glasses of brandy, having their own quiet conversation. I looked in at them and the talking ceased.

"Lost?" Geoff said.

The dirty dishes piled on the counter glistened with fat and butter, with the remains of the turkey bones. "Are you going to do the dishes?" I asked.

William said that Anne had a maid who would do them the next day. Randy shuffled his boots on the slate floor. "Are you looking for the bathroom?" William asked.

"Are you planning a bank robbery?" I said.

Joseph slapped the counter. "Hah!" he said. He kept the cigar in his teeth and used both hands to tuck his hair behind his ears.

William raised his eyebrows at me. He was the odd man out in this group. I got the impression that he was avoiding the living room and the Milton girls.

"I'll show you the way," he said, and he came toward me and slid his hand into mine. He led me to a narrow back staircase, which we climbed, single-file, our hands joined between us. Upstairs he stepped into a small room with a twin bed and a painted pine bureau. He closed the door behind us. I looked around for the bathroom, but it was clear that there wasn't one.

"What's this?" I said.

He pulled me in. I smelled the roasted poultry on his sweater, and I almost told him no before his mouth found mine and quieted me, his hands slipping beneath my clothes, cool and quick. One plunged down the front of my jeans, and I knew that we would have only a short amount of time, but we were good at this, having found ourselves able to complete the act any number of places at short notice—his office, with a line of students in the hall, at the back of the library, behind the last stack of books, beneath the dust-filled light of the projector, the only patrons in the little cinema downtown. The coolness of his hand on me made me tremble, and I bit his lip, and he moaned and turned me facedown on the bed. He unzipped his pants, and then he was on top of me, inside me, and the bed's old springs recoiled against his thrusting, a sound amplified in my ear, my face flat against the raised pattern of the bedspread. There was no explanation for his sudden desire, there never really was. Just the darkness of the stairs, our bodies in that close space, the idea of the other, and the pleasure that could be ours in a matter of moments.

Afterward, in the bathroom downstairs, I rubbed at the mark of the bedspread on my face and swung my hair over my cheek to cover it. I felt slightly abject. It never occurred to me to protest or refuse him, yet he'd refused me just that afternoon. Back in the living room, I took a seat on the floor by the fire, separate from the others. I knew they all knew. "It's obvious they're fucking," the girls would say to each other out of my earshot.

"Mary Rae would have liked you, Del," Alice said across the room. "You're just the right amount of smart and crazy." An irritating remark. Mary Rae had chosen me.

I felt too warm by the fire and regretted sitting there. Anne was watching me, making me feel odd. William's semen seeped into my underwear.

"Have the police found any clues about what happened?" I said.

A log fell into the flames. Kitty, sitting the closest to me on the floor, bit her fingernails, smearing her lipstick. Alice played with the fringe on the afghan she'd wrapped around her and Del's shoulders. I'd made yet another mistake.

"No one seems to know anything," Anne said, her cigarette dangling from her bony fingers. "Her mother has been hounding the police. But they aren't used to this sort of thing. This is a small town."

I angled myself away from the fire and imagined the heat of it catching the loose pieces of my hair. I smelled the singed pelt of the stag mounted above my head. "Was she seeing someone?" I asked.

What if it had been a situation like the one in the movie *Laura*, in which a spurned lover decides if he can't have the woman, no one will? In the dim room the pale faces of the Milton girls seemed detached from their darker clothes and hair, from the green velvet of the couches they sat on.

"Not recently," Kitty said, her voice hard.

Anne reached out for her sherry glass on the table in front of me, and I handed it to her. "Who was she seeing last?"

"We don't know," Anne said, bringing the glass to her lips. "She was taking a break from boys."

"She only loved one boy her whole life," Alice said quietly. Her hair had fallen partially over her face. She fiddled with the afghan fringe, her fingers as nervous as Mary Rae's were spinning her locket.

Anne stubbed out her cigarette. It sent up a small spark that singed the couch cushion.

"And who was that?" I said. I knew, but I wanted them to tell me.

"She and Billy were a couple senior year," Kitty said. "She never really got over him."

"Everyone wanted to date Billy," Alice said, abandoning the afghan fringe and brushing her unruly hair from her face. I sensed the word "date" was used for Anne's benefit, that to say "fuck" might have been offensive to her. Del, slumped against Alice under the afghan, gave me a sad little smile that I didn't want.

"Mary Rae kept thinking they'd get back together," Lucie said.

Their voices were soft and seemed sorry to break this news to me. The boys in their fast cars took turns with all the local girls, and William played the elusive, handsome, older guy—though his hanging around with high school girls was a little disturbing. Was this why the Milton girls disliked me? Had I landed their star local guy?

"Alice, you saw her last," I said.

Alice held her long hair in one hand, an unlit cigarette in the other. The wind rattled the windows in their panes, and the front door blew ajar. Everyone turned toward the door, startled, before Kitty got up and went to shove it closed. I waited for someone to ask me why I'd taken it upon myself to play amateur sleuth. I felt sorry for Mary Rae, I wanted her body found, her death declared. I wanted her to stop hounding me with her blue eyes and her anxious fingers on her locket. She refused to tell me anything, and like Sister in the barn, her silence weighed on me.

"She was supposed to go to work the next night and she never showed," Alice said, her voice solemn.

Mary Rae's bartending job at the Viking Lanes had been a new one. She stood to make a lot of money there, which she could use for school.

"Maybe she met someone there," I said.

We'd driven past the place—it was on the way to Anne's—a low white structure, the word "Viking" spelled out on the roof, and I imagined inside the roll of the balls, the eighties music, the smell of the bar.

"Someone knows what happened," Del said. "Mary Rae knows what happened to her."

A few of the girls flinched. Alice's eyes welled with tears.

"We have to know what happened," Lucie said.

Alice stood and shrugged off the afghan. "We do," she said. "We've decided."

"Maybe she'll show up one night and surprise you," I said. "Maybe she'll walk right through that door and whip off her coat and say, 'Hey! I'm back!'"

I didn't mean to sound as heartless as I did. Del had instigated all of this. Anne gave me a pitying look. The Milton girls seemed to recoil from me. Lucie rose from the couch and began gathering glasses. Kitty collected the ashtrays to empty. One after another, the girls slipped down the hallway to the kitchen, until it was just Anne and I by the fire.

"I'm a fan of your work," Anne said, her voice soft. "Each image seems to vibrate with something more than its parts."

When I looked confused about her having seen my work, she said she'd sat on the admissions committee. "One of the last things I did before I took my leave."

"Well, thank you," I said, slightly flattered.

"When William was an undergraduate here I took him under my wing. It seems as if he is doing the same for you."

I smiled but wasn't sure how to respond, uncertain what she meant by that. I'd asked William about his relationship with Anne, and he'd told me she was his mentor, that she was his set of eyes when he wasn't sure if something worked. I had shown some of my photographs to William, hoping to get him to reciprocate, but I could only convince him to reveal his older work—his Polaroids—pastel light, the figures dark, blurred, at a remove, and the settings overpowering—a rocky shoreline, a field rimmed by dense trees, a house's roof against a wide, startling sky. I almost asked Anne now about his "sleep studies," but William came into the room, forced out of the kitchen, I guessed, by the Milton girls. He had our coats, and I rose and went to meet him.

"It's late," he said.

Geoff followed him, pulling his car keys from his pocket. "Taking this group home," he told Anne.

What kind of car had William driven when he was a local boy, and why didn't he drive it anymore? I tried picturing him behind the wheel of a Mustang. He had told me about his Triumph motorcycle, as if that information should impress me, and it did give me a new image of him in a leather jacket and boots, leaning into the curves on Route 13.

We finished putting on our coats in the vestibule of Anne's house. William wrapped his arms around me and pulled me in.

"Isn't she something?" he said to Anne, who remained on the couch.

She gave us a wan smile. "She is that," she said, and I had no idea what she really thought about me.

Del rode home with us. In the backseat I gave in to the effects of the wine, the cold air whipping into the back from Geoff's cracked window. I paid little attention to the dark landscape, lost in worries about William's past relationship with Mary Rae, and annoyed with Del.

She faced the window, her nose nearly pressed to the glass, and I tugged on her coat sleeve.

"What was that back there?"

"What do you mean?" she said. She was using a low, incredulous voice that infuriated me even more.

"That whole bring-back-Mary-Rae scene," I said. "I mean, they did everything but light the candle."

"You two aren't going to have a fight now, are you?" Geoff's voice was jolly.

Del turned back to the window, the snow-covered fields blurring beyond it.

"Why are you spending so much time with these Milton girls?"

Del began to sing then, quietly at first. It was "A Lovely Night," from Rodgers and Hammerstein's *Cinderella*. As angry as I was, I started to laugh, and then we were both singing, and Geoff eyed us in the rearview mirror, and William ignored us, irritated, I supposed.

Just then the car slid on a patch of black ice and spun, and we clutched each other, dizzy and shrieking, and I had a flash of fear that we would join the town's list of the dead. But the car skated, smooth and untroubled, like a fish, into a small field, and Geoff quickly regained control, and the car lumbered over the grass, the frozen hillocks scraping its undercarriage, and we resumed our path, all of us silent.

17

Despite my misgivings, we continued to attend two or three dinner parties a week at Anne's—food Del prepared from Anne's vintage cookbooks or meals Geoff expressed fond memories of as a child in England, and that Del and I, exposed to our mother's meager cooking skills, had never tasted before. Duck, goose, venison, lamb. Rice and plum puddings and cakes with sugary frostings. Geoff would roll joints on Anne's antique tavern table, and the room would fill with the smoke and music, the hushed voices of the Milton girls, who did one another's hair or flipped through issues of *Glamour* magazine. Preparations for the holidays included a large tree brought over in Joseph's truck and decorated by Anne's acolytes. There were the expected stories about holidays past with Mary Rae. William revealed no emotional connection to them. When someone told a story in which he played a part—the time Mary Rae bought him a puppy and hid it in a hatbox she decorated as a cake—he left the room, and in this way it was an unspoken acceptance that he had once dated her.

It was Del who worried me. She'd been cool to William from the beginning, barely talking to him when we were all together. At times, it felt as if she were ignoring him entirely. At first, I assumed she needed to get used to the idea that he and I were a couple. But it was odd how long it continued. They would pass each other in a room as if they didn't see each other. One evening at Anne's, two weeks before Christmas, we gathered for a game of bridge. I wondered how Del had learned to play. Had my grandmother somehow taught her? Or had she played the game in the hospital? Bridge was a confusing game for me. I was never good at cards, and Del knew this. When we were children she always won—gin rummy, crazy eights, hearts. I only agreed to play at Anne's because of William. He described his parents having friends over to play when he was a child. He'd told us his mother had made a toffee apple cake for bridge nights, and he'd snuck into the kitchen to steal slices.

For bridge night at Anne's, Del replicated the toffee apple cake. Without fanfare, she cut slices of it onto our plates. William's surprise was genuine. He reddened, whether with pleasure or embarrassment or the rush of nostalgia, I couldn't say.

"This is exactly the cake," he said, almost formally, his fork in his hand. "This is simply amazing."

Del gave him a small smile and dealt the cards. I knew I should feel grateful to my sister for being so generous, but I felt suddenly cold. A draft had reached us at the kitchen table from the terrace, but this chill I felt seemed something else. I took a sip of my coffee—coffee was always laced with brandy at Anne's—and my hand shook. Del paused in her dealing.

"What?" she said. "What's wrong? Did I misdeal?"

She grew confused, and everyone had to give their cards back so she could start again.

She was too smart not to know what I felt that night. She'd orchestrated things perfectly as she always did, even as teenagers when it came to boys. David Pinney with his blond hair, the way it curled around the nape of his neck. His dark eyes, so striking against the sun-bleached hair, like two agates. I smelled the chlorine from the pool on his swim trunks, and I was afraid to glance up in Anne's kitchen, fearful I would see David Pinney standing there, his trunks dripping water onto Anne's slate kitchen floor. I surveyed my hand of playing cards, barely comprehending what I held. The old resentment rose up, and I knew I should discount this as childish emotion, and I knew that people rarely changed. Del, no matter her mental state, was still the sister who stole my earrings—she wore them now: Jane's earrings dangled from her own ears. Yes, I'd stolen them myself, but once they landed in my possession, they should have been mine.

The game would end badly for our side, William's and mine. I couldn't focus on any of it. I spent the entire time caught up in the memory of David Pinney, and watching Del, waiting for her to give William some secret look. Every so often I swore I saw it—a tip of her head, her eyes—the look of a coquette in an old movie. I felt as if a hand had tightened around my throat. I could feel the pressure of the fingers.

Del and Alice won the game. "You'll get better with practice," William said. We all pushed back our chairs to rise from the table.

But something was off. Maybe the memory of David Pinney was edging out everything else that evening. I excused myself and slipped up the back stairs to the little bedroom with the pine bureau. But William did not look for me. I heard him downstairs, laughing, and then music came on—more classical music I couldn't identify—and the sounds of the voices were lost under the tones of the bassoons. I lay for a long time on the bed in the darkness. I may have fallen asleep. When the door creaked open it was just Del, her face a shadow peering in.

"What are you doing in here?" she said.

"Nothing," I said, dully, lying back down. "That music is so loud. I didn't hear you on the stairs."

I sat up on the bed. "Is someone with you?"

Del laughed, her voice almost silvery-sounding. "No."

"But I hear someone," I said. I did hear movement in the hallway, a shuffling, a disturbance of air.

Del slipped into the room and closed the door behind her.

"Someone is out there," I said.

Del laughed again. "All right, it was Randy," she said. "My God, Martha, you're so nosy."

She stepped to the bureau and turned on the little lamp. Her feet in woolen socks appeared in the circle of light. "I've been in here before," she said.

"Where did you think I was?" I said.

"We all thought you left with Geoff," she said. "He went to the liquor store."

Geoff often asked if someone would ride with him to the grocery store, and I'd sometimes volunteered, to be kind, to get away from the Milton girls.

"I'll leave the room if you want it," I said. "I was feeling sick."

Del reached out her hand and placed it on my forehead, and I shrank back. "You don't have a fever," she said.

I went to the door, opened it, and looked out into the hallway, but no one was there.

"Your boyfriend must have gone back downstairs," I said.

"He's not really my boyfriend," Del said.

"Well, whatever he is," I said.

"He's shy," she said. "You know that."

Randy was quiet. When I spoke to him he looked at the floor. I rarely heard him in conversation with anyone. He mostly sat, amid the men, tipping back a beer, flicking his ashes into his empties. Not the type to let Del lure him up to this room.

I went down the front stairs and entered the living room. Anne sat in her spot on the couch, talking to Jeanette. Alice was by the fire knitting and flirting with a boy I'd met that evening—Hurley or Harley. Her knitting needles flashed, and she tipped her head and laughed, shaking her hair back. Lucie, and a new girl, Shenoa, who was a copy of the rest of the Miltons—long, dark hair, the same pretty features—sat on the other side of the green velvet sectional. When I'd told the girl, earlier, that I thought her name was interesting, she'd smiled that Milton girl smile—a grudging compression of the lips— and said it meant "dove."

Mary Rae would have sat on the velvet couch twirling her neck-lace, bored by her friends, ready to move on. I knew their stories about her weren't entirely true. Some nights I dreamed of her. I didn't try to verify the information I learned through my dreams—though I might have. She wasn't interested in working in a day care center; she'd changed her major to accounting. Once, she'd been in down-town Syracuse and watched a group of young people in expensive clothes in a Starbucks. One of the men had stepped behind her in the line, and she'd learned he was a CPA, that they were all working across the street in the high-rise.

"We're pulling an all-nighter," he said, laughing. "It's tax season."

Mary Rae wanted to be one of those people—a woman with high-lighted hair and cashmere sweater sets. The more I learned about Mary Rae Swindal, the more I liked her and the more I felt aligned with her whenever I was at Anne's, ignored, an outsider. Downstairs in the living room I didn't see Randy or William.

But Anne was nearly as surprised to see me as Del had been upstairs.

"When did you get back?" she said.

"I never left," I said.

And I headed off through the hallway to the kitchen. Del, who must have come down the back stairs, stood at the sink, rinsing out one of the many pans she'd used to prepare the meal. Beyond the slid-ing glass doors William, Randy, and Joseph stood shoulder to shoul-der on the snow-covered terrace, their breath huffing out above their heads. Joseph held a shotgun in the crook of his arm.

"What are they doing out there?" I said.

"They saw something moving," she said. "They think it's a wolf."

I could smell Anne's Chanel perfume arrive in the room behind me. "There have never been wolves in those woods," she said.

I thought of the taxidermy heads on her living-room wall, and William saying they were her trophies. "You hunt?" I asked.

Her presence behind me was slight, like a sliver of moon. "Oh, I did once," she said. "It was a thrill to capture the first Windy Hill eight-pointer of the season."

The outside light shone on part of the wide backyard. Beyond that lay the forest where the dead waited on All Hallows' Eve. Maybe Mary Rae was out there now, maybe they'd seen her in the yard and mistaken her for an animal, though I'd never seen Mary Rae at Anne's before. Or was it David Pinney out there? I stood at the door and felt the cold through the glass, and as if he could sense I was there, William turned and saw me. Joseph lifted his chin to the sky and howled like a wolf, and William and Randy shoved each other so that Randy nearly fell off the terrace. Geoff came in behind me, bustling to unload bags on the counter—three bottles of wine Anne had requested.

"Your ladyship's special vintage," he announced, the smell of snow coming off his clothes.

William looked back again, almost tentatively to see if I was still there, and when he saw me he smiled, a quizzical look on his face. After a few moments, the men all filed inside, and Anne began to oversee the uncorking of the wine. Randy slipped past me to the living room, his chin low, his blond hair a bright swath over his eyes. In the hallway I took his sleeve.

"Sorry I interrupted your little tryst," I said.

"What?" He seemed baffled.

"Your meeting with Del upstairs," I said.

I could hear everyone in the kitchen asking where I was. Randy's befuddled gaze shifted to over my head, to William, who was suddenly there behind me, his arms sliding around me, reeling me in. His mouth was in my hair, searching for my neck. He growled, and then Joseph, who must have heard him, let out another howl in the kitchen.

Randy took that as his opportunity to slip away, his cowboy boots shuffling down the hall. If he'd been upstairs I would have heard him, at least retreating once Del discovered me—the sound of his boots impossible to miss. Del had told me he never took them off—he'd lost two toes to frostbite as a child. I felt the same cold I'd experienced during the bridge game and wondered if I really was sick.

I told William I didn't feel well, and we borrowed Geoff's car and went home, leaving Del and Geoff to finish out the night with Anne and Randy. Maybe it was Joseph Del had lured upstairs while Lucie, who was drunk, chatted with Shenoa. Del was indiscriminate—everything to her was a game. On the drive home, when William asked me what was wrong, I didn't know how to respond, and after a while he let his own silence match mine, and the car was filled with everything we wouldn't say. Every so often he would look over at me, sadness in his gaze, and I felt almost cruel for suspecting him of anything but loving me.

18

A day later, the newspaper reported the discovery of a woman's remains in an abandoned trailer in Cortland County, and while the cause of death couldn't yet be determined, or a formal identification made, she was thought to be the missing Mary Rae Swindal. The trailer was an old Silver Streak Clipper—rusted metal abandoned in an area that hadn't been searched in the early days of her disappearance. It sat at the edge of some woods in a snow-covered field marked with deer tracks, an area remote enough to be beyond, even, the realm of hunters.

I knew it was her—the narrow room, the field, it all made sense. After another few days she was identified, and the questions swirled about how she'd gotten there. Had she simply been lost, wandering, and stumbled upon the trailer? Or had she been abducted? There was simply no way to know until investigators did their work. At no time was it released to the public that she'd been nude, that her clothes had been piled neatly beside her—the jeans and the sweater, the down coat I'd seen her wearing under the elm.

Now the Milton girls were finally able to mourn. A service was scheduled three days before Christmas, and though William and I didn't plan to go, Del came up to my apartment to announce she'd be attending.

"If you change your mind, you can ride with me," she said.

"We aren't going," I said.

I wasn't sure why Del wanted us there. William had said it was sad and tragic and he was sorry for the family's loss, but he wasn't going to sit in a church and watch everyone cry. "I knew her so long ago," he said.

I'd never asked how Anne had grown so close to the Milton girls and their boyfriends. Had she met them in town? Did she know their parents? I suspected there was one girl she had befriended who brought the rest—and I guessed this girl was Mary Rae—but when I broached this with William, he said that the gatherings at Anne's were new, prompted by Mary Rae's disappearance and Anne's imminent death. "I never saw Mary Rae there," he said. He gave me a level look, as if he wanted me to take him seriously. "I hadn't seen her in years."

The next morning just after sunrise, I awoke to William moving around the apartment. We were on break from classes, spending a lot of time at home, and his early activity seemed curious. Through the fogged glass the day promised to be gray and cold. William stood in the center of the room, distracted. He'd been having trouble sleeping. His eyes were ringed with shadow. He had Geoff's car keys in his hand, and I could tell that at some point in the middle of the night he'd slipped from the bed and left me and gone elsewhere.

"Where have you been?" I asked him.

"Get up," he said. "I want to show you something."

"Let me dress," I said.

"No, just put on your coat and get your camera," he said, as if the idea of presentable clothing was unnecessary where we were going.

He left the apartment, and I followed him out the front door onto the porch wearing the sweatpants I'd slept in, my coat over a cotton T-shirt. The air stung my face, my lungs.

"It's too cold," I said. William seemed not to hear me.

We got into Geoff's car, which was parked in the gravel drive alongside the house. The interior was warm, as if William had just driven it home.

"Where did you go?" I asked him.

He drove expertly, one hand on the wheel, the other fiddling with the Leica in his lap. He didn't answer me, just focused on the road beyond the windshield. There weren't any other cars—it was too early for anyone to be out, save the people who'd been out all night. These were dark shapes in doorways, smoking last cigarettes.

I'd assumed we were going to a site he either wanted to photograph or thought I would like as a scene for my work. Occasionally, we went on outings in Geoff's car to scout places. William found roofless barns for me, structures with weathered gray boards and lichen-covered stone foundations. Sometimes, we would be run off the property by landowners or frightened off by the report of a hunter's gun. We were always trespassing, but neither of us cared. We wanted the shots we wanted. Abandoned places often surprised me with a subject, so those were the sites I liked best.

This time, heading out on the cold morning in my pajamas, I felt unnerved. In profile, William's brows were set in a low scowl, his lips cracked and dry.

He was being evasive. I was suddenly awake, alert. "Where are we going?" I said again. "I might like some coffee."

He flipped on the turn signal and pulled into a gas station, stopping at the door leading into the convenience store.

"Make it snappy," he said, a phrase that Del often used.

"I'm not even dressed," I said.

"Dressed enough to get a cup of coffee."

Inside the overheated store it smelled of the hot dogs that had been turning on their spit all night. My shoes stuck to the linoleum. I poured my coffee and took it to the cashier. William hit the car horn, impatient. It bothered me, his repeating Del's little phrase. Del spent a lot of time with the Milton girls at Anne's. Maybe William spent time there, too. The cashier, her graying hair held back with a childish barrette, eyed the car beyond the door.

"Are you all right?" she asked me.

"He's in a hurry," I said.

He's an artist, I wanted to add, but realized how ridiculous that might sound.

I got back into the car and we drove out of the city, along Cayuga Lake, and farther still, until the trees thickened along the roadside, and the pale sun that had risen during the drive barely made it through the snarl of bare branches overhead.

"Why won't you tell me where we're going?" I said.

William's hands tightened on the steering wheel. "You're acting like I'm abducting you."

"You aren't answering my questions," I said.

"I thought you liked surprises." William pulled onto the shoulder suddenly, almost randomly.

"Here we are," he said.

I got out of the car. William began to walk into the woods along a path that seemed to have been trampled earlier. We usually followed old roads—those grown through with saplings, but this seemed more a path. Every so often William would stop as if he'd lost his bearings, and we had to backtrack and head a different way. The snow clung to my pajama bottoms. There was no point in complaining about the cold or turning back. I couldn't have said which way we'd come. It was as if we'd found ourselves dropped into the middle of a wilderness—a pair of explorers on a reality TV show.

Once, I asked him if he knew where he was going, but his frustrated glare prevented me from asking again. Finally, after thirty minutes of scrambling and climbing, we reached what seemed to be a sort of summit—a clearing in the middle of taller pines where a small stone house sat, its walls covered in lichen.

"Is it gingerbread?" I asked.

William was smiling, more in relief at having found the place than at my attempt at humor.

"Hungry?" he said. He pulled me in and kissed me—a slow, deep kiss. His chapped lips scraped mine, but just as I leaned against him for his warmth, he pulled away. I wondered at his behavior.

Footprints led to the house. William tugged me along beside him. The door wasn't barred or locked. It had an old-fashioned iron latch that William lifted, and the door swung with a rusty groan. From the doorway, his pleasure in the way the light came into the room was evident. The place was just that, one room with a fireplace, a sink, a few cabinets, a rusted refrigerator against a wall, a small couch, a table with four chairs. The dust muted the color of everything, all of the furnishings in various forms of dissolution. Mice had eaten into the couch cushions. Trails of feces and matted animal hair carpeted the wood floor. The old wool braid rug had unwound itself. In the corners of the room twigs and grass formed burrows and nests. An intricate coating of mold swaddled the plates arranged on the table. You could see that at one time food had covered the china surfaces. The whole scene suggested that a family had gotten up from a meal and left; their belongings, the accoutrements of their lives forsaken.

An open doorway beyond the living and dining area revealed a bedroom and a small stairway. The roof had partly given way above the bed, and the bedclothes had been shredded by animals. I felt as if the house was a crime scene that hadn't yet been cordoned off, and I expected a figure to emerge resembling Mr. Parmenter, with his bloodied hair. But no one appeared. I could hear William's camera, its mechanical whirring. I went outside. The weak sun flitted off the snow. Birds darted, frantic shapes winging from the canopy. I smelled the pine and took a breath to clear my lungs of the smell of the house.

William came out. "What do you think?" he said.

Del would have said it was a nice place to leave a body.

"Kids probably come here to have sex," I said.

He looked back at the little cottage, then he came up close to me in the snow and wrapped his arms around me and kissed me again, and though I would rather not have had sex in the cottage, I could tell he had brought me here just for that.

"Isn't this place amazing? Did you see the table still set? The metal toy cars? I think I had a set of those when I was little."

The house, the parents and children each with their own place, the mildewed calendar on the wall, the decaying stuffed animals, the doll with its mangy hair and moldering pink dress—these things were poignant reminders of what a family could be, of something he might have. I was touched but uneasy.

"I wonder what happened?" I said.

William took my hand and brought it to his lips.

"Marry me," he said.

The sun was up now, and the house seemed more benign in its slant of light. "What?" I said, foolishly.

"Let's do it," he said. "Let's get married."

I thought of Del and Rory and their commune marriage ceremony that may or may not have happened, of Del's love of sex in the outdoors, and in abandoned cars, and my envy at her ability to live her life in extremes. I remembered my story about the Eve of St. Agnes, how I'd awakened to him in my apartment, and how that had seemed, at the time, almost fated. Was marriage—a husband—the next step? Would my mother offer to plan a wedding at the house like she had for my sisters? And then I remembered the night at Anne's, Del and someone else in the hallway outside the little upstairs room.

I wanted to make him happy. I wanted to have him for my own. I let him draw me back into the cottage, and down onto the old rug, where we consummated our childish yearning for something beyond ourselves. If there were ghosts to watch us, I did not see them. I stared up past his shoulder at the way the sunlight came through a hole in the roof, and I stared at it until the brightness blinded me to everything else around me. Like the barn, I thought, watching the spot on the ceiling.

*She lies on the narrow bed. The sun filters through the curtains onto her bare legs, leaving strips of light, and when the curtains flutter the shadow moves like light on the surface of water. The field is alive with bees, chicory, the low drone of dragonflies. Summer. Like those afternoons we'd spend in the field by the old house, stamping down the long grass to make rooms, and corridors leading to rooms. She moves, suddenly, swinging her legs to stand—*not dead, *her long hair flying out around her shoulders, and the narrow trailer door is flung open, a shadow stretches across the floor from the doorway and footfalls come up the metal steps. The room is a swirl of movement, of arms and legs, two bodies falling together on the bed. Heat. A pan drops from the shelf above, the quilt slips, the bodies send up dust. I see his back, the white T-shirt, the jeans, her hands sliding the shirt up to reveal the pale skin, the ridges of the spine, the mole on the shoulder blade, shaped like a heart.*

19

William and I drove home, gripping each other's hands, and went to the courthouse downtown and applied for the license. I'd decided we were a perfect match—each of us devoted to our art and each understanding what a life as an artist meant—hours of every day spent working, and then a late dinner, and talk about unrelated things, the secret of our projects kept close. I vowed that as his wife I wouldn't pry—that I'd accept his need to remain quiet about his work. When he was ready he would share his new images with me.

The next afternoon, about the time that Mary Rae's body was lowered into the frozen ground in the Our Lady of Perpetual Sorrow's cemetery, we were married by a registered leader of a church I'd never heard of before. He was also an accountant with an office in his house on Cascadilla Street, within walking distance of my apartment. The man was short, round, with wire-framed glasses and wisps of long hair. *Ben Franklin*, William whispered, his mouth by my ear. We were nearly giddy. The officiant had a few children we saw scatter as we were led down a dim hall to the office. The house smelled of the meal cooking for dinner—a roast seasoned with sage and rosemary, and the strong scent of pine from the Christmas tree I spotted in a room we passed. I superimposed, fleetingly, the abandoned cottage in the woods on this happy scene.

The accountant's wife, tiny, with dark, bobbed hair, was our witness. On the shelves in the office were heavy books with moldering spines, the gilt of their titles indecipherable, and I was reminded of my grandfather's books that lined the shelves of the old house, and of Sister's missal hidden away in my bedroom there, and then, in a crushing way, of all the childhood dreams of dashing, potential suitors I was giving up, as if in marrying William I was entering an entirely different type of abbey. I had a moment of indecision in which it seemed I'd agreed to marriage to prevent Del from taking him away— as if the rings, and the vows, and the "till death do us parts" really meant something. At the same time I believed this was all a game, and that once tired of it, I could simply undo what I'd done with another trip to the courthouse and more paperwork. I regretted agreeing with William not to tell Del what I was doing, not inviting her to be present. She would have tried to talk me out of it; I suspected William knew this as well. In my confusion, I began to cry.

The notary's eyes widened in alarm, but the wife stepped alongside me and looped her arm in mine and gave it a squeeze. When I looked down at her, she smiled up at me warmly, her eyes filled with her own tears. She might have been fearful we would call it all off and they would lose the honorarium we were expected to provide, but at the time I felt she understood my sadness and my loss as something universal to all brides. The man said the few words required by law, and I verbally agreed, and William did the same, our voices sounding strange and foreign in the little office. William slid the rings we purchased that morning, plain gold bands, onto our respective fingers, and kissed me gently on the lips, embarrassed maybe, in front of these strangers. My signature on the required documents looked like my second-grade cursive, and I fought the urge to cross through it and try again.

Del came up to the apartment the next morning. She never came by in the morning. It was as if she knew about the ceremony and wanted to verify it for herself. She still had on the black dress and black tights she'd worn to the funeral. William had gone out—kissing me on the mouth before he left, a quick press of his lips.

"That's a married person's kiss," I said, and he laughed but offered nothing more.

"I'm late," he said. "If I *kiss you* I won't make the meeting."

Del came in after he'd gone and sat in the duck-carved chair. "Oh, so sad," she said. "Anne was there. She looked so frail and weak."

"You didn't have to go," I said. "It's not like you knew her."

Would Del see anything out of place in the apartment, some evidence of the marriage? Laundry lay piled on the bed, and I pulled out one of William's shirts to fold. I felt strung tight with my news, unsure how to share it.

"Her mother asked about William," Del said. "She asked how he was doing. I don't think she likes him much."

"You talked to the mother?"

"We went to the house after—to Mary Rae's mother's house. Just us, Alice and everyone."

"Why wouldn't she like him?" I said. "Because they broke up years ago?"

Del seemed thoughtful. "I don't know," she said. "Where is he?"

I buttoned William's shirt up the front and folded it like a shirt in a department store display. "He had to go out. A meeting or something."

Del squinted at me. "Well, we were supposed to go back to Anne's, but then she canceled. Said she was too tired."

"Do the police know how she died?" I asked Del. "How she got there to the trailer?"

"Officer Paul was there at the funeral," she said. "He's not so bad when he's not in his uniform." She raised her eyebrows at me, and I laughed.

Del pushed herself out of the chair. "We're going back to Mary Rae's mother's house today," she said. "She wants us to have Mary Rae's clothes. To go through and see if we want anything."

"That's weird," I said.

"No more weird than how you're folding that shirt," Del said. "You should come with us."

Maybe she'd seen my wedding ring right away and had simply refrained from mentioning it. She walked over to the kitchen area and pulled open the refrigerator. "Remember when we used to buy boxes of Cracker Jack and dump them out because we only wanted the ring prize?"

I held my hand out. "It's real," I said, a little ashamed of the emotion in my voice. "We got married."

Del shut the refrigerator door and crossed her arms over her chest. "You're kidding me," she said. "Right?"

Her eyes were wide, but something about her stance, her expression, made me wary. It was as if she were merely acting surprised, as if she had known about the wedding and was waiting for me to tell her so she could pretend to doubt me.

"You don't really seem surprised," I said.

"I don't?" Del cried. "Seriously? This is a huge surprise to me."

We stared at each other, and I could see Del holding her surprised expression, waiting for a cue to let it drop.

"What do you think?" I said. "Why don't you say congratulations?"

"Congratulations!" Del said. "I guess. If that's what you want."

"Yes, it's what I want. I wouldn't have done it if it wasn't."

"Then wonderful," Del said. "Perfect timing."

"What do you mean by that?" I said.

"I mean you timed it so well, right on the day of a funeral."

"I didn't know that girl," I said, but I did know her, and she was part of it all, in some strange way.

Del and I stood in the middle of my bedsit, watching each other.

"So are you going to come with us to her mother's house?" she said. "Mrs. Bell?"

I smoothed the shirt I'd folded on the bed. "Maybe," I said.

Randy picked us up an hour later, his red Firebird like a tropical fish at the dirty curb.

Del opened the passenger door and held the seat up so I could climb in back. Alice was there, wedged into the corner, as if afraid of being in close proximity to me. She and Randy had had little time to express their irritation about my presence before Del opened the car door.

"Hi, Alice," I said.

She didn't even bother offering her Milton girl version of a smile in return. She appraised me as if I'd worn the wrong outfit or said something offensive.

In the front seat Del was talking to Randy, pattering on about the funeral, and the parts she thought were nice, and then she looked at Alice. "I liked what you said about Mary Rae," Del said.

"I made most of that up," Alice said, quietly. "For her mother."

Del smiled. "I thought so."

Randy pulled out a fifth of blackberry brandy, and he passed it to the backseat to Alice, who tipped it back to take a long swallow. "What?" she said to me, though I hadn't said a word. "We need some kind of fortification." She held the bottle out to me. I accepted it and took a drink, the brandy sweet and burning the back of my throat.

We'd come to a streetlight, and Randy twisted around in the driver's seat.

"Del said you weren't a snob," he said in his low voice.

We drove down Route 13 and into Milton, but we kept driving, Randy, Alice, and I drinking the brandy, and Del taking a rare sip, so that I didn't feel the need to chastise her. We ended up at a local park, the lot recently plowed of snow, the woods surrounding us marked with hiking trails. I could hear the whine of snowmobiles, and Randy said how much he missed going out, how he had to sell his snowmobile to pay for technical school. "So I could have steady work for the rest of my life," he said, without any hint of sarcasm.

We sat in the parking lot like teenagers. Alice lit a joint, and the car filled with the smoke. If Randy or Alice noticed the ring I wore, they didn't mention it, and Del kept quiet about the whole thing, so that it seemed almost as if it had never happened. The sun came out for a moment above the bare trees and lit the inside of the car—the salt on the car windows, the strands of our hair, full of static and stuck to the upholstery—then disappeared again behind the masses of gray clouds.

"We should go," Alice said. "She's waiting for us."

Randy put the car in drive and we headed out of the lot, down a narrow road piled high with snow. Mary Rae's house was a white Cape with a detached garage. The picture window in front was lit by a lamp, and as we pulled into the driveway a woman rose from a couch and her shadow moved toward the front door. In each of the house's windows was a candle with an electric bulb flame, a bit of holly wrapped around the brass holder.

"In colonial times they used to put candles in the windows when a family member was away," I said.

"That's so sad," Alice said.

We were drunk and stoned, and climbing out of the car Alice slipped on the ice and fell, with a loud *whoop*, into a snowbank. By the time we got her up, Mrs. Swindal was at the storm door, her face in its makeup like a mask.

"Are you all right?" she called out.

Randy was stumbling up the path, and Del and I had Alice under both arms, all of us trying not to laugh. Mrs. Swindal held the door open and we stepped into her warm house, into the living-room lamplight, our footsteps muffled by beige carpet.

"Take your shoes off," Mrs. Swindal said, sounding resigned.

How irresponsible we were being—showing up at this woman's door smelling of brandy and pot, our boots bringing ice and snow into her clean house. I looked up at her to apologize and saw how much she resembled Mary Rae—her eyes, her hair, the shape of her mouth—all of it surprised me, as if Mary Rae had opened the door herself.

"What is it?" she asked me, concerned. She reached a hand out to touch my arm.

I shrugged off my coat.

Alice was crying now, wiping her eyes with her mittens, and Mrs. Swindal shifted her attention to her and asked us all to give her our coats.

"We're drunk," Alice said. "We're sorry."

Mrs. Swindal patted Alice's head and offered us coffee.

We sat in the living room, Alice and I perched awkwardly on the Swindals' reproduction Louis XIV armchairs, Del and Randy on a deacon's bench. The house was filled with reproduction antiques—fussy things that seemed easily breakable, the windows hung with sheers and heavy drapes. Mrs. Swindal brought in the coffee and sugar and cream.

"Mary Rae used to decorate the house at Christmas," she said to us, as if she felt the need to explain the absence of a tree, of windup decorative Santas and ceramic snowman figurines.

She told us to take our time and offered us food—there was so much food, she said, distractedly. Then whenever we were ready we could go up to Mary Rae's room and have a look at the clothes.

"I've already taken what I want," she said. "Her old Raggedy Ann doll. And her report cards. That sort of thing."

She eyed Alice and then looked down at her hands. "She's got shoe boxes of stuff—notes to friends—from high school, you know. I read it all last winter, thinking I could find some clues about where she might be. I gave it all to the detectives, but they brought it back, said it wasn't any use to them, they already talked to everyone."

Alice stared at Mrs. Swindal, wondering, maybe, what the woman had read, whether Mary Rae had written about the abortion the Milton girls had mentioned that day at Anne's, or other things that might have shocked Mrs. Swindal about her daughter, about all of them. But the woman seemed calm. Medicated.

"I'm just going to go lie down," she said now. "I get so tired lately." She stood, and told us to let ourselves out after. Then she disappeared through a doorway, and we all eyed one another.

Del stood first. "Well, where's her room?" she asked Alice.

Alice seemed unsure, her eyes filling with unshed tears, her nose red. "What are we doing?" she hissed. "This isn't right."

Randy had kicked his legs out in front of him and closed his eyes. He'd taken off his cowboy boots, and his sock was misshapen where his toes should have been.

"I like her idea of a nap," he said, softly.

I sensed then that this visit was about something more than picking through Mary Rae's hand-me-downs. "What is going on, Del?" I said.

She stood on the stairs, clinging to the banister. "We're going to figure out what happened to her," she said. "Alice says she kept journals. They're hidden somewhere in her room."

Alice's face seemed drawn; she looked as exhausted as Mrs. Swindal. "I'm not sure about this," she said.

"Alice said she was seeing someone," Del said. "She wouldn't tell anyone who it was."

I rose from my chair. "Did you tell Officer Paul?"

Alice shook her head no. "Anne told us not to," she said.

Del was resolute. "Come on," she said, and she took Alice by the hand and pulled her up.

The three of us climbed the carpeted stairs, suddenly sober. Randy stayed below, like a lookout. Two doors were at the top of the stairs, and Alice opened the one on the left. Mary Rae's room was dark. Alice flipped the switch on the wall, and we stepped inside, onto pink carpet, the room decorated with French provincial–style furniture, the bed neat with a flowered quilt. It might have been any high school girl's room from a movie—she'd never redecorated when she left high school, and had clearly been planning to leave her mother's house, to move on. I'd read that her cell phone had never been found, that her car had been left in the Viking Lanes lot. How had she spent her evenings bartending in the Viking Lanes, and returned here, to this childish room—*Anne of Green Gables*, *Little Women*, *Caddie Wood-lawn*, the shelves of girlish collections that Del and I had abhorred—jewelry, candles of all varieties in glass jars, little troll dolls with different colored hair and outfits, their ugly faces and glass eyes staring down at us?

Alice began pulling out bureau drawers, all of them emptied already by Mary Rae's mother, who'd left the folded clothes in careful piles on the bed. Del felt under the mattress and checked beneath the carpet, as if she might find a loose board to pry up.

"This is a waste," Alice said. "Everything's been gone through."

She opened the closet door, tugged a string, and a light came on.

There on the closet floor was a built-in wooden shelf, a platform for shoes, maybe, and I went to it and pulled the wood up and revealed a hidden niche. Alice rushed over, and from within this hiding place she pulled a journal—black faux leather, the pages gilt. She reached in again, and pulled out more, years of journals, the sort you'd see on the shelves of a bookstore—the covers brightly colored, embossed, decorated with flowers. She held the stack of books out to Del, who took them in her two hands and set them on the bed of clothes.

"Very clever," Del said, eyeing me.

"Well," I said. Neither Del nor I kept journals—we'd read Leanne's and Sarah's, and didn't want anyone knowing our business. But I did have things I kept hidden in our bedroom in the old house, and they were beneath a similar built-in shelf. I almost pitied Mary Rae for this invasion of privacy. Even though she was gone, it still felt wrong. "You've got a lot of reading to do."

"We're supposed to bring them to Anne," Alice said. She glanced almost longingly at the stack of journals.

"Let's go," Del whispered, and I reminded them that they were supposed to be picking out clothes, so they both sifted through and chose a sweater each, and then we went downstairs to awaken Randy on the bench.

Mrs. Swindal never reappeared. She'd probably taken a pill and was out for the night. I said we should pick up our cups, but Del and Alice were nearly out the door, Del grabbing the storm door before it could close all the way, letting the cold rush in.

"Just make it snappy," she said.

I brought the coffee cups into the kitchen and discovered the Formica counters and the small kitchen table covered with casseroles—foil spread beneath each lid. The smell in the kitchen was of food slowly going bad—shepherd's pie and lasagna and beef stew spoiling in their containers, leaving circles of condensation beneath them. I set the cups in the sink, and I stood in the kitchen, waiting for Mary Rae. Surely she would be here in her old house, in the room where she once opened cabinets to retrieve a cup or the ingredients for a cake recipe, where certainly she had once sat at the little table with her mother having a quiet dinner. There was a small glass ball hung on the end of the light pull over the sink, and I touched it, and the Silver Streak appeared to me, the fields around it filled with Queen Anne's lace, and Mary Rae with a man whose back was familiar to me—broad and pale, the mole I saw every morning when he emerged from the shower—my husband's.

20

On the car ride back from Mrs. Swindal's, the journals sat on the backseat between Alice and me. From above, the car might have looked like a slash of red against the black asphalt, the white, snow-covered hills, the trees' crosshatched branches a complicated nest. William would have found the trailer on one of his explorations—another abandoned place to have sex. The trailer might have been their own little place, like a playhouse. Despite what evidence I had that William and Mary Rae had been together in the trailer, it didn't mean that he was the mysterious man she'd been seeing at the time of her death. He wouldn't have told anyone about the trailer, for fear of implicating himself. I couldn't be jealous of a dead girl, but for some reason I was, and I wanted, more than anything, to see what the journals held.

"Anne wants them," Alice said, when I suggested we take a look, but I knew, from her expression, that she would give anything to go through them herself.

"Let's go to Del's place first," I said. "We can get something to eat, and you can tell Anne it got late, and you'll bring them by Windy Hill tomorrow."

Del turned to smile at me from the front. She punched Randy in the shoulder.

"You heard her," she said.

To keep themselves in Anne's good standing, they would say it was my idea.

We stopped at the Korean place in Collegetown, the front window steamed up, the interior nearly empty—everyone was away on break. We brought the food back to Del's. I'd tried to call William, but his phone had gone to voice mail, and I left a message. I assumed our married life would simply be a continuation of what we'd had before, and if he wanted to talk to me he'd call me back.

Del's apartment was neat and spare. On one wall were shelved books: volumes of classic works in the original Greek and Latin that the professor had collected and her own translations. There were two wing chairs, their upholstery worn. The lamps were old-fashioned, with large silk shades and alabaster bases shaped like pitchers. Assorted pillows—beaded and tapestried, plaid and paisley—decorated the couch. Randy sat at the small bar in the kitchen and ate from the cartons. Del, Alice, and I settled on the carpet under the lamplight with plates of food, the journals spread out on the floor between us.

"Anne will be mad," Alice said.

"Why does she care?" I said. "Why would she even want them?"

Del had set her plate to the side and was thumbing through a journal with a cover of a seascape. "She must suspect there's something in here she doesn't want anyone to see," she said. "Don't you think?"

I spun the ring on my finger. It felt odd to be wearing it. "You mean about William," I said. I wasn't sure why I said it out loud.

Alice had taken a mouthful of food. "God, no," she said. "Why do you think that?"

"How many entries will we find in here about Billy?" I asked her.

Alice wiped her mouth. "Rae was obsessed with him. You'll find a lot, I'm sure. That doesn't mean anything."

"It doesn't mean he was the guy she was seeing?" I said.

"He broke it off with her and that was that."

Alice's voice was hoarse from all her crying, like the keening women on the tapes in my Women and Grief course. Alice put her hand over her mouth as if to stifle a gasp. Her hair was an unruly mop of curls she'd fastened up. She wore a Syracuse University sweatshirt, a pair of plaid flannel pajama pants.

"He broke her *heart*," she said. "She *hated* him. She would never have had anything to do with him."

Del looked at me a little sadly. The Milton girls weren't jealous of me at all. In their show of support for Mary Rae they hated William, too. If they had indeed been a coven, they would have summoned spells to bring him grief.

"He's nice at first," Alice said, as if this excused my stupidity for getting involved with him. "But he changes, you know?"

Randy came over and stretched out on the couch with a sigh. He looked over at us sitting on the rug, then pulled a throw pillow over his face. "I'm really going to sleep this time," he said.

I didn't know what to say to Alice. Del continued to thumb through the journal. The room was cold, as usual. The elm threw its shadowy form on the window, a reminder that Mary Rae might be there beneath it, the snow piling up on her coat's shoulders. I wished I could invite her inside to set us all straight.

"Maybe you're the one he was looking for all along," Alice said, softly. "Maybe he'll be different." She pointed to the ring on my finger. "But he tried to get her to marry him, too."

I was suddenly angry, and I stood. "I can't believe I even care what's in these things," I said.

Del clutched the journal to her chest and pulled her knees up. "Martha, stop," she said.

"You might not know as much as you think you do about her," I said. "She might not even have *liked* you very much."

Alice paled. She set her plate aside. "How can you say that to me?"

"She hated everything about that horrible town," I said. "She dreaded ending up like all of you."

Alice looked confused. "What's she talking about?" she said to Del.

Del stood with her plate. "Can I get anyone more food?"

"You and your stupid karaoke, and your crush on that Shurfine deli clerk—'Oh Dougie, Dougie,'" I said.

I hated knowing these things, and I was usually so very good about keeping them to myself, but I felt purged, suddenly, and I didn't regret having said them for Mary Rae. Not at all.

Alice's eyes widened and she began to tremble. She looked to Del, not with solidarity but with mistrust.

Del went into the kitchen and scraped her food into the sink. I didn't wait to hear Del's explanation. I left her apartment and climbed the stairs to mine. Inside, it was dark, colder than downstairs. I slammed the door and fumbled for the light, and then I heard a noise in the darkness, and the lamp came on across the room, and William was sitting in the duck-carved chair.

"What are you doing in here?" I asked him.

"I live here," he said.

"I mean in the dark," I said. "Sitting in the dark. I had no idea you were here."

"It wasn't dark when I sat down," he said. "Then I fell asleep, and you woke me up coming in."

"Didn't you get my call?" I went over to the bed, anxious, distracted. Even the bedclothes were cold. "It's so cold in here."

William had on one of his heavy wool sweaters. He had, in fact, been reading. The book was open on his lap. "Where were you?" he said.

"With Del, downstairs," I said.

"What's wrong?" he said. He moved the book from his lap to the floor. "Why are you acting so oddly?"

I sat down on the bed. "I don't know," I said. "It's Del. She drives me crazy."

He chuckled then, and rose from the chair to sit beside me on the bed. "How did she take your news?" he asked me.

I felt the warmth of him through his sweater, and I leaned into his shoulder.

"You know, once," I told him, "I thought I wanted to join a convent. You had to give up everything you owned to go there. You could choose one of two paths—work in the fields, or spend all day in prayerful contemplation."

"Which would you have picked?" William said. He ran his hand through my hair.

"I couldn't choose," I said. "I liked the idea of having nothing, but I was afraid of having to live with my decision."

"The idea of living without sex never occurred to you," he said.

"I didn't think of that," I said. "This was before."

He probably believed I meant before him, but I didn't mean that. I meant before David Pinney, but I let him think what he wanted.

"This wasn't about changing my mind, anyway," I said. "It was a decision to live a certain way *forever*."

I knew it was possible to acclimate to the results of irreversible conditions. Like death, I thought.

"Like marriage," William said. His eyes grew serious then, almost worried. He took my hand.

"They used to think marriage saved men and women from being sinful," he said. "That there was a vein or nerve that ran directly from the ring finger of the left hand to the heart." He spun the band on my finger.

"You're kidding, right?" I said.

"It's just something I read," he said, then he rose and went back to his book.

I looked at the room and its disarray. The unmade bed, the clutter and closeness of the place, suddenly reminded me of the cottage in the woods. On the small stove the few pots I owned sat on the burners with their previous contents congealing. My clothes lay scattered on the floor, over the bed—my books and notes, the remains of meals on plates abandoned on other surfaces. Our first Christmas tree, a pathetic little thing, still sat in its pot on the table by the window, its branches absent of green life. The glass ornaments slipped off, one at a time, at night. In the darkness, they made small splashing sounds when they shattered, like spilling water. I suppose this carelessness reflected our life at the time—and it occurred to me that even before our marriage had begun, William and I had fallen into a kind of decline.

I told him I was tired, and I changed and climbed into the bed. Though I sensed there were things he didn't tell me, I convinced myself they were things I didn't need to know. I would learn to let the undiscussed spaces in our life together flourish. I would practice pretending all was well.

21

⌐

Our father spent Christmas in Acapulco. Our mother called and tried to entice me to come home with Del, claiming she'd decorated a tree with all of our childhood ornaments. A Christmas album played—Robert Goulet singing "Do You Hear What I Hear"—and Sarah's baby, born in September, wailed from a distant room.

"Convenient for a live nativity," I said.

The door to the back terrace swung on its squeaking hinges, and the baby's crying faded. I pictured my mother outside, shivering with the phone, and behind her the dead grass, the bare horse chestnut trees.

"I think we may have a white Christmas," she said.

I could have told her Del and I had had enough of snow, and that I had a husband now, but I said we'd made plans of our own.

"We'll miss you," my mother said, her voice convincingly wistful.

I didn't tell Del about our mother's invitation. Our Christmas would be at Windy Hill, with all of the Milton girls. I agreed to stop by and visit and have some of Del's eggnog, but I told William I didn't want to stay very long, and he agreed. We'd purchased each other gifts that we'd already exchanged on Christmas Eve. I'd gotten him a cashmere sweater—a forest green that went with his copper-colored hair. He gave me a vintage camera—a Pentax that I had been searching for. We showed up at Anne's with Geoff at noon, and opened Anne's gifts, and smiled at everyone, as if nothing had changed. Del was exuberant and silly, and I wondered if she'd been drinking too much. I was doing a poor job of monitoring her, if that was still my role. I wasn't entirely sure anymore.

"I'm glad I'm spending my last Christmas with all of you," Anne said, holding her eggnog up with a trembling hand. "I'm looking forward to ushering in the New Year."

She wore a red wool dress, a beautiful scarf. We'd all agreed to return on New Year's Eve for a party, and it felt, in many ways, as if that might be a final event. Anne again patted the sofa next to her and had me sit beside her, and she picked up my hand with the ring, and gave it a gentle squeeze, as if this were all she needed to do to show her approval of the marriage. I suffered the Milton girls' glares, and Alice refused to speak to me at all. Del said Alice would forgive me.

"She's one of those girls who forget things pretty quickly," she said.

We hadn't had much time to talk since that evening with the journals, and Del hadn't been especially forthcoming about what the journals revealed. "It's all who she's mad at, and who she talks to at lunch in the cafeteria," Del had told me one afternoon in my apartment. "Who she sneaks a cigarette with in the bathroom. Like an after-school special."

Christmas day I found Del in the kitchen decorating sugar cookies. She had colored icing in small bowls and was painting a blue scarf on a snowman.

"Remember when we used to do this with Grandmother?" she said.

We were alone in the kitchen, and I leaned over the counter toward her.

"Did you give the journals to Anne?"

"Sure," she said, wiping the brush off on a dish towel.

"You kept the newest one," I said.

"You are so untrusting," she said. She set the cookie on a glass plate. "No one is trying to hide anything from you."

When we were little Del or I would tell this sort of lie all the time. "This is my favorite dinner!" I'd exclaim when our mother made her Bisquick and vegetable soup casserole. "You look so pretty," Del would say when I woke with mascara streaks under my eyes.

"What are you talking about?" I said.

Del chose a large Christmas tree–shaped cookie and began brushing green icing over its surface.

"Are you taking your medication?" I said.

Del lifted her head; her brush paused. "Is that any of your business?" Then she bent back over her work. "What do you think our mother and sisters are doing today?"

I felt a stab of guilt that I hadn't shared our mother's invitation. "Sitting around the tree talking about us because we're not there," I said.

Geoff came into the kitchen singing "We Three Kings," and then a few of the Milton girls trailed him in, singing, too. Del's expression brightened.

"Remember when we put on that Christmas recital in the old house's living room?" she said. "Mr. Parmenter showed up at the front door, and we did our performance for him? He never took off his coat, did he?"

The unease of that Christmas Eve returned to me—our mother with the J&B out on the counter, the jangle of ice cubes in hers and Mr. Parmenter's glasses. It was snowing. Our grandmother had gone to bed. Eventually, Mr. Parmenter left, driving his Jaguar back to his miserable life, one he ended a short month later.

"Why was Mr. Parmenter there?" I said.

"His daughter, Candace, was in my class," Del said.

The memory filled me with an awful emptiness. But Del seemed unmoved. She joined Geoff in singing, and they all filed out of the room as if they were a group of carolers. It occurred to me that her memory seemed so sharp about so many aspects of our childhood, but it selected and excluded, and when it came to the summer David Pinney died it provided a blank, as if that one part had been conveniently erased.

When William and I left, Del was hanging pinecones covered in suet and birdseed from the trees in Anne's backyard. I called across the snowdrifts to her. Alice was with her, and Del turned and stared at me for a moment, and then turned away. I began to see the Milton girls forming a barricade between Del and me, and I wasn't happy about it.

ONCE WE RETURNED from Anne's, William and I sat together under blankets, listening to the elm scrape the side of the house, both of us wishing we could light a fire, and berating ourselves for not having stayed at Anne's beside hers. It was late afternoon, and the snow began to fall, the flakes like pencil shavings or ash, and William suggested we go for a walk.

"At least we'll be moving," he said. "We can stay warm that way."

Neither of us had initiated sex, and I thought I might make a joke about how marriage had so swiftly tamped down the urge, but I did not. I knew it wasn't getting married that changed things, really. It was my vision of Mary Rae with him in the Silver Streak, and Alice telling me he'd asked Mary Rae to marry him—two things I didn't know to be true.

We ended up on the deserted campus, and William headed toward his office in Tjaden Hall.

"I have to pick up some things," he said.

The office proved to be much warmer than the apartment—so warm that William tapped open one of the high windows with the broomstick he kept just for that purpose. He had an old leather couch against one wall, and while he sorted through slides in the light from the desk lamp, I lay down and closed my eyes.

"I'm going to the lab," he said. "Take a nap if you want."

Something was bothering me about the office, some smell in the couch's fabric cushions, something I noted when we walked in, before he'd opened the window and let most of the scent out. It was incense—sandalwood. Del had started burning it as a teenager—little cones she set on saucers, or sticks of it she propped in ceramic holders. I had often opened the windows of our bedroom to let the smell out, it was so strong. She insisted it would help us remember our past lives.

I sat up on the couch. The cold came in from the open window and erased the incense smell. I stood and went to the office door and peered out into the empty hallway. Once, Anne's office had been at the end—William had shown it to me one day. Her name remained on the door, though a group of graduate students had taken it over. I walked out into the hall and then stepped back into his office. The smell of the sandalwood seemed to have disappeared. I stood looking at the books on his shelf, and then, bored, I tugged on the top desk drawer. It was locked.

I would have expected to find napkins from the Green Dragon, or pens and pencils, or university letterhead. But there was something more important stored there. Despite my promise to myself that as a dutiful wife I wouldn't pry, I scanned his office, wondering where he might have placed the key. He might have hidden it anywhere—inside or behind books, taped under the shelves themselves. He didn't carry it with him on his key chain, which held three keys: one to his motorcycle, one to the office, and one to the apartment. It made sense that the desk key would be here in the office. I scanned the spines of the books, and noticed on one of his bookshelves a small tin—a battered thing that struck me immediately as special to him. He'd told me that as a child his mother sold apples, and he collected the money in a tin. I wavered, not sure if I should look, but then I gave in and took it down and pried off the lid. Inside was the key.

I stuck my head out the door to check the hallway, and then unlocked the desk drawer and slid it open. Lying flat, taking most of the space, was a leather portfolio. It was an awkward place to put something like that, and I was intrigued. William still hadn't shown me any of his new work. I slid the portfolio out and opened it on the desk. I felt a little thrill of surprise. I'd discovered some of his sleep studies.

Each image captured just a woman's sleeping form, her bare arms flung out, her legs entwined with sheets. Some of the women had their hands placed under their cheeks, their lips parted as if to speak. Their long hair fanned in disarray over their bodies. All of the women were nude. The bones of their backs showed, their skin luminous in early morning light, in late afternoon shadow, in a dark room illuminated by a bare bulb. Those whose faces were revealed seemed familiar to me, and yet I couldn't place why. And it bothered me, like the sandalwood smell. The images were strange, compelling. I had to admit that they disturbed me. I went back through the portfolio again, studying each photograph. Despite the shadows and blurred effects of light that sometimes concealed them, I felt that wave of recognition again, accompanied by a slowly growing unease.

The faces in the photographs belonged to the Milton girls. Once I made the connection I recognized each of them—Alice's ginger-colored hair, the point of Lucie's chin, Kitty's long lashes. I flipped through the pages, searching for one of Mary Rae, but there were none. I was stunned by his use of the girls in Milton as his subjects, but since I hadn't officially been shown the photographs I wasn't sure how to bring them up. His refusal to share them made sense to me now. Even more troubling, though, was the Milton girls' silence. If they hated him so much, why would they agree to pose?

Anne had sketched a portrait of Mary Rae before she died, and it was displayed in a prominent spot in the living room—the girl, nude, on her side, an arm thrown over her face. It was eerily similar to William's photographs. I told myself William was simply imitating his mentor, a woman with obvious talent and, we were constantly reminded, not long for this world.

The door at the far end of the hall opened, and William's footsteps approached. I wanted more time with the portfolio, so instead of putting it back in the drawer, I slid it beneath a stack of folders he'd packed into a cardboard box on his desk. I locked the drawer, replaced the key in the tin, and then returned to the couch to feign sleep. He entered the office, and I felt him standing near me, the shadow of him over me. I assumed he was watching me, but when I peered up at him he was not looking at me but at the desk, his hands on his hips. I must have moved something on its surface when I opened the portfolio.

He readjusted some papers on the desk's surface, then turned toward me, and I smiled up at him.

"What time is it?" I asked him.

"Did you fall asleep?"

I sat up. "I must have," I said.

Something between us had shifted. We were each tense, and whatever we wanted to say remained unspoken. "No one is trying to hide anything from you," Del had said. Clearly, she'd intended me to believe someone was.

"What?" William said. His eyes had grown hard to read in the office's half-light. Beyond the high window it was night, and the walk home across the dark, windswept campus loomed ahead of us.

"It's going to be cold," I said.

"I already called Geoff," he said. "He's coming to pick us up."

And then he hefted the box he'd packed in his arms, and checked the room one last time, as if for anything else he needed. His gaze took in the desk, and I knew he was thinking about the portfolio, and I almost confessed to having seen it just to clear the tension in the room, to ease my guilt. Then he reached out and tugged on the desk drawer, as if to make sure it was locked.

"Hurry up," he said. "Get your coat."

His voice was cold, distracted. Dumbly, I grabbed my coat off the couch, longing for the times we'd slipped in here to have sex, the sound of students passing in the hall, the occasional knock on the opaque class, the way we'd suppress our movements, our breath, until the person had left. I thought of the sandalwood smell, and William with Del here in the office together, and though I had no real proof she'd been there, I was filled with a rush of resentment and anger. He was mine and she had no right to him. I reached out and took William's hand, and was surprised to find how cold it was—as if he'd been outside.

"Do we have to hurry?" I said. I pressed his cold hand to my cheek. "It's so nice and warm in here."

And like the first time, when I'd awakened to find him in the duck-carved chair in my apartment, his face changed, and his hand slid around to the back of my neck, and he tugged me in to kiss. This time his lips were cold and hard. He dropped the box to the floor, and he kicked the door shut—although no one was around who might have seen us. The office, lit by the desk lamp, was filled with shadow, and he pulled me down onto the couch and tore at the clasp to my jeans. When I tried to help him he pinned both of my hands beneath his. I cried out, and maybe he took my cry for that of passion. His movements became harsh, his breathing ragged. He pulled my hair to tip my face up, and kneaded my breasts, and pressed my legs open.

I'd thought I was initiating sex—but this wasn't that. Had it been my fault for being duplicitous? For desiring proof that he was mine? I was afraid, though I tried to not show it. I hurried things along so he would be done. I left myself, and watched him as if from above, like one of the dead. Later, there would be the familiar bruises from the pads of his fingers, from his mouth. I could not erase the past. I had only spun it, like a wheel, away from me. And I had gotten a

small reprieve, but now it was back. *What goes around comes around.*
For whatever a man sows, this he will also reap. He would make a joke
about that night and tell me I surprised him, and I would think he
didn't really know what surprised was. If he wanted to be surprised,
well, I could do that.

22

That afternoon in August, the summer David Pinney died, I watched him walk across the lawn to the barn, the dry grass flattened under his feet, and I pulled myself out of the pool and followed him. I had often gone into the barn to be alone. It had been three years since my grandfather died, and my sisters were afraid of the place, but to me the barn, with its strips of sunlight and its stone floor, was reassuring and cool. I would sit in the little area where I once saw Sister Martha Mary, near my grandfather's workshop that smelled of milled copper. There was stacked hay for the sheep he'd raised once, the few cows that would get loose on the golf course, old Bonnie, the mare with her large head and frightening whinny. I'd sit on the bale of hay, draw my legs to my chest. The hay was rough and stuck to my bare skin.

Usually, I sat in the barn and waited for something. I expected to see my grandfather, busy at his bench once again, the sparks from the mill flying out onto the stone floor, his pants loose on his bony hips. I sat on the bale of hay waiting, much as Sister had once waited for me. Now I entered, looking for David Pinney. Up in the barn's rafters, swallows flitted. I didn't see him at first, and then he stepped out of the shadows. I felt a small misgiving, but I ignored it.

I showed him the old lightning rods, the coiled cable shining like a new penny. I told him how the rods worked, how the cable, buried in the ground, drew the strike away from the highest points of a church, or a barn, or a peak in a roof. The sun came in and out, blinking through the old barn's slats.

"People were afraid of lightning," I told him. "Once, they thought it was sent by the Prince of the Power of the Air."

"And who would that be?" he said.

"Satan, you know." I picked up one of the rods. "They called this the 'heretical rod.' They didn't think it was right to try to control something that came from God."

He took the rod from my hand, hefted it, and then set it down. "These must be an easy sell."

"People aren't really afraid anymore," I said.

"They don't believe in the devil so much?" he said.

Water from his damp hair ran down his shoulder.

"Playing to people's fears, that's sort of like that church you go to," he said.

"I don't go to that church," I said.

He looked at the ceiling and the scattering birds, and he laughed. He moved closer to me, and his wet shorts dripped onto my feet. I felt the closeness of his bare skin.

"But you believe in all of that," he said. "Ghosts and messages."

I wanted to correct him, but I knew I would only give him more reason to make fun of me. He made a low, wailing sound.

"Don't be so serious," he said, and I smiled, though my mouth felt stiff.

He stood in front of me with his narrow chest, his green eyes. He placed his hands on my shoulders. I watched him do it with a strange detachment. Then he leaned in to press his mouth to mine. His lips were dry. His skin smelled of chlorine. I wore Sarah's orange bikini. She had let me borrow it, soft-piled fabric with beads threaded onto the ties. His hand slid to my breast, pushed aside my suit, and I felt a rush of surprise. I knew I should pull away from him, but I liked his hand there, his mouth on mine. He sighed, and moaned, drew ragged breaths. He clung to me, holding me tight to him, his mouth covering mine, his tongue pushing in past my lips. He stepped with me back into one of the unused stalls, the floor covered with moldy hay, and I felt his hands sliding over me, sliding down my bathing suit bottom, his fingers slipping between my legs. I kicked, and pushed him off of me. I stood, unsteadily, covering myself, pulling up my suit. He reached out to grab me again, but I backed away, and he stared at me, his expression hard to read. Then he laughed at me.

"Are you just a little girl?" he said.

Outside the barn, I felt the heat of the sun hit me, felt the places his hands had touched me. My mouth felt sore and bruised. Later, I worried over what had happened. I kept feeling his mouth on mine, his dry lips. The way I'd felt when his hands slid over my breast, between my legs. I worried I should have admitted to wanting it, and not pushed him away. But I knew I would see him again, and I both longed for and feared that moment.

The next day it was Del and David Pinney, taking turns on the diving board, talking in the deep end, and that night she told me he was her boyfriend.

"You don't want him for your boyfriend," I said.

"Why not?" she said.

I told her he had kissed me, and she stared at me from her twin bed, her head propped in her hand. I wanted to describe the other things he'd done, but I couldn't find the words to do it.

"No he didn't," she said. "You're just saying that."

I knew that if I continued to object to him, Del would insist I was only jealous. All of our arguments lately had been over Del's desire for everything that was mine—the little ceramic box with its painted dragonfly, my favorite jeans. She'd been taking my things without asking and claiming them as her own. Just the other day we'd fought and our mother had stepped in. As usual, she sided with Del.

"You always want everything I have," I'd told her then, bitterly.

That night she turned off the lamp. "He is my boyfriend," she said. "I don't know why you have to pretend I've stolen him."

We lay quietly in the dark. I thought I could smell my dead grandfather's tobacco rising from the porch below.

I was filled with an unaccountable desperation. "Stay away from him," I said, and then because I'd said it I knew she would not, and it was too late to take it back.

23

New Year's Eve arrived on a Thursday. Since the evening in William's office, I'd kept my distance from him. I had become preoccupied with the photographs. In the back of my cedar closet I'd noticed a loose wood panel, and I slid it away from the wall. I'd taken the portfolio out of the box while he slept, and slipped it down behind the cedar panels and replaced the loose board. I wanted the chance to look at the photographs again when I had the opportunity. I had to admit they were beautiful, and I knew I should just confess to having seen them. But the locked drawer, the extent of his secrecy troubled me. Why hide them from me when I had already shown him my work? I vowed to keep my new images to myself. When he asked, I would counter with a request to see his sleep studies. It was only fair.

We were expected at Anne's by two in the afternoon, which I found strange. It would be hours of visiting and drinking before we ushered in the New Year, and I wasn't looking forward to another long day and night of the Miltons. I knew I couldn't look at the girls who'd posed for William the same way again. It bothered me that Alice swore to hate him, when her nude body seemed to luxuriate under his lens.

I went downstairs to ask Del what to wear. The Milton girls usually went out with dates on New Year's Eve, and Mary Rae had worn, in her last known photograph, a fancy dress. But when I showed Del what I was wearing, she asked me if I was going to the prince's ball.

"Where are your white gloves?" she said.

She was lying on the couch in her old jeans and a sweater.

"What?" I said. "What are you wearing?"

"This," she said, pushing herself up. "And a warm coat. Maybe I'll put my hair in a bun."

"What do you mean?" I said. My dress was a dark blue sheath with narrow straps. I had on black hose and high heels.

"For the hunting party," Del said.

She left the couch, went into the bedroom, and emerged wearing her faux fur hat with the flaps. "Anne has a traditional New Year's Eve hunt. For hares."

"And you're going to hunt?"

"The men are," Del said. "And Anne, if she's not too tired. The rest of us will just be the keepers of the flasks."

Upstairs, I found William loading film into his camera. He whistled at me when I walked in. "Look at you," he said.

"You like it?" I crossed the room, pivoted like a model on a runway, and walked back to the door. "It will be perfect for the hunt."

He laughed. "I forgot about that. Do you want me to bag you a hare?"

"Is that how it works? The men kill a harmless creature as a token of their love?"

He held the camera, advancing the film with his thumb. "Marriage isn't suiting you," he said.

Where once I might have felt guilty, at fault for failing to be the wife he'd expected, I felt only anger. I unzipped my dress and let it fall to the floor. "I want a white one."

"That's a snowshoe," he said, curious, unsure. "Given the foxes haven't eaten them all, I'll see what I can do."

AT ANNE'S, THE men and Anne put on orange hats and vests and filed out the back sliding doors across the terrace, towing three of Joseph's beagles, who lunged toward me on their leashes, their nails skittering across Anne's wood floors. This hunting party fanned out across the backyard and headed into the woods. Randy and Joseph had brought their own .410s and Geoff and William borrowed two guns from Anne. Anne herself looked strong and capable in her bulky clothing. It was a bitterly cold day, the sky its usual shade of gray. Somewhere beneath the cloud cover the sun shone brightly on silver airplane bodies, on other states and continents, but its warmth and light begrudged Milton and the surrounding villages.

Del and the girls had filled flasks and thermoses with schnapps. When I mused on how hazardous it might be for the hunters to drink, Lucie laughed—a pretty, tinkling sound.

"How else will they stay warm?" she said.

"We'll freeze our asses off out there," Alice said.

I'd tried to bow out. "I'll sit here by the fire and wait for you to bring back my hare," I said to William.

"Do you want to eat tonight?" he said affably, and I could see his eyes were cold and that whatever had happened between us might never right itself.

We would all have to suffer the outdoors.

Anne had hoped to catch enough rabbits for dinner, and Del said she'd found a recipe, Fricasseed Rabbits, in *A Poetical Cook-Book*. I trudged through the snowy woods beside the Milton girls, the fog from our breaths huffing out around our heads. We hung back from the orange bobbing of the hunters ahead, sipping from the flasks more than we should have. The woods were filled with thorny bushes that snagged our jacket sleeves, our mittens. The wood smoke smell of Anne's fire reached us, and over the tree line we could see spires of smoke from distant houses. Finally, we heard the dogs braying, and the retorts of the weapons ahead, and we broke out of the woods to a clearing—an open field of snow splotched with the bloody marks of the various kills. Anne's voice called out, and the men shouted congratulations, and Randy moved out across the snow to gather the hares. "Four," he called out. "Good shots."

"Disgusting," Lucie said.

Del kept walking across the field, though I tried to call her back, so I followed her. She stopped at one spot in the snow where a rabbit lay, spread out as if sleeping, its eye open, a vivid red spray around its hind legs, and then she turned, her face white, and walked back past the other Milton girls and into the woods. The girls called her. Anne approached me and put her hand on my arm.

"Is she all right?" she said.

Her face was full of color, and her eyes clear and blue. I could see the papery texture of her skin, the way it was scored around her eyes. "She'll be fine," I said. "She gets faint at the sight of blood."

"All snowshoes," Anne said. "The dogs are good ones. They flushed out quite a few."

The men decided to stay out, the dogs were excited and racing back into the woods, and Anne said we should head back with the girls. "I've got my New Year's kill," she said.

I held Anne's gun and let her lean on my arm. I was leery of the gun, but she laughed at me and assured me it wouldn't go off. The metal was cold through my glove. The Milton girls were ahead of us, and when Anne and I reached the house, Kitty came out to tell us that no one could locate Del. I said to try upstairs, and Alice found her in the little room with the pine bureau, lying down.

"She's tired," Alice said, though, from her expression, she didn't know what to think.

I climbed the back stairs and went into the little room. It was dim, and I could just make out Del on the bed. She still wore her boots, the treads filled with melting snow wetting the bedspread.

"Those damn dogs won't stop barking," Del said.

It was true—from the upstairs you could hear the dogs in the woods, their braying.

"They're just rabbits," I said.

"Missing their waistcoats and jackets," Del said.

I laughed, and then Del laughed, too, although it sounded more like she was crying. I went over and took off her boots and I carried them downstairs. Later, William and the rest of the men filed in— boisterous and red-faced, numb from the cold. They left the rabbits on the terrace—seven in all. Randy and Joseph drank back a few shots of whiskey, and then they skinned the carcasses outside and brought in the bodies—slimy and slick and pink—on a platter. Geoff volunteered to prepare the fricassee, claiming they ate rabbit all the time in England. No one mentioned Del's absence. Occasionally one of the girls went upstairs to check on her, bringing her bread, and tea, and later, after we'd eaten the rabbit—which was tender, and seasoned wonderfully with fresh herbs—Del made her appearance, like a fairy-tale princess.

She slid onto the couch between Alice and Lucie. Eventually other guests arrived—more Milton girls, more of Anne's friends from school, one of my own professors, who asked me about work that semester and made a fuss over me, holding his wineglass and his cigarette. It felt strange to be socializing with them, and I noticed that William kept hidden away in Anne's study. She'd lit a fire in there, too, and he and Geoff and the other men sat with brandy snifters, and cigars, discussing the hunt.

Before midnight, Anne flushed the men out of the study like the hares from the woods. After the usual fanfare—the uncorking and pouring of champagne, the countdown to midnight—she made another toast, and as I'd expected, she announced this to be her last year.

"The last year in this place, in this form," she said.

None of the Milton girls protested. They raised their champagne flutes with solemn faces. We all sat in the living room, and most of the guests left. William was drunk, his cheeks flushed, and he leaned back in the couch cushions and nudged me with his shoulder.

"Martha wants to take a trip to the old Buffalo State Hospital," he said.

I'd heard about the place from Charles Wu, who thought it might be a subject for my work. When I first mentioned it to William, he'd grown quiet.

"He's in one of my classes," William said. "Charles Wu." He drew out the vowels in Charles's name in a deprecating way.

As for my suggestion about visiting the place, William had said nothing, and I'd let it drop. Now he explained to the group at Anne's that it was an old lunatic asylum, long closed down. "I used to see the place every day when I was in grad school, and always wondered about it. Tell them, Martha."

I had no idea he had any knowledge of the place. "The main building is vacant," I said. "It has been for years."

"Urban spelunking," he said. "We'll sneak in and Martha can take some photos."

Alice chimed in, drunk and merry. "I want to go!"

Randy agreed to drive whoever wanted to come along. Geoff said he'd rather not go.

"It sounds illegal," he said.

"That's the fun of it," William said.

Lucie and Alice were already talking about the day. "We'll bring the flasks," Lucie said. "And a picnic lunch."

I blamed Del's subdued state on her earlier reaction to the dead rabbits, and I didn't think anything of it. So what if I was suddenly, thanks to William, the instigator of a fabulous plan the Miltons were all rallying around?

That night I drank too much, refilling my wineglass so many times, I lost count. Everything became a bit of a blur—William helping me out to Geoff's car, the cold of the car and the drive home, the stars overhead suddenly appearing and sliding around in the sky. I was lying in the backseat, and William was humming something, and my hand had fallen to the floor of the car. I felt among the bits of sawdust, and cellophane wrappers, a bit of cold metal. I put my fingers on it—a thin chain, and then the pendant, and I knew without having to see it that it was Mary Rae's necklace. I balled it into my palm and put it in my coat pocket, and the car turned along the winding roads, William humming to some inaudible music, the Christmas lights of scattered houses glinting on the car windows. I felt with certainty Mary Rae had lain there, in that backseat, though when and why and where she'd been taken remained unclear. The necklace told me nothing. Had it been William or Geoff in the driver's seat? Had she been alive—drunk, like me, half-conscious? Or dead?

24

Just after New Year's a driving storm settled in the valley and wouldn't leave. Snow blown by a bitter wind rattled the windows in their frames. It filled in the patches that had once, fleetingly, revealed strawlike grass. This storm had the suffocating effect of trapping us indoors for two days, William pacing, pacing, with a pencil behind his ear, his thick gray socks collecting dust. His hair was a mass of curls he kept cut short, he'd always said, so he wouldn't look *mythological*.

"Like those statues of Apollo, or Bacchus. Or those paintings of satyrs."

Since finding the portfolio, since the sex in his office, I'd begun to think differently about him, maybe even to admit I really didn't know him. Was this what happened to married couples? Did they glance over at their spouses one evening and see a stranger?

The whole first snowy day I kept under the blankets on the bed, watching an old movie on television. The snow blew past the window glass, masking the world white. Buried cars lined the street, their forms hulking and misshapen. It grew dark quickly, and every so often we'd hear the snowplows, or a patrolling police car, the chains on its tires a soft clanking. When the power went out William paused his pacing in the sudden quiet. We lit two tapers in my grandmother's sterling candlesticks, and he came over to the bed and slipped under the blankets. I felt myself tense with apprehension. He pressed his mouth to my shoulder, and then he kissed me, almost tentatively. I let him lift my shirt, allowed his mouth to roam over each of my breasts. He moved against me, his fingers groping to remove our clothes, and I remained a passive witness, letting him do these things, letting him think that nothing had changed. I assumed when he noticed I wasn't participating he would stop, but strangely he did not. It was dark in the room, the candlelight eerie, and I was reminded of the light in one of his photographs—the shadows it left on the woman's form—Alice, in that image. I pushed him away from me, my hands on his chest. He couldn't understand at first. He leaned forward to kiss me, and I turned away. He grabbed my chin, his eyes dark beneath his brows.

"Why are you doing this?" he asked me.

The snowplow roared past, the snow spraying off its dull blade.

"Would you ever photograph me?"

I knew I was being coy and that I should tread carefully. He rolled away to look at me. We breathed puffs of white around our heads. I threw the covers back, and my naked body was gleaming and slick in the candlelight. William smirked. He didn't think I was serious.

"Are you asking me if I think you're beautiful?"

"I'm asking if you'd ever take a picture of me. Not if I'm a worth-while subject."

William didn't know what to say. There was a frozen quality to our bodies. I began to grow cold.

"Why do you want to know?" he said.

I hadn't planned to admit to seeing the photographs. This would reveal I'd searched for a key, inserted it in his locked desk drawer—that I had no idea what I'd find, but that I didn't trust him enough to simply ask. Still, my curiosity got the better of me. Why shouldn't I confess to seeing them? He might be relieved and even discuss them with me. They were only photographs, after all.

"Your sleeping women," I said. "They're all the Milton girls, aren't they?"

William sat up, his back white in the dark room, the splotch that was his heart-shaped mole on his shoulder. He sat that way, statue-like, and I could read nothing of what he thought.

"It's understandable," I said, aware I might be digging myself in deeper. "They were part of your past. Your memories. I could see how they'd be significant."

I watched him carefully ease himself off the edge of the bed. He took a few steps away, toward the window, and then stopped and cried out.

"Goddamnit!"

I'd never heard him raise his voice like that before, and I withdrew back onto the bed. I felt sure his anger was directed at me. He lifted his foot in the candlelight. He'd stepped on a piece of an ornament. It was a big piece, and he must have stepped on it exactly right. His foot had begun to bleed, and I cringed and looked away.

"Oh, no," I said. "Does it hurt?" I put my hand over my mouth and felt vaguely sick. I climbed from the bed, the afghan wrapped around me. "What do I do?"

"When did you see them?" William said, his voice cold.

He hadn't removed the ornament from his foot. He balanced with his foot in his hand, hopped over to the bed, and sat down, and I stood nearby, listening to him breathe in and out in his anger.

"Should I get you a towel?"

I put on a sweatshirt, slipped on my jeans. I found a dish towel and wet it, and wrung it out. I sat beside him with the towel, my hand growing numb, and I felt odd and displaced. Accused. It had been wrong for me to snoop. He shoved the towel away.

"When?" he said. "That night in my office?"

"Yes," I said. I couldn't deny it now.

William felt for the glass in his foot and cursed, softly. Then he looked at me, our faces so close I could see the anger in his eyes, smell the sour tinge of his breath. He was struggling to maintain his composure, and I wasn't sure why he didn't discuss them—why they had to be a secret. Still, I couldn't say it.

The snow pinged against the window and the panes rattled.

Outside we could hear the plows moving up and down the grid of streets, throwing snow in high banks. I had the distinct feeling we were being buried. The candle flickered over his hair, his face, his tense jaw. Why was I the one who needed to explain? He'd photographed the girls of Milton, in bed, exposed in the intimacy of sleep. I felt a surge of jealousy.

"This is a breach of trust," he said. "You broke into my desk, went through my private things."

"I didn't break in," I said. "I used the key."

This made my prying even worse. He could now imagine me taking down the little tin, opening the lid.

"I asked to see them, and you told me no," I said.

"I'm still working on them," he said, slowly.

I handed him the towel. "I think you apply pressure to stop the bleeding."

He shoved my hand away again and stood and felt for his shirt, his pants.

"Where are you going?" I asked him. "There's a snowstorm."

He hunted around in the bureau, and then he grabbed his socks, threw open the apartment door, and started down to the vestibule. At the bottom, he put on his boots, his jacket, the ridiculous hat. He flung the front door open and his dark shape moved across the porch, down the steps into the snow. The front door wasn't closed all the way, and I slipped down and stood in the doorway, watching him go. The streetlights were out. He was a moving figure, disappearing into that darkness. The snow blew in over my bare feet, but I didn't feel the cold. I didn't call out to him or beg him to stop. He was going to his office to find the portfolio, and when he saw it was gone, he would be back.

I closed the front door, and Del opened hers. The beam of her flashlight blinded me.

"Why are you down here?" she said, her voice lit with alarm. She came to me and put her hand out and touched my face. When we were little I would unconsciously frown and Del hated when I wore the expression.

"I was looking at the snow."

I felt like a child with her cold hand on my cheek. I felt as if our roles were slowly revolving, reversing. In the darkness, with the wind rattling around outside, knocking off roof tiles, I thought about being Del, the uncertainty the world presented her, and I felt twinges of bewilderment as if I were now experiencing what she usually did.

"I want to see Mary Rae's journal," I said.

She pulled me into her apartment. She made me tea and laced it with brandy. We sat on the couch wrapped in woolen blankets with tattered satin edges, blankets that reminded us of the ones on our beds when were little. In the wavering candlelight Del was a small shape beside me.

"All of the Milton girls posed for him," I said. "He has a series of photographs, all of them sleeping."

"I wish you wouldn't call them that," Del said. "It's disparaging."

"You knew about the photographs?" I pulled away from her on the couch. The brandy made me light-headed.

"They brag about it when they aren't around Anne. They keep

talking about how there'll be a show in a gallery, and they'll be famous."

"I thought they hated him," I said.

Lit by the candle's flame, the lines around Del's mouth, at the corners of her eyes, were deep grooves that made her seem older than she really was. Her dark hair had grown out, and her blond roots were even more pronounced. "Maybe they don't really hate him as much as they say."

Around us, in other houses in town, students who hadn't gone home for break gathered in groups to talk and dance, to laugh. How had I become so removed from them? Why hadn't I ever tried to fit in? I hadn't needed to. Del had arrived to keep me company in my strangeness. She looked at me over her teacup, her brow creased, her eyes worried.

"The journal?" I said.

She set her cup on the table and pulled the blanket tighter around her. I suspected she knew other things she wasn't going to tell me, things she might have explained further, like the sandalwood smell in William's office. My suspicions about the two of them together on the office couch were ungrounded. I knew I was mistrusting, spiteful.

Del retrieved the book, shelved among the professor's translations.

"Are you sure you want to read this?" she said.

I took the journal from her hand and, using the flashlight, began to thumb through the entries, written in Mary Rae's girlish script. Soon enough it was clear she'd been seeing William, that her dream of being back together with him had come true. She met him once in the Viking Lanes lot, and they sat in her car and talked until morning. *The sun was coming up, and we were so surprised. We hadn't noticed the passing time. He is different now. We are both different.* She'd let him take her to dinner, in a restaurant in the next town. Had the necklace had been a gift from him? In December, there was a hasty entry: *Made the appointment. Will says he will take me.* And a week later: *I went into the clinic, and then I couldn't do it.* "It's not really anything yet, Rae," *Will says. Last time I was in high school, and he could talk me into anything, and then he left me. It's a baby, a real thing.* The last entry, two weeks before she disappeared, was angry, and cryptic. *How could he?* she'd written. *What good is anything now?* A pregnancy, and when she wouldn't have an abortion, a final breakup. And maybe the New Year's Eve out to make a show of being fine?

"Have you shown this to Alice?" I said.

"I hid it from her," Del said. "She was desperate to find it. She knew there must be a newer one. She even went back to the house to look."

"He said he hadn't seen her," I said.

We looked at each other. "Why does anyone lie?" Del said.

I was drunk on the brandy, and the wind howled. Del leaned against me, and I felt the urge to pull away and accuse her of being with William, but I had no reason, really, to do that, and I'd already driven one person away that night.

"Officer Paul would love to get his hands on this," I said.

William, my new husband, would be a suspect. Detective Thomson had always had a particular look on his face as he leaned in toward me, the smell of starch coming off his shirtfront.

Where was your sister, Delores, on the afternoon of August eleventh?

At the Prison Store with our mother.

What time did she leave?

I'm not sure. Before lunch, I think.

How long was she there?

You'd have to ask our mother.

When did you see her next?

Later that day. She was on the back porch with the other kids.

The ones who'd been swimming?

Yes.

Who'd run up to the porch during the storm?

Yes.

"Maybe he had something to do with Mary Rae's disappearance," Del said, quietly.

I knew she wouldn't go to Officer Paul. She'd kept the journal because of me.

"This doesn't prove anything," I said.

"You're right." She took the journal and returned it to the shelf. "He's your husband. You would know."

I ignored the sarcasm in her voice. We leaned into each other, our heads touching, and listened to the wind rattle the trees, the windowpanes. We watched the candle flame dip and flicker in the draft, and I felt as if we were reprising our old roles—the clairvoyants.

"I wish there really was a way for the dead to tell us what happened," Del said.

I didn't ever want to know things—how people died, what they felt, who they loved. I didn't want to understand the dead's complicated existence, or feel their ache of longing weighing me down. But the dead appeared, sometimes bearing an indecipherable message or an image of a place; a bed against an open window, the scrape of the sea on stones, a dark hallway with threadbare carpet, the smell of lilacs, or rot, or blood. I would never know who they all were. I supposed that one day I would recall them like old friends—confusing them at times with the living.

Mary Rae wanted to share something with me. I'd heard her voice at the encampment: "Oh, don't, Billy." I'd seen her outside the apartment, as if waiting for me. Sitting in the dark, neither Del nor I talked about David Pinney, or about that summer. That time in our lives seemed to have been snipped out by a great pair of shears—leaving a blank space we had never bothered to fill in. Wasn't that the problem, though? There remained a dark hole either of us could fall into. I felt myself there—teetering on the edge.

Del fell asleep on the couch, and I left her apartment. I could understand William's anger but not the desperation in it. I pictured him trudging through the snow to campus, his foot bleeding into his boot. Upstairs, I entered the empty apartment. I felt my way toward the cedar closet in the dark, and I took the portfolio from its hiding spot and sat in the duck-carved chair. I flipped through the images again by candlelight. I reached the last one and discovered a pocket in the back of the cover and, hidden away, a sleeve of negatives. I got out my loupe and went through each image. Despite the quality of the flickering candlelight, I could see they were of Mary Rae. Her hair covered one of her breasts, her mouth was pursed in sleep—a pouf of pretty lips.

Mary Rae's death had yet to be deemed a murder. Her face came on the evening news, in the daily newspaper—the dimpled cheek, the soft hair—and now I pictured her with William, the two of them drinking wine at Anne's, side by side on the velvet couch. I imagined her asleep in a room, and William's camera whirring and clicking, or in the back of Geoff's car. I'd hidden the necklace in a small plastic bag taped to the back of the bureau. I didn't know where else to put it where it wouldn't be found, though I hadn't been sure who I was hiding it from. Was I more sure now?

Before I hid the portfolio away, I paged through it again. Each girl was lovely in her own way, unique—bare breasts, arms thrown over heads, sheets threaded between legs. There was a sense of the abandon that sleep provided, a stillness so like death. How had William managed to capture them that way? Spagna had used a time-release camera placed in the room. But these were from differing angles, as if he'd been beside them while they slept and chosen each shot. What had prompted him to take each one? The slant of light? Maybe something in the aspect of each woman's face: the way her lips parted, the veins on her eyelids, the luminosity of her skin. Who was she, sleeping, but whatever he determined? He'd come into my apartment while I slept. Were we all someone he wished would awaken to love him?

25

I sat by the window most of the night keeping watch with my candle, frightened by the images of Mary Rae in the back of the portfolio. Had William hidden them when she went missing to avoid being implicated? I kept trying his cell, and at first the calls went to voice mail, but the thought of leaving an apology, my recorded voice saying those words, irked me. Eventually, the calls stopped going through at all, and I guessed the cell was dead. I had no idea where he might go in the middle of the night—if he had colleagues he socialized with, if he might find a business open. He'd invited people to a party he'd given the night I first met him; he had to know someone in town.

Yet, the only people I'd seen him with were in Milton. He must have stayed in his office. Surely he wasn't out in the night, just walking in the snow. I fell asleep in the duck-carved chair and dreamed of William's body covered in ice like the homeless people you saw occasionally on television, like the vision I'd had of Mary Rae in the

Silver Streak. I wasn't sure whether I was keeping watch out of fury or fear. I couldn't assess my feelings for him. I was holding my watch for Mary Rae—determined to find out the truth.

I was awakened by a scream—one I quickly identified as Del's. It came up the stairwell, and Geoff threw open his door. The power was still out, but weak daylight came in through the window and I could see my breath. I rushed to the door. Del was down in the foyer crying over and over, "Oh my God!"

Geoff stood with Suzie at the top of the stairs. "Jesus, Mary, and Joseph," he said.

He looked toward my door, where a trail of blood began, and then down the stairs, where it continued—large, vivid smears on every step. Del rushed up the stairs, avoiding the stains. "I thought something terrible had happened to you," she said.

"Call the crime scene detectives," Geoff said. He was half asleep, his hair sticking up at the top of his head.

The blood, in the daylight through the transom, was terrible. I found the trail of it in my apartment, all of it smeared over by my own footprints the night before. I'd tracked some into Del's apartment, too. Blood covered the bottoms of my feet.

"William cut his foot," I said. "I'll clean it up."

"Well, is he OK?" Del said, wiping her eyes with her shaking hand.

"He's fine," I said. I didn't want to tell her what had happened. I went into my apartment. I got a bowl and filled it with water and dish soap. Del stood in the doorway as if afraid to come inside.

"Where is he?" she said.

I carried the bowl out to the landing and began to wipe up the blood. Geoff went back into his apartment and I could sense Suzie behind the shut door, sniffing at the crack. My head felt heavy—I had barely slept.

"I don't know," I said.

Del didn't make a move to leave. I rinsed the blood from the cloth, my hand cold in the water.

"What do you mean you don't know?"

I sat back on my heels. "I mean I have no idea where he went. He left."

"He couldn't have taken his motorcycle," she said.

"Yes, we're snowed in. No, he couldn't have taken his motorcycle."

She had her arms folded tight across her chest. "So he just left? Did anyone pick him up?"

"Why do you care?" I said. I threw the cloth into the bowl and I stood. "Why do you care what happened to my husband?"

She bit her lip and looked away from me. "That sounds funny," she said, softly.

"I know," I said. I was so tired I began to laugh, and then Del was laughing. It was, suddenly, the strangest of things to have married him.

"It does look like a crime scene," Del said.

"Whatever," I said. "It's not."

She shrank back from my glare and slipped down the stairs to her apartment.

"Don't forget to lock up," she said before she closed the door.

Del had become vigilant about locking doors. Each night she moved about the house, checking them all. She'd climb the stairs and I'd see my own knob turn.

"Go to bed," I'd say.

It was almost like when we were young, but then we shared a room, and I couldn't put a door between us. Her sleeplessness had always made me anxious. It seemed wrong, somehow, to remain awake while others slept. Sleeping was a rule you couldn't break—like refusing food or water. Yet Del slept very little during the night. And I was now experiencing the same wakefulness.

I went back to cleaning. I had to change the soapy water in the bowl, and by the time I reached the bottom step I felt drained. William still hadn't returned. I climbed the polished stair treads to my apartment, and inside I discovered the television on, its screen flickering a jumbled static; the stove burner brightening under the teakettle; the lamp's yellow circle illuminating William's papers and notes spread out on the table. The power had come back on.

The domestic scene comprised of our disorder now seemed almost comforting, and my anger wavered. Had I been wrong to look through his things? Had I "broken his trust," as he'd said? Was I no better than Del had been when as children she'd gone through my things? Then I fingered the sore place on my breast, replayed the night in his office, the sex. Hadn't he broken my trust? He would need to prepare for his upcoming classes. He'd have to return for his notes, his slides. Maybe the weather had kept him away, but the streetlights had come back on; electricity hummed along the wires overhead.

I undressed and got into bed, hoping to finally sleep. William would be moving along the sidewalk beneath the elm, slipping in through the front door and climbing the stairs to me. I would play his dutiful wife, waiting for him. I remained awake and watchful, but he didn't return. Rather than try to sleep, I began straightening up the room, putting the clean pot under the sink, stuffing laundry into a basket in the closet. Through the window the elm's branches shifted, brittle with ice. I opened the apartment door. Below me in the vestibule a door's latch clicked. Del's door opened, quietly, carefully, as if the person knew the way the hinges groaned. I stepped back into my doorway and listened as whoever it was stepped into the vestibule and moved stealthily to the front door. I peered, careful not to be seen, but just missed whoever it had been. The front door closed and footsteps crunched the snow on the porch.

On the landing I felt the cold creeping under the front door and reminded myself of Geoff the time we'd caught him standing there in his robe. I moved down the stairway to Del's door, light-headed with fear, but slowed. Had it been William? He couldn't have gone into her apartment the same way he'd once come into mine—not with Del so adamant about locking doors. I tried her door and found it locked. Had Del let in whoever it was and let the person out? I felt a wave of doubt. I opened the front door and looked down the sidewalk, but there were only the piles of snow, the cold house fronts, their windows black, and no sign of anyone. Maybe it had been Randy, his car parked around the corner. But there were no cars out on the roads. I returned to my apartment and quietly closed the door.

Outside the snow still fell. The streets echoed with the passing snowplows. I sat on the bed. I could go down to Del's and ask her if William had been there. But what if she denied anyone had been there at all? Was this what I'd done to her all those years in the guise of being a custodian? Established the parameters of what was real and what wasn't?

I finished organizing the apartment—numbly folding and sorting the clothing, returning each item to its place, washing the dishes and putting them away. I piled William's things—those he'd left behind—neatly on his desktop.

Things were shifting, becoming not as they had seemed.

I climbed into bed and slept all day until evening, lulled by the sound of the snowplows, the settling and contracting of the old house's bones. When I awoke my mother's little travel clock read six thirty. The windows were dark, but the streetlights shone in. I sat up and turned on the lamp. The apartment wasn't as I'd left it. The drawers had been gone through, and not closed all the way. The cabinets were open, the closet door—things I'd purposely closed hours before.

I heard knocking at my door, a gentle, repetitive tap—Del using our old séance knocking. I rolled over and burrowed deeper. I didn't trust what I would say to Del. Since the heat had come back on the apartment had warmed a bit. William was still gone, but he'd been there, searching for the portfolio. He had every right to it. But the prints themselves weren't that precious—he had the negatives and could make new ones. The hidden negatives of Mary Rae were what he wanted. I ignored Del, and soon her knocking ceased and she headed down the stairs.

I couldn't sleep any longer. I got up and took a shower, nervously listening for footsteps. Something dark and lonely had settled over me.

In the refrigerator I found the makings of a sandwich—cheese and a bit of lettuce. Del had been cooking—I could smell it coming up the stairwell—roasted meat, like our grandmother used to make on Sundays when we were small. Still my sandwich was fine. Nothing came from Geoff through the wall and I wondered if he'd unburied his car. I took my plate with me into the cold hall and I knocked on his door. Del must have heard me. Her door opened below, and she came out into the vestibule.

"He's not there," she said. Her voice echoed slightly as it came up the stairwell. "You must have been *knackered*. You slept all day."

Del was using Geoff's slang again. I went to the top of the stairs and looked down at her. Her hair was dyed platinum blond—so bright and different, I barely recognized her. She smiled when she saw my reaction, and she ran her fingers through the long, whitish strands.

"Very Marilyn Monroe," I said. "Or Jayne Mansfield."

"Or Jean Harlow," Del said. Then she posed with her hip out, her hand in her hair. " 'Mind if I change into something more comfortable?' "

Now she looked like the Del from our childhood.

"Why don't you eat with us?" she said.

"Who's down there?" I asked.

Geoff popped his head out the doorway. "It's just me, Richard Burton," he said. He laughed as if at my expression, which must have seemed comical. Then William came out into the hallway, too.

"And me, Clark Gable," he said.

They both held glasses of wine, jewel-toned in the light that spilled from the apartment, out into the dark vestibule and up the stairs, illuminating the bottom treads. I was watching a play, a world below me moving on without me, Del and William now the happy couple.

I didn't want to join them. Del's apartment door had been left open, and the heat and the cooking smells filtered out into the vestibule, where William's beaver-skin hat was once again hung on its peg. William climbed the stairs, took my plate, and tried to take my hand in his like a gallant escort, but I shrugged him off of me and I continued down to the lighted bottom. Del's apartment was softly lit with candles, the stairs and the landing above dark and cold-looking. Del looped her arm through mine and led me to the couch. Over on the bookshelf, tucked between Ovid's *Amores* and *Ars Amatoria*, were Mary Rae's last written words.

"I'll get her a glass of wine," William said. "She looks like death warmed over."

"Where have you been?" I asked him.

William paused in the middle of the room. "I've been working up at school. I got stuck in my office during the storm."

"That whole time? Did you sleep there?"

"I did," he said.

"Did you think it might be nice to let me know?"

William shifted from one foot to the other. I knew he was thinking, *Now? Do we have to do this now?*

Yet he appeared to be no longer seriously upset. He seemed almost at ease with his wine, grinning in his usual way at Geoff. I had the negatives of Mary Rae, and he wanted them back, desperately enough to pretend it didn't matter.

I sat down on the couch. I felt wholly unlike myself.

"How's your foot?" I asked him.

"You gave the girls a scare leaving your blood on the stairs," Geoff said.

"I'm really sorry," he said. Then he reached out and squeezed my hand. "For everything, really."

As the party commenced around me, as the wine was poured, and I was given a plate of chicken coated with rich gravy, William watched me, his eyes lit with something I couldn't interpret.

We sat around the coffee table, William and Geoff in the wing chairs, and Del and I on the couch. The room's shadows wavered with candlelight—a large pillared candle Del had placed in the center of the table. The incense smell was overpowering. I sat listening to them talk, observing William and Del for signs of some affection. Tonight she seemed quieter than usual, put-out. Had she cooked this meal for William? Or had they been together this afternoon while I slept, and was this coolness toward each other an elaborate game?

Soon, the conversation lapsed into silence.

"Is it twenty minutes past the hour?" Geoff asked. "Are we listening for angels singing?"

"Let's tell ghost stories," I said.

"Let's not," Del said.

"Oh, come on! Like we used to," I said. But Del, always ordinarily open for a good ghost story, seemed anxious.

"We would hold séances in our pool shed when we were kids." I leaned forward and drew the pillard candle closer. "We brought back people's grandmothers and dead aunts."

"The neighborhood clairvoyants," Geoff said, sprinkling pot onto a rolling paper. "Anne is still waiting to see your talents."

"We had a whole system." I spread my two hands out on the table-top. "Didn't we, Del?"

Del's face was shadowed by the candlelight.

"We would alternate. Whoever wasn't playing the medium would be in charge of the tapping."

Del began to gather the plates.

"What was it we said? 'Please give us two taps if you're here,'" I said.

William looked at Del, adoringly, I thought. Why would he ask me to marry him if he was going to run around with Del? Would he ask me for a divorce because I'd gone through his things? He'd already shifted his attention, wanted or not, to her.

"Sometimes I was afraid the spirits were really there," Del said. She stood over us cradling the plates. "It was eerie in that little pool shed."

Geoff lit his joint and inhaled, then exhaled. "You two were regular flimflam artists."

"There were things that felt real." Del looked at me.

"No," I said. "It was never real."

Jane Roberts's earrings caught the light and trembled in Del's earlobes.

"Hey, now," Geoff said. "I've got a story for you." The room's shadows wavered with candlelight. The radiators clanked. Outside, the snow filled the streets and drives, obscuring the routes into and out of town. Geoff had opened another bottle of wine. His story was a confession of sorts, in the dim, incense-filled room.

"I was driving along," he said. He took a sip from his glass. "It was night, with no moon, and I didn't know the road. I'd just dropped off a girl I'd been seeing—Eloise, I think it was—soft brown hair, wonderful legs, I thought, well, from what I could see up under her skirt."

"Go on already," William said, reaching for the joint.

"Yes, please." Del set the plates in the sink and returned to the couch beside me.

Geoff liked to digress, and we knew the story might have changed if we let him go on about Eloise.

"I thought I'd hit something, but I was afraid, really, to stop in the dark. It was well past midnight. I assumed it was a hare or a stray dog."

Del reached out and touched Geoff's arm. "What was it?" Her eyes shone.

"Oh, well," Geoff said. "I'd driven through, and was miles away by morning. It came to me months later, when I'd revisited that part of the country again, and heard the story of the little girl who wandered the moor in her white cotton nightgown, how some used to see her, a daft girl, out late at night. And then how she disappeared, and how her body was found, hit by a car. It was a ghost story they were telling. And then I put it together."

The space around us swelled with the darkness beyond the candles' flames.

"You see, I remembered something when I heard the story," he said. He had set down his glass and was rolling another joint. In the morning the floor would be speckled with flakes of the pot. "It was the nightgown, you see. I had seen a bit of material, the child's gown, float across my dash."

We sat quietly then, drinking.

"Good one, Geoff!" William said, his face open with amusement. He settled back into the chair cushion. "You're actually a decent storyteller."

Del wasn't amused. "Do you think it was you that hit her?" she asked.

Geoff lit the joint from the pillard candle on the coffee table. "I tell myself it was the ghost I saw," he said. "But it wasn't something I could ever know for sure, was it? The timing was right, it could have been me."

The smoke from his joint rose from the lit end. I felt Del's body tense beside me on the couch.

"It must be awful to think it was your fault," she said.

We all sat, puzzling, drunk. Del stood and gathered the glasses, as if the party was now over, and William reached out and grabbed her wrist. "She's not done," he said, and he returned my glass to me and took Del's spot on the couch.

I watched Del's reaction to William's hand on her wrist. It was an odd feeling to suspect I was being duped. It made me feel a little sorry for myself, but it also gave me some power. I took a sip of my wine.

"If the roads are clear, maybe we can go to Buffalo State tomorrow."

I was testing him, I suppose, trying to see if he would placate me. It was fine to play these games now that I believed my feelings for him had changed.

"Sure," he said. He relaxed a little, as if he'd just been waiting for me to reveal some sign that I still loved him.

"What's this now?" Geoff said.

"The old asylum," William said. "Martha was talking about getting some shots before it's gone for good."

Del was wrapping a dish towel around her hands. "Do you really want to go there?" she said. "Should I call Randy and everyone?"

William got up from the couch and walked over to the window. He parted the curtains and made a show of looking out. "Why do they have to be dragged into it?" he said.

"That was the plan originally," Del said. "Wasn't it?"

"I'm too tired to think," I said.

Del put her hand on my forehead. "Are you sick?"

"Let's do the séance," I said to her. "Like we used to."

"Not now," Del said.

"Who would you like to bring back, William? What about your old girlfriend, Mary Rae?"

Del sat down beside me, the dish towel tight around her hand.

"We can ask her if you were a good boyfriend," I said to William.

He stood, stiffly, by the window. I thought he might yank the curtain from its rod.

"What about that boy you liked?" I said to Del. "The one they found on the golf course?"

Del took my glass before I could stop her, and she crossed the room to the kitchen. Geoff stared at the joint in his hand and leaned back into his chair. William left the window and came to the couch, the candle sputtering at his movement. The room grew cold with their silence. I almost regretted speaking up, but I sensed they were playing a game with me. I lay back and closed my eyes, overcome by a wave of exhaustion. Geoff told another story—this one about an old girlfriend who'd rejected him and later died. Though I'd been asleep all day, I felt myself succumbing again, a dizzying fall. Geoff leaned over, and I felt him lay his coat over me.

"You two might have tried to speak to her. I'd love to ask her a few questions," he said about his dead girlfriend.

Del spoke, and then there seemed a shaving away of time, and Del was at the sink, and Geoff was at the door, saying good night. William murmured, and Del spoke again, more caustic. The water ran in the sink. "What did you do to her?" Del said.

"What are you talking about?" William said.

I wanted to awaken, but I was not really asleep. I tried to sit up and accuse them but I could not. William walked across the room and then I felt him lift me in his arms.

"Be careful with her," Del said.

"She's out," he scoffed.

The door to Del's opened and I felt the draft coming from under the front door, and then I was being carried, and William was fumbling with the door to our apartment. He deposited me on the bed, and I expected he would lie down next to me, remove his clothes to sleep. I tried to reach for him, but found I could not. I sensed him standing over me, watching me, but I couldn't open my eyes. Then he moved about the apartment, opening the drawers, emptying their contents. "Damn witches," he swore under his breath.

26

I awoke shivering and sore. I had no memory of having sex, but I felt as if William had scraped my face with the beginnings of his beard. Through the ice-covered windows, light came in tinged an eerie blue. William moved around the apartment. He had emptied the bureau drawers, had slid out the drawers themselves, and was now meticulously returning the drawers and the clothing. If he'd spent the night dismantling the entire apartment, had he found the loose cedar plank and, so, the portfolio? When he had finished refitting the drawers and putting the sweaters away, he pulled the bureau out from the wall and ran his hands down the back and discovered Mary Rae's necklace. He held up the plastic bag and the light shone through the amethyst pendant. He met my gaze.

"You look like you've been turned to stone," I said.

"You're awake." He flushed.

According to my mother's travel clock, it was eleven a.m. William sat on the bed. His face seemed entirely changed. Even his eyes were

altered, the gold-colored warmth in them gone, as if he were somewhere else and dealing with a dire circumstance—not sitting with
me on the edge of the bed we'd shared as a married couple these past
months.

"Remember when you called me Galatea?" I said.

He unzipped and rezipped the plastic bag's fastener. "I do," he said.
But it wasn't enough to bring him back to me.

He held the bag toward me. "Hey, what is this?"

His voice sounded earnest, almost gentle, as if coaxing me to
confess.

"I found it in Geoff's car," I said. "I know I shouldn't have taken
it. It's probably one of his friends'. But it was so pretty."

William watched my face, like an interrogator, like Detective
Thomson, whose eyes were always assessing.

"Why did you hide it?" he said.

The weight of him tipped the bed and drew me toward him, but
I resisted. "I know it's stupid. I wanted to keep it, so I hid it. It's a
habit I've had since I was little."

William shifted and the bedsprings groaned. "What do you
mean?"

"Well, Del would take everything of mine," I said. "I had to hide
things from her."

"You shouldn't have to hide this." He slipped the necklace from
the plastic bag. "Put it on."

He leaned forward, and his hands slid around my throat to fasten
the clasp.

"What if it's one of the girls'?" I felt the cold of the stone and
thought of it held between Mary Rae's fingers.

"Just say you found it." He stood and looked down at me. "It looks
pretty on you."

I pushed myself up on my elbows. I felt a wave of weakness pass
through me, and then a trickle of something slip into my underwear.
I slumped back down. Could I ask him if we'd had sex?

"Are we still going to Buffalo?" I said.

He ruffled his short hair, almost in frustration. "We'd need to leave now, before it gets too late."

I again tried to lift myself from the bed, but exhaustion seemed to have settled in my limbs. "Why am I so tired?" I said.

I had so many questions I wanted to ask him. I wanted to move forward, past the lies we'd told each other. If we'd had sex, was everything forgiven between us? But his half of the bed was cold, the sheets like ice. My thinking was muddled. Some part of me understood that his persistence in seeking the portfolio only meant he wanted no one to see the images, and that he had something to do with Mary Rae's death. He placed a roll of film in his camera.

"I have to dress," I said, closing my eyes.

"You're already dressed," he said. "Just get up."

It was true I was still in my clothing from the night before, though my jeans were undone. "Why don't we go later?" I said. "Or tomorrow?"

But he was already out the door. His boots on the stairs echoed back at me. He was loading the car. And then below in the foyer, Del asked him what he was doing, and I knew she would call everyone, and the flasks would be filled, and the picnic lunch packed, and I would be the one left behind. I forced myself from the bed and gathered my camera, my cell phone. I put on my coat. In the mirror by the door my mouth and chin looked raw. I no longer had any interest in going to the asylum. I wished I hadn't mentioned it. I thought of him touching me in my sleep—when I was most vulnerable, stripped of all of my masks. Could I still love him despite everything? I wasn't going to let Del take away my chance to decide.

I made it down the stairs and out to the curb where Geoff's car was parked. I crawled into the backseat, leaned my head against the door. I awoke lying at a slant, an awkward position. The tires on the road made a humming sound. Telephone poles passed against a bright blue backdrop spotted with clouds, one after the other in a kind of loop. The car radio was tuned to a classical station. On the floor near my feet was William's camera bag. I felt a surge of panic, and William looked over at me from the front passenger seat.

"She's awake," he said.

I struggled to sit up. Mary Rae's pendant slid cold against my neck. "I fell asleep," I said.

"Again," Del said. She took one hand off the steering wheel and flipped the radio off.

I looked through the back window. "Where's Randy?" The road ribboned out behind us, dark and empty.

"They couldn't come," Del said. "It was too last minute."

"Alice was all excited about it," I said.

"Randy couldn't drive—his car broke down. Alice's mother, Erika, is back in town. Then the others changed their minds. They got drunk last night and they're too hungover."

"The trip should have been canceled if no one wanted to go," I said.

"That's what I said." Del slowed the car for a stop light. She flicked on the turn signal. "William said you told him we had to go in honor of Great-aunt Rose."

I wasn't going to admit I had only a vague memory of ever getting into the car, but it felt like a betrayal to have told him about Great-aunt Rose. Something wasn't right.

"I changed my mind," I said.

I thought Del exchanged a look with William. "We're almost there," he said. Up in the front seat they seemed like a conspiring couple.

Del kept both hands on the wheel as if fearful of letting go.

One afternoon when we were teenagers, I'd begged my father for a driving lesson, and Del had insisted on coming along. She'd driven his car at the time, a little MG, into a split-rail fence at the end of the road, denting the fender and scratching the hood. Our father had been furious and had refused to give either of us lessons after that.

I'd resented Del for all the things she'd ruined for me, as if she'd ruined them purposely. But had she, as she'd admitted, simply pushed on the wrong pedal?

The plows had been out in force, and the sun shone on the banks of snow. I had a terrible headache, and everything seemed overbright. Even the recent past seemed strange, a place of events I could not accurately recall.

"You don't have your license," I said. And then, "Don't push on the wrong pedal."

In the rearview mirror, Del glanced back at me with a small smile.

William rattled off details about the old asylum. It had been designed by Dr. Thomas Kirkbride. The idea was to have separate wings, so that the insane could be grouped by level of madness. Metal doors would block the wings from each other. Each wing would have its own sitting room.

"Why separate them?" I lowered myself back onto the seat and lay down, so I wouldn't have to look at the two of them.

"These places were built to help people get better," he said, "not to make them worse." I sensed he might have essentially called me stupid. He didn't seem to have an abundance of patience. I wondered how the three of us might be separated, into which wings we might be housed. And how was it that William appeared not to know anything about the necklace? Lying in the backseat of Geoff's car, like a transported body, my suspicions of William's connection to Mary Rae's death were jumbled. What confused me was her calm—the look on her face as she'd stood listening to him at the porch party that first night, her quiet plea at the encampment. Could victims still feel that sort of longing for their murderers?

For the rest of the drive I fought sleep. The world passed in a blur. Del and William's conversation was oddly fragmented. By the time we arrived at the asylum, the sky had been overtaken by building clouds.

"See the way they've planned the grounds?" William said, as we drove past scattered patches of denuded trees—beech and hickory and stands of white birch. "The idea was that looking out at the trees would ease troubled minds. This is Olmsted's work, the man who planned Central Park."

"Olmsted had designed the Institute's grounds in Hartford, too." I'd read that in the brochure about the place, though the rest, about Gene Tierney and the electroshock therapy, the lobotomies, had been excluded. The building ahead of us was dark brick and turreted in a heavy Gothic style.

"It looks like a castle," Del said, turning the wheel.

"Jane Roberts thought the Institute was a home for unwed mothers," I said. I laughed, but the color rose in Del's cheeks, so I left the topic alone.

William leaned forward—his voice was tight and alert, giving Del directions to a lot some distance away, bordered by woods. We parked and approached the place on foot through the trees. Up close we saw the missing panes of glass, the "No Trespassing" signs, the barred windows. Crows filled the beech branches and dotted the snow, black and noisy.

"How will we get inside?" Del asked.

She dragged behind us, and I fell back in step beside her. "Are you sure you want to go in there?"

The sun came in and out of the clouds, a weak splattering of light on the brick walls, the poor leafless trees. The crows scattered overhead.

"We may not be able to get in," William said, his camera bag slung over his shoulder. "But I read online that it's still possible."

Del and I followed William around the buildings to a place in the back. There was a loading dock with rusted railings, and near its base a hole, once grated, that William knelt down beside and examined with the flashlight he'd pulled from his bag.

"Here it is," he said.

We'd drop through the hole into a corridor in the basement. It was a risk to do this in daylight, but William had explained to us on the drive that photographs with natural light were best. "And who'd want to sneak into an old asylum at night?" he'd said, chuckling.

William seemed to have regained some of his old enthusiasm. He put his hand on my neck and tugged me in to kiss—a gentle press of his lips on mine.

"Come on," he said. He went first, then called up to us to climb through. "It's not that far a drop."

I peered over the edge, and Del took hold of my coat sleeve. "What are we doing here?" she said. Her gaze was drawn to the necklace.

"Why do you think I'm here? I'm here because you're here. You didn't have to come, you know."

William called out again. I pulled my arm away from Del and stepped to the edge of the hole.

"You'll be OK," William said. His flashlight left a circle on the floor below.

Del took the necklace in her hand. "Where did you get that? Amethyst is a February birthstone."

And then I foolishly slipped down into William's arms, my face pressed to his chest. The smell of mildew was sharp, as if it had infused his jacket. He called up to Del, and she appeared at the top, outlined by the gray sky, the reeling crows.

"Maybe I'll just sit in the car," Del said.

William raised his hands in the air, annoyed. "Sit in the car, then."

He slung his camera bag over his shoulder and pointed the flashlight ahead. "Let's go."

As we walked off, Del's voice echoed down the passage. "You're really leaving me?"

We would go through the underground corridors, William said, until we found stairs to the upper floors. It was no warmer inside than out. Our breath formed airy clouds in the semidarkness. We followed the funnel of William's flashlight. Now and then, he'd move the beam slowly over the walls—the brash graffiti, the huge overhead ducts—and I began to feel trapped. The malaise of the night before overtook me again. I hadn't eaten all day, and it seemed as if I were treading through waist-deep water.

I clutched my camera, slung around my neck. The sharpness of its metal body grounded me. We found the stairs soon enough and climbed two flights to the second floor, where enough light came in through large windows at either end of the corridor that we didn't need the flashlight. We passed from one wing to the other, our feet crushing fallen plaster. Beneath a layer of dust, the wood floor still shone with polish, but pieces of the walls, strips of paint, littered the way. Many rooms still held beds, their iron frames rusted, their mattresses' plastic covers disintegrating. The windows looked out over the benevolent stands of beech, the sweep of snowy lawn, but through iron bars.

William was busy taking photographs as if he had an agenda, and he didn't pay much attention to me. I followed him and waited in the hallway as he slipped into an octagon-shaped room lined with window seats. The windows were gone; the snow piled on the floor and the plaster had given way to the lathing and the brick beneath. William's camera clicked and whirred. Here patients opened letters from home to learn that a sister had given birth, that the cornfields were planted, that a brother had bought a new car. I followed him into the room and waited until he lowered his camera. The snow on the floor was crosshatched with animals' prints.

"Charles Wu told me about a grand staircase in the administration wing," I said. "He said that in one abandoned hospital people had found pills in bottles and patient records—Rorschach results, and drawings and notes."

"Charles seems to be well informed," William said, raising the camera, looking back through his lens. "Usually they were people who just couldn't fit in anywhere—depressed people or alcoholics. Some had nervous disorders, and families couldn't take care of them."

He lowered the camera. "I think the doctors meant well. They just didn't have the best treatment options."

If Del had been there, she might have told us what an inpatient's life was really like.

We were not as lucky as the trespassers Charles Wu had heard of. This hospital had been almost cleaned out, and things left behind were no longer of use. But in one room I found a shoe, and in another a paper with someone's handwriting. A wheelchair moldered in the hallway, its vinyl seat torn. We passed an open space that held a stage with tattered curtains, rows of upholstered seats blooming yellowed batting. In the lockup ward the doors had small, square mesh viewing windows. I pictured poor Great-aunt Rose in a place like this, and I began to feel guilty about Del, waiting in the car. William changed his film and pocketed the roll. Then he let the camera dangle by its strap. Our cloudlike breath fanned out around our heads.

"You're not taking any shots," William said.

I pointed my camera at him and took his photograph. "You're taking enough for both of us." On the wall immediately behind him someone had written a poem in a shaky hand. "Look," I said.

From too much love of living,
From hope and fear set free,
We thank with brief Thanksgiving
Whatever gods may be
That no man lives forever;
That dead men rise up never;
That even the weariest river
Winds somewhere safe to sea.

"Too bad that isn't the end of it," I said. I thought of Mary Rae.

I sensed that William wanted to add something, but he turned away. "Let's find that staircase for you." By the time we reached the administration wing and its grand stairway, the huge arched window over the main entrance, the elaborate woodwork that made the place seem like a hotel or a resort, it was dusk. The light had faded too much to photograph without a flash. The stairs curved down to the dim foyer below. It was gray beyond the high windows, and we could hear sleet tapping on the glass. Soon it would be completely dark.

"Well, here's your staircase," William said. "The one your friend told you about."

"It's too dark," I told him.

"Of course it is." His voice was bitter and annoyed. He stood with his hands on his hips. Other than the kiss he'd given me at the corridor entrance, and his catching me in his arms as I dropped down, he hadn't touched me. I'd spent the hour and a half we'd been there staring at the back of his corduroy jacket. I felt uneasy.

"The state should charge admission and offer a ghost tour," I said.

Except there were no ghosts. The building was just an old ruin. The dead appeared in the Big Y supermarket, not in the places we expected. They couldn't be courted or sought out. William put his camera back around his neck, his movements quick, irritated. There was nothing else to do but leave. I missed Del and Alice and the others. The flasks would have come in handy, the picnic lunch.

"We should have come with everyone else," I said.

"I came to make you happy," William said. He composed his features so that, in the dim light, I could almost believe him. "But you're never happy, are you? It's impossible to please you."

He kicked a piece of debris on the floor and it skittered toward the stairs and thumped down each step.

"Why are you so angry?" I said. The sleet tapped at the windows. The tension in the air was a sort of haze made of secrets.

"Just tell me what you did with it," he said. He seemed at the end of his patience. Had he thought that if he accompanied me here he might somehow win me over, ease the whereabouts of the portfolio from me?

"It's in your office." I took a few steps away from him.

"You know it isn't," he said.

How much easier it might have been to admit I had it, and yet as a child, caught in a lie, I had always found it easy to convince others that they were wrong: the lie mixed with what I pretended until the division between truth and untruth disappeared altogether.

"Where is it?" His voice was harsh, angry, transformed. Like the voice he used the night of the snowstorm. Then he closed his eyes, as if gathering his thoughts. "I'm sorry," he said, almost guiltily. He stepped toward me, his hands tense in the air to make his point. "You're my *wife*," he said.

I had failed in that capacity. I was supposed to support him, no matter what. If I'd loved him, this rift would never have occurred, and we'd be having sex now on one of the old beds in the patient rooms. Except Mary Rae had sent me on this chase. The circumstances never seemed to be on our side.

"What is so fucking important about that portfolio?" I said, dismayed. "Is it the negatives in the back? The ones of Mary Rae?"

William paled.

"I made a mistake marrying you," he said, his voice leaden. "You've lied to me—about other things, too. Don't think I'm such a fool. You and Charles Wu? Is that it?"

"What?" I said. "*Me?* Weren't you at Del's apartment yesterday?"

"You don't know what you're talking about." William shifted his bag to his other shoulder.

It had grown darker, the shadows sifting out from the corridor. A voice was calling me from downstairs—Del. She had somehow gotten inside and was looking for us, tired of waiting in the car. "I'm ready to go home!" she called. I felt a rush of shame—for suspecting Del of her old ways, for doubting William and being such a terrible wife. I wondered if we could go back—despite everything, I told myself I had been happy. We could forget about this and forgive each other.

"I should have known you were as crazy as she is," he said, under his breath.

I pushed past him, to the top of the stairs. "Del! Up here!"

And then he came for me, his hands gripping my forearms. His expression had altered to one I'd never seen—a dark caul seemed to have slipped over his features. He couldn't love me. What had I been thinking?

"William, don't," I said, and I realized, with a vague disappointment, that I sounded like Mary Rae's ghost in the encampment. Had this been who she faced when she died—this man, broken and disheartened by something she'd said or done or failed to do? The first time he'd spent the night in my apartment I'd watched him sleep, and his face had seemed a stranger's.

Del had gotten closer, her voice louder, more panicked.

"This is your fault," William said, anguished. "What do you expect me to do now?"

He held me at the top of the grand staircase, and I called Del again. We might have looked in the gloom as if we were dancing. His hands tightened on my arms, and I struggled to free myself, and in my struggle my legs tangled with his—the way legs tangle together in sleep under bedsheets, that twining of limbs during sex. We both lost our footing—me sprawling back onto the wood floor, William cartwheeling into the void where the staircase descended. I watched him flail for the banister, and then he fell backward, disappearing as he tumbled, his body curled in on itself. I put my hands over my ears so I wouldn't hear the sickening sound of him falling, of his landing in a pool of darkness at the bottom.

From below, Del screamed. Maybe she thought it was me.

27

Did it anger me, the summer David Pinney died, that Del had claimed him as her own? The day after I found out, I came upon my mother on the terrace reading a magazine and I told her that Del had a boyfriend.

"And who would that be?" she said, flipping one page, then another. I could tell she didn't really want to be bothered.

"I don't know, a boy from the Spiritualists' camp," I said. "They snuck off to the barn together."

My mother bit the inside of her cheek—something she did when she was nervous. She looked up from her magazine. "And what did she say they did?"

"She didn't," I said. "I thought you should know."

That afternoon Del was told she had to accompany my mother to the Prison Store. I had Jane Roberts come over, and we spread our towels in the grass and waited for our other friends. It was a hazy day, the air dense with humidity. The cicadas whined overhead. Jane was sluggish and silly, and I knew she'd taken some of her mother's pills. My grandmother came out of the house and called to me, and told me she was heading to a luncheon. She had on her pearl earrings, her floral skirt with the large peonies.

"Be good," she said, as if she knew I would not. "It's supposed to rain this afternoon."

She got into her car, and I watched her drive away, the sound of the pebbles crunching under the wheels.

We were swimming when David Pinney arrived. He dove in off the board, and then surfaced and came up to me. I felt as if I'd taken one of Jane's mother's pills—flushed and dizzy.

"Where's your sister?" he said.

The water ran down his shoulders, and his eyes were bright against his tan face. I stared at him, defiant.

"Well?" he said, annoyed.

"She's not here," I said. "And you can just stay away from her."

He laughed, and I watched him swim back to the deep end, a streak beneath the water. He pulled himself up to dangle under the diving board and grinned at me. "Jealous?" he mouthed.

Jane sat on the pool steps, talking to Katy and Paul Grant. Every so often she gave Paul a playful shove. Paul had his cooler of beer, and I swam over to him and he handed me one. David stayed in the pool in his spot, and eventually others arrived, and we got out of the water and started a game of croquet. The wind had picked up, and the sun kept disappearing behind clouds. Over the ninth hole the sky was gray, threatening a storm. I had it in the back of my mind that David was still under the diving board, and I wanted him to watch me, to want me, even, so that I could be vindicated by refusing him again. I drank more beer, and we played the game, the wickets set along the wide lawn. At one point I looked for David, and he was gone. I should have been relieved, but for some reason I was not. I was drunk and wanted the last word. I left my mallet leaning against a tree and went to look for him, stumbling a bit over the hillocky grass.

I approached the barn. The big doors were closed, as they usually were since my grandfather had died. I went in through the side door—a wooden door that stuck in its swollen jamb. I felt the familiar coolness, the smells of the stalls nearby still emanating cow and sheep. The dim light seemed to amplify sound for me and something high and lilting—a girl's laugh cut off—came through the barn. I guessed it was someone at the pool, the sound traveling between the barn's slats. The sun kept flickering in and out. I heard thunder, not too far off, and then another sound, rustling—hay being disturbed— and jagged breathing. Once I stepped around to my grandfather's workbench, I saw David. His bathing suit was lowered, and he worked, panting, furious, between two spread legs. I watched him and the girl, her knobby knees, oddly numb. David held her arms over her head with one hand and I knew the weight of him would have kept her from fleeing. There was no way to tell who the girl was, until I noticed her bathing suit bottom ringing one ankle, Sarah's orange bikini, the one I'd worn my own day in the barn with David Pinney. It was Del held pinned beneath him.

At what point she'd arrived home I couldn't say. Later, no one would have a clear memory of where we were, if we were in the pool or inside the house. No one would place David Pinney swimming that day at the pool at all. One moment David Pinney was hovering over Del, his suit down around his knees, and the next he had collapsed on top of her. She rolled him off, her eyes wide with shock. She lay there, unclothed, the pale places ordinarily covered by the bathing suit revealed in the flickering light, her hair tangled in the hay. I had taken a sharp breath in, and I felt the air in my chest, held, waiting for release. I had my grandfather's hammer in my shaking hand. My arm throbbed from the impact of the blow. David Pinney's eyes looked up from the barn floor, dark and empty. Around his head a blackish puddle had begun to form.

Outside, the leaves shuddered in the tall trees. The petals of my grandfather's hydrangea scattered into the grass. Clouds covered the sun, and the light went out. Thunder sounded again, and I smelled the ozone in the air, the scent of hay and copper wire and chlorine. The rain hit the barn roof in a torrent. The sparrows cried out in the eaves, *churee, churee*. Once, near the spot where David Pinney and Del had lain, Sister Martha Mary had sat, cool and implacable, her hands clasped in the black folds of her lap. I didn't know how long I stood there, looking down at David Pinney. Del had scrambled to pull up her suit, to fasten her top.

"What did you do? What did you do?" She was next to me, breathing in a high, panicked way.

I'd seen them together, and something had filled me—but what that was I couldn't explain. I'd taken the hammer from the workbench. I'd been too late to protect her from him. I didn't want him to ever look at me again with that mocking expression.

"He was hurting you," I said.

David's pants were still down, his limp penis pale against the dark hair. The hammer had grown heavy in my hand. Blood had splattered on my arm. Del's face, her chest, were speckled with blood. I had to do something with the hammer, and I looked around the barn—at the tool bench, the boxes of copper rods and fittings, the stalls, the loft. Despite my daze, my trembling, I remembered the cistern. Up until the 1940s the cistern had been the source of water for the barn. My grandfather had shown it to me when I was a girl. I went to the back and opened the barn door. The rain fell from the eaves. The world beyond the dark barn was shimmering and wet and green. I went to the cistern, pried the cement lid from the top, and dropped the hammer in. I found I was still trying to catch my breath. Back in the barn, my hair matted to my head, and I bent down and tugged David's pants up. Then I grabbed one of his arms and told Del to take the other. She looked at me, horrified, but took his arm, moving mechanically, taking his wrist, and pulling him. It took us over fifteen minutes to drag him through the barn's back door, to draw him under the barbed-wire fence, to roll him beneath one of the golf course's elegant weeping willows. The whole time it rained, watering the trail of blood into the pebbled drive, into the earth beneath the grass. The sky shuddered with lightning. We cleaned the barn floor with borax, scrubbing with brushes that we dropped, like the hammer, into the cistern.

No one came looking for us. Jane Roberts and the others had run up to the porch off the back terrace to wait out the storm, as we'd done so many times that summer. Since the porch was on the other side of the house, they wouldn't see Del and me leave the barn behind the cover of the privet hedges and enter the house through the front door. My grandmother would be gone for another hour or more, eating tiny sandwiches, sipping iced tea. Our mother's shift at the store ended at four o'clock. We went into the kitchen in our wet suits. Out on the porch, Paul Grant teased Jane, whose laughter rang out, a bell-like sound. Through the screen door I could smell the joint they'd lit.

Del and I stood dripping in the kitchen. Neither of us had spoken. I took two beach towels from the linen closet, and we wrapped up in them. I breathed in the smell of the kitchen—my grandmother's bread, her cinnamon tea. I expected Del to look confused, but her eyes greeted mine with a glinting alertness. We needed to join everyone on the porch. The sooner we pretended nothing had happened, the more real it would seem that nothing had.

I went outside first. Jane saw me and called me over. I took the joint from her fingers, trying to keep my hand from shaking.

"Where were you?" she said, her eyes laughing. "You missed the drama."

It seemed that a boy had nearly drowned, and Jane had saved him. He was a middle school kid, who sat on the porch steps, looking peaked.

I listened to the story, told by two or three people at once—how Jane had jumped in to drag him out, how she'd given him mouth-to-mouth. The kid looked so mortified, it was a wonder he didn't run home. Del came outside then and sat on the railing. No one questioned us about our damp hair, the bits of straw in Del's. The rain stopped, but none of us wanted to go swimming again, and eventually everyone left. Del and I were alone. When the sun came out I pictured David Pinney beneath the willow shade, his mouth on mine, the rough press of his dry lips. The moment in the barn pivoted on the horror afterward: his empty eyes, the sheen of sweat that remained on his skin.

That evening, a dog showed up at the kitchen screen door, a stray, scratching and whining to be let in. My grandmother, home by then, shooed it off the porch. But that night, the dog remained nearby, barking and howling. Below our bedroom window its nails scrabbled on the porch boards. Del had the first of what would become a series of sleepless nights, murmuring, sitting up in bed and pacing the room. She turned on the little milk glass lamp between our beds.

"You have to stop," I said. "Don't even think of it."

I didn't admit I couldn't sleep, either. I kept running through the day, worried I'd forgotten something, worried we would be approached and questioned, that David Pinney would appear, alive and bloody, sitting at the edge of my bed, holding my grandfather's hammer. There was no possibility of telling our mother. Even if our actions could have been forgiven, we were better at lying than telling the truth.

I got out of my bed and sat down on Del's. I took her arm from beneath the sheet and held it out into the light. There were bruises beginning to form, dark fingerprints on her forearm, a ring of bruises on her wrists.

"Look," I said.

Still, I hadn't really saved her. Del would suffer because of what we had done—David and me. The dog renewed its barking, on and on that night, and for several days after. Sometimes, it would appear to whine at the screen door, and once it chased me down the pebbled drive, and the sound of its chuffing breath, the pebbles kicked up by its paws, terrified me. The next day, I saw Cindy Berger. At first, I thought she was one of the summer people who sometimes cut through the yard to avoid the rocky bulkhead. I even called out to her, "Hello," foolishly, and started across the lawn toward her. But she stood completely still and luminous by the privet hedge to the pool. She disappeared just as I recognized her dress as the one they buried her in—a satin halter dress she wore to the eighth-grade dance, her last school function before the leukemia killed her.

I knew nothing would ever be the same.

28

At the top of the grand staircase in the old Buffalo State Hospital, my warm breath condensed in the cold. The dead waited in the corridor's shadows—pale arms and feet and glowing white gowns. They'd come finally, as witnesses. Del arrived at the top of the stairs, her blond hair incandescent in the darkness. I couldn't quite make out her face. Sleet slashed at the big windows, but there was no sound from below.

She held William's Leica. The camera's body was dented, the lens cracked. Its back swung away and the film was revealed. She shut the back and held the camera closed.

"It was at the bottom, beside him," she said, her voice small.

"Is he—?" I said.

William's bag sat on the floor behind me, and Del dug through it and found his flashlight. She located his wallet, his cell phone, his keys, and then stuffed them along with the camera back inside. The darkness seemed to tighten in on us where we squatted over the bag.

"We have to call for help," I said. I knew this was what needed to be done, but I let myself breathe, slowly in and out, and I told myself he would have thrown me down the staircase. I felt amid the rush of emotions a sense of relief at having been saved, and then a terrible wave of guilt.

Del gave me a hard look and shouldered the camera bag. "Get up," she said. "We have to leave."

Behind the flashlight's trembling beam we started down the long, curving stairway. As the light neared the bottom, she shined it away from a crumpled shape that might have been anything.

I made a move toward him, but Del stopped me, her hand icy on my wrist.

"I have to see how he is," I said. I watched the shadow on the floor for some sign of movement, but there was none.

"We'll call from the car," Del said. "We need to get out of here."

I sensed the urgency, the fear in her voice, and I knew William was gone. Was she afraid he might reanimate and slink after us, like the villains in horror films?

Del dragged me along to a broken lower-level window, the place where she'd come in. The glass was gone, and the sleet blew past the caution tape wetting the floor, making the window ledge slick. It was nearly dark, and much colder than when we'd arrived. The sleet had iced the branches of the old trees, the few remaining leaves, and the grounds looked like an eerie fairy tale in the flashlight's beam. We made our way through the little woods, the snow now layered with ice, and found the car, forlorn and dirty, still parked in the lot. I looked back a few times, watching for a figure trailing behind us, searching for William's furious, heartsick face framed in one of the broken windows, but the path back and the windows of the place were dark and I couldn't see anything at all.

Inside the car, we sat listening to the sleet slash the metal body, to the wipers mechanically moving back and forth. The smell of the asylum remained attached to our clothes and hair. Del had gotten behind the wheel. She kept shivering, the shaking making her whole body quake. I told her I would drive, and she refused. I got out my cell phone.

"Who are you going to call?" she said. "They'll see our footsteps. They'll know we were with him."

Anyone else might have claimed an accident, called for help and gotten it. Not us. All of this was my fault, tied as it was to another time. Del put the car in drive.

"Wait, please," I said. "We can't just leave him."

She put the car back into park. "The sooner we're away from here, the better."

I pictured William's corduroy coat, his copper hair matted with blood. Had I somehow caused him to fall? Had he really been about to shove me down the stairs? Once again, the solid truth was lost to me. After David Pinney, even when I tried to re-create those moments—taking up the hammer, the sound as it met his skull— I could not.

The ice tapped against the metal roof. The wipers made their scraping noise.

"Remember the game we all used to play at the pool?" Del said.

We'd catch each other standing along the pool's concrete rim, unaware, and push each other in.

"Have a nice fall," Del said, her voice soft.

The surprise of it, the shock of the cold water, was thrilling. It was a great joke, and once it had happened to you, you were always suspicious. Always suspecting. It got so you had that tingling feeling all day, waiting for someone to trick you. It got so that if you were angry at someone, you could give them a shove and none would be the wiser.

"This wasn't my fault," I said.

I watched another tremor move through her, shaking her arms, her torso. "Something was off last night," she said. "You sleeping like that. It didn't make sense after you'd slept all day." She sounded calm, but then she had probably been up all night, and that flatness in her voice was exhaustion. "The wine. He insisted on pouring yours. I couldn't let him take you alone this morning."

I felt my chest constrict and tighten. "You think he planned to hurt me?"

That was it—the easiest thing to accept. But I somehow doubted William had any sort of plan. I'd forced him to act when he wasn't prepared, accused him of things and held on to evidence that might convince anyone—even Officer Paul—that he might be implicated in Mary Rae's death. Del and I sat listening to the sleet, to the wipers grazing the melting windshield ice.

"This might be an efficient way to get rid of cheating husbands," Del said. She slit her eyes at me. "He didn't cheat with me. I don't know where you got that. He did come to my apartment, but he was looking for his portfolio."

Del had overheard our argument, my accusations.

"It *was* an accident," I said.

"Maybe one of the other girls in his nudie photos," Del said, tapping her nails on the steering wheel. "Maybe Jeanette."

"You sound like you're trying to throw blame on someone else to divert attention from yourself," I said.

"I wouldn't do it," she said. "I didn't even like him."

"You made him a special cake," I said.

"I did that to make you think I liked him," Del said. "I was trying to be nice."

We could go on and on and never arrive at the truth. I would simply have to choose to believe one thing over the other.

"Now that we've got that taken care of, I'm going to get us out of here," Del said. "Unless you think we should wait to see if his spirit lights up the place."

She put the car in drive and skidded out onto the road, into the middle of nowhere.

I looked behind me at the grounds, the stately trees, and the line of woods. I looked for the shape of him along the road, his figure in the headlights.

We drove through farmland spread for miles in either direction. Del fiddled with the radio, her hand shaking, and found a station playing Dixieland jazz, and we passed through a landscape distorted by the windshield ice—the wide open space, the few remaining out-buildings of an old farm, their gray, splintery wood darkened by the sleet, jutting like carcasses.

"There are bones of families out there," I said. Spread under layers of soil, compacted in their separateness. The Dixieland band played its tinny hopefulness. We drove this way for a long time until we could see nothing of the land we passed through save an occasional kitchen light in a house set off the road. Then we reached an intersection, a small town, like Milton, with a gas station and a diner, and Del pulled into the diner's parking lot. After David Pinney died we'd gone on, pretending he hadn't. I could say we were murderers now. This didn't happen to other people twice.

"We should eat something," she said.

William would be hungry and cold in the asylum. Then I real-ized he would feel nothing, and that seemed even more oppressive.

The diner was in a wood-framed building with wide panes of steamed glass in front. A large exhaust fan spit out smoke from the fryer. Inside we stood in the warmth in our coats. A waitress told us to sit anywhere. She had on a rust-colored apron, black slacks, and a plain white T-shirt. The patrons spoke in loud voices, laughing, tell-ing stories over their food. Del shrugged out of her coat.

"I want meat loaf," she said.

We walked down the row of booths and picked one along the window. I took off my coat and slid into the booth across from her. From the menus, large plastic rectangles, comically large, Del ordered her meat loaf and I ordered a cheeseburger, French fries, coleslaw, an ice-cream soda.

"Remember the old Sea Shell Restaurant?" Del said.

It would be Del and Jane and me, and two or three of the summer boys, all of us wedged into the booth to eat greasy cheeseburgers and thick fries from plastic baskets. The time right before David Pinney died was solid and clear, but it was as if there were no memories after. The dead had begun to appear to me, their pitiful expressions reeking of lost love, and they erased any other memories that might have formed.

The waitress brought our food and we ate as if we hadn't in days.

"I want to remember this," I said. "This after part."

Del put a forkful of meat loaf in her mouth and chewed. "You will."

The waitress eyed us, a teenager who probably had plans that night after work—a date with her boyfriend at the bowling alley down the street. They might kiss in the car for a long time after. She might not be able to foresee her life without him. We ordered sundaes and coffee. We watched her put on her coat and go home, and a new waitress take her place, an older woman with gray hair and ropy veins in her hands. When the waitress brought our bill, I discovered that neither Del nor I had any money with us.

I told Del I'd check William's wallet. I felt full, and warm, the grease coating my tongue. I slid out of the booth and went out to the car. I leaned into the backseat where Del had tossed William's bag and unzipped it. On top was the Leica. He was rarely without it—it was always on its strap around his neck. I lifted it and the back fell open, and the film spilled out. It was all that was left of him. The cold was awful, and despite everything I didn't want to imagine him trapped in the asylum for the night. I stuffed the camera back into the bag and quickly dug out his wallet. And then I remembered the other roll of film—the first one he'd shot, and taken out of the camera, and placed in his coat pocket. It was too late to go back, to find him and retrieve it. Once he was found the film would be found and developed, and they would see the images. And maybe he'd gotten a shot of me.

My hands were numb, but I managed to take some bills. Del sat in the booth, watching me through the restaurant window, and I closed the car door and returned to pay the bill. I couldn't tell her, not when she believed we were safe.

We got directions home from a patron sitting in a booth by the door. We were over an hour away, and I told Del I'd drive. For that length of time we traveled in silence. Del fell asleep, her head against the window. At our house we parked in the street and climbed slowly from the car and entered the vestibule. The first night William came, when I kissed him, we believed things about each other that were never true enough. His beaver-skin hat still hung on the peg where he'd left it. I thought of him slipping into Del's apartment. Had he been looking for the portfolio? I felt another rush of panic at the thought of having left him behind. And of the roll of film in his pocket.

Del reminded me, in this moment, of our mother—steadfast, stoic. She put her key in her apartment door and swung the door open. The faint scent of incense, of last night's meal, wafted out. Then she stepped inside and closed the door. The lock turned, as if she were barricading herself against me.

After we'd hidden David Pinney's body, the threesomes and four-somes continued to play the ninth hole, hitting their drives, their putts, getting caught in the rough. None of their monogramed balls ventured near the stand of willows. Our friends continued to swim at the pool afternoons, but Del refused. She'd gone out once and been confronted by the stray dog—its dark shape darting out from beneath the privet hedge. From then on she told our mother she wanted to stay inside. Some days I was able to stay inside as well without drawing suspicion, but more often than not I was the one who had to pretend that nothing was wrong. One day at the pool Jane Roberts asked me where that boy was.

"What boy?" I said. I felt a buzzing, flickering faintness.

"The one you said you liked." she said.

She had on another boy's aviator sunglasses and lounged on her towel in the grass. I told her I didn't know where he was. "I don't even know his name," I said. I laughed at my own carelessness, and she laughed along with me. I pretended I was interested in another boy at the pool, and I flirted with him, and we went out to the movies with Jane and Paul Grant. I tried not to think about David Pinney under the willow. It was the animal control people, called by my mother's report of the stray dog, who found his body. His photograph was in the newspaper, but I barely looked at it. He had on a suit and tie, the photograph taken on the occasion of his sister's wedding.

A variety of local boys were initially questioned as suspects, though none confessed and nothing tied any of them to the crime. Everyone believed he'd been the victim of a crazed drifter, someone from beyond the neighborhood, summoning a picture of a man riding the rails into town, slipping from an open car under cover of darkness to do his evil deed. His family's ties to the Spiritualists by the Sea darkened the camp's reputation further, and for a while people wanted to shut the temple down. But eventually, a sort of hush settled over the tragedy, though the case, still led by Detective Thomson, remained open.

On the stair landing I considered confessing everything to Geoff. He'd call the authorities and have the asylum searched, William's body found. We could tell the truth about the accident, and trust that no one would ask about the teenage boy found dead near our family's property in Connecticut. But Detective Thomson would know—he'd follow up. He'd come talk to me, to Del. I was too tired to play games with Detective Thomson.

> *Was David Pinney a friend of yours?*
>
> No.
>
> *Not a friend?*
>
> Not really.
>
> *What about your sister, Delores?*

No.

But he was often here, at the pool?

Sometimes.

He was a good-looking boy, wasn't he? Did any of the girls have crushes on him?

Not that I know.

But you noticed him, didn't you?

I noticed he was sometimes here, if that's what you mean.

I put Geoff's car keys under the mat, and I stood outside the door to my apartment, wondering if William, or some version of him, would be waiting for me in the duck-carved chair. I was afraid of his being there, of what that would mean. The dead had appeared to me with their awful longing, their torment at being separated from their loved ones plain in their expressions. I was afraid to see that look in William's face, to know that I'd made a terrible mistake. The room was dark. I turned on a lamp. The light cast a round shape on the floor. The place was empty and cold. And that night I was glad for it.

29

I found I was waiting for William to return, as if he had just gone off on one of his jaunts with his camera, even though the camera, what was left of it and its spool of film, was tucked away on a closet shelf among his sweaters. Part of me longed for him to return to explain himself, to settle things, and part of me dreaded it. I tried to reconstruct the moments of his fall, but they were unclear, blurred and wavering. I wondered if I was having some sort of psychotic break, like Del as a teenager. Then I told myself that if I wondered if I was having a breakdown, I probably was not. I took off Mary Rae's necklace and set it on the table by the bed, next to the travel alarm clock. I'd abandoned my husband, injured in whatever manner, in that place, and I was certainly a criminal. That he may have intended me harm was beside the point, wasn't it? I had only Del to rely on for that information. Her insinuation that he'd put something in my wine certainly explained my grogginess that night and the following morning, but I had no proof. And though I'd suspected we'd had sex that night—was I simply half-asleep and unaware? Or had it been something else?

What might have happened if Del hadn't gotten tired of waiting in the car? The possibilities were ominous. Had he planned to kill me if I hadn't provided the location of the portfolio? And once she'd insisted on joining us, was his plan simply altered to killing me and leaving Del to take the blame? I felt his grip on my arms, the way he pulled me toward the staircase. And what about Mary Rae? Clearly, it was William she'd loved and couldn't bear to be separated from. What had happened to her?

Del came to my door with food—a miniature chicken potpie, steaming in its foil pan, glasses of milk and cookies, as if I were a sick child. On the third day of William's absence she brought me a TV dinner. She plopped down beside me on the bed and set it in my lap.

"You've lost your creativity." I picked up the fork and jabbed at the chicken cutlet in its compartment. "How long are you going to keep bringing me food?"

Del fished a carrot off the tray. "How long are you going to hide?"

"I'm not sure what to do now." I took a bite of the chicken.

"Anything you want," she said.

"Well, he's been missing for over forty-eight hours. Should I report it to the police?"

Del had an aversion to police officers, doctors, and anyone involved in the role of public welfare. In her eyes they'd all either forsaken her or lied to her; their occupations involved the kind of trickery we undertook as children, misrepresenting the dead. They claimed to help, but they did not.

"That's what you want to do?" she said.

I had to admit when I considered reporting William missing I felt a terrible vertigo, as if I were peering down into the gorge. I waited for Del to talk me out of it, for her to convince me I shouldn't call anyone. Then she took Mary Rae's journal out from beneath her sweater.

"Here," she said. "Put this wherever you have that portfolio he was looking for."

I took the journal from her and set it on the end table beside the little travel clock. I was waiting for more of her plan. There was always a plan with Del; some scheme would follow.

"And?" I said. "What?"

"If anyone asks where good old Will is, you can say he took off. You two hadn't been getting along, and he said he was leaving you."

Del took a piece of the chicken and put it in her mouth, then spit it out into the palm of her hand. I handed her a tissue, and she wrapped the chicken in it.

"So, we never went to the asylum in Buffalo."

She widened her eyes, innocently. "That's right," she said.

"We borrowed Geoff's car and drove to Connecticut to see our mother," I said.

There was no body to hide this time. Only an absence.

"He's gone," Del said. "You're free."

I wanted to ask her exactly what she'd seen at the bottom of the stairs, but I hadn't wanted to force her to relive it. I knew I should have seen his body, cradled his head as he drew his last breaths, apologized for saying the things I'd said, for making him miserable, for being a hard person to make happy. After all, I had no real evidence he had killed Mary Rae, and now I had even less chance to discover it.

I watched Del carefully. "Are you sure he was gone?"

She put another carrot in her mouth, chewed, ate another. She dipped a finger in the mashed potatoes.

Outside I could hear someone chopping at the snow on the sidewalk with a shovel. "I'm sorry," she said.

"I just can't believe it," I said. "It doesn't feel real."

I covered my head with the afghan. After a few minutes, Del rose from the bed.

"You just have to forget it ever happened," she said.

Those words I'd told her once. They hadn't really done any good then, and I wondered if they would help me now. Del left the apartment and stood on the other side of the closed door. "Lock the door," she said, and I knew she wouldn't leave until I did.

I would accept that William was gone, that our life together would never resume the way it had been. He wouldn't walk into my little bedsit, take a shower, sit at the desk in the corner, lie down beside me on the bed. He would never touch me again—what I had come to see as the basis for whatever grief I carried, though I understood that our physical closeness had a terrible edge to it.

But I believed I would see him again. This is what my curse allowed me—a correspondence remained, however uneasy.

THE FOLLOWING MONDAY classes began, and that afternoon I crossed the quad toward Tjaden Hall. The shadows lengthened on the snow. Students passed singly, their heads down against the wind. A group burst from the Green Dragon, clutching paper cups of coffee, laughing, clinging to one another, the girls in knitted scarves and hats. I felt something on my face and saw that it had once again begun to snow.

Inside the hall I had a reprieve from the wind. I went first to William's office, drawn by a feeling that I might find him. I stood in the hallway, and something stirred behind the door—a rustling of papers, a movement, or breathing. I knocked, and the movement stilled. I pictured him behind the door, not wanting to be found. A man came out of the office next door and stopped beside me.

"He's not scheduled to teach this semester," he said.

"Oh, thank you," I said. I wanted to say I was his wife and that he was missing, but all of these admissions seemed almost improbable in the real world. William had not been assigned any classes, and yet he had never told me. Everything he'd said, and not said, seemed suspect.

Later in the week I went by the class he usually taught, and it was true, someone else was teaching. It was as if William had simply been erased from my life. At night I had dreams of pushing him down the long stairs, of finding his body at the bottom. I'd awaken, sweat-drenched, and tell myself it was simply a dream. Still, I didn't contact the authorities and report him missing. I thought of Detective Thomson, and I kept quiet.

One afternoon, two weeks after classes began, I took my film to the lab at school to develop the images and print contact sheets. These I poured over with my loupe. I had taken shots that day in the asylum, and in the photographs the day came back to me: the light crisp, the metal bedsteads flipped on end, the old wheelchairs with cane backs eaten through by vermin, *There but for the grace of God go I*, on a plaque and the paint coming off the walls in long, tender strips, like skin. The more frightening the objects, the more I could not stop looking—examining tables of cold rusted metal, instruments and wires and hoses and basins and tubs, all bathed in that tinted light. I imagined birds coming in and out through the broken windows, the sound of their beating wings amplified in the emptied rooms.

There was one image of a bed with covers kicked back, as if someone had just gotten up, the mattress ticking worn and stained, the blanket thin and gnawed on at the edges. I'd caught none of the dead in the frames. Then I reached the photograph I'd taken of William. He wore his corduroy jacket, his oxford shirt and sweater. I enlarged the negative and made the print, thinking the whole time that he may have surreptitiously taken one of me.

It was late afternoon. No one was around, and in the glow of the darkroom the image emerged clearly, eerily. He'd paused in the doorway, his expression filled with love and so unlike the memory of him I'd been entertaining that I felt disoriented. Who had I confronted in the asylum that day? I felt overwhelmed with guilt.

I debated destroying the print, and then Charles Wu came into the darkroom, and I shoved it into my bag. He gave me a little wave, a tentative smile, and peered over my shoulder at my contact sheets.

"You went to Buffalo State," he said, surprised.

He took my contact sheets and peered at them. I felt my face flush with irritation. Now I couldn't deny I'd been there.

"Yes, yes I did," I said. "It was incredible."

Charles Wu seemed pleased I'd taken his advice. He'd dyed the white stripe in his hair, and he wore a pair of pressed khakis, as if he'd decided to give in to his parents and accompany them to the country club. Would I need to start a list of all the people who could implicate me in William's death?

"You didn't have trouble getting in, did you?" he said. "These are really cool. I might have to go out there myself."

Charles could be the one to find William's body. That would be apt after William's accusations.

"You should definitely go," I said. "It's easy to get in."

Then I found myself telling him all about the loading dock and the hole that allowed access to the underground corridors. I told him about those tunnels and the route to take to arrive at the upper level.

"Did you find the staircase?" He was excited by my story.

"I did," I said. "It was dark by then, though. I only got a few shots. I'm not sure how they turned out."

Charles handed my contact sheets back. "Best to go early. That's what I've heard."

Although I'd never cared to read a newspaper, I'd begun buying the local paper, scanning it for a report about the discovery of a body in an asylum. Now, it seemed possible that any number of urban spelunkers, artists, or paranormal investigators might have visited Buffalo State and uncovered William's body. If the roll of film he'd pocketed had come free during the fall, and landed below the balustrades in some hidden niche, if William hadn't properly captured me in a photograph developed by forensic officers, he might become one of the thousands of unclaimed bodies in the United States, remains dis-covered without any identification and no one stepping forward for them. Maybe there would be a line drawing of his face in the record, a description of his clothes. Perhaps there would be a mention of the discovery of his body in the Buffalo news. In the old Buffalo State Asylum for the Insane, soon to be refurbished to house an outpatient hospital, he might become a ghost who haunted the rooms.

"Let me know if you decide to go," I said.

"I will," he said. He unloaded his backpack and slid strips of neg-atives out of their sleeves for the enlarger, as if sensing I was ready to leave. "We should totally have coffee one afternoon this week."

My face felt odd, as if I weren't used to conversing, and my mus-cles were underused. "I'd like that," I said.

Del continued to spend time with Alice and the other Milton girls. I would hear her come and go, or hear Alice's laughter downstairs. Sometimes, Del would invite me to go bowling with them at Viking Lanes, or snowmobiling in the fields around Milton, but I refused. I wasn't sure what she was telling them all about William, and I wouldn't know how to act. It was disorienting to have the apartment to myself—a constant reminder of him. We would have broken up eventually—I knew that now. My only question remained his obsession over the images.

I kept my distance from Geoff, too. It was March when he finally knocked and I couldn't pretend I wasn't home. I opened the door to his familiar brown eyes, his crazed hair, Suzie thrusting her nose into my palm.

"Have you got some tea?" he said. "I'm parched."

He tugged Suzie in on her leash and took a seat at the little table. I boiled water for a pot.

"So have you been licking your wounds?" he said, launching into his real reason for coming by.

I stared at him. "What do you mean?"

"It's obvious old William has flown the coop," he said, and pulled out his tobacco. "There's no shame in admitting defeat. He was always a fickle sort."

I poured the hot water in so the tea could steep and set the teapot in the center of the table. The apartment was still filled with William's things, and Geoff took this in.

"I guessed you'd notice soon enough," I said.

He gave me a sympathetic look. "At least you've managed to come out of it unscathed," he said. "Count yourself lucky you aren't in the same predicament as your sister."

I was confused by this bit of conversation, but I sensed I should go along with it. Geoff knew something I didn't, and I wanted to know it, too.

"Well, I am grateful for that," I said. The table sat by the window, and I could feel the cold panes. Below me was the sidewalk and the place beneath the elm where I'd seen Mary Rae that first night. Geoff poured out our tea, oblivious. "These are gorgeous cups," he said, eyeing the Limoges.

I drank the tea, scalding my tongue, and waited.

"Have you banned him from your place?" he said. "It might be easier on you if you packed up his things."

"I was planning to do that," I said. "I've just been so busy with school."

The truth was, though I'd continued to attend my classes, I was barely paying attention in them and had begun neglecting assignments.

Geoff eyed me over the rim of his cup. "You're going to be busy helping raise a baby," he said. "She's lost the plot, if you ask me, expecting you to be part of the whole thing."

I shrugged and set my cup in the saucer. My hand shook, and I buried it in my lap. I could hardly believe this story Del had told him.

"You're a better person than I'd be," he said. "Don't think some of us haven't put two and two together—I mean Will takes off, and Del is knocked up. Everyone is being so hush-hush."

He sipped the last of his tea and laid a hand on Suzie's head. I thought of the things we each could infer about the other through the plaster wall that separated our apartments—the pacing of the floorboards, the sounds of lovemaking. The odd pleasure it lent us to know things that the other might never confess. And then, how difficult it was to know the person we were closest with—how our bodies together never guaranteed anything.

Geoff said Anne was shocked by the turn in events. "But that's often the way with unplanned things. A bit of a surprise that often ends up being lovely."

I didn't dare sip my tea and reveal my trembling hand. I simply nodded at him, and he saw my distress and changed the subject. "It'll be spring eventually. Slow to arrive, you know. But it always does."

Though it was March, there were no signs yet of the thaw that signaled spring's arrival. Geoff didn't usually have a problem dominating a conversation, and he did that while he drank his tea, switching topics, until he couldn't resist returning to the highlight of the day.

"Where is the old scoundrel?" he said. "I haven't seen him around."

"You should ask Del," I said.

"She told me to ask you," Geoff said. He spun his cup in its saucer. "Sounds like neither of you has a clue."

I gave him a feeble smile. "That would be Del's problem now, wouldn't it?"

Geoff stood to go, brushing the excess tobacco from his lap to the floor. In the doorway I told him to wait.

"I found a necklace in your car," I said. "It was an amethyst pendant."

Geoff didn't seem too surprised. "I don't drive many women around in my car. But if you girls gave someone a ride, maybe they lost it? You might ask Will, too. He's borrowed the thing a few times in the past."

"Well, I'll ask him if I see him," I said. After Geoff left I stood listening to him cross the hall, open his door, and enter his own apartment.

I went downstairs and knocked on Del's door. She opened it with her usual flourish.

"There you are!" she said. "Mother says she's tried to reach you, and you aren't returning her calls."

"So?" I said. I walked past her into her apartment.

"She wants us to come home for Easter."

I watched Del put her hand on her abdomen, though nothing yet showed beneath her oversized sweater. She saw me looking, and then pulled the sweater tightly closed.

"I know it's surprising," Del said, matter-of-factly. "But I saw a doctor in Milton, Alice took me, and it's true. I'm due in September."

I felt a lurch of guilt. Our mother would be furious. I could hear her accusatory voice now: "How could you have let this happen, Martha?"

"Were you going to tell me?" I said.

"I thought you already knew," she said. "After what you said in Buffalo."

I'd made a comment about Jane mistaking the Institute as a place for unwed mothers, but that could hardly serve as evidence that I knew about the pregnancy. "I didn't know," I said, icily.

"I was planning on giving the baby up for adoption," Del said, "but I've been thinking, the genetic makeup might really predispose this child, you know, God, to any number of problems, and maybe someone else should take it, someone in the family who has experience and can show some compassion, and give it siblings and a nice bed to sleep in. Or crib. A crib at first, right?"

Del had scrunched her face, and her expression switched from wide-eyed to puzzled, and back.

Like a thrown switch she had gone off again. I suspected she had either stopped her medication or the doctor she'd seen had readjusted it.

"Who do you think will take it? One of your sisters?" I said.

Del sat down on her couch. Dust rose from the cushions into the slant of weak sunlight. "Eventually we'll have to tell them."

I noted her use of "we" with a feeling close to despair. I could easily pity her, with her soon-to-be-extending midsection full of something that stirred and pressed and made its presence known against her skin. I couldn't help thinking of the movies with gestating babies destined to wreak evil and havoc on the world. She caught my expression and frowned. "You have to be a good aunt," she told me. "Who else will it have?"

"All babies have a father," I said.

Del pulled her sweater sleeves over her hands. "You're so amusing." Outside a car horn sounded in the street, and we both startled. "Does it really matter?"

"That sounds like your new phrase," I said. *"Does it matter?"*

I told myself that the father might be Randy.

"Weren't you using birth control?" I said. My anger must have shown on my face. Del folded her arms across her abdomen as if she were protecting the child.

"They tried to make me use an IUD, but I took the pill, and then I ran out," she said. "Still, I honestly don't know how this could have happened."

She laughed again and looked up at me.

"Is it William's?" I said.

Del looked even more confused. "No!" she cried. I had the feeling, as I had the day I told her William and I were married, that she was faking her exclamation, that her protest was a lie. Then she said something under her breath that I couldn't hear, and I worried she was talking to herself.

"What?" I said. "What did you say?"

"'Sun, Moon, and Talia.' Remember? By the Italian author. It was in that book of tales Grandfather used to read to us."

"What does that have to do with anything?" I said.

Out the window and across the street, I saw a figure by the curb on the corner, watching the house. He lurked slightly behind a tree, almost leaning on it. Then he pushed himself off and moved away slowly down the sidewalk. A glint of sun caught in his copper hair. His shoulders were broad in his coat. He moved away with a distinct limp, a drag in one leg. I didn't think I could take a breath. My head filled with ringing. Del was asking me something, and I couldn't make out what she was saying—my head was so full of sound.

"What did you say?" I turned my back on the window.

"What is it? What's out there?" Del came to the window, but I moved away and she followed me across the room to the door.

"It's nothing," I said.

"Will you come with me?" she said. "For Easter?"

In the vestibule, William's father's hat hung from the coatrack.

"We should get rid of that," I said.

I went out onto the porch, but the figure, William, had disappeared. Had I experienced enough grief to summon him? Or was it his love for me that brought him around? I clutched the porch railing, faint and confused. His ghost might be undertaking unfinished business, but what use would the portfolio be to him now? This life and its ordeals were erased. The dead clung to a tether of love, drawn back by a loss that tormented them, and I felt my knees weaken with my own desire, and the impossibility of ever being with him again. Del, beside me on the porch, pressed her hand to her stomach. If Del was pregnant with William's baby, he might have another reason to be watching the house. I felt a fresh surge of anger. And Mary Rae was back beneath the elm.

I'd waited long enough to uncover William's connection to her death. I owed her the truth. And I was going to live my life. He'd accused me of seeing Charles Wu—as if something that preposterous had been the reason for his misery. I'd give him something to be miserable about.

30

It was after I saw William across the street that things began
to melt. Icicles dripped audibly onto the front porch. They hung from
the house's eaves, deadly threats we ducked under or knocked off with
a shovel. It was time to clean house. I left the windows open and let
the cold air blow through the place. I thought of the miniature book
by Maurice Sendak my mother had read to us as children, *Chicken
Soup with Rice*. It told its nonsensical story month by month, the
months personified, and March blowing down the door and lapping
up spilled soup. I shoved William's things—papers, bills, clothes—
into boxes and put them in the closet. I used bleach and scrubbed. I
went to Geoff's door and asked to borrow his mop, and then later,
his car. I loaded the blankets and sheets in the trunk and drove them
to the Laundromat, maneuvering around the potholes in the streets,
the slush spraying onto the windshield. Outside, without William
Bell, the world was changing.

At the Laundromat, a boy I'd met when I first came to school recognized me and called my name. He asked me what I was reading,
and what courses I was taking this semester, and then asked me more
things. I'd forgotten his name but didn't ask him for it. The big hot
dryers rolled and tumbled. Pieces of lint floated past. The boy's expression was earnest, his eyes lit with genuine interest. My hair was too
long, uncombed, my wool sweater's hem unraveling, my hands smelling of bleach. But could he be attracted to me?

"Help me take my stuff to my car," I said.

He grabbed armfuls. I opened the trunk and we put the sheets
and blankets inside. And then we stood in the slush in the cold, filling the space between us with our fogging breath.

"Come home with me and help me make the bed," I said.

He scanned the parking area, as if someone might witness all of
this occurring, as if he'd stepped into a play and been asked to read
a part.

"Are you serious?" he said, quietly, covertly.

"Sure." I jingled the car keys in my hand.

Climbing into his car, he was eager and quick. He drove that way,
too, following close behind, almost hitting me once at a stop sign. At
my house I parked at the curb and he carried everything in his arms
up the stairs. His footsteps were light, glancing off each step, careening up to the landing where he had to wait for me to unlock the door.
He caught his breath behind the pile of laundry.

Inside, the breeze had whipped things into a frenzy. Magazines
and papers had blown onto the floor. The curtains were caught up in
their rods. All of the old smells seemed resurrected—fireplace ashes,
oak polish, the walls' dampened plaster, not unpleasantly. The apartment felt cold and fiercely alive.

"It is freezing in here," the boy said.

I shut the windows and the room stilled. His name still eluded
me. We were in the Women and Grief class on the third floor of the

Andrew White House. He had lost his father recently, he'd admitted in class. He had no idea what to do now that he was here in my apartment and, without any complicity, neither did I.

"This is the bed," I said. The mattress was thin in the pitiless March light. He grabbed an end of a sheet, and we stretched it out from either side. From the pile of bedsheets we found the one to go on top, our heads bumping, sorting through everything. His hair smelled of shampoo. The room filled with the smell of clean laundry. We made the bed. He was very competent and serious, as if this were really what he had expected. When we were done, he sat down on the edge.

"I want a cigarette," he said. He looked up at me, apologetically.

"I don't smoke," I told him. I sat down on the bed next to him.

"Maybe we should go out and have a pitcher of beer," he said.

I took his hand and placed it on my leg. We both looked at it, a fine hand with long fingers and bulky knuckles. "There isn't a set way to go about this," I told him. "Either you want me more than a cigarette, or you don't."

He snorted and ran his free hand through his hair. "Do you do this a lot?" he asked.

His face was fine-boned, his eyebrows drawn together. "No, not really," I said.

"Didn't you go to Wellesley?" he asked.

I told him he must have me confused with someone else.

"Didn't you go to Yale?" I said.

He laughed. "No, I didn't," he said.

"Well then," I said. "We aren't who we thought we were."

The spot of sun on the bed was almost warm. "We are just imitations of what we thought," he said.

"Apparitions," I said.

His hand on my leg heated it up. Our bodies touched at the shoulder and hip. They sank at varying depths into the too-thin mattress.

"What if we kiss?" I suggested. Anything to stop his musing.

He put both of his hands on my face then and held it like a bowl you might tip and drink from. I felt my body thaw, my heart shift and give, dislodged from its winter hibernation. I would come to learn that most men exhibited at least one endearing gesture, and this was his. His mouth was soft and he closed his eyes. We kissed for a long time on the clean-smelling bed. He whispered my name like a summoning spell. I wouldn't have said his if I'd known it, anyway. While we kissed I felt an anxious tightening, and I imagined William had slipped into the room and taken a seat in the duck-carved chair. I sat up and looked over, and was disappointed that he wasn't there. The boy watched me, his bare chest rising and falling under my hand.

"Did you hear something?" he asked me, his eyes glazed with desire and not really seeing. He urged me back into his arms. He had a way of holding me that made me feel breakable, like a soft-feathered bird. I kissed his mouth, his chest. I slid down his body and undid his pants. When he left I made sure to walk him out onto the porch and kiss him so William across the street, and even Mary Rae, standing in her down coat under the elm, could see.

"Look at me, ghosts," I as much as said.

Mary Rae smirked. William, stonelike, stalked off with his limp.

Inside, Del was waiting for me, too. "A boyfriend?" she said.

"Not really," I said. "Just a boy."

"Be careful." She twisted her hair into a bun and slipped an elastic band from her wrist to secure it. "You don't want to get knocked up."

I didn't want to be angry with her. "Thanks," I said. I gave her a halfhearted smile.

"Sometimes I don't understand it, either," she said. Her eyes were so sad, I was sure even if she was guilty of sleeping with my husband, I should have had some sympathy for her. But neither of us deserved any sympathy at all. Del went into her apartment. Later that I night, I went down to see her, but Alice's quick laughter came from behind the door, and I felt glad for Del and Alice's friendship, even if the Milton girls weren't friends of mine.

⌒

It occurred to me that Del had become the steady, responsible one, and somehow I had taken on her old high school promiscuity.

"I'm already ruined," she'd said then.

I wouldn't let the boys I brought home interfere with my goal of finding out what happened to Mary Rae. I pored over the journal Del had given me. It covered the year prior to reconnecting with William, and during that time Mary Rae had dated a series of boys— ones she named and described, providing details of their various dates—to the Regal Cinemas at The Shops at Ithaca Mall, to the Antlers restaurant, swimming at Buttermilk Falls. I took Geoff's car, the air rushing in through the open windows smelling of melting snow and wet earth, and I drove to Milton or the nearby villages and I tracked them down—Jimmy Cahill sorting bulbs at the Agway hardware store, Russell Watkins tending bar at Viking Lanes, Frankie Duncan carting gravel at the Milton Department of Public Works. Each of them seemed to emanate a sorrowful sense of loss.

Jimmy Cahill sat behind the store alone, eating lunch, a book opened in front of him. Something about the way he tucked a pencil behind his ear spoke of his grief. With Russell the ache was in the way he hitched his pants walking across the Viking Lanes parking lot, in the shape of his hands below his rolled-up sleeves.

"You don't know me," I'd say. "But I was a friend of Mary Rae's, and she always used to talk about you."

Seriously? A mix of disbelief and gratitude.

There was always a reason to draw them close. Each reason presented itself, like a blessing. Sudden rain. A desire for coffee. Russell and I ducked back into the Viking Lanes. We drank and played pool. I leaned over far enough, let my hair fall onto his arm. With Jimmy we walked to the diner down the street, past the funeral parlor, the bed-and-breakfast. I whispered to him, my hand cupped around his ear. As with the boy in the Laundromat, it would just happen. I'd say we could go to my place. I'd feel a satisfied thrill when they agreed—though I couldn't admit I wanted to flaunt them in front of a ghost.

The day with Jimmy was chilly, and we walked back to my car in the Agway lot. He wore a T-shirt.

"Aren't you cold?" I asked. I reached out and touched his bare arm.

He looked at me in the slow, lazy way of boys who know exactly what you're doing. He didn't say anything. By the time we reached my car and climbed inside, we were both dizzy, breathing fast, falling into each other's arms with one long exhale, our mouths too busy for words, the car windows steaming up.

When I took Jimmy home, Geoff came out of his apartment with Suzie as we stood on the landing, my key in the lock. He didn't admonish me. I was an abandoned wife, and he pitied me. He shook his head in disapproval and silently descended. Only Suzie glanced back, and then he gave her a tug with the leash, and a harsh word that was surely meant for me. Jimmy wrapped his arms around my waist and I sank back into his shirtfront, into the muscles of his chest, the bones of his rib cage, wondering if Mary Rae felt the way I did when she was with him.

I stopped locking my door. Sometimes I dreamed William's boots stomped up the stairs, scraping mud on the landing. He would come in and stand by the bed in the gray light. His gaze did its usual sad dance over the body he no longer held, and sometimes he would take a seat in the chair, and at others he'd turn and leave the room. Once in a while I awoke to his retreating footsteps and I chased after him, slipping out of bed and down the stairs, out the front door onto the porch. There I stood shivering, half-dressed, fooled by what was dream and what was real, no longer able to tell the difference.

One morning Geoff stepped onto the porch from the sidewalk and found me. I had no idea where he'd been—if he'd been out all night or had just stepped out for some air.

"What is it?" he asked me. His eyes were alert, watchful, taking in my feet, bare and white on the porch.

"It's nothing," I said. I went inside, and he followed me. I shut the door and headed toward the stairs. And the boy that had been with me, Frankie, from the DPW that time, came down, groggily, carrying his boots.

"I have work," he said, and he sat on the bottom step and put his boots on. I watched him, his dipped head, the white place on the back of his neck. He pulled on a jacket. "Maybe I'll see you later," he said, as they all had. I told them that they probably wouldn't. I didn't want to foster closeness, to become attached.

They all said the same thing when I asked about Mary Rae—when I worked my way around to mentioning her name. Sometimes I wondered if I was inviting a murderer into my bed, but each of them replied the same way.

"I would have married that girl," they said. "But she was in love with someone else."

Mary Rae had refused to have sex with any of the boys, and I could only think what a waste it had been for her not to. We'd both been virgins until William, but she'd lost her chance with anyone else.

Before the boys left I always provided the briefest of messages to them from their dead: "Your aunt Lila is so happy her tulips have come up" or "Your grandfather wants you to major in music."

This boy, Frankie, hesitated, unsure whether to kiss me in front of Geoff. I walked him out onto the porch, and then he pulled out a wool scarf from the sweatshirt pocket and leaned forward and draped it around my neck.

"The old guy," he said. "I've seen him around somewhere."

The sun wasn't yet up, and it was chilly. "Really? Where?"

The boy shrugged, but he seemed uneasy. "Mary Rae didn't like him," he said. "We saw him talking to a group of girls outside the Viking Lanes snack shop one afternoon. She wanted to avoid him."

"Did she ever say why?" I tugged on the scarf and wrapped it around my hands.

But Frankie only shook his head, sadly. "No reason to worry about it now, huh?"

Mary Rae refused to appear under the elm when I had one of the boys with me.

Inside, Geoff stood at the foot of the stairs, as if he were waiting for the boy to go. "Another one?" he asked.

I held the scarf over my face and breathed in Frankie's smell. I told Geoff that when the boys left, they always gave me something. I didn't say the gift was prompted by an unexplained relief at the message I provided, at having the sex turn out to really mean nothing more. "You're sweet," they'd say. I'd have put on his undershirt, and when I began to remove it he'd tell me, No, keep it. Small things. One gave me his Saint Christopher's medal on a tarnished chain. Another his L.L.Bean windbreaker.

"You're lucky they didn't give you anything else," he said, his voice harsh.

I wasn't sure why Geoff was angry with me. He never seemed the type. I attributed it to his feeling something for William. "Good old Will," he would always say. Maybe he felt torn to choose sides, and even my abandonment wasn't enough to sway him to mine.

31

I could have predicted it. In April, Anne called me and invited me over. "I'd like it to be just the two of us," she said. "A little tête-à-tête."

As far as I knew, Anne's dinner parties had continued without me and William. Del would relay the menu she'd planned, but like our mother and her halfhearted invitations, I was never expected to attend. Anne had gotten word from Geoff, and probably resented my involvement with other men—especially if she'd heard, as I suspected she had through Randy and Del, that they were local boys. So I was leery. Anne always had some ulterior motive. She would want to know where William was. She would quiz me about how we left things, about what was said. I could tell her William's ghost was keeping a vigil and watching the house. I might say Mary Rae was beneath the elm, warding him off, waiting for me to solve the mystery of her death. When Anne said she'd pick me up, I agreed.

Spring had begun to show itself—the elm's buds were bright. Crocuses sprang from beneath the spot where Mary Rae stood. Other
bulbs—jonquils, daffodils, tulips—came up in surprising places along
the perimeter of the house in beds I hadn't known existed. The yellow
grass grew spongy and speckled with robins. William's Triumph leaned
against the back of the house. It had begun to rust, and weeds had
grown through its wheels. I wasn't quite sure what to do about it, so
I left it there.

I planned to bring William's portfolio to Anne's. According to Del,
the Milton girls discussed the photographs when Anne wasn't around,
which led me to assume Anne knew nothing about them. I hesitated
to be the one to show them to her. But I decided to pretend William
had left them behind. I got dressed and slipped Mary Rae's necklace
into my pocket.

Anne arrived at five o'clock to pick me up. It was dark and a surprising spring snow was falling in the lamplight. Her car was an old
Mercedes-Benz—a beautiful blue two-seater. As I got into the car
Anne said that if the snow got too bad I could spend the night at her
house, and just then I wanted nothing more than to be fed and tended
to. She drove expertly along the whitening roads, downshifting on
hills we might not make it over. I told her I liked her car, and she gave
me a little, secret smile. I worried she thought I had designs on it—
another item I wanted her to leave me after she died.

"It was my mother's," she said. "My father bought it for her in 1960
from the New York showroom. I shouldn't be driving it in this weather,
but it was spring, wasn't it?"

She had the radio tuned to the local NPR station, and she talked
brightly over a BBC news report—holding back her mention of
William's strange disappearance, I guessed, until we got to her house.
I settled back into the leather seat. I had William's portfolio with me
in my bag. When we turned up Anne's drive, the gravel and the snow
pinged beneath the little car, and one lamp burned in the house.

Usually every floor was illuminated, the light spilling out of every window, and I felt a woozy anxiousness—as if something inside the house, in one of those dark rooms, lay in wait for me.

Anne pulled into the garage alongside a Jeep with thick tires—the car she should have driven out in the snow. The headlight beams hit rakes and galvanized buckets hung on hooks on the wall. She explained that her husband used to tap the maples for syrup and that William had taken over when her husband had left.

"He should have started already," Anne said, sounding miffed.

The car's engine cut off, as did the lights, and we were thrown into darkness. We made our tentative way up the path to the front door and Anne stopped in the middle of her snowy lawn.

"Isn't this a fabulous night," she exclaimed, taking deep breaths of it.

At the door, she fumbled with her keys until I nearly offered to do it for her. The snow fell and landed on our shoulders, powdery and soft. Finally, the door swung open and we stepped inside. There was a fire in the hearth, but only one lamp illuminated the room.

"Welcome to my world," Anne said. "Dreary without my usual company, isn't it?"

We draped our coats over a chair, and Anne led me back into the kitchen, into the smell of something roasting in the oven. She had on a wool cap, and she went into a small mud room and emerged with her usual scarf—a paisley silk that made her eyes seem violet. The dimness was explained by the candle she had lit on the counter. I watched Anne step over to the bar.

"I'm going to have a vodka martini," she said. "My parents and their friends were avid martini drinkers in their forties. When I turned forty last year I just fell into the tradition."

I admitted I'd never had one, and she insisted I sample hers. She held her glass toward me by its stem, and I took a cautious sip. I said it was like drinking partially melted snow, and she laughed and poured me one, too.

"It's a glioblastoma," she said, eyeing me over the rim of her glass. "The tumor."

I didn't know what to reply. I composed what I hoped was an expression of sympathy.

"I plan to come back as a cardinal after I die."

My first instinct was to reassure her that she would be fine, but I knew that was pointless. "They're beautiful birds," I said. "My great-grandfather was an ornithologist."

Anne brightened. "Really?" she said. "I'm an enthusiast."

I sipped my drink. "You don't have any taxidermy birds on display," I said.

Anne gathered her glass and the shaker. "I don't kill the birds. I watch them," she said. "Why don't we take our snow by the fire?"

In the living room, we sat on opposite sides of the velvet couch, and I could smell Lucie's patchouli in the dense fabric. Most meals at Anne's were hearty meat dishes, and Anne said she had made a beef Wellington, and it was her first try, so anything might come out of the oven. When would Anne arrive at her reason for inviting me? Del had always said that I was too suspicious, that I never believed in the goodness of others. She was right about that, but I had never yet been proven wrong. I leaned into the velvet cushions, comfortable but cautious about what might come next. I kept watching the stairwell, expecting to see William in his beaver-skin hat, or Mary Rae twirling her pretty necklace.

The drinks seemed to sharpen my senses rather than dull them. Since the day in the asylum I'd felt in a fog—even with the boys, I'd been trapped in a dreamlike existence. Now I could see the points of the stag's antlers on the wall, the dewy moisture of their eyes, the shine of their pelts, as if they might leap from their spots to charge across the oriental carpet. The fire sparked and hissed with Anne's addition of a new log. She sat back down and gave me a searching look.

"I just want you to know that I'm here, for a little bit longer at least, if you need anything." She lifted her martini glass from the table where she'd set it and held it toward me for a toast. "To friendship."

The first step in luring someone in was to offer support. I'd seen the mediums do this at the Spiritualists by the Sea camp. I held my glass up and she tapped hers against it, making a bell-like sound.

"We all know about Del and the baby," Anne said. "I'm here for her, too."

Anne was smart enough not to indulge the rumors about Del and William. "That's very sweet of you," I said. "Maybe the father will be supportive as well."

"Randy is trying. But I don't think your sister is falling for it. She doesn't seem like she wants a husband."

"No," I said. "I don't think she has many good examples."

Anne set her drink down carefully on the table, and I sensed her friendly facade falling away. She pushed the button on her cigarette box; the music played, and she retrieved the cigarette and lit it. She brushed the ends of her scarf over her shoulder like a swath of hair. William had been her protégé. Was she making it clear that she wouldn't hear any disparaging comments about him?

"Mary Rae and I had a get-together after she and William broke it off," Anne said. "We'd grown so close. She was an absolute mess."

Anne blew smoke to the ceiling. What would she make of the news that William and Mary Rae had reconnected more recently? Was she assessing me—trying to gauge my own level of despair?

"He made his choice," I said, leaning back into the couch cushion. "I have to accept it."

Anne reached for her drink and took a sip. "He's had a difficult life."

I tried not to correct her usage of the present tense. It unhinged me. Contrary to the last, threatening physical contact I'd had with him, William's spectral presence was benign, and I'd grown used to imagining him tormented by his love for me.

"He told me about his mother," I said.

Anne raised her eyebrows. "Did he tell you that his father abused her? That rather than let her divorce him he had her committed to the hospital in Binghamton? I knew his mother. She had a drinking problem." Anne tipped back her glass and finished her drink. "But honestly, who doesn't?"

"Why did he drop Mary Rae?" I asked.

She refreshed our glasses and stood with the shaker. "I'm going to check on the Wellington," she said. "And make more of these. Come with me."

We went back into the kitchen, and Anne mixed another shaker and poured us new drinks. I told her I'd had enough, and she smiled.

"One martini is never enough."

I didn't protest, I simply took another sip, and another. The kitchen grew warm from the stove. I understood why the Milton girls gathered at Anne's. It felt lovely to be taken care of, to have Anne's attention, all of it tinged bittersweet. Each moment with her was special, and there wouldn't be many more times like this, you told yourself. She asked me about my classes, about my own work. We talked for a while in the kitchen. Anne grew tipsy, laughing. She leaned over the stove and the ends of her scarf caught fire and she batted it out expertly with a damp dish towel, as if this kind of thing happened all the time.

My bag with William's portfolio sat on a chair nearby, and I wondered why Mary Rae's images were separate from the others, why he hadn't chosen to print one as a sample.

"Did they have an argument?" I asked. "William and Mary Rae?"

Anne put on oven mitts and leaned over to take out the roast. She stood, took off the mitts, and busied herself with a pot on the stove.

"They had a misunderstanding," Anne said. "It had to do with his work."

"The sleeping women." I tipped the shaker over my glass but it was empty.

I expected Anne to seem curious, to ask what I meant, but she did not. Her face flushed from the heat of the oven. "Yes," she said, simply.

The series wasn't a secret to her at all.

"You haven't heard from him?" she asked me. "Not a word, after all this time?"

We were finally getting to the point. "Have *you* heard from him?"

Anne faltered. "No, I have not. But I'd only been seeing him with you. He'd stopped coming by. I thought it was too hard for him, with my illness."

"He told me we were through and not to contact him. I'm not going to crawl after him."

Anne swung the refrigerator open and then closed it without taking anything out. She did the same to a cabinet door, as if hiding her expression from me. I must have seemed the most horrible person in the world. Finally, she placed her hands on the counter in front of me. "He truly loves you," Anne said. "I believe that."

How much I wanted this to be true. "I'm sorry, but you're mistaken."

Anne reached for the shaker. I watched her tip it over her empty glass, then bang it down on the counter.

"What do you really want from me, Anne?"

She fiddled with her scarf. "Before he disappeared from our lives William mentioned some prints he'd made. He'd said you had them."

"He mentioned them?" I sat down in the chair at the counter bar.

"Yes. It was months ago. He told me about the argument you had, how you'd seen the photographs, how he thought you might have, well, taken them."

I knew Anne, upset about Mary Rae's disappearance and her death, had wanted her journals. I didn't think her interest in the photographs was in any way related to William's. I believed we might have a common interest.

"I do have them," I said. "With me, actually."

I went to my bag and pulled out the portfolio and brought it back to the kitchen island. Anne grabbed her glasses and came to stand beside me. She went through the prints slowly, looking closely at each one. She was unsteady, and my head spun from the martinis. The glass doors leading out to the backyard were black, and the cold seeped through. They were big, glass sliding doors and my gaze was drawn to them, waiting for someone to appear. Anne looked up at me, her eyes magnified behind the lenses of her glasses.

"Where did you get this?" Anne seemed disappointed in me, as if she knew I'd stolen them.

"It's all of them—Alice, Lucie, Kitty, and Jeanette." I pulled the portfolio over and leafed through the prints so Anne would see, but she wasn't even looking.

"Mary Rae was jealous of the girls," she said. "She didn't understand the photographs. William wanted her to be a part of the series, and she told him emphatically no. Silly, isn't it?"

"It takes a certain trust to fall asleep with someone watching," I said. I paused at the photograph of Alice, her bare leg entwined with the sheet. "I don't think they're faking."

Anne closed the portfolio. "No, they aren't."

She went over the stove top and stood looking down at the Wellington. "I'm not so hungry," she said.

She came around the island counter and placed a hand on the portfolio. "I gave him my sleeping pills. The girls were fine taking them. They all agreed. They thought it was a hoot. They loved the idea of it, loved their bodies. They loved William, too."

Beyond the sliding glass doors the snow had covered the terrace. Anne's hand on the portfolio trembled slightly.

"The more Mary Rae protested, the more he wanted her to pose."

Had William given me Anne's sleeping pills that night at Del's?

"Don't you think pills are a bit extreme?" I said.

"You know how it is with him," she said. "His work is everything. And look how these turned out. They're beautiful—you have to admit it. Exceptional. I set up a show for him—a solo exhibition at a gallery in Chelsea. It's a well-known place, one that's made the careers of many artists. He felt the pressure of that, I think. He claimed the camera knew when the girls weren't fully asleep—and of course none of them could fall asleep at the drop of a hat."

She took the portfolio in her arms and held it, and I had a strange feeling that she had gotten what she wanted from me. The meal, everything else was forgotten.

"Mary Rae did pose," I said.

Anne shook her head. "No, she didn't. She's not among these prints."

I held out my hands for the portfolio, and she seemed reluctant to give it to me. I took the sleeve of negatives out of the back. "See."

Anne took the plastic sleeve with a shaking hand and held it to the light. She shook her head. "No," she said. "No, this just doesn't seem right."

"You can see more clearly with a light table," I said. "I have my loupe."

"The studio," she said, her voice thin and anxious. She told me to follow her.

We went back through the living room, grabbed our coats, and left by the front door. Anne led the way toward the dark garage, her bright scarf flapping in the darkness. Snow covered the driveway's gravel, and the pretty bulbs that had come up would all be frozen now. Anne went up a set of stairs along the side of the building, and I waited below, unsure.

"There's a rock down there," she called to me. "It's a piece of granite. Get the key out of the back."

I looked at the base of the steps and discovered the rock. Beneath it was a hinged panel, like the one in the cigarette box. This was how the Milton girls all retrieved the key, letting themselves into this room. I took the key up the stairs to Anne, and she opened the door and flipped a switch. The snow that fell in the light that came on was fluttery—flakes that seemed to have lost conviction.

"This is his," Anne said. She stepped into the studio and leaned against a wall, as if she were usually prohibited from entering the room. A mattress covered in a white sheet lay in the center of the floor. If I hadn't seen the photographs the setup would have struck me as odd. The photographs felt far more organic—their play of shadows, the sensual poses, and that he'd managed to create them would have seemed like a feat if you didn't know the girls were drugged, that he could move their lifeless limbs into any configuration he wanted. After the dimness of Anne's house, the room felt overbright, dazzling. A worktable stood against a far wall, and on it was a light box.

"Over there," I said, and I crossed the room to the table.

Anne stayed behind near the door. "I don't usually come here," she said.

I had no fear of William catching us, but Anne seemed worried he might.

"Do you want to see these or not?" I said.

Anne, usually a forceful presence, looked small and helpless in her flimsy scarf. "I don't know if I want to see them," she confessed.

I set the negatives on the surface of the light box. When I looked through the loupe I could enter each image, its shadow and light reversed, the depth of each scene three-dimensional, like a diorama.

"It's definitely her," I said over my shoulder. "I can see her necklace."

Anne made a noise from across the room. It was a sound like a sob or a gasp. She stood against the wall, both hands over her mouth. I had given something away—and I was usually so careful. Anne stared at me and let her hands drop.

She crossed the room in a rush, and I handed her the loupe and she bent to look at the images.

"These weren't taken here," Anne said.

"The light is different, and the wall, and the wood floor," I said. I hoped that if I talked about something else she would forget I'd mentioned the necklace.

"And these at the bottom," I said. "Some field. Do you know where this is?"

Anne's eyes were terrified and bright, her face chalky and lined in the studio lighting.

"The Peterson field," she said.

Anne went to the door of the studio, and I gathered the negatives and followed her. In her hurry she neglected to turn off the light. We went down the snow-covered stairs and then back to the house, Anne scuttling along. Inside she dug through her bag, searching for something.

"I can't find my keys," she said. "The keys to the Jeep."

"Where are we going?" I asked her. "What about the Wellington?"

Anne ignored me. "We'll just take the Mercedes," she said. "It will have to do."

I couldn't understand Anne's reaction to the negatives. We stepped out into the night. The snow had stopped falling but the cold was piercing and viselike. I worried about Anne in her thin scarf, but she seemed even less concerned about the cold air than I was.

We got into the little car and the space filled with our exhalations—white clouds ballooning out from our mouths. The windshield was hoary with ice. Anne turned on the heat and used the wipers to scrape it clear. I trembled in my coat, but as the heater did its work I felt my alertness overtaken by a dreamy malaise. "I have to cancel our plans for dinner," she said, finally. "I'm going to take you home."

"Why are you so upset?" It didn't seem as if she planned to explain anything to me.

The tires slid a bit as we took off from the driveway.

"I'm a fine driver under any circumstances," Anne said, her gloved hand fumbling with the dashboard gauges. "I'm sorry about this. I really am."

"You haven't told me what's wrong," I said.

Anne drove on and passed under dark trees, the moon occasionally appearing between the boughs, the only sound the hum of the engine. Her demeanor had changed—from friendly to preoccupied, almost severe. I felt a slow, building dread. Her gloved hands clung to the wheel. We drove for a long time, it seemed to me, but I had become a poor judge of distance and of time. I grew warm in the little car, my unease building. I watched the side of the road but saw nothing familiar.

"This doesn't seem the way," I said.

"I gave Mary Rae that necklace," Anne said.

I'd admitted I knew about it. I suspected that the next thing Anne would ask me was how I knew. But she didn't.

"She'd seen it in a jewelry store window in Ithaca and told me about it. It was her birthstone, an early birthday gift," Anne said. "The next day she was gone. No one could find her."

I was about to mention that I'd found the necklace in Geoff's car, but then we hit the second patch of ice, and neither of us had much chance to even voice our surprise. From Anne, just a small "Oh." I felt a swirling disorientation as we spun, and then the whipping and cracking of tree branches as the car slid sideways down what seemed to be a hill. We stopped, abruptly, a jolt that took my breath away.

The headlights lit the underside of a pine, its branches laden with snow, and I wasn't sure how we were situated. The engine had stalled and the silence of the woods we'd fallen into was thick, muted by the snowy boughs. Just beyond the headlights' misaligned beams, a shadow flickered, and I imagined the elk and deer from Anne's wall stepping delicately over the limbs we'd broken to nose the debris of the car that enclosed us. I watched, waiting to glimpse their bright eyes at the windshield. My cheek pressed against my own window, and the cold came through, numbing the side of my face. The inside of the car began to fill with our scent—a mix of fear and alcohol, of the beef Wellington that clung to our coats. Anne's beautiful car.

I pushed myself upright, away from the window, and shuffled my legs and shifted my hips. I felt for Anne and found her arm and I shook it and called her name. The two of us were wedged in the sideways-leaning car, the headlights weak beacons. In the dim light inside the car her face leaned close, her eyes hooded. The space was tiny and warm from our bodies. She reached out and moved my hair from my face and cupped my cheek.

"Such a pretty girl," she said. "You're bleeding."

I must have banged my forehead on the window when we stopped. I felt the blood on my face.

"Are you OK?" I said.

"Just fine," she said. She laughed a little. I felt her shift in her seat, and then she made a sound that frightened me—a small cry—and she fell still.

"Anne?" I said. "Anne?"

I dug around in my bag and found my cell phone, but the battery had died. I was as irresponsible as Del. My door was tight against a tree. I had to struggle with Anne's door, and then clamber out over her into the snow, apologizing inanely for having to do it. We'd slid into a ravine. Briefly, I tried to pull Anne from the car, but I couldn't dislodge her and figured that it was best to leave her there and get help. I managed, somehow, to climb out of the ravine, clinging to saplings, sinking into snow up to my knees. Lit only by moonlight, I reached the road.

I had no idea where I was, where Anne had taken me. I had been lulled into a martini stupor, and now Anne was trapped in her little car, with me her only hope of survival. A figure appeared ahead and I called out, believing it was someone walking their dog, or someone who had stepped out into the night for a cigarette. But the person simply stood in the road and my feelings sank as I approached and the figure materialized in the moonlight as Anne, or not Anne, a version of her that seemed to bubble and warp like an image seen through plastic wrap. She wore her skirt and blue sweater and black boots. Her scarf had fallen off, and her bald head shone cold and white, wisps of fair hair remaining in patches. On her hands she wore her black driving gloves. This incarnation of Anne didn't care about her uncovered head, her damp, wrinkled clothing. More sorrowful to me than this evidence of her death was that her plan to come back as a cardinal had not come to fruition, and a terrible hopelessness stole over me, and I began to cry.

Anne appeared to get her bearings, and then began to walk down the road. I knew she wanted me to follow. She wasn't there to offer me any comfort, but she had a mission to fulfill, and I was the only one who could fulfill it. We walked for a length of time that grew to become indiscernible, and I was aware again that I was not paying attention to where we were. As we walked I said that I knew Anne believed William had lied when he denied seeing Mary Rae before she died. I said that he was the last to see her, that the necklace in the photographs proved it. And I told her he was dead, too, and that I was sorry she would have no answers. I had hoped that Mary Rae might reveal to me who her murderer had been, but even the dead had secrets. You were privy only to those they felt you were ready to hear.

"I think I'm frozen," I said. My head had continued to bleed, to flood my collar, which had begun to stiffen.

Incredibly, I did begin to see lights ahead through the trees, and then mailboxes appeared along the side of the road, and Anne stopped. Maybe she'd been leading me to safety after all. We'd arrived at a long set of steps descending to a house below. Beyond the house was a lake, its surface vast and frozen and ringed with lights, a cold wind coming off it. The house at the bottom of the stairs, a wood-shingled cottage, was partially lit by a streetlight. The windows were dark, reflecting the sheen of the snow. Certainly, Anne couldn't have meant to bring me here—to this dark house at the bottom of the long set of treacherous, snow-covered steps?

I kept walking to the next mailbox, this one on the opposite side of the road. The paved driveway rose up, and the house at the end of it was brightly lit. People moved about—a man passing by with an armful of plates, a table in another room filled with people holding glasses of wine, the women's heads tipped back in laughter. I regretted having to interrupt their gaiety, but I went to the door anyway. I would call the phone in Del's apartment and have her find Geoff to come get me.

A woman answered after I rang the bell, her dark hair framing a blurred face. She smiled at me, as if from a distance, and then her expression grew alarmed. She took my arm and led me into the house—brightly painted, filled with books and photographs, rugs and lights. I wondered if I could use her phone, and I was taken to a warm bench by a table and a phone was placed into my hands. The woman hovered over me, and then word must have spread, because a group formed around me, their faces peering at me. Someone brought a damp cloth that she pressed to my head. When it was removed it held a bloom of bright blood.

I managed to dial Del's number and she answered, her voice far off and small. I told her to come get me or to send Geoff. I asked the dark-haired woman where I was, and she took the phone from me and gave an address to Del, who must have written it down.

The woman said I should get my head looked at. "You've got a nasty cut," she said, applying the cloth to my forehead. "Were you in an accident?"

Anne was back in her car in the ravine, and I needed to tell someone, even though in the warmth of this happy house the accident felt unreal. The details of the evening had begun to fade—the martinis that tasted like snow, the beautiful car, Anne herself, her bare head. I might have doubted any of it had happened at all if my coat hadn't smelled of wood smoke, the beef Wellington.

"Yes," I said. "I was."

The woman's eyes darkened with concern. She told someone to call an ambulance. She offered me a change of clothes, and I was led up to a softly carpeted room and helped into a warm shirt, a pair of jeans. Downstairs I was given a glass of water, a plate with a piece of chocolate cake.

"You can't say no to cake on someone's birthday," she said. "It's just not right."

I felt awful I had brought this tragedy to someone's birthday. I took a bite of the cake and the sugar made me queasy. The sea of faces around me shifted and receded. I wanted to lie my head down, and another woman, this one smelling of sandalwood, lifted me onto my feet.

"Are you one of my past lives?" I asked her.

"Don't go to sleep," she said. "Stay awake now."

She walked me up and down the hall and I looked at the photographs—groups of smiling people posing on sloping lawns, on a rock jetty with the sea behind them, on the porch of a large house surrounded by pines.

"Someone needs to get Anne's car out," I said. "And Anne."

This was when the EMTs arrived, a police car. I was asked questions that I couldn't answer. "Where is the car?" a police officer said, his face marked by a growth of beard, his eyes filled with sympathy.

"It's up the road," I said. "I walked here."

I was given a temporary bandage for my head, and I got into the officer's cruiser and we set off to look for the place where Anne's car went off the road. But nothing seemed familiar to me, and the dark, wooded roadside revealed nothing.

"I don't know the area," I said, and I sensed the man was frustrated with me.

It was decided I would be transported to the hospital for assessment, even though I protested that my ride would be arriving. As I was taken off in the ambulance, the group of people gathered at the door, like a send-off. At some point, on a stiff-sheeted gurney, I did fall asleep, and then Del was there. She stood beside me, her face white, her rounded belly protruding from the folds of her sweater.

"What happened?" she asked me.

Beside Del stood Alice, and beside Alice was Randy, the three of them smelling of cigarettes, their eyes dark with worry. "Where's Anne?" Alice asked.

My head had begun to throb, and I closed my eyes.

"She has stitches," Del said to Alice. "She has a concussion."

"What time is it?" I asked.

"Can you tell us what happened?" she said slowly.

I opened my eyes. "I don't know," I said. "Anne was taking me home, and we went off the road."

I pictured Anne's car in the ravine, the snow covering it up, the wet eyes of the dead stag's head mounted on her wall. But these images came as flashes, flat images, like something I'd invented.

"You weren't found anywhere near our house," Del said. "You weren't anywhere near Anne's."

"I know she's dead," I said.

Alice sobbed and covered her mouth. I'd given her another reason to hate me.

Del made a shushing sound and smoothed my stiff hair back from my forehead like our mother used to do when we were sick. I closed my eyes and I held Del's hand and felt the shape of her fingers, the texture of her skin, grateful to be delivered back into the world of the living.

32

I have never had a confidant to whom I could describe the feeling of being in touch with the dead. It's an intimacy that I would have trouble explaining, one that lingers long after I've seen them, after whatever message they relay, though most of the time I am given no message at all. If one of them is standing innocuously outside the post office, or lingering after everyone has left a room, I can try avoidance, but the effects of having seen them cannot be ignored. I experience a sweetness, a warmth like a flush of embarrassed surprise. The encounter's unpleasant if you're the type of person who would rather be alone, who generally keeps far away from others, who allows only a few to get close.

Anne's farewell event was a week after the accident. The authorities had found her car late that evening and hauled it out of the ravine. Her body was transported and taken care of per explicit instructions she'd left with a sister none of the Milton girls knew she had. The sister, Tara, was notified by the authorities after Anne's doctor reported her listed as "next of kin" on Anne's medical records. Tara came to Milton from Saratoga Springs—a foreigner placed in our midst. The Milton girls grieved more for Anne than I'd seen them do for Mary Rae—though Mary Rae's prolonged disappearance before her body was found might have had something to do with that. Anne's death, though it had been imminent, was sudden, and the cause was unexpected. Since Anne had planned to return as a bird, no grave site had been purchased. There was no service. Instead, we were invited to meet at Anne's house.

The girls sat in the living room passing a box of tissues. Joseph, Randy, and their friends stood outside by their cars with cigarettes and beers, and few of them ventured into the house. Del assigned herself the job of chef, preparing small sandwiches and crudités, and Lucie and Alice played hostess, serving on Anne's sterling trays. Geoff was too sad to do much more than sit on the couch beneath the stag heads with his bourbon. Every so often he would sigh and say, "Oh dear, Annie, Annie," and put his face in his hands. Someone would pat his back and refresh his drink. The living room filled with the smoke from the Milton girls' clove cigarettes. Lucie kept pushing the cigarette box's button, and "Smoke Gets in Your Eyes" played so often that someone had to ask her to stop. Alice put the cigarette box on a high shelf.

Del had talked me into going to Anne's. I'd suggested that my lurid injury might make the others upset. And I didn't want to go back there, to the beef Wellington I expected was rotting on the stove top, to the cold glass doors. Del had come to my apartment door almost cautiously. "You *have* to go," she said.

"Why?" I said. "So no one thinks I killed her?"

Del blanched. "Who would think that?" She twisted a wooden toggle button on Mary Rae's hand-me-down duffle coat. "You were the last to see her and the girls will want to know what she said."

It wasn't something she said; it was more what she hadn't said that they wouldn't like. That William had been the last to see Mary Rae alive. Even if I had the necklace to show them, Anne was no longer present to vouch for when it was given to Mary Rae. The girls might be slightly surprised that their friend had given in, envious even. But they wouldn't have understood Anne's shock, her intimation about William. Since the accident I'd thought about Anne's behavior that night, how I'd felt afraid of her, and how she had refused to explain what was wrong or where she was taking me. Now, I reasoned that she'd probably been taking me home, as she claimed. She'd been upset, and drunk, and had gotten turned around somehow.

At Anne's, someone, presumably Tara, had cleaned the house. There was no rotting Wellington. The day was a rare one—infused with sun and the beginnings of warmth. The new snow had melted away. Crocuses came up around Anne's lamppost. There were university friends at the house, and many had taken their drinks out onto Anne's deck. Though it was still chilly, the sun was enough to send them out, like the crocuses. Tara approached me and told me she had my bag.

"It was recovered from the car," she said. She led me up the narrow stairs to the guest bedroom and handed it to me. "I did look through it, I'll admit. I had to find out whose it was. The photographs are, well, *intriguing*."

I explained they weren't my work.

"They're Will's," she said. "Right?"

"They are," I said, surprised that she knew William.

Tara was taller than Anne, more robust, though I didn't know Anne before she was sick. And Tara's eyes were green, not Anne's blue. But there was something about Tara's gaze reminiscent of Anne's, a canniness.

"They were close when he was a student," Tara said. "She talked about him all the time. He helped her out around the house, taking over in a sense when her husband left. But I wish she hadn't gotten mixed up with him. With these photographs, and these girls."

"They're like her family," I said, and then I saw Tara's expression. "Of course they aren't."

"I absented myself," Tara said. "But that girl's death upset her. She called me, drunk, when they found the body."

I looked around at the little guest room, at the narrow old pine bed and at the worktable in the corner. Tara's suitcase was nearby on a chair. I'd only been in this room in the dark, and now the blinds were open, and the view of the backyard revealed. Out there, on All Hallows' Eve, the trees had been strung with little lights.

Tara sat down on the bed and gestured for me to sit as well.

I said I'd met Anne right after Mary Rae died. "And she had me here for dinner the night of the accident," I said. "She saw these photographs, and then she got upset, told me she would have to bring me home."

"She would get confused easily," Tara said, reassuring me. "It was the tumor."

I stood from the bed and walked to the window. "I don't know how we ended up where we did."

"I'm sure this is quite traumatic for you," Tara said.

If I'd taken Anne's offer to stay the night, I would have woken up here, and everything might have been different.

"I feel it's somehow my fault," I said.

Tara looked, for the first time, sad. "It was going to happen soon anyway. And let's face it, she shouldn't have been driving."

She ran her hand over the coverlet, smoothing out the wrinkles we'd left. "Ready?"

Back in the living room the Milton girls held plates of food and talked in subdued tones, passing the tissues. When I came in the room they grew quieter.

"We want to know what she said," Alice said.

"We're just curious about her last night." Jeannette's voice was squeaky from tears.

"It's not like she knew it was her last night," I said.

"She made beef Wellington," Geoff said from his end of the couch. "For God's sake. She must have sensed something."

They were wondering why it hadn't been them with Anne.

In the living room, dust motes mingled with the smoke from everyone's cigarettes. Del stood in the doorway wearing her apron, her hair so blond and fine, it seemed translucent. The fireplace was cold, but the sun streaming through the living-room windows made up for it. Tara walked a few of Anne's colleagues to the door. None of them ventured into the living room or disrupted the Milton girls' interrogation of me.

"I want to know where Billy is," Alice said. "Why isn't he here?"

They looked to me, even though Del, with her expanding midsection, was only a few feet away. "Tahiti?" I said. "Singapore?"

Alice wouldn't be deterred. "What did you and Anne talk about?"

"We talked about William's work," I said. "About the photographs he took of all of you."

Alice's mouth flattened and seemed to seal itself up. The girls readjusted their positions on the couch.

"Why would that be a topic of conversation?" Lucie said.

"We were talking about him," I said. "I found the photographs and I showed them to her."

The girls shared a look.

"Where are they?" Alice blurted out.

I opened my bag, took out the portfolio, and handed it to them.

The Milton girls rose as one from their seats and gathered in the center of the couch. It seemed they had never seen the images, either. They slowly turned the pages, their heads touching, their faces unreadable.

"It doesn't even seem like me," Lucie said. Her face reddened. "I hardly remember."

Alice and Jeanette concurred. "It was like a dream," they said.

Del came into the room and sat on the arm of my chair.

"The secondhand smoke won't be good for the baby," Alice snapped.

Del wrapped her arms around herself, as if to ward it off.

"Anne told me," I said. I caught Del's eye. "Sleeping pills."

The Milton girls slowed their page-flipping.

"What are you talking about?" Lucie said.

"You've lost the plot," Kitty said.

Geoff roused himself and inched forward on the couch.

"That's ridiculous," Alice said. She grabbed her hair in her hands and twisted it into a long rope. "I mean I don't remember really falling asleep," she said. "I remember waking up in the guest room."

"Anne made breakfast," Kitty said.

"I had chocolate chip pancakes," Alice said quietly.

I was surprised they hadn't discussed these experiences before. Had jealousy made them guarded?

Del left the arm of my chair and sat beside Alice on the couch. "They drugged you," Del said. "The two of them."

At Del's dinner party, the night before the asylum trip, I'd been confused, fighting the sleep that overtook me despite my efforts to hold it at bay. I felt as if I'd had sex, though the details escaped me.

Tara stepped into the doorway from the hall. "I think it's time you leave," she said, firmly. "Anne is gone. You've paid your respects."

This might have produced renewed crying earlier in the day, but now it did not. We got up, Del and I and the Milton girls. Del helped Geoff from the couch. He stood in the center of the room and looked around, as if he'd lost something. I tugged on his arm and he came along with us, reluctantly. "That's it?" he said.

Had Geoff been involved in the sleeping pill scenario? His befuddled air, his sorrow, seemed to reveal that he had not. We left the house slowly, funneling through the front door, down the stone steps to the yard, aware that it was probably for the last time. Randy and Joseph leaned on the hoods of their cars. Randy approached Del, and she told him she'd call him later. He turned away, dejected, scuffing his worn-down boots. Del helped Geoff into the car and got behind the wheel. My head ached, and I couldn't drive. I opened the door to the backseat, but it occurred to me that the girls might fill in part of the mystery of the night with Anne.

"Where's the Peterson field?" I asked.

The girls, gathered on the lawn in a clutch of winter coats and long, dark hair, turned their white faces toward me, stricken.

Joseph pushed himself off the hood of his car, accidentally kicking one of his glass empties into the driveway. "They found Mary Rae in the trailer there," he said. And then, to the girls, soothingly, "She probably didn't know that."

I hadn't known. I got inside the car and, as Del pulled away, Anne's farmhouse receded through the back window.

"The plot thickens," I said.

But did it matter anymore? Even if William had murdered Mary Rae, he would no longer be a threat to anyone.

Del flashed her eyes at me in the rearview mirror. Geoff sat slumped in the passenger seat. Poor Geoff.

Tara had turned on the lights inside Anne's house, and the Milton girls stood on the yellow grass, in the spring mud, like statues in the game of freeze tag we'd play as children. The town was a place to escape from, and in some ways they understood that and in others they were destined to remain prisoners—marrying the local boys, having babies who would grow up to fulfill the quota of the town's tragic losses. On Anne's lawn they made a tableau. Geoff's car tires reached the asphalt of the road and left the gravel drive behind.

33

I called my mother and told her I wouldn't be coming home for Easter. She said, "Oh," and then the rusty spring on the screen door to the terrace grated, and the little finches that came around my grandfather's old birdfeeder made their piping sound. "I'm sorry," she said. She pulled out one of the iron chairs—the metal feet scraping against the slate—and sat down with her morning coffee.

Del would be there, I said. "She can stand in for the two of us." I laughed, thinking of Del's pregnancy, and my mother's reaction to it, but when my mother asked me what was so funny I said, "Oh, nothing." I wondered if she could hear my sullenness. I didn't know for sure if Del and William had been together, if I'd killed an innocent man—loyal to me and unconnected to Mary Rae's death—or a man who'd slept with my sister and killed a girl who by all accounts was devoted to him. Until I knew more, I decided to believe my sister.

Geoff began his quiet pacing at night again, perhaps in his grief over Anne. The breeze rubbed the elm's branches, bright with leaves, against my window. Geoff's footsteps shuffled across the wood floor, followed by Suzie's clicking. Once in a while I'd hear something suppressed—a moan or a cough. And then the pacing. A few times I considered going to his door but lost my nerve. We had come full circle, back to a place from which I had believed we'd been freed.

Sleepless in bed, I listened for William's footsteps on the stairs. Lover? Predator? Startled by a noise, I caught sight of myself in the little mirror by the door—my hair disheveled, my eyes blank, the awful mark from the accident branding my forehead. I went to classes but ignored the boys who seemed to surround me like bright coins. Back in my apartment, I burrowed into my bedclothes and read through Mary Rae's last journal—sifting through the pages, obsessed and searching for clues; her handwriting, girlish and rounded, its own sad reminder of a future she'd once planned. With William. The baby. He'd been the last to see her. Had she told him she hadn't kept her appointment for the abortion? How would he have reacted? Had they met at the trailer? Wouldn't there be traces of William there? Del and I had scrubbed the concrete floor of my grandfather's barn with the borax, erasing the blood, tossing the hay over the spot.

Though the Miltons hadn't told me where the Peterson field was, I had my own sources. I called Jimmy at the Agway. It seemed the field could be accessed by an old railroad line that ran near the store, a line that had only recently been turned into a nature path. I met Jimmy at the Agway one Sunday afternoon. He wore a red ball cap pulled low, a T-shirt, and jeans. It was his day off, and he took my hand as if I were his girlfriend.

"The path's through here. The field's a ways down," he said. "It's a hike."

"The weather is nice enough," I said.

Jimmy was hesitant. But I assured him I only wanted to look from afar.

"That's probably all you'll get," he said. "A look."

The place was a crime scene—I understood that. We started down the path. The old ties had been taken up, and loose gravel marked the way through the woods. Every so often the sun broke through the canopy of trees. We passed families out walking, the little girls picking violets. The air was crisp, and snow lay beneath the low-hanging pine boughs. We crossed a trestle over a swift-running brook, and small birds darted about. Soon there were no more people. I felt as if I were in the middle of nowhere. Jimmy walked quietly by my side, nervous, shy. He wasn't sure what to make of me or my interest in Mary Rae, and I almost wished I could tell him that she'd appeared to me and asked me to do this, but even that wasn't exactly true.

Soon we emerged at a place where the path opened and fields stretched for miles on both sides. The sun was high and bright, and Jimmy stopped walking and pointed.

"Up there," he said.

I could see the rise of the field, the grass waving, the bluets and buttercups, and then along the line of the woods batches of day lilies. If he hadn't pointed it out to me, if the sun hadn't hit the Silver Streak's metal body, I would never have been able to spot it. I slipped my hand from his, and I stepped off the path and ducked beneath the farmer's barbed-wire fence. Jimmy shook his head at me—a caution not to go, maybe a little angry that I'd lied to him. It didn't take long to cross the field. A path led beside the trees that rimmed it. Every so often I looked back at Jimmy, and he waved his arm— whether in greeting or to call me back, I wasn't sure.

In winter, when Mary Rae came here in her down coat, the snow would have been high, though along the tree line where I walked now there might have been less. Even so, she would have had to break off through the field to reach the trailer, as I did. The Silver Streak stood beneath an oak, below the field's rise, and hidden from view from the path. I'd thought there'd be yellow crime scene tape cordoning the trailer off, but there was nothing—only a trailer's rusted hull, and the concrete blocks that formed steps up to the door. The detectives must have gotten everything they needed. I took a step up to the door, turned the knob, and pushed the door open. The inside was nearly the same as I'd seen it—though the mattress on the narrow bed was gone, and the interior was empty of its contents—the tattered drapes, the clothes that once hung on the rod. The kerosene lantern was gone, the clothespins. The shelf above the bed was empty, and the little window was broken. I guessed kids came up here, too, and, afraid to approach the trailer, threw rocks.

Despite the changes, this was the place. This was where Mary Rae had died. During the spring and summer months her body had decomposed. Now the pollen and new grass smells filled the trailer. Hornets had begun to build a nest in a corner. The floor was soft with rot. Soon the whole thing would slump into the soil. There would be nothing I could find that the investigators didn't, yet I closed my eyes, listening. Why would she come here in the dead of winter? Had she made the trek, heartsick, and shut herself in the trailer to let the cold consume her? Somewhere I'd read that hypothermia often caused confusion, that people experiencing it shed their clothing. Maybe she'd given in and let William take his photographs, then found that wasn't enough to win him back. If so, William played only a small part in her death—he'd confessed to not loving her—and she'd done the rest.

As I stood there someone called. It was Jimmy. My name echoed over the fields, bouncing off the line of trees. I left the trailer and went to the rise of the field where I could see his red cap, and I waved, and he waved back—this time clearly signaling for me to return. I stood at the peak, and I turned to take in the view behind me. The field led down to another large crop of woods, but I was high enough to see beyond them to a house—the yellow siding of Anne's Windy Hill farmhouse, miles away, but visible. Mary Rae had been here above us that October evening of the All Hallows' Eve party. I'd imagined her in the line of trees, waiting to emerge, and I'd been partly right.

Jimmy met me in the middle of the lower field. He said one of the local officers had approached him on the trail and asked him questions, and he'd told the truth—that one of Mary Rae's friends wanted to see the place where she died. The officer had seen me walking along the tree line and told Jimmy it wasn't safe for me to be there.

When I asked Jimmy what he meant, he shrugged. "I guess he means there's a murderer loose."

The sun dipped behind a bank of clouds, and I felt a chill as we started back along the trail.

"I had to give your name," he said. "I hope that's all right."

"That's fine," I said, although I'd lied about being Mary Rae's friend, and the officer would probably find out.

Jimmy escorted me back to Geoff's car. He tried to talk me into a movie, or dinner, but I told him I couldn't. He leaned on the car and crossed his arms. "You're a cagey one," he said. "But I'm a good sport."

I kissed him on the cheek and drove the long way back to Ithaca, thinking about his blue eyes below the brim of his cap, the lovely curve of his arms in his T-shirt.

THAT NIGHT I awoke to footsteps on the stairs, the sound like the clomping of William's heavy boots. They paused outside my door, and I waited, breathless. The knob turned, but I'd locked the door, and the footsteps retreated down the stairs. I lay in bed, holding my breath, straining to hear the front door open and close, and then rigid with fear, unable to sleep for a long time after. Was this what it was like to be haunted, to have someone return from the dead for you? The next morning Del was at my door, frantically knocking. I opened it, half-asleep, and she pushed past me into the room and slammed the door behind her.

"Are you OK?" I asked.

"I saw him," she whispered. She wore a pair of leggings and a misbuttoned work shirt, Randy's name embroidered on the pocket.

"What are you talking about?" I said.

She went to the window and peered around the frame. "I saw him," she said, her voice strained. "He's out there."

I joined her by the window, and she pulled me back.

"Nothing's there," I said. It was true, William wasn't in his usual place.

"He *was* there," Del said. "He was."

Del's face was drained of color, the shade of her platinum hair. I didn't know what to say. I'd never confessed to seeing the dead to anyone, not even to Del. I led her back downstairs, and she pointed to the hat stand.

"He had it on," she said.

William's beaver-skin hat was missing from the vestibule. I had never packed it. I'd left it there, almost afraid to touch it, tangible evidence of William's existence, almost more than I could bear. Geoff must have tired of seeing it and thrown it out. It had been months since William's disappearance. To wonder now if he was alive was irrational.

The spring sunlight lit the vestibule's fading wallpaper, including the edges where it had begun to peel. Del had left her apartment door open, and she followed me inside. I pulled the door closed and locked it behind us.

"What did you see?" I asked, firmly.

"I saw him standing across the street," Del said. She went over to the small table by the window where she'd abandoned her breakfast— an English muffin, a cup of tea—and she slid into her chair.

"No," I said, angrily. "*That night.*"

Del picked up the muffin and set it back on her plate.

"His eyes were closed."

"Did you feel for a pulse?"

"Of course I wouldn't touch him! There was blood, around his head. What are you saying?" Del stood. She pulled Randy's shirt tight around her.

Perhaps I had *lost the plot*. Alive? Dead? I could no longer tell the difference.

Del moved over to one of the wing chairs and fell into it. "He couldn't have gotten out of there. We had his phone," she said.

"It might not even be him," I said. I tried to keep my voice calm. "Lots of people have odd hats. Even you." I laughed, and reminded her of the day she'd been trying on the hats. I sat down in the chair across from her. "Why don't you finish your breakfast."

"It was him," Del said. She picked at the tapestried upholstery, pulling threads loose.

I waited for her to insist she wasn't crazy, but she did not. She decided we should visit Sybil Townsend in the encampment. Partly to appease her, and partly because I felt in need of guidance and lacked anyone else to offer it, I agreed. I warned Del she couldn't tell Sybil the truth. "We can't really trust her," I said.

We walked the same route we'd taken the night of the snowstorm with William. Now, window boxes of pansies decorated the houses' front porches.

"What do we ask her?" Del kept so close beside me, she bumped my shoulder.

"Let me talk." I had no idea what I would say. Could Del see William as I did? I had considered that possibility when she'd gotten sick as a teenager. Could she have been following the dead around town? Conversing with them? This seemed unbelievable, and I told myself it was wishful thinking—but maybe she couldn't accept the voices she heard and the people she saw who asked her to follow. Maybe her breakdown had been a result.

The encampment path was muddy. The brook had swelled its banks, and the rank mud smell was almost overpowering. Under the pine shade patches of snow remained, the tarps stained and faded in comparison. Daylight revealed the camp for what it was—harsh, dirty. Without the cover of darkness and the enchantment of the strung twinkling lights, the place lost any aspect of magic. No one glanced up to spot us or wave hello. The people moved between tents, or traversed the narrow paths, bundled in grubby winter clothes. I hesitated, but Del tugged on my arm and we set off farther down the path, farther into the smoke from the fires, the odor of rotting garbage. Some of the inhabitants, wrapped in blankets, came out of their tents. They stood in front of the entrance flaps, stern and protective. A man approached us and shouted at us, demanding to know what we wanted.

"We're looking for Sybil Townsend," Del said.

The man, older, wearing mismatched gloves, marched in place in the mud, the mud squelching around his shoes.

"What do you want with her?" he asked, like a sentinel. His breath was foul, tainted by whiskey and coffee and bad teeth.

"I want to talk with her," Del said.

The old man gave us a strange look with his head to the side. He was blind in one eye, the color a vague and milky blue. With the good eye he was looking us up and down. I didn't know why Del believed she would be recognized.

"She knows me," Del said.

I smelled something cooking, a heavy scent of fatty broth.

"She's not here," the man said, roughly. He turned from us and walked away down the path, his shoes sinking into the mud. Del began to follow him.

"What do you think you're doing?" he shouted into the air ahead of him. He seemed astounded.

People put their heads out from under the tarps. Tent flaps opened, and I glimpsed the insides, the piles of bedding, the low-lit lamps. From one tent came the spicy scent of Constant Comment tea. "You're insufferably persistent," the man said, continuing to tromp away from us.

Once, he may have lectured children this way as a severe parent or a schoolteacher.

"Can you tell us where she's gone, then?" Del begged.

The man stopped. He was waiting for us to go. Neither of us moved. And then his shoulders seemed to relax, and Sybil Townsend approached, picking her way along the path toward us, chuckling.

"Oh, I can't hide from you two," she said.

Del hugged Sybil. In the daylight she was younger than I'd thought. She was missing a tooth. I regretted agreeing to come. What could she possibly relay? Still, I let her lead us down the path to a tarp stretched over wooden posts, and we sat beneath it at a small table, the legs of the chairs sinking into the earth, Sybil in her layer of brightly colored shawls.

"I had a shop once," she told me. "I sold books, and incense, and that sort of thing." The breeze buffeted the tarp like a parachute. A distant radio played jazz. "I was chased out by the townspeople," she said, her laugh deep and rheumy.

Del fidgeted, waiting for me to fulfill my end of our pact.

"Del has seen someone," I said. I didn't say she thought she'd seen someone. I didn't want her to doubt herself.

"Why are you really here?" Sybil Townsend said. "Don't you have other means of discovering the truth?"

I wanted to say I'd tried everything I could. I was confused. The dead had secrets, but no dead were offering them up to me. Around us a small group had gathered. They began to make a queue outside the tarp's posts. Sybil smiled a mysterious smile that might have served her well in her little shop. I wanted to slap her. My last conversation with Reverend Earline, I'd wanted to know why my mother visited the spirit circles, who she wanted to hear from, and Reverend Earline had said a man was trying to reach her. He was a suicide—a special case—someone who hadn't been able to abandon the lower astral plane. Mr. Parmenter. My mother was the woman he'd been in love with, the woman who'd never shown up at the Stardust Motel. I was the one to put this together, but Reverend Earline saw the recognition, the shock, on my face.

"We don't always hear the things we want to hear from the dead," Reverend Earline had said.

"Especially when they have to speak through people like you," I'd said.

Like the old game of telephone—a message passing from one person to the next becoming distorted and muddled, the dead pretending to be someone they were not, the messengers unable to tell the difference. In my great-grandfather's manuals "A Student" made it clear that the practice of contacting spirits through mediums was prone to error.

"What are these people doing?" Del said.

Beneath the tarp we could see the boots of people lining up in the slush.

"They're here for your sister," Sybil Townsend said. She stood, her large bosom heaving under her shawls. She led Del out from under the tarp just as a woman in a fleece jacket, her hair dirty and her face lined, ducked under and sat down across from me. She took my hand and gave me an imploring look across the table. Her hand was chapped, the palms calloused.

"I want to know about my father," she said. "He was living in California."

The light wavered around me. Water dripped from the fringe of the tarp, overbright and shimmering. I pushed back from the table and reeled with anger out from under the tarp and through the encampment.

Del was in Sybil Townsend's tent seated in a camp chair. I pulled Del out of the tent, down the mud path to the creek. My anger receded as we climbed toward the road, and I breathed, deeply, once we'd left the place behind altogether. You couldn't expect the dead to provide answers. Those lingering behind, trapped on the lower astral plane, were filled with desire. They only wanted what they'd always wanted. William had stood at the curb multiple times. I'd told myself that he always appeared the same, his outfit the last he'd worn in life, like Mary Rae, but that wasn't true. Sometimes he wore his corduroy coat, his green sweater, his faded jeans. Sometimes a gray sweater, khaki pants I'd never seen him wear before.

34

Del was quiet on the walk home. The sidewalk was bright with tree pollen, and the warmth of the sun was like a balm. As we approached the house, she slowed and seemed apprehensive.

"I suspected you saw things," she said. "After, you know, that summer."

It was easier to let her believe in what she'd seen. It was a relief to have her understand what that was like.

We went right into her apartment, and I helped her pack for Connecticut. She'd asked me again to come with her, but I told her I couldn't.

"I have classes to finish," I said.

"Will he follow me?" Del asked. I'd loaned her a suitcase, and she folded hand-me-down sweaters and T-shirts from the Milton girls.

"No," I told her. "He won't."

At first, she'd surprised me by making plans to go home on her

own, but now I was glad. I guessed my mother and Del had kept up
a regular conversation, regained ground they'd lost, and now I was
on the outside of things. I drove Del to the airport, and said good-
bye in the car. Before she got out she handed me a folded piece of
paper. "It's Alice's phone number," she said. I put the paper in my bag,
but we both knew I wouldn't use it. I watched Del enter the airport's
glass doors and had a fleeting, childish resentment that she was going
and I was not.

True, I wouldn't have to endure my mother's elaborate preparations for our arrival—the cut-glass bowl of pastel mints, her suit and
her pumps and her hairdo. My grandmother would hold court in a
chair in the living room, talking about the past as if it were the present. I didn't understand how my mother could continue to live in that
place. The old house hadn't fallen into disrepair; my mother wouldn't
let that happen. It was simply deserted; its many rooms filled with
dust, were cleaned, and slowly refilled with dust. Dust clung to chair
skirts and caught in bedspread fringe. Dust filmed my grandfather's
books, Sarah's and Leanne's yearbooks, and my English Lit paper-
backs. Dust coated my grandmother's antiques, Leanne's collection of porcelain butter plates, and Sarah's sea glass.

In my and Del's room the shelves were bare save for an odd stuffed
animal or two won from the Catholic church carnival, a wooden box
with two miniature drawers filled with old earrings and periwinkle
shells.

"Do you even go into the rooms upstairs?" I'd asked my mother
once.

"I sleep upstairs." She'd yanked open a kitchen drawer, hunted
through matchbooks, twine, and dried-up pens. "I'm up and down
those stairs twenty times a day."

The old neighborhood housed the same old families. The same old
children, grown into adults, returned for visits with their own children.
But there was less socializing and a kind of closed-off feeling to the
neighbors' homes tucked behind their privet hedges. The cocktail

parties on summer patios, my mother's friends mixing their whiskey sours—all of that had been eradicated by divorce and alcoholism. The flight from Ithaca to Hartford had a stop in Philadelphia, and I assumed my mother would tell Del to take a cab to the house. By that time, Sarah, who'd been waiting with her new baby to see Del, would have already left. Leanne, more patient, and childless, would have progressed to her second or third sherry. They'd have eaten pizza from the Greek place in town, the same pizza from the same place we had ordered out from when we were children, where we'd meet with friends as young teenagers. The pizza was heavy with tomatoes and strewn with oregano. The ancient jukebox played "A Whiter Shade of Pale," and the boys sat red-faced and gangly in the booths, while we girls made chains out of chewing gum wrappers.

I couldn't imagine the taste of that pizza without remembering David Pinney, how his death had stained everything that came after. When a boy leaned over to kiss me in a dark car it would be David Pinney's lips and the pressure of his hand on my breast. I'd sequestered myself in the tomb of a house during my teen and young adult years, sealed off from anything that might trigger my memory. And what was that memory, exactly? Whichever version of the past might not match Del's. I had rid the world of a violent boy, but she once claimed she knew what she was doing, that the sex had been her idea. "That doesn't make what he did right," I'd said. And at the look on my face, she'd changed her story to match with mine.

IN MY APARTMENT, the little travel clock let me know that by now my mother would have met Del by the door, would have given Del one of her usual hugs, applying a faint and cursory pressure with her sinewy arms. My mother would have invited Del to sit down in one of the wing chairs, and would have tried to appear as if she weren't evaluating her—jumping to gather drinks from the kitchen, to offer snacks, to close the windows so the breeze wouldn't blow the napkins around the room. My mother would be kind and accommodating, and would exhaust herself with the effort.

Del's pregnancy would be immediately apparent, and my mother would know I had slipped in my responsibilities in more ways than one. She would suspect this was the reason I hadn't come, and it had been, originally. I didn't want to face my mother's disappointment in me. Since it was late, my mother would soon usher Del into our old bedroom, where the cold, spring night air would come in, smelling of forsythia and sap. The spread would have been turned down on one of the twin beds, the same spread that had been on the beds for years—white, with raised threads that made intricate designs on your skin if you slept on them.

On Easter morning at the old house, everyone would leave for Mass at the Sacred Heart Church in town, the whole family in two pews. Sarah and Leanne would skip their own church services and come with their husbands, and with the baby. Of course Del's pregnancy might alter this tradition a bit. I couldn't be sure about my mother's reaction—if she'd wonder aloud about the possibility of getting rid of it, or if she'd call our father to consult.

Most of my predictions were proven correct when Del called me a week later and recounted everything, nearly exactly as I'd imagined it, except for one startling revelation: she would stay in Connecticut with our mother. They'd had a long talk Easter evening, she said, sitting on our mother's bed. Our mother thought it would be easier to have the baby there. She had offered the support I had not, and while I had to admit that staying in Connecticut was a more practical option—the availability of our sister's gently used baby furniture, our mother as experienced babysitter—I was suspicious. Why would our mother with her newfound freedom from child rearing, and the drudgery she so hated when we were young, agree to help Del? Del said that they went out shopping at Nordstrom and A Pea in the Pod, and I pictured Del laying out each outfit on the twin beds in our old bedroom. I was reminded of the days when we'd choose our clothes for the first day of school. The whole scene was so redolent of the past, I felt a wave of sadness. How leery I was of any attempt to recapture lost happiness. I'd learned that it was impossible, an endeavor pit-holed with disappointment, and I steered clear.

"Who will break the news to Randy?" I asked her. "I hear he's got the trailer all set up with a crib."

Del closed a door and the hush, as if she'd shut herself in a closet, dampened her voice. "I wish you'd leave there," she said.

She told me she'd sent me something, and the next day I received a small package that contained Sister's missal. As a child I had often slept with the missal; it had been a comfort. I'd held the small book in my hands or tucked it under my pillow. During the day I knew I would have to hide it from Del, who sought out anything I valued. I'd slipped the missal beneath the bottom shelf of the built-ins against the wall, a white-painted shelf that lifted like the lid of a box. Like Mary Rae's hiding spot for her journals. Del must have realized how I'd know where Mary Rae's journals had been and explored my hiding place once she got home.

I took the little volume out of the envelope. Its cover was mildewed, and as I thumbed the gilt pages, so thin and fragile, most of them stuck together. I turned on the desk lamp and sat down at the table and looked again at the illustrations with a sense of having merged with the past, the younger version of myself somewhere, living out her days. On the inside cover, my great-aunt had placed her signature, and the date, 1943. She'd died at twenty-nine, in 1962; she'd been about ten years old. She'd written in the book with pencil, but underneath I noted there'd been another name, one erased, presumably by Martha Mary. I pulled the light closer and saw the etched-in name: Rose. The missal had been Rose's, but Martha had claimed it as her own. I understood that. Someone had given Rose the missal, and Martha had wanted it, coveted it, and taken it, as I had.

In her phone call Del had reminded me of the pink inflatable rabbit she received one Easter as a child. It had been nearly as big as she was, and she'd taken to sleeping with it each night. It sprang leaks, and by morning it was out of air. We had to keep blowing it up, and our mother patched it with black electrical tape. "How sad for me," Del said.

Would Del start another life with our mother and Leanne and Sarah, a life of babies and tending and birthdays and occasions for celebrating? During the years she'd been at the Institute, and then at Ashley Manor, the old house had been as much mine as my mother's. We'd had our routine—tea in the Brown Betty pot, toast with orange marmalade in the afternoons. Like two spinsters, we'd spent our evenings reading under throw blankets. Would Del heat the water for the tea, open the back door and feed the gray cat? Would she move back into our old room, sleep in her long-empty bed, hang her new clothes in the closet where I'd left my summer dresses? My mother and I were often at odds, but we'd slipped easily into a pattern of life together. Would Del now step into my place and reestablish my and my mother's old routine? And if she did, what was left for me? I felt a strange sadness, much as Del must have felt remembering her dependence on the pink plastic bunny, bandaged again and again with the shiny black tape.

Through the small window the sky is gray with burden, and out of that brushed charcoal shade the snow tumbles, delicate and dizzying. The flakes make a sound like pinging on the metal roof, and I try to imagine each cluster of crystals—hexagonal plate, crystal with broad branches, stellar crystal, ordinary dendritic, fernlike—like the images classified in the book we found on Grandfather's shelves. Dark boards, a gilt snowflake on the cover, and inside thousands of photographs, the images so beautiful we spent hours turning the pages.

Snow Crystals by W. A. Bentley. Where is that book now?

The trailer is empty, everything is still and cold. Outside, the silence is broken by the sound of footsteps in snow, and then the door thrown open and someone struggling in with a burden, breathing with exertion. Mary Rae, wrapped in her blanket, her hair trailing dark along the floor. It is a man, lumbering in heavy winter clothes, who places her on the bed, who takes the blanket from her body, and sets a pile of clothing nearby, neatly folded—jeans, wool, sweater, bra. The down coat. She wears her panties, nylon bikinis, twisted, on backward, clearly a fumbled attempt at getting dressed. He stands over her for a long moment, but not long enough to hint at any regret, before he huffs—yes, huffs, as if he's angry, and then, his bulk hidden in the winter coat, he trundles out, taking the blanket. His footsteps recede. The thin layer of ice breaks. Snow pings gently on the roof. I sit down on the edge of the bed and watch her expel breath—a soft filament of moisture that rises from her lungs.

35

I was certain that once the semester was over I would leave the apartment. I emptied the bureau and stacked my clothes on the floor. I piled my books and papers. I was waiting for more from William, waiting for him to make some move, whatever that might be. I began to look for him at the Korean place, walking up College Street, or through the Commons, mingling with students. We were playing a game. I wouldn't leave the apartment until the game was finished.

One afternoon I came across the old flyer of Mary Rae, pinned to a pole on State Street. And, like the first time I'd touched one tacked onto the Wegmans bulletin board, when I grabbed it down, I saw the Silver Streak, the snow falling beyond the window. I was almost sure that William had left Mary Rae there to die. Though I hadn't seen his face, I recognized the angry huffing sound he'd made. That was William's impatience, his irritation with the sequence of events, his inability to start over, his helplessness.

We'd both done terrible things. After David Pinney's death, when it seemed I wouldn't be caught, my sentence came from the astral world. When Del was admitted to the hospital, I worried that I would emerge unscathed once again, and then I worried about the repercussions of emerging unscathed. How would the balance be righted?

The weather grew warmer and people shed their clothes, revealing whitish limbs. They sunbathed on the flat rocks in the gorge. At night they sat on balconies and drank, lining their empties on the wooden railings. And then exams were over. I was restless, ready to leave, but so much remained unresolved, and I didn't feel I had a place to go. One evening, Del called.

"It will be summer soon," she said. "The Spiritualists will be back."

She laughed, pretending she was joking, but I suspected she thought this might really lure me home.

"She's spring cleaning," Del said, about our mother.

She told me that our sisters came over to the old house and stood around complaining while our mother made a big pile for the League of Mercy.

"If you don't take these things now, they will be gone," our mother said.

Boxes came up from the basement, down from the attic. One full of ice skates, the white leather cracked, the blades dull. Out of others came the relish trays; old spectator pumps; a seersucker sport coat; a fox stole with the head intact, its tiny teeth still vicious; piles of old high school texts with illegible penciled marginalia; heating pads with frayed wires; eyeglass frames missing the prescription lenses; my mother's discarded handbags; the dresses she wore to her senior prom, her spring wedding, a formal dinner, a cocktail party on New Year's. Spread out on the living room floor were years of our family's lives—mildewed Barbie doll clothes, snowsuits and red plastic boots, gloves and hats I could donate to the people in the encampment. My mother discarded these things with vigor, her eyes shining, her movements quick.

"I hardly know her," Del said.

I didn't want to live with my mother and Del, with a baby that might or might not have been my husband's. My sisters, my father—they had separate lives. Del mentioned Detective Thomson, briefly. He was reviewing old evidence—especially a long, blond hair found on David Pinney's body. He'd come by and "sat and chatted, as usual," Del said. She'd done her bland replies, her struck-dumb stare.

"He must have gotten bored with me," she said. "He asked when you were coming home."

But our mother did not want to be bullied. She called her attorney, who discovered the strand of hair contained no root or follicle and that conclusive DNA could not be acquired from it. "Lots of long-haired blond girls in town six years ago," the attorney said.

I wasn't sure that would be the end of Detective Thomson. I couldn't sleep, and some of the disturbance seemed to come from worry about where I'd end up.

Then, one afternoon I came in from the grocery store and my mother's travel alarm clock was missing. I glanced around the room, wondering what else might be gone. I opened a bureau drawer and sifted through my clothing. Then I knocked on Geoff's door, and he stuck his head out, his hair dirty and wild.

"Did you borrow my clock?" Geoff's apartment was oppressively dark, though it was a bright, spring day outside.

"If I borrowed it, I would have asked first, correct?" he said.

"Where could it be?" I said.

Suzie thrust her head out from behind Geoff's pant leg, and he blocked her from leaving the apartment. "How should I know?" he said, closing the door on me.

The next day my mirror was gone, and the day after that the lamp that sat on my end table. I felt part of some art installation, the contents within the frames dissolving piece by piece. I told Geoff I wanted to change the locks. This time when he came to the door the window blinds were open in the apartment behind him. He'd washed his hair.

"That's a chore," he said. He yanked Suzie's leash and stepped around me into the landing.

"Someone is coming into my apartment," I said.

Geoff moved to the stairs and started his way down. "Are you sure you didn't misplace these things?"

"A mirror?" I said. I found I was shouting, and I'd never gotten angry at Geoff before.

He paused on the stairs. "No need to raise your voice."

My heart dipped with remorse. I watched him slip out of the front door, dragging Suzie behind him.

The next morning, rubber-soled shoes bounded up the stairs. Unless Geoff had gotten a new pair of shoes, it was a stranger. Whoever it was hesitated at the top step and knocked on my door. Out the window, parked beneath the bright buds of the elm, was a police cruiser. I felt entirely alone and vulnerable. I was sure William's body had been discovered, the film in his pocket developed. Somehow, I had been identified. I found I couldn't summon the strength with which I'd faced Detective Thomson, but those times my mother had been with me.

I would pretend I wasn't home. But the knocking continued, and Geoff came out into the upstairs hall and told whoever it was that I had been there earlier.

"Perhaps she's in the shower," Geoff added.

The knocking was louder, and there wasn't a possibility for me to slip away—no escape route out a window, down a trellis. I opened the door, resigned, and was surprised to see Officer Paul. In the daylight, his expression was kind. Despite his large ears, he resembled the ruggedly handsome men in old cigarette ads. I understood why Del had found him attractive. He had on his uniform, the one I'd thought was a costume at Anne's cookout.

"Are you Martha? I wonder if you have a few minutes?" he said. His voice was soft. He smelled of shaving cream. He introduced himself as Officer Donaldson, and I peered at his badge, confused.

"The little kids call me Officer Paul," he said. "The others do it to be funny."

"I'm sorry I didn't answer the door. I was asleep. I was up late last night, packing."

And I showed him the piles of clothing and the boxes. He stepped into the door frame, but he didn't come inside.

"You're probably wondering why I was walking around in the Peterson field," I said.

"We get morbid people up there poking around," he said. Then he waved his hands. "Not to suggest that about you, of course."

"I'm a photographer," I said. "Abandoned places interest me."

Officer Paul placed his hands on his hips. His belt was thick and slung low, weighted down by his holstered gun. "I don't want to keep you," he said. "I'm really inquiring about William Bell."

"What do you need to know?" I'd managed to keep a level tone, though I felt weak with fear. I sounded so much like my mother I wanted to laugh, but of course I knew not to. "Can I get you anything? Water? Tea?"

"No thank you. Is William Bell at home?"

I tried to gauge from his expression what he suspected, whether he already knew William was gone and was feigning ignorance, whether he wanted to find him at home for some other reason. "I'm sorry," I said. "He doesn't live here anymore."

"Some of the girls mentioned you two got married," he said. I'd long since removed the ring.

"We separated," I said. "It didn't work out."

"I'm sorry," Officer Paul said, and I believed he truly was.

"Can I help you with anything?" I said.

He explained that he was investigating the Swindal case, following up on a few things.

"It's so sad," I said. "I guess it wasn't an accident, if you're investigating?"

Officer Paul stepped away from the door toward the stairs. "We aren't disclosing the cause of death yet."

"Well, I'm glad you're looking for clues."

He thanked me for my time and began to descend the stairs, and then he stopped, and turned back.

"You wouldn't know where I might find him?" he said. "I have some questions for him."

Officer Paul's radio issued a burst of static, and his presence transformed the familiar stairwell to reveal the worn banister, the railings' peeling paint, the stair treads scraped of their varnish. "I haven't spoken to him," I said. "Not for months."

It felt wonderful to tell the truth.

Officer Paul seemed convinced. Maybe that was all it took—a statement that wasn't rearranged to stand in for the truth. He jogged down the stairs, and I was grateful that William's hat was gone from the hook at the bottom.

Once Officer Paul had left, Geoff came out of his apartment. I had my door open. I sat on the floor, packing William's things, eager to get them out of the place, but uncomfortable handling them. Geoff leaned in the doorway.

"What in God's name was that?" he said. "Did you call him to report your theft?"

I folded a pair of corduroys, the knees worn, feeling disoriented. "He was looking for William."

Geoff didn't come in. From the doorway he rolled a cigarette and handed it to me, like a peace offering. I didn't have the heart to refuse it. Then he rolled one for himself. William's things were scattered about. We smoked quietly, tipping our ashes into a teacup.

"How did Anne ever meet the girls from town?" I said.

Geoff exhaled. "She was always looking for models for her paintings," he said. "And I'd see a pretty girl in town, and start a conversation—get around to asking if she wanted to pose."

"For Anne," I said.

I hadn't seen a lot of Anne's work—the one nude of Mary Rae, a few studies upstairs in the guest room—but I understood that was her subject, and that William had, in a way, patterned his own work after hers.

"Funny how easily girls are swayed when you tell them they're beautiful," Geoff said. "When you say there's an artist who wants to use them as a subject."

Being approached by a wild-haired, older man with a British accent might have seemed thrilling to the girls. He'd invited Del and me to the All Hallows' Eve party, and Anne had immediately asked us to pose.

"Not for William?" I said.

Geoff had wood chips in his hair from working in his shop. I resisted the urge to brush them out. "Why no," he said. "What makes you say that? I thought he was more of a landscape type?"

"Maybe," I said. Mary Rae must have known the girls were being pawned off on William, talked into being part of his work, and she'd resented them.

"He left a lot behind," Geoff said.

I hadn't thought about how it would look—having all of William's things in my apartment, and I cursed myself for not getting rid of everything sooner.

I stacked folders of his notes one on top of another. "Well, he never came by for them, so I'm getting rid of them," I said.

"Will you go now, too?" Geoff slid down the door frame and sat half-in, half-out of my apartment.

"Yes, I guess." He would need to know the date I was leaving so he could rent the place. I flipped my cigarette's ash into the cup and took another drag. The smoke burned the back of my throat, but I liked the light-headedness the cigarette gave me. I felt almost happy, almost free.

Geoff leaned over and grabbed the teacup. "And what about your husband? No chance he's coming back?"

"Do you think he'll come back?"

Suzie lay patiently near Geoff's apartment door. The cool spring air came in through the window screen, smelling of lilacs.

"I'll give him a piece of my mind, if he does," Geoff said.

I laughed and dropped an ash into a box of William's sweaters, and before I could put it out, it singed the wool. I dumped the box and his battered camera fell from where I'd hidden it at the bottom, the film dangling out its broken back. Geoff slowly extinguished both of our cigarettes in the teacup. He bent down and picked the camera up, hefted it in his hands. "He must have gotten a new one?"

"He must have," I said. I gathered the sweaters and began to refold them.

"He wouldn't go anywhere without this," Geoff said, fingering the film.

"He probably has a new favorite," I said.

Geoff dropped the camera back onto the pile of sweaters. "It's funny, though," he said. "Can't see him letting his film get spoiled."

We both knelt over the box, and Geoff's eyes seemed darker, almost sly.

"No," I said. "You're right. He was very fastidious about his film. But I was also surprised he seemed so eager to move on."

Geoff pushed off the floor and stood, his joints cracking. "As if he just dropped the camera and kept running."

"Maybe," I said. I finished replacing the sweaters in the box. Geoff held his hand to me and pulled me up.

"It's a mystery," Geoff said. "When someone disappears without any explanation, it's like a death, isn't it?"

I agreed with him, uneasily. The cool breeze came through the open doorway from my apartment. Then Geoff said he had to head back to the shop, and he turned, wearily, toward the stairs. After he left I decided to walk to the campus to have lunch. I had signed up for classes for fall, but I wasn't sure what I'd be doing then. The woman who'd helped me after the accident had contacted me about returning my clothes. I wanted to tell her to throw them away, but she'd sounded so kind on the phone, I'd agreed to stop by to pick them up.

I stepped out on the porch. William was across the street in his usual spot. He wore his beaver-skin hat, a dress shirt tucked into khaki pants. I stood on the porch, watching him, almost hoping I might make out his expression, and then he spun on his good leg and started off down the sidewalk. Rather than let him go, I crossed the street and went after him. It was a beautiful spring day—the dogwood blooming and shedding its petals on the ground, the air warm and filled with birdsong. I kept a steady pace behind him, but he turned toward campus and joined a great throng of students. It was so unlike the dead not to wait for me. Maybe he'd simply disappeared. Or maybe at some point he'd taken off his hat and ducked into one of the campus buildings. Either way, I couldn't find him. My heart raced—not from exertion as much as from anxiety. I knew I didn't want to catch him. I had nothing to say to him. I suppose I could have cleared my conscience and apologized. Ordered him to leave me alone. I had the strange feeling that I wasn't being haunted but stalked. The missing items in my apartment, the feeling that someone had been there and gone through my bureau drawers—the dead had never taken anything from me before.

That afternoon, after I'd eaten and spent an hour or so in the lab, I returned home to discover my apartment nearly emptied of its contents—William's boxes and the remaining furniture had disappeared, and only my belongings and my suitcase were left. I examined the stair treads and the muddy footprints. Geoff was at work, so I knocked on Professor Whitman's door, but he, too, was out. That night I made a pallet on the floor, and I slept there and dreamed I lived in the encampment, working as the local clairvoyant. The place was shrouded in green growth, the tarps stretched in the sun smelling of wood smoke and melting snow, the creek rushing its banks. In the dream, I went to bed and little strung lights left spangles on the canvas like stars. But it was a fake, like a stage backdrop. In the morning I walked out of my tent to the mud, and the smell of rot and decomposition.

I awoke, startled, and sat up. Gray light filled the window, and the tree's leaves fluttered in shadows on the wall. The room with its cracked plaster and blown dust made me think of the asylum, as if I had come to live inside one of my photographs. The throaty rev of a motorcycle idled outside my window, and it took all I had to restrain myself from looking out. Downstairs, I found Professor Whitman at home, and he admitted that he'd come in the day before to witness an old box truck at the curb, and two movers on the stairs.

"Can you describe the men?" I asked him.

Professor Whitman adjusted his glasses over his nose with his age-mottled hands. "I don't know. I didn't pay attention. It's that time of year, people moving in and out."

When I talked to Geoff later that morning, he was lugging grocery bags up the stairs. "Your mother probably sent movers," he said, huffing. He unlocked his apartment door and disappeared inside.

My mother had bought me an airline ticket. I tried to call her, but she wasn't home, and I left a message. My flight left the next day, and I wasn't sure what to do in the meantime. Then I remembered the woman who had helped me after the accident with Anne, her hopes that I would come by to pick up my clothes. I called her back, and we arranged to meet. Outside, I stood in the gravel drive under the elm's shade. I looked into the tree's branches. Once, I had imagined myself in love, my heart warm and rapt. The elm had chafed in its coat of ice, and the frozen world had held a silent promise. I went down to the end of the driveway and glanced at the back of the house. William's Triumph was no longer there. Like my furniture, it was gone.

36

The woman's name was Marcia Fuller, and her house was on a road that wound around Cayuga Lake. I drove, troubled by the missing furniture, the motorcycle, but told myself Geoff had been right—my mother had sent the movers. Someone had stolen the motorcycle, like he'd said—they'd seen it there, unused, and had wheeled it off in the dead of the night. I had a hazy memory of the lake from the night of the accident—the snow and the darkness, the sense of wind blown off a frozen surface. I'd followed Anne for what turned out to be over two miles, according to the officer who found her car. I recalled, vaguely, the house at the bottom of a long set of steps. The road now was bordered by verdant green—brambles and trees and heavy brush. Though I searched as I drove, I couldn't find the place where Anne's Mercedes went off.

I'd dropped Geoff at his shop so I could use his car. He'd gotten out and patted his pockets and realized he'd left his phone behind. "Don't forget to come for me at five," he'd said. "I can't call to remind you."

At two thirty I arrived at Marcia's, a pretty mid-century ranch at the top of a long, sloping tarred drive. Nothing about the house seemed the same except the front door, painted bright yellow, a stand of white birch which that night had been lit in the landscape spotlights. I parked in the street and went up the front walk. Marcia answered the door right away and took my hand. I recognized her dark hair, her smell—like freshly ironed clothes.

"You look healed up," she said.

"Thanks to you." The scar on my forehead was all that remained from that night.

She drew me inside and offered me a drink, a glass of wine, a cup of tea or coffee. She had some crackers and cheese set out, and the late afternoon sun came in through wide windows at the back of the house in a cheery way. "Sit down," she said. "I've thought about you a lot since that night."

I asked her why, and she explained that she'd read the newspaper report of the car and the woman inside. "It was eerie, in a way," Marcia said. "After you'd told us your friend led you here."

Much of the night had dissolved out of a desire to forget. "Did I *say* that?" I said. I took a sip of the wine she'd poured me.

Marcia nodded, emphatically. "Oh, you did! We all heard you!"

"I must have been delirious," I said.

She seemed a little disappointed. Something dimmed in her eyes. She had wanted me to confirm some ghostly evidence she might share with her guests like a party trick, and I would not. We talked a little about Anne and her work. There once was a showing in a gallery downtown, and Marcia had attended and enjoyed it. Then I told her I had to get going, and she left the room and came back with my clothing in a soft, laundered pile—the sweater I'd had on, the blouse and my jeans. I felt a welling of emotion I couldn't explain, as if that incarnation of myself was lost forever. Marcia reached out and squeezed my hand. "You were lucky," she said.

Then she took out an envelope and handed it to me. "This was in the pocket," she said.

It was Mary Rae's necklace. I'd lost track of it after the accident. I might drop it back into Geoff's car for him to find again, its cycle as evidence completed.

"Thank you!" I said. "I thought I'd lost it."

Marcia, trying to be kind, slipped the necklace out of the envelope. "Let me," she said, and she undid the clasp and fastened it around my neck before I could really protest. I felt the weight of the stone, the cold, gold chain, and twirled the pendant in my fingers. Then Marcia saw me to the door, and I went down the walkway to the street. Here the trees shaded the road, and I felt the chilly presentiment of evening—even the summer evenings were cold. I paused at the car, placed the clothing inside, and then crossed the street to the long set of stairs leading down to the house on the lake. Faintly, music played. It was the same cello piece from Anne's party on the night of All Hallows' Eve. Orange lilies bloomed along the slate steps, and the trees were green and full, their leaves flapping. The night Anne died the snow had covered the grass, the stone steps. The trees had been stark shapes against the night. Along the lake that night I'd seen the lights of other houses. Now, the motor of a boat puttered past on the water.

The notes of the cello piece that drifted up the long flight of steps and the familiarity of the house frightened me. Yet, I gripped the iron railing and started down. Some of the house's old clapboards, faded gray, were missing in spots. Paint chipped from the window ledges. On the terrace beside a pot of snapdragons I listened to the music. There was a wooden screen door, the main door propped open behind it with a doorstop, an iron dachshund. For some reason, perhaps because of the things I could see in the room beyond the screen, rather than knock I pulled the screen door open and stepped inside. The house was cool, with a breeze blowing through its opened windows.

The sound of the cello played with the sunlight on the ceiling. The walls were covered with William's photographs. His little metal tin sat on the desk, books of his lay on the coffee table. The duck-carved chair was tucked into a corner. A pair of his shoes were aligned in the mudroom as if he'd just slipped them off.

My heart beat wildly.

A table from my apartment was being used as a desktop. On it was my mother's little clock, which I closed and held in my hand. Prints of sleeping women were spread on the tabletop, and I reached out, tentatively, and shuffled through them with my fingertips, recognizing those I had in the portfolio and others I'd never seen before. William had developed photographs of the asylum, but within the frame, placed in that empty, decaying place with its tumble-down walls and snow on the floor—was a superimposed image of a sleeping woman. There were several of these. The mattresses had been excised, and only the woman's form, her bare arms flung out, her legs entwined with sheets, remained. One lay in the middle of a hallway. The chips of salmon-colored paint from the asylum walls surrounded her on the floor, a strange litter of leaves. I'd always suspected he'd photographed me, but it was a surprise to find this image of myself— the last afternoon sunlight striping my bare thighs, my arm thrown out in sleep—taken the day he'd slipped into my apartment. He'd placed this image of me into the photograph of the octagon-shaped room we'd seen in the asylum, the walls the color of the bottom of a swimming pool. Even in sleep I looked troubled, as if my dreams would not let me forget my waking life.

I set the print down, distracted by one beneath it of Del. Up until this point I'd not known for sure if she and William had been together, and not even the image of a nude Del tangled in sheets was evidence of that. She was asleep. But I knew she would not have volunteered to be photographed. She'd been duped, lured to sleep the way the other Miltons had been—only to awaken in the spare room the next day to Anne's waffles and gourmet maple syrup. Del had mentioned an old tale to me weeks ago—"Sun, Moon, and Talia"—a version of Sleeping Beauty. A piece of flax beneath the girl's fingernail threw her into an unconscious state, and she was placed in a country manor by her father, who could not bear to lose her. A king from another land was hunting in the woods, and when his falcon disappeared inside the manor, he broke in to retrieve it and discovered the girl. Overcome by her beauty, he attempted to rouse her, but when he could not he raped her and returned to his kingdom. The sleeping girl became pregnant.

Across the open room, through a set of sliding doors out to a porch over the lake, William appeared. The glass separated us, and I thought of the dead that had appeared to me through windows and doors, staring in with their pining looks. William wore a gray T-shirt, faded jeans. His hair was long and his gaze through the glass level, calculating. Then he slid the door open, and he stepped through the doorway into the house. I could smell the soap on his skin. His face was flushed from the sun. He held a glass of water in his hand, and he set it down, carefully, on the top of the counter in the kitchen. He came toward where I stood in the living room, his leg with that perceptible drag, and he took a seat in the duck-carved chair, his head thrown back, listening to the anguished cello.

"It's Elgar," he said.

The sound of the concerto filled the room. I wasn't the slightest bit relieved we hadn't left him to die in the asylum.

William crossed his legs at the ankles. He put his hands behind his head. "I'm not one of your spirits."

It hadn't occurred to me until that moment how similar William was to David Pinney—the coldness behind their eyes, their need.

"You thought I didn't know that?" My hand shook holding the print of Del, and I set it down on top of the others.

William moved his arms to his knees and leaned forward. "I'm not sure how you found me. Anne was sworn to secrecy."

"You have my chair," I said.

"I ran into Geoff, and he told me you were leaving. I figured you wouldn't need it." He patted the ducks' heads on the arms. "We're married. Equitable distribution."

He smiled at me, sadly. "That's all you care about? A silly chair?"

"Of course not," I said. "I'm so happy to see you."

"Really? Geoff seemed to think you were over me completely."

Geoff had been sworn to secrecy, like Anne. He must have told William that Officer Paul was asking for him. I looked around at the house, the pine wood floors, the light coming in through the glass doors.

"You photographed Mary Rae here," I said.

William groaned. "Stupid of me to keep the negatives."

"She died that night," I said.

"Yes," he said. He rubbed his face in his hands. He leaned forward, businesslike. "It was an accident. We came here and after the shoot we argued and I went out to pick up some food and when I came back—I found her. I found the empty pill bottle." His voice faltered. He'd planned out this story for Officer Paul, if needed. I was the first to hear it.

"I panicked," he said, his palms up.

"Why didn't you photograph her at your studio?" I stepped away from the table of photographs and stood in the middle of the room. I could see the lake beyond the sliding glass doors, the porch. Behind me stood the door I'd come in through—two exits should I need them.

"She wanted it to be here," he said. "Away from Anne's."

Mr. Parmenter had waited for my mother at the Stardust Motel. What might have happened to her if she'd decided to go? And Mary Rae had been lured here for a final meeting, William maybe begging. I remained in line with the door, knowing Geoff's car was parked on the road, that Marcia Fuller might glance out her large picture window, curious about where I'd gone.

"What kind of person leaves someone for dead in a place like that?"

William said. "Who doesn't report her husband missing? I've had a lot of time to think out here."

"You were trying to hurt me," I said. The accusation seemed childish now.

He rose from the chair and walked over to the door. I felt dizzy with fear, the Elgar concerto an eerie accompaniment.

"I got what I deserved? Is that what you're saying?" He spoke facing the screen door, as if someone else were out there. "Have you ever spent the night in a freezing mental hospital?"

"You left Mary Rae to die in that trailer," I said.

He stood by the screen door, his hands stuffed into his pockets, staring out at the little stone patio, the long set of stone steps up to the road.

"Trusty Anne came to save me," he said. "That was my backup phone in my bag. I had a phone on me. I like to be prepared when I head out to remote locations. Anne thought we'd broken up already, that I'd gone there alone."

"We used the same lie," I said.

William pivoted on his good leg to face me. "Elgar wrote this piece in a cottage like this one, in Sussex. They say that during World War I, he could hear the sound of artillery echoing across the Channel."

The concerto's tempo slowed, and the piece ended with three haunting chords. The breeze blew the frames on the wall, a gentle thudding sound. Outside a boat passed, and the water from its wake rushed the grasses near shore.

"This was my mother's place, and her mother's before her." William grasped the door handle, as if for balance. "You weren't coming to look for me, were you? You and clever Del thought you'd gotten rid of me."

"You took my photograph. My sister's." My voice sounded too loud. I couldn't keep my indignation out.

He tottered a bit on his bad leg, moving away from the doorway toward the table.

"I have an exhibition next month. Anne set it up." He carefully sifted through the prints on the table. "Tell me what you think."

"You drugged us." I was wound tight with fear and anger.

"I convinced Anne it was best if the girls were sound asleep," he said, his voice soothing. "She didn't know I'd photographed Mary Rae. I planned to stop, to forget the whole series, but the gallery owner wanted to set a date. And I thought I needed a couple more models." William sighed. "I didn't need any more."

Anne would have done anything for William's art, whatever he needed. But did she realize she hadn't been helping him with his art? William was attracted to girls sleeping, to us unconscious. I'd known it from the images, the poses, from the way the Milton girls blushed when they looked at their likenesses.

"Did you have sex with *all* of them?" I said, slightly breathless.

His face was such a mask of despair, I almost pitied him.

"You're sick," I said.

"I know," he said.

He came over to me and took my wrist and turned my hand to reveal my mother's clock in my grip. "What do you have there?" he said. Then he chuckled. "Your little clock. I knew that would bother you."

I felt sure he could feel the race of my pulse. Then he reached to touch Mary Rae's necklace.

"Anne gave it to her, didn't she?" he said.

"It must have fallen off her in the car."

"Geoff's car, yes."

"Anne figured out what you'd done, you know," I said. "She was coming here the night she died."

He slid his hand up and down my arm. "A shame about Anne," he said. "She might have had a few more good days in her."

I felt a chill on my skin, felt our pasts intersect with a terrifying speed, a shining zeroing-in. He'd tried to dress Mary Rae, fumbling with her clothes, then wrapping her in a blanket, carrying her up the

long set of steps to the car in the cold. This had been the thing con-
necting us from the beginning. The weight of David Pinney's body
as we dragged it across the grass, under the barbed wire, beneath the
willow. The cold of his hand in mine, our frightened breath, Del's
refusal to pull him, to touch him, and my pleading with her: "You
can! You have to!" But William had transported a living body—one
he'd only thought was dead. Mary Rae's pulse, slowed by the pills,
must have been nearly indiscernible. Even if she'd taken the over-
dose herself, William was a murderer.

"You found the trailer for the two of you, like you found the
cottage for me," I said.

"I still love you." He shook his head as if these feelings disappointed
him. He threaded his fingers with mine. "Even if you did try to kill
me. Even if you didn't waste much time finding someone new."

"You asked Mary Rae to marry you," I said.

He squeezed my hand. "You don't believe that I love you?"

I considered William's eyes and the smooth curve of his shoulders
beneath his shirt. You don't ever know what someone is capable of.
You can suppose, you can guess. Maybe he loved me once, or thought
he did. I couldn't tell anything from his face.

"Do you ever wonder if it would be easier to confess?" I said.

I felt his breath in my hair, along my neck.

"I just did," he whispered.

Out on the water a bell sounded.

"The church in Aurora," he said. "It's evening services."

"Bells used to be blessed," I told him.

He slid his hand to my cheek, and I tried not to flinch.

"They were struck by lightning in the church spires. The bell ring-
ers, too. The clergy believed that demons lived in the air and caused
the storms, so the bells were blessed."

"Always the lightning expert," he said, softly.

And there was a moment, a slip of something fleeting and lovely,
in which I imagined Del and my mother settling down in the old

house, and another version of William and me, settling down in this place by the lake. I could imagine evenings during warm-lit sunset, watering the pot of sad flowers, the sound of the lake slapping the shore, the bugs pinging the screens.

"Could two people stay together knowing what we know about each other?" he said. "You never told me what you thought about the prints."

I couldn't erase the photo of Del, the fact of her pregnancy, her confusion about how it had happened.

"They're beautiful," I said, and it was the one, true, honest thing.

I felt him begin to gather me in his arms, and I let him lean in to kiss me before I shoved him away. He was unprepared and he lost his footing. I could have taken the iron doorstop and struck him. There were weapons at my disposal, a variety of ways I might have killed him, dumped his body into the lake, and let the currents sluice him into the northern marshes. I could have revenged Mary Rae's murder, Del's rape, the rapes of the other girls who had no idea he'd violated them in their sleep.

I could have taken the candlestick from the mantel.

But I had something better planned for him.

He stumbled back against the duck-carved chair, and I left the cottage and ran up the long set of steps to Geoff's car. I felt my progress slowed by panic, a heaviness in my legs I experienced attempting escape in nightmares. I'd left the car door unlocked. ("Nothing to steal in there, eh?" Geoff had always said.) I tossed the little clock onto the seat and started the car. William's footsteps sounded on the stairs, and as he stepped out into the road I pressed the gas, and he leapt out of the way of the car. I could have run him over. All of these things might have been deemed self-defense. They would have fit into the story I planned to tell Officer Paul.

I drove to my apartment first. I expected William to pursue me on his Triumph, to appear at any moment, but he did not, still confused, puzzling out his next move. He would call Geoff. But Geoff didn't have his phone at work. The apartment was as vacant as I'd left it—my pallet on the floor holding my shape from the night before. I went to the closet and slid the cedar panel aside and slipped the port-folio and the journal out from their hiding spot. I got back into the car and noticed my phone had three missed calls from William. Rather than listen to his messages, I drove the long route into Milton, watching in my rearview mirror, my heart racing and jubi-lant. I arrived on Main Street not knowing where the police depart-ment was. I pulled into the Viking Lanes parking lot and clasped the wheel with my shaking hands. I wasn't sure if I could do what I'd intended to do.

I scrambled through my bag and found the scrap of paper Del had given me with Alice's phone number. I punched the buttons, clum-sily, getting the wrong number at first, redialing twice before she answered. Alice met me in the parking lot and together we took Offi-cer Paul the negatives, the necklace, the journal. The Milton pre-cinct was across the street from the Shurfine market, and I sat in a molded plastic chair and watched through the front window as women pushed carts across the uneven tar lot, loaded bags of groceries into their trunks. When Officer Paul came out I told him my story. I felt like a child again in elementary school—reciting the correct responses, watching the teacher's face beam with pride. Paul put a hand on my shoulder and patted it. He wrote down the address to the lake house and promised to let me know immediately when all was safe.

Alice and I went to her grandmother's. It was late afternoon, and Alice's mother, Erika, greeted us at the door in a bikini worn under a white linen shirt, looking like exotic evidence that, beyond the dark confines of Milton, bright oranges hung from glossy trees, and beaches stretched white and blinding—the water a rare green, like malachite. Erika grabbed each of us by the hand and ushered us into the house, through the living room to the kitchen. She mixed us gin and tonics, and we took them outside, where we sat in her lounge chairs in the backyard, telling our story until fireflies emerged, tiny, weightless embers bobbing over the place where Alice and Mary Rae had practiced their twirling.

I told Alice and Erika how Del and I had held our séances on summer nights, a candle throwing our shadows onto the pool shed walls. Outside, the fireflies had dipped between horse chestnuts and honey locusts. Luna moths had flitted around the pool shed's yellow outdoor light. For a dollar we'd communicate with the dead with the sole intention of collecting money for lip gloss and gum. Sometimes, I would know the color of a dress. I would smell lavender. I'd get an urge to sing part of a song I'd never heard before. I didn't tell them that any of it had been real. I let them speculate—another clairvoyant's trick.

Alice and Erika and I sat outside until late, startling at any sudden noise, imagining William's Triumph revving down Milton's Main Street, his silent approach around the side of the house. Erika slipped inside to make up a bed for me, though it would be a sleepless night. I planned to call Del and tell her everything, so she would know that it wasn't William's ghost she'd seen but the man himself, but I did not. I sat on the bed and I played William's messages—the first an angry attempt to reason with me, a promise not to reveal what had happened in the asylum. The second message was more of the first—spiteful, hateful, a threat to find me, to do what he should have done to me before. The third message was blank, at first. Then water sloshed against a boat's sides, buffeted by wind, by William's slow breaths. "Why couldn't you love me," he said softly, despondent.

The next morning, under ash-colored skies, Officer Paul arrived to tell us in person that William's body had been found in a small boat on the lake, a self-inflicted gunshot wound to the head.

We stood in the driveway, Officer Paul scuffing his dark shoes. It began to rain—a soft drizzle. "He won't hurt anyone else," he said.

He ducked back into his cruiser, offering a quick nod of sympathy, imagining the ordeal I'd been through. Alice put a tentative arm around my shoulder. The rain misted the grass, the tar road, the metal street signs. All I'd ever wanted was to be loved. All William had wanted was for me to love him. Even Mary Rae, under the elm, had wanted something. As much a mystery as the appearance of the dead was the way none of our wantings could ever be aligned.

37

Del had her baby six weeks early, in July. She held him, briefly, then she took off with a man she'd met while pregnant, a yachtie who'd invited her sailing. At times I imagined she was fleeing Detective Thomson and his questions and, later, that she was running from the baby and the predictability of the life she would have lived with him. The baby—she'd named him Owen—was born blind. His eyes were like Del's, the same color and shape, heavy with lashes. For five years I saw only photographs of him, and from those I couldn't tell for sure if he was William's son. I thought that on meeting him I would sense it, that I would somehow resent him. But by then he was school-age, sturdy and thoughtful. I hadn't been around children much and had no idea the things they taught you about yourself.

My mother and I would get postcards and e-mails from various ports of call—Grenada, Tobago, St. Vincent—the boats Del was on and the men she was with constantly changing. When she was in town she went by our mother's to visit, but only for an hour or two. My mother, when I asked how Del was, would say that she'd warned her to use sunscreen, but that Del had a dark suntan.

"And what else?" I'd say.

She'd shift the phone to her other ear, her hands busy in the kitchen sink. "Her usual impulsive self."

Del would bring Owen spice drops, watch him play, read him *The Velveteen Rabbit*, then go. Later, I would get an e-mail from Del about how the visit went—a humorous description of our mother's attempts to satisfy Owen's every whim, and play hostess. *Tea on a tray*, Del would write. *For God's sake.* About Owen she said little. *He is a clever little man*, she wrote. *He asks more questions than any human being I've ever met. Even You-Know-Who.*

We'd stopped hearing from Del in May—no cards or e-mails. Last we knew she'd been on a yacht called *The Pearl*, anchored off a small island in the Grenadines. My mother had put out inquiries, but Del couldn't be located. We assumed she'd taken off with someone new. But it wasn't like her to stay out of touch. Together, my mother and I had invented a story for ourselves: Del had decided to stay put on some island, and was eating papaya and roti, entertaining yachties at the island bar with her stories.

The first week of June, my mother called and asked me to come home. Ordinarily, I would have made some excuse. This time I did not.

"Why do you want me there?" I asked.

"It's your birthday. And it's time you met your nephew." The pendulum of the old regulator clock echoed through the kitchen. "Stay for a few days. Stay for a month or the whole summer. It's up to you."

"You've heard something about Del," I said.

"No, I have not." My mother's voice was crisp, annoyed.

I took the train into the Old Saybrook station and called a cab to take me to my mother's house.

The morning was cool, the weather always changeable near the shore. Driving down our road I smelled the Sound, the remains of morning fires lit to ward off the damp. Overhead the trees shook their bright leaves. The house was the same, the windows flashing the sun. The barn was gone. My mother had called me two years before to tell me we'd lost it, but I'd forgotten. "Fire," she'd said, and nothing more. As the cab pulled into the pebbled drive the missing barn was all I could see. My mother came out onto the wide front porch.

She was thinner. She'd let her hair go gray, though it was still long to her shoulders and styled. She wore no makeup. "You made it," she called.

The driver went to the trunk for my bag, and then the cab drove away. I stood below my mother on the pebbled drive. "What really happened to it?"

She put her hand up to shade her eyes. "Lightning," she said. Then she did something astonishing. She tipped her head back and laughed.

"Are you my mother?" I asked.

"Oh, Martha," she said. "Still the same."

I followed her inside the house, where the sea breeze came through the windows into the kitchen. The Spiritualists by the Sea camp had opened—I could smell the scent of oil paint. And then Owen came into the room with a little white cane, tapping it in the doorway. He held his two hands out and my mother told me to kneel down onto the kitchen's worn wood floor. I smelled his breath, cloying and sweet. He placed his small hands on my face.

"This is how he knows you," my mother said.

His little fingers were nimble, searching me out.

"Girl," he said, quietly, his hands on my hair.

"Auntie Martha," my mother told him. "Run along and play while we visit."

He put his small arms around my neck and squeezed. His cane *tap-tapped* along the wood floor into the living room.

My mother set out two cups of coffee and poured a shot of Baileys Original Irish Cream into each. Though Del had claimed she and I would raise Owen, we both knew that would prove impossible. I'd stayed in Ithaca to finish school, and my mother had taken on the care of Owen. As we drank our coffee, the breeze through the screen door riffled the linen tablecloth, and I wondered if she forgave me for never visiting, even on holidays, for never offering to help with Owen. I'd come for my grandmother's funeral last year but left immediately after. My sporadic phone calls and texts relayed only basic information about my own life—a new apartment in the city, a small show at a gallery—and never inquired into hers except to ask about Del.

My mother had put swatches of fabric on the door frames, on Owen's chair at the table, until he'd learned which was his. His toys lined the shelves in the old den, where my grandfather once watched his documentaries—Braille lettered blocks, stacking cups, puzzles with little knob handles, textured books. Owen's artwork hung on the walls—brilliant and full of colorful dabs and smears. I put my finger out and felt the dried paint on the paper. I closed my eyes and listened to the tapping of the little cane.

That afternoon, Leanne and Sarah arrived—Leanne with her baby, and Sarah with her two, a boy and a girl. We chatted, sitting at the old iron table in the iron mesh chairs, and watched the children play on the steps of the pool. They each, grudgingly, acknowledged my birthday.

"Mother says you don't want to celebrate," Sarah said. "Here's this, anyway."

She handed me a small wrapped box. Inside was a silver cuff bracelet of my grandmother's that Sarah had owned for years.

"You always wanted it," she said.

Leanne gave me a silk scarf that reminded me of Anne.

Neither of my older sisters mentioned Del. We managed not to argue about anything, but they both ended their visit by claiming they had to get going—Leanne to the grocery store, Sarah to get ready for a dinner party. Even in my apartment in the city, I had nowhere pressing to go. I'd abandoned any friends I'd made in Ithaca; they'd served their purpose in that part of my life, and felt temporary, as if

I were supposed to let go of them. I had made a few new friends in the city. I had a job at a gallery. I had my photographs. But I was often alone.

Before Sarah left, after the children were buckled into their car seats and she had gotten into the driver's seat, she called me over.

"Remember that birthday you were banished from the house?" she said. She wore a small smile I couldn't quite read.

"No," I said, though she must have meant the time I'd spent the night.

"You had gotten into it with Del," she said. "And one of you threw something that shattered that framed picture in the living room? Glass was everywhere. Mother went crazy."

The heat from the car fanned my face, and I took a step back. "I don't really remember."

Sarah snapped on her seat belt, reprimanded her younger child in the backseat. "Well, we all knew *you'd* broken it. Del never got angry, if you think about it." She gave me that odd smile again, a little sorry for me. "I guess you put that memory aside."

I watched her drive away. *Aside*, I thought. As if that could be accomplished with pieces of the past.

Later, I sat in the living room wing chair with a book, not reading, just thinking. Owen came tapping into the room where I sat, and I remained quiet, believing he wouldn't know I was there. After a moment, he left, and the tapping moved down the front hallway, up the front staircase, and down the back kitchen stairs, a circuit of the house. My mother called him for his bath, and I went out onto the porch.

The site of the leveled barn was shaggy with weeds, the remains of the cement and stone foundation like a ruined mouth. The golf course, its stands of weeping willows, was visible now from the porch. Near the debris of the barn, the hammer rusted in the cistern. Would I ever see David Pinney's ghost peering at me from beneath the willow? I had hidden my crime and gotten away with it. I had continued on as if it had never happened, but I was wrong. I would always carry my blame. I'd thought my mother believed that she and I were covering for Del, but she'd known from the first it had been me.

The sun setting beyond the rise of the golf course lit the sky a deep orange. The wind picked up and scattered geranium petals across the porch, shuffled the horse chestnut leaves together like a deck of cards. Evening blotted out the place where the barn once stood. I left the porch and went inside. As part of Owen's bedtime ritual, my mother read to him, and after she'd left his room I stuck my head in the doorway to say good night. I didn't know what he expected of me or who I might be to him. In the dark of his bedroom his face and hair were pale against his spaceship-patterned pillow.

"You were in the living room today, Auntie Martha," he said. His voice was clear and soft.

I stood in the doorway. Was he listening to my breathing, to the beating of my heart? "You knew."

He propped himself up, as someone might who wanted to see you better. "You smell like yellow."

Outside the cicadas sounded. A bicycle passed in the lane beside the house, its tires shushing over the sandy road.

"What does yellow smell like?" I asked him.

"Aunt Martha, quiet, lemons."

I AWOKE AT dawn to Owen's voice in the room across the hall. I listened to him turn the pages of a book. Every so often he would ask a question: *Will the rabbit ever become real?* There'd be a silence, and more turning pages, and more of the one-sided conversation. Soon after, he came into my room, stood beside the bed, and touched my face.

"It's time," he said. "Don't you hear the birds?" The light played in his hair, swept over the shoulders of his pajamas where stars and blasting rockets dotted the dark blue background.

"Your grandfather used to say that about the birds," I said.

My heart caught with sorrow, imagining William, Owen's age, collecting apple money in the little tin.

The Spiritualists' organ's notes came through my open window, and he pressed his face against the screen. "Where does that come from?"

I wanted to say it was the sound you heard on the astral plane, as my grandfather had once told me. Instead, I helped him dress, and we slipped downstairs, unhooked the porch screen door, and left the house. I took him along the path through the woods, shadowed and cool from the recent rain, to the gravel lane that led to the Spiritualists by the Sea camp. We moved through the silence of the tree canopy to the open meadow, where the sun colored the blowing grass, and then down the little tarred lanes, Osprey to Nehantic, to the bulkhead. I told Owen about the cottages with their gingerbread trim. I described the hand-painted road signs. We took the path between the swamp rose bushes to the beach, where the tide was out, the Sound glazed and calm. We gathered jingles and arks that littered the wet sand.

A pair of mute swans passed overhead, their wings disturbing the calm of the water, making a sound like singing. Owen tipped his face to them, and the breeze moved his fine hair, jostled the swamp roses, heavy on their stems. We listened to the organ in the temple, its notes flung out to sea. In the camp, we passed the meditation garden, where Reverend Earline, now a spirit herself, sat alone on a bench wearing her Diane von Furstenberg sheath, her scarab bracelet. She followed our approach with a yearning expression.

"Aren't you going to say hello?" Owen said.

"No," I said. "No, I'm not."

Could he read my surprise in the dampness of my palm?

I circled the shell paths through the camp, and when we passed one of the dead Owen would squeeze my hand, and then we'd walk on. When I asked him how he knew them, he said they were quiet, like me.

"Do they smell of lemons?" I said, smiling.

"No, never," he said. "They smell like anise."

It was the spice drops that Del brought him. Then I caught the scent myself, jumbled with that of the mown grass, the wildflowers, the gasoline of a boat powering out.

His one-sided conversation over *The Velveteen Rabbit* in his room earlier suddenly struck me as odd. Despair filled me, and I scanned the camp grounds for Del, for the blouse my mother had bought for her when she was pregnant, the last thing I'd seen her wearing in a photograph she'd sent me in Ithaca: *C'est Moi, Garden Club Secretary.* But I saw nothing and reassured myself that Del, the living, breathing version of her, was still somewhere, sailing the Caribbean Sea, asleep in an island hammock, toasting an approaching hurricane with a glass of *rhum agricole.*

Owen tapped his little cane along the shell path. Up at the old house, my mother would have made coffee, set out cups on the linen cloth. She'd wait for Owen and me on the porch, and when she saw us her expression would alter—*happy sad*—the closest to joy we would ever allow ourselves. Sister Martha Mary had shown herself to me on a summer day in a cold barn, the sun on her face, her hands clasped in her dark robes' folds. And later, innumerable dead had disclosed their heartbreaking faces; Mary Rae had kept her frozen vigil beneath the elm. I'd believed the dead had expectations of me. But what if they asked nothing but that I serve as a witness to their longing?

I told Owen that it was time to go home. My grandfather had a book with an Irish tale about the swans I'd find on the shelf and read to him. And maybe all that could happen to us in our lives was portended in fairy tales. I held Owen's hand, warm and smelling of copper pennies. We made our way back along the wooded lane to the old house.

ACKNOWLEDGMENTS

My gratitude begins with my family—storytellers all, who contributed to the mythic landscape of my childhood, a place from which I've drawn my own stories. I am indebted to my late uncle, Christopher Nicholas Brown, for poems that shaped my writing life, especially the elegies for my grandfather, the lightning rod man: ". . . sharp eyes of Lyme fishermen / and North Bloomfield growers / knew the talk of his toned nonsense / that electricity was life / that after rain / the grass was so green blistering because of static / in the air." I owe inspiration, friendship, and thanks to Valerie Wilson, who first told me about Pine Grove Spiritualist Camp, and Susan Wolf Johnson, who graciously read this book's convoluted first draft and offered encouragement. Thank you to everyone at Henry Holt, especially Barbara Jones, gifted editor, who inspires me to be a better writer, line by line. To Samantha Shea, I owe my deepest gratitude. Her patience, direction, and tireless reading of this book's many versions gave me a reason to keep writing it.

ABOUT THE AUTHOR

KAREN BROWN's *Little Sinners and Other Stories* was named a Best Book of 2012 by *Publishers Weekly;* her previous collection, *Pins and Needles,* received AWP's Grace Paley Prize for Short Fiction; and her first novel, *The Longings of Wayward Girls,* was published in 2013 by Washington Square Press to rave reviews. Her work has been featured in the PEN / O. Henry Prize Stories, Best American Short Stories, *The New York Times*, and *Good Housekeeping*. She teaches creative writing and literature at the University of South Florida.